MW00576461

BOOK 2

BASTARD OF BLESSING

THE LEGACY OF LUCKY LOGAN

J.R. FRONTERA

Published by
TIN CAN

An imprint of Wordwraith Books, LLC
705-B SE Melody Lane #147
Lee's Summit, MO 64063
http://www.wordwraiths.com

Version 1.0

http://www.jrfrontera.com

Cover art and dust jacket by Julia Jin
Cover typography by J. Caleb Design & Julia Jin
Formatting by Charity Chimni
Maps by renflowergrapx
Interior Illustrations by Taylor Park

BOOKS BY J.R. FRONTERA

All books available on Amazon.com and most other online retailers, wherever books are sold.

THE LEGACY OF LUCKY LOGAN

(scifi western)

Bargain at Bravebank

Bastard of Blessing

Bones in Blackbird

Demon at Devil's Deep

(and more coming soon)

N'SPACE

(humorous space opera)

Galapalooza

The Starburst Inn

(and more coming soon)

STARSHIP ASS

(humorous space opera)

Of Sporks, Overlords, and Moon Worms

Of Donkeys, Gods, and Space Pirates

Of Donkeys, Dogs, and Rogue Bits

Of Donkeys, Cogs, and Hot Bodies

COMPLETE

For a fully updated book list check out https://jrfrontera.com.

FREE BOOK ALERT!

Before he was a rancher and a family man, Logan Delano was a 15-year-old orphan, running in an outlaw gang led by the ruthless Paul Johnson. In the wilds of the Independent Americas, under the merciless eye of Kill 'Em All Paul, having any kind of conscience just might land you dead.
Unfortunately for Logan, it seems he's still got part of his...

Download your free copy of LUCKY LOGAN at the link below and saddle up for a gritty, gun-slinging tale of just how far one young outlaw will go to survive...

https://bit.ly/LuckyLoganFREE

DEDICATION

Once again… thank you, thank you from the bottom of my heart to every single one of my Kickstarter backers. The incredible book you hold in your hands only exists because of YOU. Be proud! YOU did this! Thank you so much for believing in me and the stories I create! This one's for you…

DEAR READER,

This book wasn't supposed to exist.

This book, and the one before it, (and the one that will come after it) were all originally meant to just be backstory. Backstory that would never be drawn out and detailed. Backstory that would only become known through small hints here and there, maybe an offhand comment from some secondary character, an afterthought now and then from the protagonist.

Originally, I'd only meant to release the first chapter of book one as a standalone short story. And that was that. Or, that was *supposed* to be that.

Except the group of people I recruited as my beta readers before I published that short story unanimously gave me the same feedback: "This isn't a short story," they said. "This is a whole novel. Where's the rest of the story?"

If only one or two of them had said that, I probably would have chuckled and published the short story anyway, and written books 1 – 3 as I'd originally envisioned them, starting a whole five years from where we currently are in this series. And I'd have three fewer books in this series. And I wouldn't have gotten to have so much fun writing these three books. And probably, even *I* would have never known about a lot of what happens in these first three books.

As it stands, I'm so glad I listened to those wise folk who read that short story (ahem, *first chapter*).

But... writing out that story that was never really supposed to be a story has been a bit of a challenge, if only because a back-story not meant to be published as a whole apparently does not land in my brain like those stories that were always supposed to be published.

It took some reorganizing. And so... perhaps the ends of

these books will not exactly feel like *ends*. For that, I apologize. But also, I do not apologize. Yes, I basically just said #sorrynot-sorry... but I am a *little* sorry. I think of this series more like episodes of some of my favorite tv shows, where each book is an episode, with some things within wrapping up, but other things within being left open, to be closed in another, future episode.

And like some of my favorite tv show episodes, the very end of the episode creates almost a teaser for the next episode, establishing one of the problems or conflicts ahead of next week. AH! The suspense! The anticipation! I don't know about you, but personally, I absolutely *love* that giddy expectation.

Some may not like it so much. Some may find it unpleasant or torturous... but personally, *I love it*. That's what I want people to be feeling when they get to the end of each book in this series. I suppose you can leave a review (or write me an email!) and let me know if I actually succeeded, since that's the only real way I'll know if my grand evil master plan is working... but golly gee I do hope it's working... otherwise I'm quite sure it will blow up in my face!

In any event, writing this series has been the most fun I've ever had writing books, so it's unlikely I'll stop till I'm good and tired of them, even if my grand evil master plan *does* blow up in my face. So I suppose there's that...

Until then, I want to thank you for being here. For buying (or borrowing) this book, for showing your support of an indie author, and for actually reading this very-possibly-boring author's note! It really means *the world* to me!

So, with that, I'll let you get on with the tale. Just remember... it's all that original group of beta readers' fault! ;)

Much love,

J.R. FRONTERA

WORDWRAITH BOOKS

PRESENTS

A NOVEL PRODUCED BY

J. R. FRONTERA
VICKY MEYER \ PAT STEVENS
AMY CAMPBELL \ ANDREA VIEGAS
AUDREY HUGHEY \ BARBARA CLEVELAND
ADAM NEMO \ CLINT HOUSE
CULLEN BUNN \ DANI HOOTS
DREW TABB \ E.J. MCKENNA
GERALD P. MCDANIEL \ HANK ALWARD
JO ABYONA PHOENIX \ JAS PENNOCK
KACI BRYSON \ KALIE REID
KATY WILLCOCKS \ MICHAEL + KRISTI CATALANI
KRISTIN HELLING \ VALLYSON LINDT
MATTHEA W. ROSS \ MELANIE B.
MICHAEL DAVID ANDERSON \ MICHEAL W. KERR
MONICA LEONELLE \ NICOLA BACON
NICOLETTE ANDREWS \ PAUL + LAURA TRINIES
ROD GALINDO \ RYAN SCOTT JAMES
SAMANTHA LANDSTRÖM \ SARAH H. HIGGINS
SCOTT CASEY \ SYDNEY STOKOE
TAMI CLARK \ TAYLOR PARK
WARD LENZ \ DENNIS RACKERS
MANDI LYNN BRIELLE \ VIRGINIA KERR

COVER ART AND DUST JACKET BY

JULIA JIN

COVER TYPOGRAPHY BY

J. CALEB DESIGNS
JULIA JIN

FORMATTING BY

CHARITY CHIMNI

MAPS BY

RENFLOWERGRAPX

INTERIOR ILLUSTRATIONS BY

TAYLOR PARK

There were three silhouettes standin' in front of me...
(An Especially Bad Day) page 51

"So nice to see you again..."
(On The Same Side, Maybe?) pages 176 & 177

"There's your damn lockbox..."
(Patience Is a Virtue) page 403

AND STARRING

ROGER CLARK

IN THE AUDIO PRODUCTION

SPECIAL ILLUSTRATED EDITION

THE LEGACY OF LUCKY LOGAN
BOOK 2

WRITTEN BY

J.R. FRONTERA

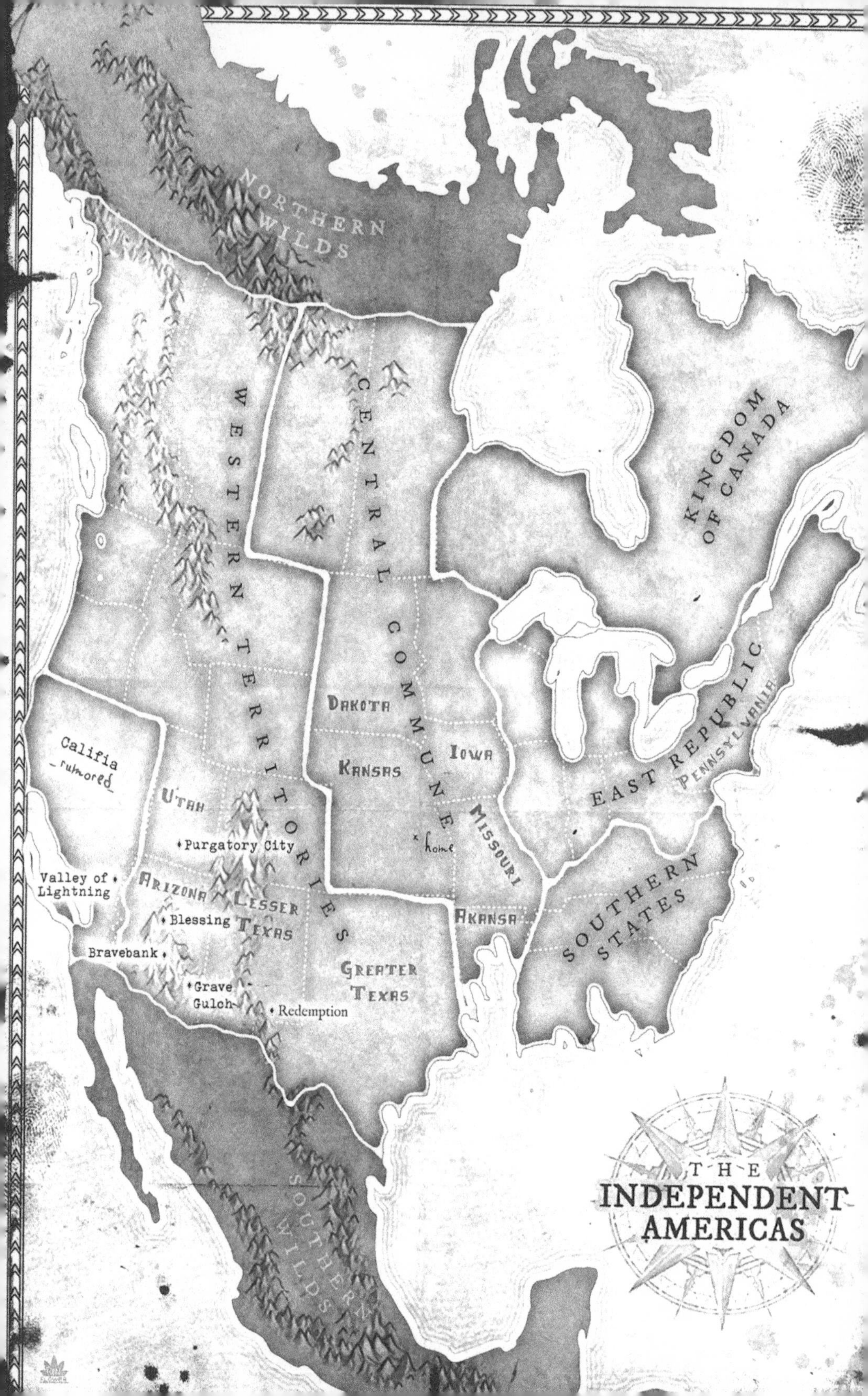

NORTHERN WILDS
WESTERN TERRITORIES
CENTRAL COMMUNE
KINGDOM OF CANADA
EAST REPUBLIC
PENNSYLVANIA
DAKOTA
KANSAS
IOWA
MISSOURI
AKANSA
SOUTHERN STATES
Califia
rumored
UTAH
Purgatory City
Valley of Lightning
ARIZONA
LESSER TEXAS
Blessing
Bravebank
Grave Gulch
Redemption
GREATER TEXAS
home
SOUTHERN WILDS
THE
INDEPENDENT
AMERICAS

WESTERN TERRITORIES
CENTRAL COMMUNE
Califia
—rumored—
UTAH
KANSAS
Purgatory City
alley of
ightning
ARIZONA
Sonoita
Blessing
LESSER TEXAS
Bravebank
Nan's hideout
Holding Tank Pool
Peridot
Grave Gulch
GREATER TEXAS
SOUTHERN WILDS
THE INDEPENDENT AMERICAS

ACES HIGH

The sonuvabitch was cheatin'.

I may have been shit at poker, but I'd learned enough about it in the last few weeks to know when a man was cheatin'. And the sonuvabitch sittin' across from me at the table right now was cheatin', sure enough.

So when he laid down his winnin' hand with a cocky grin and made to grab for the stash of money in the middle of us, I put my hand over the top of it first. His grin slid fast into a murderous scowl, and the other four men sittin' with us pushed their chairs back a mite, not wantin' to get caught in the middle of this. They glanced to each other, then toward the barkeep, but I paid 'em no mind.

This here was the Stag Saloon, under the ownership of none other than Nine-Fingered Nan, the oldest and most feared outlaw in the Territories, and around here, I was Nan's man.

No one had much wanted to pick a fight with me before, and they certainly didn't want to do so now. So I kept my glare on the man across from me, my hand atop his money, and he glared right back. His left hand was below the table, but I happened to know he only wore one gun, and it was perched on his opposite hip. If he tried to draw, I'd beat him easy.

"I don't much like cheaters," I said.

His face reddened.

The other four sittin' with us pretended to look surprised, but I had a hard time believin' they hadn't suspected somethin'. I was shit at poker, and the room was on the verge of spinnin' on account of all the whiskey I'd downed since sun-up, but even I had seen it.

Maybe I was shit at poker, but this fella was even more shit at cheatin'.

"Yer drunk, Delano," he said. "You should mind the words comin' outta yer mouth. Might getcha into trouble."

"Might," I agreed. "But I still don't much like cheaters. And yer a cheater. And a bad one, at that. If yer gonna do it, you should at least get good at it before you come in here tryin' to rob me and the rest." I tilted my head toward the others at our table. "So why don't you go ahead and get outta here. Before yer cheatin' gets *you* into trouble, yeah?"

His face got even redder, and his eyes darted from me to the other fellas sittin' round. They were watchin' him, tense on their chairs, ready fer him to try somethin'. Or fer me to try somethin'.

His eyes finally came back to me, glarin' somethin' fierce. "I ain't no cheat," he hissed. "You shut yer lyin' mouth 'fore I gotta teach you some manners!"

The conversations nearest to us faltered at his shoutin', people turnin' to see what the commotion was about.

I smiled at him. Truth be told, I was itchin' fer a fight. But then, it seemed I was always itchin' fer a fight these days. Three weeks I'd been holed up in Bravebank now, waitin' on word from Nan over what she wanted from me in exchange fer my sister—beyond that twenty-five thousand dollars I'd already given her.

Three weeks of waitin' with nothin' to do but drink, sleep, and gamble. And avoid goin' near Dr. Balogh's shop, which I'd discovered was set up over on the east edge of town.

All that time, and not a word yet from Nan.

Holt were convinced no word would come. He figured she'd

said such things just to get me outta the way. Just to fuck with my head while she sold Ethelyn off, anyway.

That coulda been true. But if that's what she'd wanted, it woulda been easier for her to just gun me down three weeks ago when I'd showed up at her cliff-side hideout with the gutted body of one of her men in tow.

She coulda just ended it all then.

But she hadn't.

I had to believe she wanted more from me. I was bankin' on her greed. Bankin' on the fact that would be enough for her to keep her word, enough to save my sister.

But there was always that doubt in the back of my mind, made manifest in Holt's conviction of Nine-Fingered Nan's dishonesty, and his certainty she was only manipulatin' me.

That, and the fact no one in this damned town seemed keen to talk when I inquired as to the details of Nan's operations, was enough to drive a man to madness. So I only smiled at that cheatin' sonuvabitch across the table, and stood slowly from my chair. I rocked a bit as the room tilted, but reached out to steady myself on the table. Well, maybe I'd had more whiskey than I remembered.

"I'm gonna give you one more opportunity, Mister," I said slowly. "You can leave now on your own two feet, quiet-like, or we can make a nice scene and I'll throw you out."

He stood then, too, but fast, knockin' his chair over.

More people turned to look now, and I saw his right hand dip toward his sixgun.

I coulda drawn then and put him down, even drunk, but there was too much fierce anger roilin' around inside me, and it wanted out. So instead I grabbed the edge of the poker table and flipped it over toward him just as his gun was clearin' leather.

He had to jump back to keep from bein' hit by it, throwin' off his aim. Cards and money went everywhere.

The other four men sittin' there yelled and dove fer the money, likely tryin' to recover their share of it before anyone else could claim it.

Someone somewhere shouted out in alarm.

And then the cheatin' bastard recovered his balance and took aim again. I launched myself at him, tacklin' him just as his gun went off.

It was loud, right in my damn ear, but I still heard the barkeep swear and yell for us to take it outside.

Too late.

We crashed to the floor, and a commotion erupted all around us. Seemed the other patrons were quick to pick sides in this fight … or quick to get the hell outta there.

The cheater's pistol jarred out of his hand as he hit the ground and went spinnin' off across the floor. And all his aces fell outta his sleeve. But I ignored all that, rollin' over the top of him to land a few good fists into his face before he could bring up his forearms to block my pummelin'.

He struck out with a fist of his own and caught me on the chin, ringin' my bell pretty good. I fell sideways and caught another fist to the jaw, then I was the one on the floor. He made a grab for my left gun but I twisted away outta his reach, and then the other four fellas we'd been playin' cards with found him and hauled him up to his feet.

From the beatin' they proceeded to lay on him, seemed like they'd sided with me.

Hands found me then, too, grabbin' my upper arms and draggin' me upright. I winced as their fingers dug into the mostly healed burns on my right bicep. The burns were mostly healed, sure, but the skin there was still kinda sore, and I didn't much like people diggin' into it.

Too bad fer me, they weren't friendly hands. Seemed the cheatin' bastard had some people on his side, too.

A fist landed in my gut and I doubled over, the breath goin' out of me. Then another cracked into my face and I staggered sideways before bein' caught again by more hands.

I ducked the next blow and sent my own fist into someone's middle, then reached out fer a half-empty bottle on the closest table and came up swingin' it, catchin' the nearest man on the side of the face.

The bottle shattered. The man howled and spun away as blood painted his cheek.

His friend stepped up to take his place, and another fist sailed at my face.

I dodged that one, too, but stumbled. Damn the whiskey. I'd drunk more than I thought. The room was spinnin' now, and I caught the back of a chair to keep from pitchin' over onto the floor again.

Someone was yellin' fer the sheriff, and the barkeep was cursin' all of us.

A blow landed in my right kidney and sent me down to my knees, but I let myself roll with the momentum even as I gasped in pain, and took the chair with me to use as cover.

The next fist punched the solid wood of the chair back instead of me, and then that man was the one cryin' out in pain as he shook out his hand. I kicked at him with my left boot, the one that had a metal foot in it, and made solid contact with his right shin.

It knocked his leg out from under him and he fell forward. His face smashed into the chair on the way down and I grimaced. *Ouch. That had to hurt.*

Sure enough, he wailed and rolled away with his hands over his nose.

It was probably broke.

Well, at least my metal leg was cooperatin' better these days. It almost even acted like a real leg now.

Three men loomed over me then, one of 'em a big, burly fella with a bushy beard. He didn't look friendly, neither.

I threw the chair at 'em, but the big guy knocked it away easy and it bounced off his meaty forearm to crash into another fella and knock him sprawlin'. Then the big guy reached down and grabbed the front of my shirt.

Well shit.

He pulled me up as easy as he'd knocked away the chair and grinned into my face. "Hey there, Delano," he drawled. "Remember me?"

I frowned at him as the fightin' went on all around us, the sounds of yellin' and shoutin' and shatterin' glass makin' a real ruckus. I had a feelin' I shoulda remembered him, and he had the kinda build that was hard to forget, but I couldn't recall crossin' paths with him before. "No," I admitted.

But then, I *had* been awful drunk lately…

Maybe the swill was startin' to affect my mind.

Maybe I needed to lay off a bit.

"Well then, let's see if we can't refresh your memory," he said.

He drove one of his big, meaty paws into my middle hard enough to send black spots burstin' across my vision, and then I was on the floor on hands and knees, retchin' and gaggin' fer air.

He didn't give me time to catch my breath.

He caught the back of my shirt and lifted me again, then threw me at the nearest table.

I crashed into it and knocked it over, and what food and drink had been left atop it clattered to the floor, addin' to the mess. I landed myself in a tangle of chairs, but I still couldn't breathe. I rolled onto my side, gaspin', tryin' to blink the black from my eyes.

A pair of boots stomped up next to me, but they didn't look like the big fella's boots.

Then a shotgun roared out over the noise of the fight, and I flinched at the closeness of it. I fumbled fer one of my own guns, but all the damn chair legs was in the way.

"All right, that's enough!" a familiar voice boomed into the little hole of quiet the shotgun blast had bought him. "All of you, that's enough! Party's over!"

I shoved some chairs outta my way and rolled over onto my back, a hand over my achin' stomach and feelin' like I might vomit. I looked up into the angry face of Sheriff Earl Jennings, the man who passed fer the law around these parts. So those boots had belonged to him.

He stood over me with his shotgun ready, three of his deputies fanned out behind him.

The sound of people runnin' quick out of the saloon marked the hasty retreat of several of the fight's worst offenders, and the sheriff motioned fer his deputies to go after some of 'em. I hoped that blasted cheater wouldn't get away.

I wasn't quite sure what to hope for that big, burly fella. On the one hand, I wouldn't mind him spendin' a few days in a cell while I recovered my wits. On the other hand, if the sheriff had scared him off now, maybe he wouldn't chance comin' around again if he managed to escape this time.

Least, I was pretty sure Sheriff Jennings had scared him off. He weren't comin' fer me anymore, anyway. And fer that, I was grateful. I smiled up at the lawman standin' over me and ignored his scowl. "Howdy, Sheriff. Mighty nice timin' you got."

His frown deepened beneath his gray mustache, and his dark eyes glittered. He looked awful angry this time. "Delano," he growled. "You start this again?"

"No, sir." I touched gingerly at my jaw, already feelin' a spot swellin' up. "I didn't start nothin'. Only called out a man fer cheatin' at cards, is all."

"He started it, all right," the barkeep called from across the room, and I pushed myself up sittin' to glare at him.

He was glarin' back at me, and his slicked-back hair and hooked, narrow nose sure made him look somethin' like a vulture, waitin' to pounce on a meal.

"He was *cheatin'*," I said again. "You wanna harbor cheats at your establishment? I thought you wanted to be a respectable place of business?"

He scoffed, throwin' up his hands as he looked around the saloon. "Respectable place of business? Delano, look at this place! You've trashed it!"

I gave the room a glance-over. Everyone else able-bodied had cleared out now, leavin' only me, the barkeep, and the sheriff. It *was* quite the mess. Tables overturned, chairs broken, glass and shattered bottles all over the floor, and some bodies, too. Looked like they was all breathin', at least, though they'd likely have some awful bad headaches in the morning.

It seemed things had escalated, sure enough. But I hadn't been the one to cause such a mess. I'd only called out one man fer cheatin'. "What was I supposed to do?" I asked. "Let him rob me and the others? That don't seem smart. All I did was call him out, give him a chance to leave quietly." I prodded at a new split in my lower lip. "He refused my offer. But ya can't say I didn't give him a chance."

"This is the third time I've had to come in here 'cause of brawlin' in just as many weeks," the sheriff said. "And every time it seems I find *you* in the center of it."

He was lookin' at me.

I lifted my hands and shook my head, then winced as that made the room start spinnin' again. "No, sir. I ain't at the center of nothin'. Seems there's just an excess of cheats and swindlers in this town. Maybe you should work a little harder on cleanin' them up, yeah? Then we wouldn't have so much of a problem."

One of his thick gray eyebrows lifted up into his hat brim. "All right," he said. "We're gonna go have a little talk."

He grabbed the collar of my shirt before I could protest the notion, and I found myself once again hauled to my feet. Sheriff Jennings was an older man, but he'd lived in the Territories all his life, and the sun and the heat and the outlaws he'd been chasin' most that time had whittled him down into a hard, unyieldin' man.

It made me wonder what Nine-Fingered Nan had on him, to bend such a man to her whim.

I had no such leverage, least not yet, and so he was none-too-gentle as he dragged me across the mess of the saloon floor to the back door and shoved me through it.

I tripped across the threshold, partially 'cause of too much whiskey, and partially 'cause of that damnable metal leg, and landed hard in the dirt on the other side. All the places I'd been pummeled in this most recent tussle started to make themselves known, and I groaned as I picked myself up onto hands and knees.

I was gonna be one sore mess soon enough.

But for now ... for now I had to decide what to do about Sheriff Jennings.

He rounded on me in the back alleyway behind the Stag, and I noticed he kept his shotgun in-hand, as if unsure whether or not he might need to use it.

Smart of him, 'cause I wore both my own sixguns, and I weren't sure whether or not I might need to use those, neither. I sat back on my heels and regarded him through a haze of alcohol and a deep, throbbin' pain that was startin' up in my temples.

"Listen here, you cocky little shit," he snarled. "You might be in Nan's fold now, but that don't mean you have free rein to go around causin' trouble whenever you damn well please!"

I scoffed. "Don't it? Thought you and her had an *under-standin'*." I remembered clearly the sneering face of Taggert, the handlebar-mustached bastard who'd double-crossed Nan and me both the first time I'd tried to make a bargain in this town. He'd also been the first to clue me in to the fact Bravebank was ruled by Nine-Fingered Nan.

And now, he was dead.

"Yeah, we got an understandin', all right." Sheriff Jennings stepped up closer to me. "We got an *understandin'* that this town is gonna run business as usual. None of her crew goes around shootin' up folk or causin' trouble, and we let some of her questionable business practices go unnoticed, let her use the place as a base of operations for her industry expansion out further west."

"Industry expansion?" What the hell was he on about? The only industry Nine-Fingered Nan seemed interested in was robbin' and murderin' and the sellin' of innocents as slave labor, and that was an industry I was keen on bringin' to an end.

"Yeah," the sheriff said. "And you're givin' the Stag a bad reputation, Delano. Word's startin' to spread that it's a good place for bad men, and that's just what we *don't* want. Word like that scares away the honest folk and brings in people who might be lookin' to move in on Nan's territory. You startin' all these fights and wreckin' the saloon every week is *bad for business*, got it?"

I only scowled at him. Frankly, I didn't give a damn about the success of his business, or the Stag's business, or Nan's business. Far as I were concerned, they could all go to Hell. But I was stuck here, bidin' my time, until Nan sent word on what she wanted next from me.

And if most of the town was loyal to Nan, it wouldn't do much good to make enemies out of 'em all. Not yet.

Maybe this Sheriff Jennings was the one I shoulda been tryin' to talk to about Nan's operations these last few weeks. Seemed he knew an awful lot about 'em. I wondered how loyal he really was to their *understandin'*, given he was a lawman and all.

He was at least loyal enough to be upset over my recent

public disturbances, I supposed. I wondered if he'd tell me anythin', either, in that case.

"If there's one thing Nan hates most," he said now, "it's people gettin' in the way of her business. You best watch yourself, Delano. She ain't got no qualms about cuttin' loose dead weight. You best make yourself of more use and less trouble, else…" He broke open his shotgun and made a show of pullin' out the spent cartridge, puttin' in a new one, and snappin' it closed again. "Else she's gonna cut you loose, and then there won't be nothin' between you and the law. Nothin' between you and me. Understand?"

I grumbled and scrubbed at my eyes. It all made sense, sure. Made sense I'd backed myself into a nice, tight corner, and I didn't much like that feelin'. "Yeah," I growled. "Sure."

"Glad we have an understandin' now too, then," Sheriff Jennings said. "Cause I'm gonna need you to come back to the jailhouse with me. Take a little time to cool off and sober up."

I stared up at him, pretty sure I'd heard him wrong. "You wanna lock me up?"

"That's right."

He was starin' down at me steadily, shotgun in hand. Close-range. Real close. If he wanted to take me in, there weren't much I could do about it. But even still, that restless anger flared again inside, heatin' up my blood. Why should he go after *me*? I weren't the one cheatin', or tryin' to kill a man over cards. And I'd had nothin' to do with what anyone else did in that saloon. "Like hell—"

He didn't give me time to finish.

He whipped that shotgun around and cracked its butt into my skull, and I went out cold.

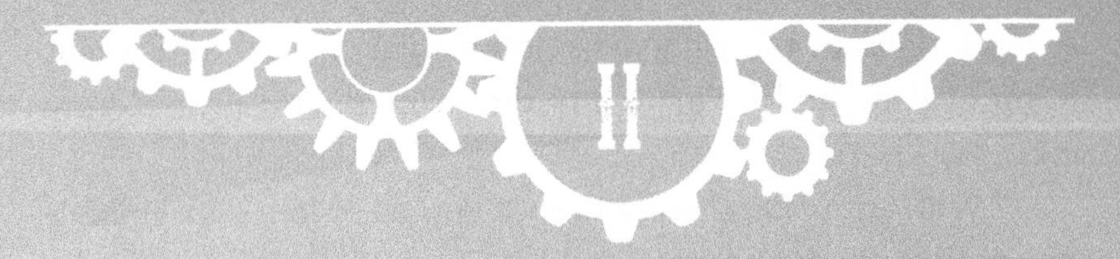

MORNIN', SUNSHINE

Consciousness came back slow, and the pain came back quick.

I groaned and rolled over, feelin' a thin mattress underneath me. My head was splittin', my jaw achin', and bruises all over my body throbbin'. My middle was especially sore, and I put a hand over it as I forced my eyes open.

The place I were in was dim, lit only by a single lantern sittin' across the way on the corner of a desk. There was one window, high up and small and barred, but not much sunlight came through it.

Barred?

Shit.

I brought my focus back to my more immediate surroundin's and found a whole wall of bars right there not three feet from my face.

The jailhouse. That damned sheriff had got me here, all right. I muttered foul words and shoved myself up sittin' on the cot, then grabbed for the bucket meant as my chamber pot as nausea rolled up my throat.

I emptied out what was left in my stomach and sat there fer a minute gaggin', then grimaced and spit, and shoved the bucket away into the far, far corner of the cell. Then I lurched back to the cot and collapsed down atop it, pushin' myself back into the corner of the wall to keep me upright.

Fer Chrissakes, I felt like I'd been ran over by a whole herd of cattle.

The door to the jailhouse opened then, spillin' in a bright beam of light, and I winced and threw up an arm to shield my eyes.

"Well," came the sheriff's deep, resonant voice. I imagined it probably made the ladies around here swoon. "Look who's finally awake. Mornin', Sunshine."

The door shut and mercifully closed off the light, and I squinted toward his voice.

He clomped across the room to his desk, spurs janglin'. He had a folded newspaper under one arm, and a steamin' cup of joe in the other hand. He eased himself down into his chair and sipped at his coffee, and I realized that's what I very much needed right now: a good, strong cup of joe.

He smiled over at me and put his boots up on the corner of his desk. "Thought maybe you'd sleep all day."

I growled at him, fingers brushing my left temple where his shotgun butt had come into contact with my skull. The spot was tender to the touch. A fine match fer the place on my right temple I'd had to have stitched not too long ago after my run-in with Baron Whittaker. Still had a scar there from that one, still pink. "Didn't have to hit me so hard," I muttered.

The sheriff shrugged. "Couldn't take any chances. I gave you an opportunity to come quiet. You refused my offer. But you can't say I didn't give you the chance."

I peered through the bars at him, wonderin' if he was usin' my own words against me on purpose. Who was bein' a cocky little shit now? I sighed and rolled my eyes, leanin' my head back against the brick wall behind me. "Where's the rest of 'em?" I gestured weakly to the other two cells in the place, which I'd noticed were empty.

"Gone already," the sheriff said. "Had a few in here overnight for all that ruckus you caused at the Stag, but I think they got the message. Let 'em free this mornin'."

"Yeah? You get that cheatin' bastard?"

"He got ran outta town. But after that beatin' he got, I don't think he'll be back."

I grunted. Not exactly what I'd wanted, but good enough, I supposed. "What about the big guy with the beard?"

The sheriff's brows lifted at that one. "Thomas Withrow?"

"Don't know his name. But he's a big, ugly fella with a beard that could use a trim."

Sheriff Jennings shook his head and chuckled. "Sounds like Tommy. You get sideways with him, too?"

"I dunno. Maybe. Seems so. I don't rightly remember."

The sheriff let out a low whistle and set down his cup. "Good luck with that one, Delano. Tommy's a mountain man, tough as they come."

"Mountain man?" That didn't make no sense. "What the hell's he doin' down here, then?"

"Came to visit his sister awhile back. She lives close by. Married to a railroad man, though last I heard he'd taken pretty sick. Guess that's why Tommy showed up. Maybe to help her out for a spell."

Huh. Somethin' about all that seemed kinda familiar, but I couldn't quite place it.

"But no," the sheriff went on. "Tommy weren't in here. He didn't do nothin' wrong, far as I could tell."

My hand still rested on my stomach, and I could almost feel the shape of that man's fist in the bruise there. It ached every time I breathed. "I think he wanted to kill me," I said. "Or else come real close to it."

"Well. Maybe if you'd stop stirrin' up trouble, you'd stop makin' yourself so many enemies."

"Real helpful, Sheriff," I drawled. "Thanks."

"Just statin' facts, Delano."

"And what about me? You gonna let me free now, too?"

He sighed and pulled his boots off his desk, leanin' forward in his chair. He tossed the newspaper to his desktop. "I dunno. You gonna stop causin' trouble 'round here?"

"I said so, didn't I?"

"Yeah, well, sayin' and doin' are two different things, ain't they?"

"This is a strange town you run, Sheriff. Gotta say I ain't never been jailed fer callin' out a cheater before."

"That ain't why you're here and you know it." His voice turned sharp. "You're scarin' the townsfolk and interruptin' business. I had to bring you in here to give 'em a little reassurance. Let 'em know there's still law and order in this town."

I laughed despite myself. "Law and order? That's rich, comin' from a man under Nan's thumb."

His face went all stormy at that, and he pushed his chair back and stood, leanin' over the desk to glare at me. "And just where do you think you're at, Delano? Right there with me, ain't you? Only I heard you volunteered for the job, which makes you one of the worst kinda people. Either that or stupid. Or maybe both."

I glared at him through my bars, heat risin' up under my shirt collar and makin' my head hurt even worse. *Volunteerin'* was a funny way of puttin' it. But I didn't feel like explainin' myself to him. So all I said was, "I have my reasons."

"Yeah? Bet you do. Same as me. So why don't you cut the shit? Least I know my place … least I *have* a place outside of Nan's arrangements. What do you got outside of that, Delano? Huh? An appointment with a noose somewhere? How many towns in the Territories got bulletins up with your face on 'em, I wonder?"

I managed to hold his glare, but I had nothin' to say about that.

It was true enough. Outside of tryin' to save Ethelyn, I didn't have much else. I had Holt, if that could be counted fer anythin', considerin' we hated each other most the time. And I had our little camp in Grave Gulch, the closest thing to a home anymore. And my two guns, and a mule that'd been stolen once, but was now bought and paid fer.

None of that mattered much. And it didn't matter at all if I couldn't get Ethelyn back.

"Yeah, you can go," Sheriff Jennings said abruptly. He fished a heavy ring of keys off his belt and sorted through 'em till he found the one he wanted. "For now. But I'm tellin' you … watch yourself. No more brawlin', no shootin' no one—"

"What if they try to shoot me first?"

He paused mid-step on the way over to my cell and pursed his lips under his neatly groomed mustache. "Then you'd better hope you got witnesses. Otherwise I swear to God, Delano, I'm gonna try you for murder."

"Awful biased operation you got goin' on here," I grumbled as he turned the key in the cell door's lock.

"You ain't given me any reason to trust you," he snapped back. He pulled the barred door open with a horrific screechin' of hinges, and I winced. Then he turned on his heel and marched back to his desk, where he retrieved my gun belts from a hook on the wall behind it.

I grabbed up my hat from the floor and shoved it back on my head, then made my way slowly off the cot and stood unsteadily, rocked a minute, then stabilized. I was stiff and sore, all right, and my head pounded somethin' terrible. I limped toward the sheriff as he held my belts out toward me.

"Your rig," he said. "Just remember what I said."

"Yeah, yeah. I'll remember." I took my belts from him and buckled 'em both back around my hips, then checked both guns to be sure everything was still in place. They looked fine, and, satisfied, I slipped 'em both back into their holsters. "One more thing, Sheriff."

His eyes narrowed, his hand goin' straight to his gun grip. "What's that?"

I lifted my own hands, not wantin' him to get the wrong idea. "Just wonderin' what you can tell me about Nan's operations, is all," I said. "You mentioned she was lookin' to expand her industry out further west. What industry is that, exactly?"

He raised his eyebrows. "She didn't tell you?"

"No."

"Well then," he gave me a smile, "that means she don't want you to know. And that means *I* sure as fuck ain't gonna tell you."

I sighed. But I was too tired and too sore at the moment to push the subject, or to do anythin' about his reluctance to share, so I only rolled my eyes and turned away from him, then hobbled toward the door, grimacin' with every step. Maybe we could resume this conversation later. When I felt more myself. "Can't wait to leave this godforsaken town," I muttered.

"Can't wait till you're gone," he said from behind me. Then he stalked past me and yanked open the door to the outside, blindin' me with that sunlight again. "Now get the fuck out of my jailhouse."

He didn't have to tell me twice.

A jailhouse was the last place I wanted to be, though the irony of my situation weren't lost on me, neither. Any other day, before I'd made a deal with Nine-Fingered Nan, I likely wouldn't have had the chance to be *walkin'* out of a jailhouse, not unless I was walkin' out to make my way to the gallows. Most certainly I wouldn't be walkin' out free. Least, not if the sheriff took any time to investigate my background properly.

Course, I never woulda stayed in one town a whole three weeks, neither. And likely wouldn't have downed so much whiskey, or been itchin' so much fer a fight, or played enough cards to be able to know when a fella was cheatin'.

I sighed again as I made my way slow and careful out of that brick buildin' and into the street. Sheriff Jennings slammed the door behind me and I cringed again. Goddamn. He have to do everything so goddamn loud?

I squinted in the daylight despite my hat, and swept a look down the street both ways. It was late mornin', thereabouts, and most folk were on about their daily business now. The streets were quiet, mostly empty.

I had nothin' to do still, seein' as Nan hadn't seen fit yet to retrieve me.

The anger flared up again, hard and bitter, but I tried to shove it back down, somewhere deep where it'd stay buried and stop gettin' me into trouble. Just like the sheriff had said.

What I needed was coffee. Coffee and food. Maybe that'd improve my mood. But I figured I'd better stay away from the Stag fer awhile. Had a feelin' that barkeep was mighty tired of me by now.

No matter. There were plenty of other saloons in Bravebank. I turned in the dusty street toward another of 'em, this one called, amusingly, First Chance, and ambled that way, instead. I was just passin' the tailor's place when a shadow moved in the alleyway between the buildings and came right at me.

III

AN ESPECIALLY BAD DAY

I swung around toward the shadow with a yell and went fer my gun, only to stop mid-draw as I saw it were Holt.

I swore at him somethin' awful and shook my head, then leaned against the nearest hitchin' post and waited fer my heart to slow. "*God damn*, Holt. Yer fixin' to get yerself killed, sneakin' around like that."

The old man scoffed. "I weren't sneakin'. You weren't payin' attention."

"Why you always gotta be lurkin' around in the shadows, anyway?"

Holt looked both ways down the street, same as I had just a few minutes ago. "Cuz I don't like towns. They ain't nothin' but trouble waitin' to happen."

Well, that certainly seemed true enough. Least fer people like us. Funny how when I was a boy, livin' with Mama and Pa, towns hadn't seemed to be much trouble at all. "Seems all right to me," I lied. I pushed off the hitchin' rail and resumed my walk toward First Chance, and Holt joined me, though his eyes kept dartin' around all fidgety like.

"Yeah, sure," he said. "That why you spent the night in the jailhouse?"

Damnable nosy old man. I'd been hopin' that had escaped his notice. "Yeah," I said. "Wanted a sample of the sheriff's hospitality. That Sheriff Jennings, he's a real friendly gent."

Holt snorted. "Sure he is. You just be careful, Van. I heard what trouble you've been causin'. Yer the talk of the town, pretty much, and it ain't nothin' good. I know Nan's got some kinda agreement with that lawdog, but I don't like the look of him."

"You don't like the look of no one. Not even me."

"Yeah, and that's why I ain't the one bein' locked up."

"It weren't nothin'," I insisted. "Just a misunderstandin'. Sheriff and I got it all worked out now."

"Uh huh."

We walked in silence fer awhile, and I turned my attention to nursin' my multiple bruises. A covered wagon rattled by at a trot, and the driver and his missus gave the both of us condescendin' looks as they passed.

We ignored 'em. Weren't nothin' we weren't used to.

"By the way," Holt said at last, reachin' to the inside pocket of his duster. "You got a telegram from that girl. Charlotte."

My stomach lurched at the sound of her name, and my heart picked up pace again.

Holt pulled out a folded piece of paper and held it toward me. "Was at the Grave Gulch post office when I went back there last week. Post master said it'd been waitin' there awhile."

I took it from him and swallowed hard. I gave a nod, suddenly findin' no words, and shoved it into my back pants pocket.

Holt looked at me funny. "Ain't you gonna read it?"

I shook my head, then cleared my throat and managed to speak. "Naw. Later." I already knew what it would say, anyway. If she'd sent me somethin' in the first place, it meant she'd made it home safe, and that was all that really mattered.

I didn't want to read the rest of it. She'd be askin' about Ethelyn, most like. Wantin' to know if my sister was home safe, too. Wantin' to know why I hadn't written her myself yet to tell her so.

But of course I hadn't written her myself yet.

I didn't have nothin' to write about. I still didn't have my sister. And I didn't need any more reminders of that.

"Suit yerself," Holt muttered.

There was another long minute of silence between us, and truth be told, I was happy fer the quiet.

Too bad it didn't last.

"How long you gonna stay here, Van?" Holt asked abruptly.

I sighed. We'd already had this conversation. More than once. "I told you. I'm stayin' here till Nan says what else she wants fer my sister."

The muscles in Holt's jaw flexed, visible even under his scraggly gray beard. "Fine. Let me say it a different way. How long you gonna stay here 'fore you give up on hearin' from Nan?"

I stopped walkin' and faced him. "If you need to move on, you just go ahead and move on. I ain't stoppin' you."

"Like hell." He tossed back the sides of his duster coat and stuck his hands on his hips. "You still owe me a job."

"I ain't forgot that."

"Good, cuz I got somethin' lined up." He dropped his voice. "Another bank."

I shook my head and wet my dry lips, feelin' at the place where a fist had bloodied 'em. It was all dried and scabbed over now. "Not now, Holt."

"See, kid, that's the problem. You wanna wait here fer who knows how long, maybe forever, and I ain't got that time to just sit around. You still owe me a job, and that job needs doin'!"

"After I get Ethelyn, I told you."

"And what if you never get her?"

I said nothin' fer a long minute, just starin' at him as we stood in the oppressive heat of that dusty street. *What if I never get her?* I couldn't think about that, so I hadn't. And I wouldn't. "After I have her, I'll do the job. I swear."

Holt threw up his hands, pacin' away from me angrily. "Goddamnit, Van. Yer swearin' don't mean shit to me. I don't got time fer this nonsense!"

"Then leave," I shot back. "But I ain't goin' nowhere, Holt, not till I hear from Nan. You do what you gotta do, and I'll do the same." I turned away from him and strode off toward the saloon, but he weren't gonna let me go so easy.

He caught up to me and grabbed at my shoulder, yankin' me around.

He caught me on a bad day. Hell, I hadn't had a good day in a long, long while. But this day was an especially bad day.

I weren't in no mood for his shit, and that anger I'd tried to bury deep turned out to not be buried so deep, after all. It came roarin' back up at his man-handlin', and I lashed out with a fist and got him good in the left eye.

He stumbled backward and I saw the surprise go quick across his face. Holt and I had had our share of spats in our years travelin' together, sure, but I'd never started nothin' before. Not like this.

He straightened, and the surprise got replaced by fury.

This time I hadn't been so much itchin' fer a fight, but it seemed I'd be gettin' one, anyway. 'Less I could make amends real quick. "Holt—"

He came at me like a rabid dog, and I cursed the impulse that had made me want to deck him in the face. I weren't in no condition for another fight so soon after the last one, least of all with a mean old bastard like Holt. But I weren't gonna let him beat on me without defendin' myself, neither, so I dodged his rain of blows as best I could and landed a few of my own, too.

If only I hadn't already felt like I'd been trampled by a herd of cattle, or that my skull was splittin' open. I staggered as I blocked one of his fists with my left forearm, exhausted and just wantin' him to stop already, but in doin' so I left my already much-bruised middle wide open, and he took advantage of it.

He didn't hit me that hard, in truth, but he got the spot big ol' Tommy Withrow had hit the afternoon before and it was enough to draw a yell outta me and send me down to my knees, folded up with an arm over my belly.

Holt grabbed the back of my neck soon as I was down and dunked my head straight into the nearest water trough.

It weren't cold, and it weren't pleasant, and I weren't sure he didn't intend to drown me right then and there. We'd nearly shot each other a time or two before ... him drownin' me wouldn't be much different.

I braced my hands against the edge of it and tried to leverage myself upward, but he had a hold of me good and was leanin' his weight on me, and I couldn't budge him from that angle. I struggled, kicked, flailed, but I couldn't find nothin' of him to grab onto. My hands slapped against the sleeves of his duster and I took fistfuls of 'em and tugged, tryin' to loosen his grip.

Nothin'.

I kicked out with my metal foot, hopin' to find one of his legs, but he weren't stupid. He was standin' close, too close fer me to get any good force behind my struggles.

My lungs burned, everything in me screamin' for me to open my mouth and take in a big ol' gulp of air. But there weren't no air to be had. It was all I could do to fight that urge ... and the burnin' in my chest got worse, till I realized it was gonna happen whether I wanted it or not.

My mouth opened, lettin' out bubbles, and my chest spasmed as I sucked inward, bracin' myself to drown.

But instead I got air.

Mostly air. Some water.

I choked and coughed, gulpin' at the hot, dusty air like it were the sweetest thing I ever tasted. And right then, it was.

Holt threw me sideways and I fell into the muddied dirt and just laid there, relishin' the act of breathin'. So he still couldn't bring himself to kill me. Well, that was somethin'. I supposed I still didn't want to kill him, neither.

Maybe.

"Fine," he spat down at me. "That's it. I'm done. You want me to leave? I'm leavin'. Good luck, kid. Yer gonna need it."

I watched his boots turn and walk off, but I didn't have enough air yet to call out after him. Not that I had anythin' to say, anyway. I had no right to make him wait here with me, or to ask him to accompany me on any errand Nan might eventually have fer me. I was the one who'd made the deal, and the deal'd had nothin' to do with him.

If he couldn't have patience enough to wait till my deal was done … well … like I'd said … I wasn't stoppin' him. He had to do what was right by him. Same as me.

Even still, there was a strange sorta melancholy in my burnin' chest as I watched him stalk off down the street and turn the corner out of sight. Sure, he mighta just almost killed me, but in the end, he hadn't. And we'd been runnin' together fer a long time now. He'd been the one to keep me from starvin' after Mama and Pa were killed.

I wondered if he'd really be gone fer good this time.

Swearin' and scowlin' and breathin' hard, I shoved myself up sittin' and sat back against the side of the trough I'd almost drowned in. I fished my hat out of it and tried to shake the water off best I could. "Ain't … ain't no such thing as luck," I husked.

I stuck the drippin' hat back on my head, and that's when I noticed several folk in the street, all starin' at me. I wondered if they'd been drawn outside by the noise of the fightin', or maybe by all my splashin' around.

I wondered if they was the real reason Holt had spared me.

Well. Guess I'd never know, now.

I glared at 'em all. "Whatcha lookin' at?" I snapped. "Go on back to yer business. Show's over."

They milled about, some havin' the grace to at least look sheepish. Others of 'em didn't seem to have no shame.

I ignored 'em. I didn't have the strength left to yell anymore. Didn't even have the strength left to get up from where I sat. So I just pulled my damp hat down over my face to block out the light, block out the folks starin' at me, and let my head rest back against the lip of the trough.

I closed my eyes and let myself relax, not carin' what happened next.

Surely this day couldn't get no worse.

Someone kicked at my boot and I startled awake, pullin' my hat down off my face and then squintin' in the sun. Seemed I'd been out awhile. Looked like afternoon now, and the heat of high summer was swelterin'. No one sober or sane was out and about at this hour, but there I was, still sittin' next to that trough.

My head still throbbin' and my bruises still achin'.

Someone kicked at my boot again, and I forced myself to focus. There were three silhouettes standin' in front of me. The one front and center had a familiar shape. Tall and thin, with a wide-brimmed hat and two pearl-gripped pistols, one on each hip.

She had her thumbs hooked into her belt, and she was starin' down at me with those hard, pale eyes. "Didn't realize I'd hired the town drunk," she said flatly.

Fuck.

Nine-Fingered Nan.

The outlaw boss herself. Come all the way to Bravebank. And here I was passed out in the middle of the street.

"I ain't drunk," I rasped. Least, not anymore. I could use a drink right then, though. Preferably of somethin' like coffee. I reached out to grab the edge of the trough and used it to pull myself up sittin' straight, then struggled to my feet.

And anyway, *hired* wasn't what she'd done to me. Forced, extorted, ransomed … one of those descriptors woulda been far more accurate.

"Sheriff Jennings tells me you've been causin' him a lot of trouble," she said.

I glanced down the way toward the jailhouse, a squat brick buildin', and scowled. There was two ways to approach this situation, but there weren't no way I was apologizin' to Nan fer anythin'. So instead I brought my gaze back from the jailhouse and put it right on her, lookin' her square in the face.

Ignorin' the two lieutenants flankin' her.

"I was bored," I said.

To my surprise, a corner of her mouth quirked upward at that statement, almost smilin'. "That so?"

"Yeah."

"Good."

I hadn't expected her to say that, neither, and I didn't know what to say in reply. Besides maybe somethin' like, *Fuck off, ya old cunt*, but I didn't think that'd probably get me very far in gettin' back my sister, so I kept my mouth shut.

"Well," she said then, "I've had a nice, good think on what I want from ya, Mr. Delano. You ready to talk business, or ya wanna continue yer nap there in the mud?"

I swallowed back the swell of anger at her derisive tone and shook my head, then brushed futilely at the dirt crusted to my clothes. "Naw, I'm ready. Let's talk."

"Fine. This way, then." She nodded at her lieutenants, then turned and headed straight fer the Stag.

Shit. But this time I had no choice in the matter, so I went after her, limpin' and wincin'.

EST
PARK
2023

Her two lieutenants fell into step behind me. I didn't like 'em there. The hair on the back of my neck prickled, but there weren't nothin' I could do about them, neither.

So I walked quiet in the shadow of Nine-Fingered Nan, and tried not to dwell on the fact I felt an awful lot like a steer bein' driven off to slaughter.

IV

IF THE MATH ADDS UP

She marched into the Stag Saloon like she owned the place.

I suppose that's 'cause she *did* own the place.

The barkeep snapped to proper attention as he realized it was *her* walkin' in, only sparin' me a quick, annoyed glance. He'd made a lot of progress in cleanin' up the place since yesterday afternoon. Except fer a few new stains on the floor, and a missin' table or two, the place looked pretty much same as it usually did.

Weren't many people in there, though, for this time a day.

Nan seemed to notice the sparse patronage, a flicker of somethin' passin' over her face before it went neutral again. But I saw it. Saw it, and noted it.

"Get out," she snapped, wavin' at the barkeep, then sweepin' her glare across the rest of the place. "All of you. Out."

No one said a word in protest. No one argued. The barkeep marched straight out the back door, and the few other fellas in there just stood and filed past us toward the front door, givin' Nan a wide berth, and not one of 'em makin' eye contact.

That didn't make me feel no better.

Nan went to a table in the middle of the room and pulled out a chair, then sat down, facin' the front door.

One of her men went to that door, too, and posted himself just inside it. I guessed to be sure no one else wandered in durin' our discussion.

The other of her men went back behind the bar and poured a few drinks.

Of whiskey.

Nine-Fingered Nan nodded at the chair across the table from her and pushed it out with one boot. "Sit," she commanded.

I did so, slow and stiff. I didn't like my back to the door, or to her fella over there. But then, I didn't like a whole lot about this situation. Didn't like the situation as a whole, altogether.

Her second man came to our table and put the drinks down in front of us. One fer Nan. One fer me. One fer himself. He downed his and set the empty glass on the table, then moved around to stand behind Nan's right shoulder.

As if she needed him lookin' out fer her.

Even at my best, I weren't sure I could beat her.

And I most certainly weren't at my best today.

Nan reached out with her left hand, the one with all the fingers, and picked up her glass. "Well, Mr. Delano. You sure yer up fer this? Yer lookin' a little worse fer wear."

I surely felt worse than even that. But I'd waited three long weeks fer this. I weren't gonna wait any longer, not if I'd been at Death's door, itself. "I'm up fer it." My voice was all hoarse, and I cleared my throat. Reached fer the whiskey and stared down into it.

If only it were anythin' but whiskey.

"Good to hear." She took a long, deep drink from her glass, savored it, and set the glass back to the table. "In that case..." Her left hand went up again, the fingers gesturin'.

The man behind her reached into the satchel he had slung over one shoulder and pulled out some documents. He put them into her waitin' hand.

She put them on the table between us, pullin' off the top paper to unfold it—with both hands this time, and I couldn't help lookin' at her stump of a finger.

Least it weren't a stump of a leg, like she'd given me.

'Course, missin' a leg didn't much matter to my shootin' abilities. Losin' the trigger finger of yer dominant hand, though, weren't no small thing. But she'd managed. More than managed.

She'd built a whole terrible empire out here in the Territories. An empire that seemed to be stretchin' awful far to the east, if Charlotte were right about Nan's crew bein' the ones who'd grabbed her out of the Republic.

And an empire Nan seemed awful keen on stretchin' out further west, too, based on what Sheriff Jennings had told me. And I didn't like the thought of either of those things bein' true.

She smoothed the paper out, and I saw it was a map. A couple routes had been marked along it to the north of us, comin' down from Utah and goin' toward Blessing.

That was a town I surely had no wish to return to any time soon.

"What I need from you, Mr. Delano," Nan said, tracin' the marked routes with the gnarled middle finger of her right hand, "is to intercept a stagecoach that'll be along one of these roads here, goin' south. I'll need you to get to it, and stop it, before it comes anywhere near its final destination."

"All right. Where's it headin', then?"

"Blessing."

My breath hissed out between my teeth before I could catch it.

Nan looked up at me, then sat back in her chair. "There a problem, Mr. Delano?"

"No." I shifted on my own chair. "No problem. Just don't much like that town, is all."

"That's good, 'cause if that stagecoach gets to Blessing, then ya didn't do the job, did ya? And then we're gonna have a problem."

"We won't have a problem," I said. "I'll stop it before it gets there." I wasn't gonna step foot in Blessing again if I could help it, that's fer sure.

"See that you do. Yer sister will be countin' on ya."

A shot of somethin' went through me at the mention of Ethelyn. A shot of somethin' like fear. Anticipation. Hope. All the things I couldn't afford to feel. I straightened on my chair and fought to keep my voice even. I didn't want her to see any of those feelin's. Didn't want her to hear the desperation clawin' around in my belly. "So I stop a stagecoach. Make sure it don't reach Blessing. That all?" It almost seemed too easy.

"Not quite."

Of course not. I shouldn't have asked.

"Stop the stagecoach. Kill everyone aboard it, and be sure they're dead." She pulled another piece of paper from her pile of documents and slid it over across the table toward me. "It'll be carrying a lockbox that'll look something like this. Fetch that from the coach—might be on one of the people ridin' in it, or maybe in the coach's treasure box—and bring it back here to me."

I picked up the piece of paper. It was a pencil sketch of the item in question … but it only looked like somethin' you might see in any someone's home who had a bit of money, protectin' their valuables. I raised my brows. "A lockbox in a lockbox?"

"That's right."

"Must be some mighty fine valuables in there."

"You could say that."

"But it looks like any other lockbox," I said. "How will I know if it's the one you want?"

"Not like any other lockbox," she said, sittin' forward in her chair and givin' me a look of disapproval that woulda rivaled Holt's. "Lookit." Her middle finger jabbed the paper in my hand. "Lookit the lock."

I squinted at the sketch. Sure enough, it weren't *quite* like any other lockbox, after all. This one didn't need a key to open it. Instead, there was a row of small dials across the top, each with their own set of numbers, kinda like one of those combination safes. "Ah."

She plucked up a third paper and pushed it at me. "And this is the coach yer lookin' fer. Seems like a hired coach, same as all the rest, but it ain't. It belongs to Baron Haas and his family."

My stomach turned at the mention of another of those metal barons.

"It ain't much, but if you look close, you can see the difference. There's no company name across the top. The rear boot is smaller'n most. And it won't be loaded up with passengers. You find this coach, and it'll have that lockbox I want in it somewhere."

I put down the sketch of the lockbox and considered the picture of the coach. This was a real picture, an actual photograph. It showed a nice-lookin' stagecoach pulled by four tall, glossy horses. Well, that in and of itself woulda stood out. Most public coaches had seen their share of miles. They were roughed up a bit, the paint chipped and faded, and the horses more of the workin' variety.

This one had a sharp-dressed gentleman and his similarly sharp-dressed lady standin' in front of it. Baron Haas and Lady Haas, I reckoned. I swallowed hard. "Will the baron be aboard?"

Nan shook her head. "Nah. He wouldn't risk such a thing. Just be some of those he employs on-board. The driver and a few armed guards."

I looked up across the table at her. This was gettin' more and more complicated by the minute. Don't know why I was surprised. "How many armed guards, exactly?"

She shrugged. "Fer anythin' transported by the barons? Three to five marshals is pretty standard fare fer their types."

I muttered a curse and tossed the photograph back to the table. "So all I gotta do is stop the stagecoach, kill the armed, angry men accompanyin' it, the driver, and whoever else is aboard, grab that lockbox, and bring it all the way back here to you. That sound about right?"

Nan smiled, then picked up her whiskey and took another long pull. "Precisely, Mr. Delano. Must be those smarts you got from yer mama at work."

I glared at her fer a long minute, but before I could think of a proper retort that wouldn't also get me shot, she leaned forward again and spoke.

"Just one other thing."

"What now?"

"See that you don't open that lockbox."

"Shouldn't be a problem, seein' as I don't know the code to open it."

"Some might try and open it usin' other means," Nan offered.

"Well, *I* won't."

Her pale eyes stared at me, flat and even. "Good. If I see that lockbox has been tampered with, or opened, the deal is off."

I had no intention of tryin' to open that lockbox. But my mouth went all dry at the finality in her tone, anyway. "I ain't gonna try the lockbox," I growled. "You'll get it, safe and sound. And then I want my sister. In the same condition, safe and sound, understand?"

She gave me that bland, disturbin' smile again. "Of course."

I got the feelin' she mostly didn't expect me to live through this escapade.

Well, that was fine. She hadn't expected me to live through the last one, neither. That time she'd left me stranded in the desert with no horse and a bullet in my leg. Yet here I was. "Good," I croaked, then cleared my throat again. Why did my insides feel so jumpy?

I'd run down stagecoaches before.

I'd murdered more folk than I liked to remember.

Hell, I'd even dealt with those bastard barons before … and this one weren't even gonna be aboard his own coach.

None of this should be much trouble, really. Especially once I got my hands on one of those long rifles Holt liked so much. All I had to do was this one more job, and I'd have Ethelyn back. A small price to pay.

I pulled the map toward me and looked it over again. "When exactly are you expectin' this coach to be comin' south?"

"Accordin' to my source," said Nan, "it should be passin' through Sonoita in about six days or so. Should give you plenty of time to head up north and get situated afore it comes by."

"Sonoita?" I squinted down at the map, searchin' fer such a town. "Never heard of it."

Nan thumped a finger down on a particular spot, then tapped at it forcefully. "Right here, Delano. You *can* read, can't ya?"

"Yeah," I grumbled. Course I could read, with Mama havin' been a schoolteacher and all. But Arizona was a big place. It helped to know the general area to look in, first. I found the town easy enough after she pointed it out. Then frowned. "Why Sonoita? That don't make much sense if they're headin' to Blessing. You sure yer source is reliable?"

Nan's gaze went cold at my question. "They're reliable," she snapped. "I ain't the only one after this stagecoach. And Baron Haas knows that. He's got it runnin' all over the country, tryin' to confuse those lookin' to steal from him. And he's got a few decoys out there, too. So you be sure the stagecoach you stop matches that one in that photograph, got it? That's the one we want. That's the one that'll have the lockbox."

I slumped in my chair and rubbed at my burnin' eyes with one hand. A nonsensical route, decoys, armed guards, a disguised coach … what in the hell could possibly be in that lockbox? I didn't ask. Certainly she wouldn't tell me, of that I had no doubt. So I only said, "Sure. Got it. Can I take the map?"

She waved her hand as if shooin' me. "Yeah, yeah. Take the lot of it. That's what it's for."

I refolded it, then tucked it into my shirt pocket. The sketch of the lockbox and the photograph of the coach followed it.

Nine-Fingered Nan watched me, then sat forward and leaned her elbows on the table just as I was about to stand and take my leave. "You know," she said, "I heard the Bank of Blessing got robbed 'bout a month back. Was all over the papers. If I recall correctly, that was right about the time you managed to show up with thirty-five thousand dollars for that swindlin' sonuvabitch Taggert, weren't it?"

I sat back in my chair. So maybe I weren't goin' nowhere yet. But I also weren't about to freely admit to Nan where I'd got that money. "Dunno. Maybe. I don't keep much track of the days, to be honest. They all kinda run together after awhile."

Her eyes narrowed. Clearly she didn't believe me. "You by chance get all that money from Blessing, Mr. Delano?"

I shrugged. "Don't matter where I got it, does it? It all spends the same."

She smiled a little at that. "Sure. Yeah. Guess it does." She leaned away from the table, and her chair creaked as her weight shifted. Her left hand turned her whiskey glass around in circles as she kept starin' at me. "But a lot of those metal barons had their money in that bank. They sure are sticklers about their money. Boy, that robbery got that town all in a fuss, all right. *And* it seems one of those barons got murdered. His house burned down and all his slaves freed and everythin'. Same night as the bank robbery." She shook her head. "The town of Blessing had a bad night that night."

"Sounds like it," I agreed. I'd had a helluva bad night that night, too. I eyed my own glass of whiskey and contemplated downin' it. She was wearin' on my nerves, and I didn't like the feelin' of sittin' so on-edge.

"How long you been here in the Territories, Mr. Delano?"

The question made me look up from the whiskey and I frowned across the table at her. "Awhile."

"How long?"

I did some rough estimations in my head. "'Bout four years. Maybe five. Like I told you, I don't much keep track of time."

She grunted. "You ain't learned much about the barons of Blessing in all that time, have ya?"

"Can't say I have." Unless, of course, you counted the time I blew up Whittaker's house, burned down his barns, freed his slaves, and then got treated to his very special *brand* of hospitality.

My right arm twinged with a phantom pain just thinkin' about it.

She fixed me with a full-on grin, then, and it was truly the most terrifyin' expression I'd ever seen her wear. "You should know better than to lie to me, Mr. Delano."

I tensed, but she only lifted her left hand again, gesturin' to her man who stood there behind her.

He pulled another folded piece of paper from his satchel and handed it to her. She took it from him and unfolded it, and her steady stare never left my face. She slid it toward me. "Seems you'll be just as popular as yer sister 'fore too long, at this rate."

Frownin', I dared to tear my eyes away from her to look down at this new document.

And my throat closed up at the sight of the face that stared back at me.

It was mine.

Or … real close to mine. Not a photograph, but a sketch. And a fair good one, too. Across the top of the bulletin were those bold, fat letters: WANTED. And below the drawin' of my face was my price: *fifty thousand dollars.*

All the breath went out of me. Felt like that brute Thomas Withrow had buried his fist in my gut again. I kept starin' down at the paper while the rest of the room went to tiltin' like it had on me yesterday afternoon after all that whiskey. The rest of the words printed there all ran together, but a few of 'em stood out clear enough:

Murder. Arson. Theft.

The bounty had been posted by the Whittaker family. Whatever was left of 'em.

And they wanted me *alive*. At least there was that.

Maybe that's why Nan hadn't shot me yet.

But then … this poster didn't make no sense. All those who'd seen my face—or Charlotte's face—were dead. I was sure of it. Couldn't say the same fer Holt, of course, since I hadn't been there when he'd robbed the bank. Not fer sure. And maybe that's why he was so keen on movin' along and stayin' out of Bravebank in general. Maybe he knew someone had got a good look at him.

But that seemed doubtful. That woulda been sloppy of him. Holt knew better than that. He hadn't lived to be so old by bein' sloppy.

Guess I couldn't say the same about me. Who could have escaped my notice that night? Who could have escaped with a good look at my face and also been a person strongly inclined to go tell the rest of Baron Whittaker's family just who exactly had murdered their patriarch?

"Looks an awful lot like you, wouldn't ya say?" Nan quipped.

Slowly, I lifted my eyes from the poster to look at her.

She still had that horrible grin on her face.

"There's no name," was all I managed.

"Indeed there ain't," she agreed. "But it does mention a lame left leg." Her head cocked to one side. "Which, coincidentally, you got. It also mentions that lame left leg is made outta metal. And that, Mr. Delano, is what I find of *particular* interest. There may be other familiar-lookin' stupid young fools out there wanderin' the Territories with lame left legs … but I'm willin' to bet an awful lot there'll only be *one* of those legs that's made outta metal."

I didn't say nothin', didn't so much as twitch, but I was sure calculatin' just then what I would do if she decided she wanted to hand me over to the Whittakers. Or if she decided she wanted to know more about my metal leg, or even wanted to take it fer herself, as it seemed so many others had been wantin' to do of late. Calculatin' who I'd need to shoot first, and tryin' to figure out what she might find more valuable—the offer from the baron's family, or the possibility of workin' Old World tech.

She must've seen somethin' change on my face despite my best efforts, 'cause she held up her hands and shook her head. "Now, now, don't you worry yer pretty little head none. I just gave you a job to do fer me, didn't I? Why would I do that if I planned to hand you over to those barons?"

I could think of a few reasons, but then, I didn't want to encourage her none. So I kept my silence, not hardly darin' to blink, havin' no idea what kinda plans she mighta had in her head right then.

"Hell, if you wanna know the truth of it, Mr. Delano," she went on, "*I'm* the reason the people of this town ain't killin' each other fer the chance to truss you up and cart you off to Blessing to get that reward fer themselves. These posters came down maybe a week after you showed up and planted yerself here. I instructed Sheriff Jennings not to post them. He burned the lot of 'em, in fact. All except this one, of course, which I saved special just fer you. Don't know what other bounties you might have on yer head in other places, but it looks like you done pissed off the Whittaker family somethin' awful. They've sent these out all over the Territories. And with a price that high…" She shook her head again and gave a low whistle. Her pale gaze gleamed.

She sure loved talkin' about that cold, hard cash.

Either that, or she sure loved twistin' that knife in me just as often as she could.

I remembered what Holt had said about her hatin' my pa more than anyone else she'd ever hated. Had she possibly hated him so much she could now hate his son just as much?

I swallowed hard at the thought, wonderin' if maybe … maybe this was a game I couldn't win, after all. But then, she didn't know how stubborn I was. If she thought any of this was gonna scare me off, convince me to stop tryin' to free my sister, she was sorely mistaken. And anyway, neither she nor anyone else had managed to kill me yet. Seemed I had some tricks up my sleeve, myself.

She reached out and plucked up the poster, then rolled it. "Just consider this a friendly warnin', Mr. Delano. Ya see, I did the math. Turns out that lockbox I'm sendin' ya to fetch is worth more to me than the fifty thousand the Whittakers are offerin' fer you." Her pale blue gaze dropped to the table, and she nodded toward my left leg, currently tucked safely underneath it. "Worth more to me then that leg of yers, too, even if it really *is* made outta metal." Her eyes came back up to my face. "So fer now, I'm doin' what I can around the Territories to keep this poster out of circulation. *But*," she pointed the rolled up paper at me, "if I don't get that lockbox, then the math don't add up. And in that case, I'll take the next best thing. Meanin' I'll be keen to learn all about that leg of yers, especially concernin' where you managed to get it. Then I'll go ahead and take it off you. Then I'll hand you over to the barons and let them do whatever the hell it is they're plannin' to do with you. Do I make myself clear?"

I glared at her steady, but every muscle in my body was all coiled up, braced and ready in case she changed her mind. In case this was all another trap. In case she was lyin' about not wantin' to take me to the barons. It was makin' all my bruises ache even worse, and the headache pulsed in my skull. "I'll get yer damned lockbox," I whispered.

As if it weren't enough she was already holdin' Ethelyn over me.

Now there was the goddamned barons and their bounty to worry about.

And Dr. Balogh and his family and the consequences of their foolish, misguided kindness.

"I should hope so," Nan said. "I hafta admit, Mr. Delano, you *do* keep surprisin' me. And that ain't an easy thing to do these days." She handed the rolled-up poster back over her shoulder to her lieutenant. He jammed it down into one corner of his satchel, and Nan's eyes narrowed at me. "Ain't never heard of anyone gettin' away from Baron Whittaker. Much less gettin' away from him and burnin' down everythin' he owned. And … *murderin'* him, to boot…" She shook her head again, then blew out a breath and caught up her whiskey glass.

I didn't bother to mention it hadn't really been me at all who'd murdered Baron Whittaker. Charlotte had done that. Hell, it hadn't even really been me who'd gotten away from him, neither. That had been Charlotte's doin', too. If not fer her, that night woulda turned out a whole lot different, all right.

But I kept my mouth shut. Nan hadn't mentioned Charlotte yet, and if by some miracle the old hag didn't know of Charlotte's involvement in all that, I sure didn't want to be the one to tell her. She didn't need nothin' more to add to her extortion of me. That list was growin' long enough all on its own.

"You might be just the man to pull off this job," Nan said. She leaned back in her chair. "Long as you don't let that coach get to Blessing. That's a town I got no jurisdiction in. Be plenty of people on the hunt fer the likes of you around those parts."

"I got no intentions of settin' foot in Blessing, or anywhere near it," I said, and that was the whole truth. "Much less entanglin' myself with any of those barons." And that was even more of the truth. I surely didn't want to meet another baron of Blessing so long as I lived.

"Good. Guess you really are smarter than ya look."

I scowled and shoved my chair back away from the table. If she weren't gonna shoot me or collect the bounty on me, I was done sittin' here and takin' her insults.

"Somethin' wrong with my whiskey, boy?"

Her sharp tone stopped me. I looked up to see her man's hand on his gun. Nan was glarin' at me now. She stuck her chin out in the direction of my glass, still full. I hadn't touched it.

I hesitated, then twisted to look over my shoulder at her second lieutenant. He had his hand on his gun, too. And was blockin' the door.

I faced Nine-Fingered Nan again and cleared my throat. Guess I still weren't goin' nowhere. I shook my head. "No," I croaked. "No." Of course there weren't. I'd downed enough of the stuff in the last three weeks to last me months. And the headache throbbin' in my skull reminded me well enough how much I'd had of it yesterday. I hadn't drank so heavy since before I'd had a good lead on the whereabouts of my sister.

If only Nan coulda served me coffee now instead.

I picked up the glass and raised it as if in a toast, then took a breath and downed it. I set it empty back to the table between us, and Nan gave a nod.

She raised hers in turn and finished it off, then set her glass next to mine. "Well then. Seems we've got ourselves a suitable arrangement." She stood and touched the brim of her hat. "I shall be eagerly awaitin' yer return from this errand. As will yer sister."

A whole swell of feelin's rushed up inside me at her mention of Ethelyn, all the things I'd been feelin' and fightin' since the day I'd come back to find her missin': anger, desperation, fear. But I swallowed it all back, kept my gaze hard and even.

Kept silent.

"Good luck to you, Mr. Delano," Nan said then, a hauntin' echo of Holt's last words to me. "Yer gonna need it." She smiled again and nodded to her two lieutenants.

Then she went toward the Stag's front door, and as she passed me she clapped a hand down hard on my shoulder. I recoiled at her touch, but her grip was strong, sharp and bony, diggin' into my flesh. Then she let go and went on, her two lieutenants trailin' after her, and I turned in my chair to watch her leave … mostly to convince myself she was actually goin'.

She was.

Her tall, black-clad figure stepped through the door and out into the white heat of the afternoon, and then she turned right and was gone. One of her men shut the door after them, and I was left all alone in the middle of the Stag Saloon.

I heaved out a long breath of relief and dropped my head into my hands, rubbin' at my achin' temples.

Truth be told, that coulda gone a lot worse.

And the job coulda been a lot worse, too. A whole lot worse.

In the end, it really weren't so bad. All I had to do was stop a stagecoach and steal a lockbox. That bounty would complicate things some, sure, but I didn't plan to get too close to any kind of civilization. I'd need to hit the coach before it reached the town of Sonoita, anyway. The bounty wouldn't change that fact. If I played my cards right, all this shouldn't really be that hard.

And I was gettin' better at cards, at least.

The sound of a door openin' and shuttin' from somewhere in

the back made me lift my head with a grimace. I heard footsteps across the floor, and soon enough the barkeep reappeared. He stopped short at the sight of me, a look of clear disgust twistin' at his features.

I ignored his distaste as a spark of hope lit in me. "Hey … you got any coffee?"

OVER THE EDGE

Turned out that barkeep disliked me more than I'd thought.

He'd had coffee, all right. He'd even brought me some. And then he'd spit in it.

I'd thought about shootin' him fer his trouble. I was far too tired and sore to suffer such nonsense. I wondered if Nan would care any.

Most likely not.

Sheriff Jennings, though, he probably woulda cared. And he'd seemed awful serious this mornin' about not wantin' me to shoot no one. If I was too tired and sore to suffer havin' my coffee spit in, I was surely too tired and sore to suffer bein' tried fer murder.

And so the barkeep of the Stag Saloon got to live another day.

I'd left him standin' there, holdin' that cup of joe he'd spit in and givin' me a look like he dared me to shoot him fer it, and I'd limped on down the street to the First Chance and got myself a fresh cup there. And some good grub.

Spit-free.

I pulled out the map Nan had given me and studied it as I ate, makin' plans. There was a decent spot to plant myself with one of those long rifles, looked like. The coach was takin' a path southwest out of Utah, accordin' to Nan, then cuttin' back eastward to hit Sonoita before goin' south again toward Blessing.

I could catch 'em easy enough on that eastward leg. Get

my own sharpshootin' rifle and take out the driver and as many guards as I could from a distance. I weren't as good with those rifles as Holt, but I weren't about to take my chances up close and personal with a group of armed marshals, that was fer sure. Not when I was havin' to do this job all by my lonesome.

Briefly, I wondered if Holt might try to pull off that new bank job of his all by himself, too.

But then I shook my head and grumbled, took another swig of my coffee. I didn't have time to be worryin' about Holt. He was a mean old bastard. He could take care of himself. I had plenty to worry about on my own here.

Stoppin' that coach. Gettin' that lockbox. Killin' those marshals.

Watchin' fer anyone comin' after that fifty thousand dollar bounty.

Freein' my sister.

And I only had six days till that coach was scheduled to arrive in Sonoita. That was … if Nan's *source*, whoever that might be, could be relied upon. I sure hoped this person was more trustworthy than her man Taggert had been, anyway.

In any case, I figured I'd better head on up that way just as soon as I could manage. It'd be a few days ride to reach the spot I wanted. And with no time to retrieve any more supplies from Grave Gulch, I'd have to buy anythin' else I needed here. To include that rifle.

I sighed, folded the map, and stuck it back in my shirt pocket.

It'd be a long ride, indeed, in my current condition, but the coffee and the food *was* helpin'. A bit. Still had the headache and the bruises, but those would pass too, in time.

Well, I'd stay one more night in Bravebank. Buy the rest of what I needed once I finished here. Get a proper hotel room and sleep in a real bed. Get proper rested up so I had a clear head startin' out tomorrow.

There was an awful lot ridin' on this little errand.

I surely didn't want to fuck it up.

We headed outta town late the next mornin', me and my mule. He weren't such a bad animal, really. Overly social, sure, but generally steady. He didn't spook easy, and mostly did what I asked.

I was workin' on teachin' him to ground-tie and to come when I whistled. And I'd named him Joe. Holt had always insisted namin' yer mount was a surefire way to get 'em killed … but that had only happened to me once … and had only happened recently.

The horse Nine-Fingered Nan had shot out from under me the first time I'd come across her. The one I'd called Ace. Despite his name, his luck had turned out even worse than mine.

I'd really liked that horse.

But Joe … I was pretty sure he was safe with a name like that. It weren't considered lucky or unlucky, it just was.

So we went, Joe and me, and we kept a consistent and steady pace northward. I stayed well off the roads, and didn't stop to camp that first night till after sunset. I braved a small fire, bein' as I was off the beaten path and not yet too near Blessing, but truth be told I only wanted it fer a little light to see by.

I pulled Charlotte's telegram out of my back pocket as I sat cross-legged on my bedroll in the cool desert's night, and wondered why I was nervous to read it. The plan had been fer her to write me when she got home safe, and fer me to write her once I had my sister and had ended Nine-Fingered Nan.

If Charlotte had sent this … it meant she was home.

It meant she was safe.

That surely weren't nothin' to get worked up about.

I shoulda been happy about the telegram. Relieved.

And I guess I was. But there was somethin' else there, too. Somethin' that was tyin' my stomach up in knots as I sat there starin' down at that paper.

Was it only 'cause I hadn't been able to write her myself, yet? 'Cause I didn't have Ethelyn yet? Not only that, but I hadn't ended Nine-Fingered Nan yet, neither. Nope, instead here I was, actin' as her errand boy, headin' straight back toward the wasps' nest Charlotte and I had kicked up real good those weeks ago, hopin' I weren't about to get swarmed and stung.

I drew in a breath, then let it out long and slow, and tilted the telegram toward the glow of the flames:

DEAREST VAN

AM HOME SAFE STOP HOPE AND PRAY YOU AND SISTER ARE THE SAME STOP EVER SO GRATEFUL FOR YOUR AID STOP PLEASE CALL UPON MYSELF OR MY FAMILY IF YOU NEED ANYTHING STOP WILL SEND PROPER LETTER VERY SOON STOP PLEASE WRITE AS SOON AS YOU CAN

I let out another long exhale, feelin' as if I'd been holdin' my breath, and blinked hard. I read it over a few more times, mostly to convince myself she'd really made it, that she was really home safe. Then I rubbed a hand over my mouth and sighed, and slipped the note back into my pocket.

Well, she was safe. That was all that mattered.

Fer now. I wondered again if there was a bounty out on her for what had happened to Baron Whittaker. I wondered if I should write her now, after all, and warn her that such might be the case. The Republic didn't usually honor bounties posted by the Territories—hell, they mostly didn't honor those posted by the Commune, even—but if the reward fer her was anythin' like the reward fer me, there'd be more than enough greedy types out there who might be determined enough to track her down … even all the way out to Pennsylvania.

Maybe that's what had me all worked up; concern she'd made it all the way back home just to be hunted again by more lowlifes. Concern they'd catch up to her eventually, and she'd be brought right back here to face whatever unpleasantness Baron Whittaker's family had in mind.

I stood at that thought and paced in front of my small fire.

Joe was hobbled behind me, already dozin'. He felt no concern at all over my predicament, nor Charlotte's. The sky was black overhead, a thick carpet of stars visible in the absence of any moon.

I had to warn her. She seemed to come from money; maybe her family could just pay off the Whittakers. The baron himself had mentioned somethin' about monetary retribution before proceedin' to torture me … if I'd had enough money, maybe it woulda saved me all that pain.

Maybe Charlotte had enough money to spare her any of that.

My fists clenched and I paused in my pacin', lookin' up at the stars.

Even if she didn't, even if the Whittakers wouldn't take her money, I wasn't gonna let them—or any bounty hunter—get their hands on her again.

After I got this lockbox fer Nan, after I freed Ethelyn, we'd head east. We'd find Charlotte. And we'd get ready fer anythin' they sent after us.

It weren't enough—weren't nearly enough—but it was the best I could do.

Fer now, I'd write her that letter I'd promised. Only it wouldn't have the news she'd been hopin' to hear.

I reached the place I'd wanted on the fourth day, in the late afternoon.

By then, I had a pretty good idea of what I was gonna write to Charlotte. Once I got back to a town with a telegraph station, anyway. Maybe I could pass through Sonoita myself on my way back to Bravebank and send it from there.

After I took care of this coach and got that lockbox.

I pulled Joe to a halt at the top of one of the numerous hills that marked this area, then took off my hat and brushed at the sweat runnin' down my face with a sleeve. Squinted down at the road that ran below us.

This spot would do just fine.

The road ran along the side of the hill here, with a steep incline on one side and a steep drop on the other side. I could set up my camp here and get a good shot at 'em with the rifle as they came eastward. And they'd have nowhere to go but straight backward or straight forward, and my bullets would be waitin' fer 'em either way.

I was high enough they shouldn't be able to get too good a shot at me, in return, and there was some brush around I could lay behind to help hide my location and the glare of the sun off the rifle.

All I had to do now was wait.

There was another day and a half or so, maybe two, before that coach was due to come through here. So I made myself comfortable. Found a tree a little ways away to tie Joe to, and set myself up under its shade to keep an eye on the road. I kept my binoculars handy, too.

Anyone comin' down this way now was worth a good look at, just in case.

I settled back against the trunk of the tree and took out the photograph of the coach. Studied it long and hard, till I had all its features memorized. There was bound to be more than one such vehicle pass through here in the next day or two, and I didn't want to be shootin' up the wrong people.

Then I occupied myself by draftin' up my message to Charlotte, scribblin' it out on the edge of the brown paper my cheese was wrapped up in with the little stub of a pencil I kept in my pack. And checked over my new sharpshootin' rifle; made sure it was ready fer shootin' on short notice. Took a few practice shots at a rock far down the road when I sure there was no one comin', just to get a feel fer how it handled.

And kept on waitin'.

Night fell, and I wished suddenly I weren't doin' this job alone, after all. That coach could come by at any hour. If I missed it 'cause I was asleep … that wouldn't be no excuse Nan would accept, I was sure of it.

So I moved myself down the hill aways, takin' my binoculars and my rifle with me, and rolled out my bed closer to the road. Where I could hear anyone comin' through, and I only dozed off in fits and starts, joltin' awake at every rustle and snort from Joe.

It weren't a restful night, fer certain.

The next day passed in much the same way as the remainder of the first, only now I were more tired. A few riders came by, and I checked 'em all through the binoculars, but no sight of any coach, yet.

Not till nearly dusk, when one came thunderin' down the road and made me jump to my feet, heart racin'. But then I saw it was pulled by six horses instead of four, and my heart fell again. Still, I made sure to get a closer look at it, just in case … but the build of the coach was all wrong. Older and bigger and with a lot more missin' paint. A mail coach, looked like.

I scowled in disappointment. Blew out a breath and eased

back down to sit against my tree. I knocked my head back against its trunk and scrubbed a hand over my eyes, really hopin' Nan's source hadn't gotten their timin' wrong.

Really hopin' this wasn't some elaborate game Nan was playin' with me…

Holt's incessant warnings about that woman kept ringin' in my head, but I did my best to ignore 'em. She'd come fer me in Bravebank, after all, hadn't she? She'd said she would send fer me, and she had. That hadn't been a lie. Why would this be?

Especially somethin' so complicated and involved as this particular coach robbery. Why invent somethin' so complex? If she was gonna send me off after somethin' that didn't exist, why not make it somethin' a lot simpler?

And so another restless night came and went, and I was awake again at dawn, sittin' there watchin' the road, my eyes burnin' now.

Today was the day. If it didn't come today…

No, I weren't gonna think about that. Not yet. One problem at a time.

I shook my head and set about makin' another small fire. I wanted coffee, damnit. And it just so happened I'd brought some with me.

I'd brought whiskey, too, of course, but I still had the remnants of a headache hauntin' my temples, and the thought of drinkin' that stuff right now made the pain flare up again. I'd really overdone it that day I'd gotten in that fight in Bravebank. I hadn't been that drunk in a long, long while.

And I didn't want to be that drunk again fer a long, long while, neither.

I was sittin' there, sippin' at my cup of joe as the sun climbed into the sky and began to warm the day, when a cloud of dust rose on the horizon. I didn't let myself get excited this time. Just kept sippin' at my coffee as I lifted the binoculars and focused on the bend in the road. They'd be comin' around it any time now…

Four horses in harness came into view, movin' at a brisk trot. They pulled a coach … a mighty familiar coach.

I set my coffee down quick, sloshin' some on my hand. I scowled and shook my hand off, wiped it on my pants, and stood, grabbin' up the rifle. I left Joe at the tree and moved down the hill a bit to the bush I'd picked out to be my cover. I flattened myself behind it, layin' out on my belly, and propped myself on my elbows. I slid the end of the rifle barrel through the bush's sparse branches, and put my eye to the sight.

I tracked the coach as it came right at me, and double-checked its features. The horses weren't the same four glossy ones I'd seen in the photograph, but that weren't unusual. The rest of it looked right enough. No company name. Smaller boot. Shiny paint. The shades were drawn, so I couldn't see who was inside, but that didn't matter so much. There was one shotgun rider in front, next to the driver, and another in the back. That meant there'd be another two to three marshals ridin' passenger.

This was the coach Nan wanted. Had to be.

I aimed fer the driver first. Needed to slow 'em down so I could shoot 'em all from afar before they had time to pass me by. I took a few breaths to try and calm my nerves. Remembered what Holt had told me about shootin' these rifles. Be still. Be patient. Exhale.

I did so, breathin' out long and slow, and squeezed the trigger.

The crack of it echoed out loud as dynamite, rollin' back and forth between the hills.

The driver jerked, blood sprayin' out from his chest. He slumped on the bench, and the reins dropped from his limp hands.

I watched through the sight as the marshal next to him

sprang into motion, reachin' over to try and catch the reins before they fell out of reach. I pulled back the rifle's bolt action, expellin' the spent cartridge, then pushed it forward, loadin' a fresh one. Took aim again, this time fer the marshal scramblin' fer the reins.

The rifle barked a second time, the bullet catchin' him in the right shoulder and throwin' him back against the coach's cab. Shoutin' rose up into the mornin', though faint at this distance. Some of the shades rolled up. The sun glinted off gun barrels as they poked from the windows, searchin' fer a target.

But I paid those no mind; focused again on the marshal in front. He cradled his injured arm against himself and shoved the dead driver off the bench. The body hit the dirt and rolled. The marshal took the vacated seat and struggled to gather the lines with his one good hand.

I buried another bullet in him and ended him. He, too, slumped, and this time the reins dropped free, bein' as there was no one else to catch 'em. The horses slowed, confused and unsure of all the ruckus. They tossed their heads and chomped their bits.

The marshal at the back of the coach had started to make his way toward the front, goin' around the far side of the cab so I couldn't get a clear shot at him.

Smart.

But he'd have to come out into the open eventually.

So I waited and watched through my scope. Stayed still. Stayed patient. Anticipation ran hot through my blood, and I took another few deep breaths in efforts to calm it. I saw his hand grab the back of the driver bench and braced myself, finger wrapped around the trigger.

What emerged next, though, weren't a body. It was what looked like a big piece of metal. Rough and pitted, but big enough to cover him from knees to head. He kept it angled in my direction as he clumsily clambered around the corner of the cab and up onto the driver's seat.

The hell was this?

Nan had never mentioned anythin' about no metal shields. I'd never seen anyone with anythin' like that before, neither. Not on any coach.

I laid there fer a minute on my belly in the dirt behind that bush, tryin' to decide what to do now. Would it really save him from my bullets? I squeezed off a shot, just to test it.

The *ping* of the bullet ricochetin' off that metal sheet reached me even from my hidin' spot, and the force of it knocked the man back onto his ass. But he didn't fall off the bench, damn him. He only struggled back up to his feet and hunkered down behind his shield as he groped for the fallen lines.

Their horses had picked up their pace again now, and, swearin', I switched my aim to the coach's windows. Maybe I could get at some of the bastards inside, at least, while I figured out what to do about that man in front.

There were two gun barrels pointed at me, and I only barely had time to recognize that fact before the muzzles flashed, and the shots rang out into the hills, and a double spray of dirt kicked up right in front of my bush.

I flinched back despite myself and spat more curses, then steadied myself and resumed my flat-out position, cradlin' that rifle again as I looked back down the scope. I tried to even out my breathin', tried to focus, and honed in on one of the dark shapes I could just barely make out inside the cab. His barrel was pointed up toward me, but I resisted the urge to scramble away from my cover. No way could they have a good shot at me from down there. If I moved now, I'd only give away my position fer certain, and make myself a much clearer target. So instead I stayed put, and made the last shot in my first clip count.

One of the guns hangin' out the window jerked and fell

away, and a splatter of blood painted the window edge. I'd got one of 'em, at least. Couldn't be sure if I'd killed 'em, but at least I'd hurt 'em awful bad.

The second gun re-positioned itself in the absence of its fellow.

I dropped the rifle to reload it, and in the time it took me to slide in another five cartridges, the man in the front with the metal shield had pushed the dead marshal off the bench and gotten control of the horses. I heard him shout at 'em as he slapped the lines and urged them up into a canter.

So they were gonna try and run.

At that pace they'd pass me by right quick, sure enough.

And me and Joe coulda caught up to 'em, yeah, but I weren't fool enough to face down two or three armed marshals all by my lonesome. Especially not with that armor of theirs.

I took one more shot at the cab's window, but their speed made it harder to track 'em with the rifle, and the bullet buried itself in the back corner of the coach, sprayin' out wood splinters.

They cracked off another shot at me, and this time their bullet whizzed through the branches of the bush only a foot or so above my head.

Instinctively, I ducked, and my swearin' turned truly vile. They musta had a rifle in there somewhere themselves. One with a scope. Or some binoculars, maybe. In any event, they'd managed to pinpoint my position with more accuracy than I would have preferred.

And that man in front was workin' the horses up into a full-on gallop.

I was runnin' out of time. Runnin' out of chances.

I scrambled to adjust my aim again, this time fer one of the front horses. I hesitated, then, as they charged up the road straight toward me, and gritted my teeth. That horse hadn't done nothin' wrong. Animals usually didn't. Only their no-good masters usually deserved the killin'.

But I *had* to stop this coach.

I had to get that lockbox.

For Ethelyn. And Dr. Balogh and his family. And myself.

"*Shit,*" I hissed, rememberin' my own horse, Ace, gunned down by Nan. "I'm sorry. I'm sorry, I'm sorry..."

I pulled the trigger.

The front left horse dropped in the harness, and the other three, still gallopin', stumbled at the sudden dead weight that dragged 'em down and tripped, then went down themselves, fallin' onto their knees. The coach lurched into almost a dead stop all at once, and the marshal in the driver's seat was thrown forward, his metal shield goin' flyin', and him landin' on the wagon shaft, right in-between the two rear horses.

They didn't like that none. They staggered back to their feet and tried to shy away from him, but they were still in their harness, and tied to their dead fellow, to boot. The third horse wasn't too happy, neither, and was tryin' to jump sideways ... away from the dead one. But in so doin', he was gettin' awful close to the edge of the road where it dropped away into nothin'...

"*Shit,*" I hissed again.

Forgettin' caution, I slung the rifle over my shoulder and jumped up from my cover, pullin' one of my pistols as I headed down the hill at a run. Or half-slid down the hill with all the gravel, more like.

Don't you do it, I willed that horse. *Just stay put, stay calm, it'll all be over soon...*

But he didn't listen. Not one bit.

The marshal in the front was flailin' around, tryin' to untangle himself from the traces. He'd just managed to right himself and sit up as his companions inside the coach also appeared to regather themselves, because that gun emerged from the window again.

I saw it from the corner of my eye as I raced toward 'em, and saw the man sittin' between the horses grab fer his gun, too, his eyes goin' wide as he spotted me comin' at him.

I drew my second pistol and shot at both of 'em simultaneously, not even breakin' stride. My left gun's bullet hit the front man's left shoulder and he yelled and swore. My right gun's bullet went into the dimness of the coach's interior, but I heard a grunt. That gun fired anyway, but the shot just missed me.

The marshal in front brought his own gun up and took aim, but I already had him in my sights again.

Didn't matter, though.

The horses were all riled up, and that's when the one in the lead stepped a little too close to the edge of the road. The ground of that steep incline gave way under its hoof, and it slipped and fell, jerkin' the coach along after it … just enough to unbalance the horse behind it, who also slipped and fell, and then the whole coach tipped precariously to the side, all of it bein' dragged inch by inch toward that drop.

The man in front had abandoned his gun now, clingin' to the wagon shaft, tryin' to climb around the flailin' horses to get free of the coach entirely. There was a commotion comin' from inside, too, and the side door started to open.

I stumbled down at last onto the flat of the road with my guns at the ready, just in time to see the terrified expression on the marshal's face as him, the coach, and all its horses disappeared over the edge.

VI

ONE PROBLEM AT A TIME

"*Fuck.*"

I stood there in the road with no company save the two dead men lyin' a ways back, at a loss, and grimaced at the noise of that coach and its horses and its passengers all tumblin' down that slope.

I shoved my guns back into their holsters and rubbed a hand over my face, the sweat tricklin' down my neck. I glanced back over my shoulder, up the hill I'd just come down, back toward my bush and beyond that, my makeshift camp and the tree Joe was tied to. Couldn't even see it from down here.

Well, I didn't want to take Joe down the slope. He'd be fine up there fer now.

I didn't want to go down the slope, neither, but I didn't have much of a choice. I had to get that lockbox. At least maybe the fall woulda killed the rest of those marshals fer me. Though I was hopin' it hadn't killed all the horses.

I'd feel awful bad if that were the case.

'Cept you weren't the one who killed 'em. They did that all on their own. You can only take the blame fer the one. I shook my head, shovin' the guilt down where I kept all my feelin's, and waited till the commotion of the rollin' coach stopped. Then I took a breath and stepped up to the edge of the road myself. Looked down over it.

And grimaced again.

It was a mess, but mostly intact. It had landed on its side, and one of the wheels had come off. The marshal that had been in the front was dead fer sure, but I couldn't tell what had happened to the men inside. The horses had come unhitched from the coach in the tumble and looked, miraculously, mostly fine. Looked like maybe they'd managed to just slide down instead of roll like the coach. The three alive were still harnessed up together and staggered around a bit, then shook themselves, seemin' dazed.

Good, let 'em stay that way fer awhile ... maybe they'd stay quiet long enough fer me to get down there and unharness 'em before they could try and kill themselves again.

But I had to hurry. There'd be more travelers along this road before long, and the bodies lyin' along it would be a clear sign of trouble. Any curious folk, whether vultures themselves lookin' fer an easy score, or Good Samaritans lookin' to involve the law, might stop to investigate. And we weren't that far out from Sonoita. If anyone *were* inclined to go and get the law, it wouldn't leave me much time to get clear of this whole disaster. And if anyone stopped lookin' fer an easy score, well, *I* had to get to that lockbox first.

So I sighed and took the rifle off my shoulder to hold it. Didn't want it gettin' caught on anythin'. Then I grumbled and eased myself over the lip of the road. The slope was steep, all right. Too steep to do much walkin' or runnin' down it. Mostly I just went down on my ass, lettin' the loose dirt and gravel carry me down, usin' a hand now and then to keep my semi-controlled descent from turnin' into an uncontrolled fall.

I got to the bottom soon enough and without much trouble, just covered in dust now and with a few scrapes on the hand I'd used to steady myself. Goin' up, on the other hand ... that was gonna be a whole 'nother problem. But I couldn't worry about that right now.

One problem at a time.

Sure seemed I was sayin' that an awful lot these days.

I jogged over to the horses first and cut 'em free of their harness. They snorted at me, but seemed content to stay put. Of course. *Now* they weren't keen on dancin' around and bein' stupid. If only they'd have kept their heads while up there on the road, we wouldn'ta been in this situation.

I waited, then, and listened fer any sound of life comin' from inside the sideways coach. But things stayed quiet. There was only the soft noises from the horses shiftin' and snortin' around, and the buzz of flies that had found the nearby dead already. I crouched, anyway, and moved up quick and quiet-like to take cover right behind the cracked driver's bench. Then I waited again, and listened again.

Still nothin'.

So I propped my rifle up against the broken bench and helped myself to the front boot, slicin' it open with my knife and rippin' the canvas apart. Then I sat there and just stared into it. It was empty. Completely empty.

All right. Well, Nan had said it would be *somewhere* around here … didn't mean it had to be in the front boot. So I stood and moved to the rear boot. Did the same there; sliced it open and ripped it apart.

This time there *was* somethin' there, and my heart did a little jump as I realized it was a lockbox. But not the one I was lookin' fer. This one was too big, and had a regular padlock keepin' it shut. But it coulda been holdin' the one I wanted. So I pulled it out into the sun, into the open, and shot off the padlock. The lid creaked as I swung it open, and despite myself, I held my breath as expectation sparked through me.

But then all the anticipation soured, and I snarled and spit into the dirt.

Empty again.

I stepped back away from it and chewed at my lip. I rested

my hands on my gun grips, the fingers drummin' restlessly. A very bad feelin' snaked its way through my gut just then, and I didn't like it. Didn't like it one bit.

My eyes went to the cab itself. Guess it was time to see if anyone was alive in there. Time to see if any of 'em was carryin' that lockbox on their person.

And what if they ain't?

The thought shot through my mind before I could stop it, and I took a deep breath against the dread that rose in my throat. Tried to swallow it down. It had to be here somewhere. *Had* to be.

Nan had said so. Her source had said so.

If whatever was in that lockbox was valuable enough to garner decoy coaches and routes wanderin' all over the map, they was probably just makin' it right difficult to find.

Though why there weren't nothin' else at all in either boot, and why they had a locked lockbox that was empty, didn't add up right. But then, not much about those metal barons seemed to add up right.

I hissed out my frustration in a long breath and clambered up atop the side of the coach. I peered through the windows; saw a tangle of limbs and splattered blood. Didn't look like no one was movin', but I wouldn't take no chances. I pulled at the door, but it was locked, too. Another shot from my pistol made short work of that, and I yanked it open while keepin' it between me and anyone on the inside.

I waited a second, but no one came out shootin'. No one so much as moved or made a sound. I peeked cautiously around the edge of the door and down into the mess of bodies below. Stared at 'em fer awhile. Couldn't see no one breathin'.

Satisfied they were dead, I swung my legs over the side of the doorway and hopped on down, tryin' not to step all over 'em, but only partially succeedin'. I winced at the look of the place.

Some limbs were clearly broken, bent at odd angles. The two I'd managed to shoot through the window had gotten blood all over the place. One was missin' part of his face. The other had taken a slug to his chest. There was a third man in here, too, and he didn't look like no marshal. He was sprawled underneath the body of one of those armed guards, but he weren't wearin' no guns, himself.

And he was dressed fancy. Even had a monocle danglin' out from his vest pocket, the lens shattered.

Fer a minute I worried it might be Baron Haas aboard his coach after all, but his suit weren't as nice as the one Baron Whittaker had been wearin'. Maybe not all barons dressed the same, sure ... but this man's outfit reminded me more of Dr. Balogh, instead.

Maybe just another learned man, then.

But why was he on Baron Haas' coach?

And why hadn't Nan mentioned him?

Maybe she'd known he didn't carry and hadn't deemed him a threat, seein' as how he weren't wearin' no guns.

Well, none of that mattered. I shook off the questions, the curiosity, and refocused on my job. It didn't matter who that man was, or why he was aboard this coach. All that mattered was that I found that lockbox with those coded dials and got it back to Bravebank. To Nan.

A cursory glance around the grisly interior revealed no lockbox.

Of course it wouldn't be that easy.

Reluctantly, I bent down and started movin' bodies and limbs around, tryin' to see if maybe the box was loose in here somewhere and had ended up buried by one of these gents.

I'd just shoved the man missin' part of his face aside to check under him when a gunshot blasted from behind me, deafenin' in that small space. My hat blew off my head as I flinched away and spun, drawin' and firin' almost without thinkin'.

To my surprise, a shriek of fear answered my return shot instead of a cry of pain, and I found myself starin' down at the man in the fancy clothes.

So he weren't dead. Coulda fooled me.

He was still under the body of the other marshal, and it seemed my shot had gone into the dead guy instead of the live guy. He was usin' that body as a shield somewhat, and pointin' one of the marshal's guns at me.

Though from the way his gun hand was shakin', I weren't too worried about him hittin' me, even at this range.

I kept my gun trained on him, anyway.

And my hand weren't shakin'.

"D-don't shoot!" he yelped. "D-don't shoot or I'll … I'll … I'll shoot you back!"

I blinked at him. Did he not understand how these things worked? But as long as he was alive, I figured I should take advantage of the situation. "All right," I said. "I won't shoot you then. Long as you tell me where the lockbox is."

His face scrunched up in confusion. "L-lockbox?"

"Yeah. You know, it's a box with a lock on it? Usually holds expensive stuff inside?"

"That's what this is? All this murder, all this pain … for a … a robbery?"

I gave a huff of impatience. "Look, Mister, I don't got all day. Start talkin' or I'm gonna start shootin'."

He tried to steady his hand, bravado hardenin' his features. "You shoot and I'll shoot back, I told you!"

I rolled my eyes and stepped forward, snatchin' his gun before he had time to blink. I shoved it into my belt and stepped back again. "There. Now you don't have to worry about it. Let me ask you again: where is that lockbox?"

His mouth dropped open, and his eyes got real wide.

I waggled my own gun at him. "Mister? You'll want to be talkin' right about now … my trigger finger is startin' to get real itchy…"

"It's … it's in the back," he blurted. "In the back!"

My shoulders slumped. I really didn't have the patience fer this right now. I scrubbed a hand across my eyes and sighed at him. "No, not that one. I already found that one. It's empty. I want the other one. The one with the dials."

His eyes got wider. His breathin' quickened and he swallowed. "How … how did you know about that one?"

"A little bird told me. Just like yer gonna tell me where it went to. Right now. Ain't you?" I thumbed my hammer back for emphasis.

He went very pale. Silence stretched out between us for a heartbeat, and his eyes darted around like he hoped to find some way out of this predicament.

But he was stuck under a dead body in the cramped sideways space of a turned coach, and there weren't no more guns within his reach. His scared eyes eventually came back around to me. He opened his mouth.

The creak of wood sounded from outside, like a boot climbin' up the side of the coach, and I twisted quick toward the open doorway.

Just in time to look down the barrel of a sixgun.

The man behind it smiled lazily and touched the brim of his black hat with his free hand. "Howdy there," he said. "You the one who made all this mess?"

I swallowed, hesitated, lookin' him over, tryin' to judge how fast he was. I still had my own pistol in my hand … pointin' in the wrong direction. And my left hand had come up to my left grip, but stopped at the sight of that barrel in my face.

"Now, now," came a new voice, a woman's voice, and I

looked over my shoulder to the other side of the open doorway. She was lyin' on the side of the coach on her belly, all casual-like, her dark hair spillin' over her shoulders as she smiled down at me. She had a pistol, too, silver-plated and bright in the sun, leveled at my head. "Don't even think it. You won't beat him. Won't beat me, neither."

"That's easy to say when you sneak up on a fella," I growled.

Her smiled widened, and she shrugged. "You wanna square off? Who's it to be? Me or him?" She nodded toward the man in the black hat. "Moses has been real bored lately. I'm sure he'd take you up on it."

"Sure," the man agreed.

I turned back to him.

"Just say the word."

And I could tell from his tone he'd shot down plenty of men. His eyes were mostly blue, squinted under his hat brim, and they'd gone all flat and cold.

I cleared my throat. "No. I don't wanna square off. I wanna finish up my business here and ride on, understand? I got no quarrel with either of you. I don't want no trouble."

"Hrm," the woman mused. "Seems a man who don't want no trouble probably shouldn't go around robbing stagecoaches."

"I ain't robbin' it," I snapped. "I found it like this."

"That's not true!" the man in the fancy clothes blurted. "You were just asking about the lockbox!"

I closed my eyes and exhaled quietly. He didn't have no foreign accent like Dr. Balogh, but clearly he weren't from around here, neither.

"A lockbox, you say?" the man called Moses drawled.

I opened my eyes again at his question. He was starin' straight at me.

"There's a lockbox out here," the woman said. "But it's empty."

"There another one around here somewhere?" Moses asked, and his tone had switched from cold-blooded killer to all kinds of curious.

My stomach tightened at his interest, and suddenly I prayed the man in the fancy clothes had more spine than I had judged him to have.

"N-no," he practically squeaked. Seemed he had realized right quick now these two newcomers weren't exactly on his side. "No others. We're not carrying any valuables. None at all!"

"You're just carrying around an empty lockbox?" the woman asked. She sounded mighty skeptical. "Locked up for nothing?"

The man in the silk vest craned his neck sideways in an attempt to look up at her. "I don't know, I suppose? This isn't my coach! It belongs to Baron Haas. Maybe they were carrying it for whatever they were supposed to pick up later in the day."

Moses grunted. "Seems highly unusual to me."

"I'm telling you, I don't know anything about any other lock-boxes or any other valuables," the man in the fancy clothes insisted. "I swear!"

Relief flickered through me. At least he hadn't mentioned the box with the dials.

"So it was just you and four armed escorts on this here coach?" the woman asked. "What the hell were they protecting, then? You?"

The man had the courage to look affronted at the question. "Yes!" he blustered. "Of course! Is that so hard to believe?"

"Maybe," Moses said. "Who are you, then? Someone important?"

I turned to look at him too, curious despite myself. He glanced between all of us, and tried to push the dead marshal off of himself. But his leverage weren't so good, and he only barely managed to budge the body. He gave up, pantin' from exertion, but puffed up his chest as best he could from his undignified position, anyway. "Yes, in my own way," he said. He reached for his monocle, frowned as he saw it was shattered, and sagged back against the coach wall. He let the monocle drop again. "Name's Professor Christopher Morton. I'm Head Curator of the Royal Museum for Her Majesty Victoria the Third, Queen of Canada."

Moses let out a low whistle. "The queen, huh?" He snorted a laugh. "I don't buy that fer a minute. You?" His gaze shifted over my shoulder, presumably to his lady partner.

"Nope," she said. "Canada is a real, real long way from here, Mister."

"Yes, well..." the man tried to shove the body off again, and again, failed. "It's true. All of it. And if you'll just be so kind as to get me out of here, and safely escort me to the residence of Baron Haas in Blessing, I am quite sure he would be most pleased. Probably offer you a nice reward to show his appreciation."

"That so?" Moses looked again to the woman behind me.

He mighta been the killer, but it appeared she was the boss.

"That so?" she echoed. "Well, we didn't come all the way down here for nothing. Let's get you boys out of all that blood and gore and have a *proper* chat about all this, shall we?"

I remembered then how Nan had been quite explicit in wantin' me to kill everyone aboard this coach. But then, she hadn't ever said nothin' about no museum curator from Canada. Was he included in her kill order? And even if he was, if these two new folks decided to take him to Blessing, I didn't think there was much I could do about it. "Look," I said, "I told you, I don't want no trouble. I ain't a part of any of this. You let me ride on now, and I'll leave you to whatever you get from here. From him. Ain't no business of mine what happens after I'm gone." I glanced to the man still trapped beneath the dead marshal.

He gave me a look like he weren't quite sure if I'd meant that in a good way or a bad way.

But I hadn't meant it in any particular way. I only needed to get myself clear of Moses and his lady boss so I could watch from a safe distance and see if they ended up makin' the deal with Professor Morton. Then figure out my next steps fer how to find that damned lockbox with the dials, dependin' on whether or not that deal was made.

One problem at a time.

But Moses shook his head and somehow managed to look genuinely sympathetic. "Don't think so, partner. You'll be stayin' put fer awhile. And I'm gonna need you to hand over yer piece." He paused, his eyes shiftin' between all three of the guns currently on my person. "All of 'em."

The click of a hammer sounded from behind me.

"Go on now," the woman prompted. "Do as he says."

I gritted my teeth, fingers tightening around the grip of my pistol. But there was nothin' to be done fer it. They had me dead to rights.

Seemed I was gonna have a whole lot more problems to work through, after all.

Fuck.

VII

IF

It was almost high noon now, and the blisterin' heat made the sweat roll down my face even under the brim of my hat, which the woman had so kindly returned to me. It had a brand-new bullet hole in it now, but better it than my head.

I sat cross-legged on the dusty ground, my back against a big boulder. And my arms tied behind me, around the boulder's bulk. The so-called professor sat on the other side of the rock, his arms tied as well in a similar fashion.

And he wouldn't shut up.

He shouted relentlessly at Moses and the woman as they turned the coach inside out, very thorough, indeed, in their search for valuables. At first he'd been pleadin' with them to take him to Blessing, promisin' rewards and treasures. But they didn't seem to believe him. So then he'd tried threatenin' 'em with the queen's justice … but they'd paid even less attention to that. Even laughed at him a few times. So now, he'd resorted to insults. Callin' 'em all sorts of foul names.

They were ignorin' those, too.

Professionals, these two.

"Would you *shut up*?" I finally hissed. "Please, for the love of God, *shut up*."

He went silent for a blessed moment, then directed a string of muttered insults at me.

I twisted best I could toward him, but couldn't see him around the curve of the boulder. "Look, Mister, you want them to come over here and put a bullet through yer forehead? 'Cause I gotta admit, if I was them, I'd have already done that. They ain't killed us yet, and I'd like to keep it that way. Yeah? So please, if ya wanna stay alive … *shut it*."

Stony silence answered my plea.

Maybe he'd realized I'd made a good point.

Well, I'd take it. I breathed a sigh of relief, closed my eyes, and leaned my head back against the rock behind me. It was hot as fuck out here. And I was wishin' fer a drink out of my canteen about then. But all my supplies—and Joe—were up at my makeshift campsite.

I kept quiet, though. God hadn't ever seemed real keen on grantin' me favors, but by some kinda mercy, it didn't seem Moses or his lady partner had seen the bounty posters with my likeness on 'em yet. At least, I was prayin' that were the case. And if it was, I wanted to keep it that way.

I wanted 'em to forget about me. To leave me be. I wanted to show 'em I weren't no trouble. Maybe convince 'em they could untie me and let me go on about my way.

A cry of triumph from the woman made me snap my eyes open and sit up straighter, heart jumpin' with fear they'd found that other lockbox. But when I looked toward the coach, they were only draggin' out two trunks.

Must have been a hidden compartment in there somewhere.

Still … one of those trunks could have the lockbox with the dials inside it…

I tugged at my wrists again. Tied tight, damnit. The skin already raw, and my arms achin'. If they did find that lockbox … well, I didn't have a plan fer that yet.

I watched as they jimmied both trunks open with their knives and started sortin' through the contents.

Clothes. It was all a bunch of clothes.

From the noise of despair that came out of the professor, I guessed those trunks had belonged to him.

That was sure a lot of clothes fer just one man.

Moses and the woman rifled through it all, tossin' pieces here and there, to the growin' frustration of Professor Morton.

"So that's all you are, then?" he finally growled, unable to hold his silence any longer. "Nothing more than a pair of scavengers!"

"Hardly," the woman scoffed. She pulled out a pair of nice, polished boots and raised her eyebrows. She held 'em down by her own feet, checkin' to see if they might fit her. "I'd call us … *opportunists*."

Professor Morton gave a disgusted grunt. "If you were true opportunists, you'd see the benefit in taking me to Blessing! You wouldn't be rummaging around through my baggage and throwing my wardrobe all over the desert!"

"Yeah, there's just one problem with your offer, there, Professor," the woman said. She set the boots aside and held up a white dress shirt so clean it hurt to look at it in the sun.

"Pray, do tell," Professor Morton quipped.

"You see…" She paused as she put the shirt up against Moses and tilted her head to one side, clearly considerin' what a man like him might look like in such a garment. His current get-up was a standard button-up that may have been white once, but was now more a beige color, with faded blue stripes.

Moses, fer his part, gave her a glower.

She only raised an eyebrow and threw the white dress shirt over her shoulder, then returned her attention to the trunk and cleared her throat. "You see," she said again, "the problem is that Moses and I got no love at all for those metal barons. Can't stand 'em, if I'm to be honest. So we ain't going to Blessing, I'm afraid."

"Not even for a reward of thousands of dollars?"

The professor sounded truly confused. But I understood well

enough. I wouldn'ta gone to Blessing fer thousands of dollars, neither. Not after meetin' with Baron Whittaker up close and personal.

"Nope," the woman said.

"But … but if you like my wardrobe so much, you could buy a whole trunk-full of similar clothes for yourselves with the reward money!"

"No thank you," the woman said again. "These'll do just fine." She collected a few more shirts and a pair of trousers while the professor continued to bluster on, appalled.

I started to relax, finally, after they'd emptied out both trunks with still no sign of that dialed lockbox.

But then a shout echoed out from up on the road and made me tense up again.

Moses and the woman twisted around to look up the slope, both of 'em pullin' iron faster than I could see.

Shit. Good thing I hadn't tested 'em. Either of 'em.

Up on the road, the small figure of a person could be seen leanin' over the edge, peerin' down at us. I imagined we made quite the sight. At least at the moment I looked like one of the victims … instead of like the murderer I was.

But the person up there only turned, talkin' to someone else, and then he disappeared from view, only to reappear a second later on the back of his horse, goin' on down the road. Another man rode with him, and they both took off at a gallop.

Toward Sonoita.

"That's our cue to leave," Moses said. He pushed his pistol back into his holster and went quick to gather up the things they'd deemed worthy of keepin'. He threw 'em over the back of his horse, a tall, shiny black gelding. Woulda put Holt's gelding to shame.

The woman did the same, tyin' stuff to the back of her own saddle. Her horse was a white mare. And a true white horse, at that, with a pink nose and everything. Didn't see those very often.

Moses finished loadin' up his saddlebags, too, then grabbed up my long rifle from where I'd propped it against the turned-over coach.

Now it was my turn to make a noise of despair. I'd just bought that damn thing! "Hey," I blurted. "Come on, not the rifle. Please?"

He paused, lookin' at me dubiously from under his hat brim. "I'm doin' you a favor, boy. You want this weapon here when the lawdogs arrive? Anyone can see this rifle is what put those holes in those marshals … and you want me to leave it here, lyin' right next to you?"

I considered his point. Though I had no plans to still be here by the time any law arrived, that was fer sure. We were close enough to Blessing they could have seen that poster. And even if they hadn't, they'd be askin' questions I surely didn't want to answer.

But before I could say anythin' further, he'd shouldered it and swung up onto his horse. "And anyway, we're leavin' you yer irons." He nodded toward my gun belts, rolled up nice and neat next to the coach. Far out of my reach. "I'd say that's mighty generous, wouldn't you?"

"Like I said," the woman chimed in as she also mounted up and reined her mare around to face me and Professor Morton, still tied around that boulder, "we're opportunists, not savages." She grinned at me, and turned her mare away. Kicked up into a trot, leavin' a little trail of dust behind her.

Moses touched the brim of his hat again, like he had when he'd first caught me unawares in the coach. "Pleasure doin' business with you gents." He turned to follow after the woman, and as he caught up to her, they both spurred their horses into a nice, easy canter, ridin' off into the desert.

And just like that, they were gone as quick as they'd come.

And I was stuck here, tied to a boulder, like a snared rabbit waitin' on the return of the hunter.

This job was really not goin' my way.

I sat there fer a minute thinkin', tryin' to figure out how I was gonna get myself free before someone *less generous* came along and found us … or until those men got back with the law.

If that's even where they were goin' in the first place.

If.

That's when the idea came to me. I twisted around toward the professor again. "Hey, Mister … Professor … help me out, would ya? I think we can get free if we work together."

He'd been mutterin' something about wishin' he'd never come here—I couldn't fault him fer that sentiment—but he paused in his lamentations long enough to scoff at me. "Oh, is that so? And just what makes you think I'd want to help out a man like you? You *murdered* those men! You robbed me! And you might have murdered *me*!"

I winced at his accusations. I was afraid he'd feel that way. "Now, now … I didn't rob you. Those other two did that."

"But you *would* have. If they hadn't come along!"

"Look, all I'm interested in is that lockbox with the dials. I wouldn't have taken any of yer other stuff like those other two did. And now … well, now we're both in trouble, ain't we? We're both in a right predicament, meanin' fer now, we're on the same side. So let's get out of these damned ropes, yeah?"

"I'm not in any predicament," he protested sullenly. "I have no reason to fear the law. I'm perfectly content to wait here till they arrive to cut these ropes. And then I'll be giving them a *full* account of what happened here. And don't think I'll leave out *your* part in all this. Oh no. You're the one who started it! I was having a perfectly fine day until you started shooting up my escorts!"

I winced again. I was afraid he'd feel that way, too.

But that's where the *if* came in. Uncertainty could sway a lot of folks.

So I gave a little laugh. "You think the law is comin'?"

"Yes. Why else would that man called Moses and that woman have taken off so quickly?"

I scoffed at him now. "Because when you're a thief, it ain't smart to stay put in once place too long." I shifted against the hard, rough rock pressin' into my back. "Look, Mister, two men ridin' off in the direction of a town after seein' a turned coach and a buncha dead bodies ain't no guarantee they're goin' to retrieve the sheriff. More likely they run off scared. More likely they wanted to make it clear they didn't want no part of this. I guess you couldn't see Moses and his lady friend draw, bein' as you were facin' the other way, but I can tell you, friend, they were lightnin' fast. And I've seen a lot of people draw, mind you. Anyone with any sense woulda high-tailed it outta here at seein' their speed … maybe that man up there on the road saw it, too. And he and his friend did the sensible thing and made a hasty exit."

He was silent after my speech, and hope stirred in my chest. Maybe I was gettin' to him.

A shadow slid across the ground in front of me and I looked up to see a vulture glide overhead. It circled around over the coach, no doubt quite pleased to see such a feast laid out beneath it. Where there was one, more would follow.

Damned buzzards. Seemed they was like my own shadow … always there and waitin' when I turned around, no matter where I went or what I did.

"And that's another thing," I said, watchin' the vulture circle. "See that buzzard, there? He ain't the only kinda animal out here. There's others, too. Like those mountain cats. You ever seen one of those?"

"No…"

"Yeah well they'll be attracted to all this meat same as the buzzards. Except they're not just scavengers. They like live meat just fine. And here we are, all trussed up nice fer 'em. One of those finds us … they may not even kill us before they start eatin' on us. That's if, of course, we ain't dead already from thirst or exposure to the sun."

I paused then, but the professor still said nothin'.

So I went ahead and made my closin' argument. "Sure, Mister, yer right … we *could* just sit here and do nothin' and wait fer the law to show up … and sure, that wouldn't be too good fer me … but if I gotta be honest … it's probably not gonna happen. Or if it does happen, they'll come too late. Some other *opportunist* will find us first, and they might not be so generous as Moses and his lady friend. They might decide we're both better off dead so we can't go around describin' their deeds to the authorities."

The vulture finally landed on one of the bodies. It looked right at us and raised its wings, lettin' out a screech, as if challengin' us to take away its prize.

"Or one of those cats will find us first," I said. "Or the desert will kill us first. And I don't know about you, Professor, but I don't much like those odds. I don't much want to take that kinda chance. Maybe none of those outcomes are particularly favorable fer me, but only one of 'em is favorable fer you. You willin' to take that kinda chance? You willin' to bet yer life on it?"

More silence.

This time I let it stretch. Let him think it over.

The vulture started peckin' at the body.

One of the harness horses snorted at the dirt. They'd wandered a bit, but hadn't gone too far yet. I wondered why Moses and the woman hadn't taken the extra horses with 'em.

Maybe they'd figured it was too much trouble. Maybe that was part of their "generosity", leavin' us some kind of mounts.

The professor cleared his throat. "If I help you get free … how do I know you won't just shoot me afterward?"

The flicker of hope in my chest solidified. This might just work… "Didn't you say Baron Haas would reward anyone who brought you safe to Blessing?"

"Well … yes. That's what he paid those marshals for. But now that they're all dead, I imagine those funds could go to someone else. To whoever ended up fulfilling the job they were meant to do."

"All right, then. So that means yer worth more alive than dead, Professor. If I killed you now, I'd be throwin' money away, wouldn't I?"

"That's an awful way to put it."

"But it's true, ain't it?"

"So you're saying that if I help you get free, if we both get free of this rock, you'll escort me all the way to Blessing? Safely? Even though you already tried once to rob and shoot me?"

I shrugged as best I could with my arms wrapped backwards around the bulk of that boulder. "What can I say? Circumstances have changed, Professor. Like our friends who left us like this … I consider myself an opportunist. But *unlike* them, can't say *I* can pass up such an opportunity. Like you said, thousands of dollars is a lot of money. So, yeah, that's what I'm sayin'."

Again, a long stretch of silence.

More vultures arrived on the scene, circlin' over us.

"All right," Professor Morton said at long last.

I breathed a quiet sigh of relief.

"All right, fine, I'll help you. But I want to get free first. And I want to keep hold of your guns for the journey."

A snort of laughter escaped me. "Professor, just how do you expect me to protect you on the way if I don't have my—"

"You can have them back if we run into trouble."

"*If*? No sir, it'll be *when*. And if I have to get 'em off you before I can shoot, it'll be too late to do anythin' about the trouble!"

"Then I suppose we'll just take our chances here."

I ground my teeth and rolled my eyes. Why'd I always have to get stuck with these kinda bull-headed idiots? "Fine," I spat. "Fine. You get free first and hold onto my guns. That agreeable to you?"

"Quite."

"Wonderful. Thank you. Let's get free of these ropes then, yeah?"

"And just how do you plan to do that, anyway?"

VIII

WHEN

I explained to him another of the "generosities" left by Moses and the woman. Maybe they hadn't done it on purpose, but it seemed a pair of professionals like them probably woulda been more thorough with the method of tyin' us if they'd wanted to leave no chance at all of us freein' ourselves. As it was, they'd tied each of us to the boulder with a separate rope, and there was just enough slack in it to let us move around it, if we wanted. Weren't easy, but it could be done.

So I grabbed my rope on either side in my fists to take some pressure off my wrists, and slowly, bit by bit, shuffled myself around the rock until my right hand met with Professor Morton's left. Then I worked at the knot around his left wrist one-handed, pullin' at it with my fingers.

"You really come all the way here from Canada?" I asked. I didn't really care all that much if he had or hadn't, truth be told, but I was hopin' he'd get comfortable enough with me to answer the questions I was gonna ask him later. And also to not leave me here to rot once he got free himself.

"Yes. I really did."

"Huh. So why in the hell are you here, then? And why go to Blessing, of all places?"

"I'm here on business for Her Majesty, as a matter of fact. As I said, I am the Head Curator for the Royal Museum, and Her Majesty is very interested in acquiring some of Baron Haas' antiquities for her collection. I'm here to make an offer on her behalf. Not only that, but the baron himself is quite interested in my appraisal of his most recent finds." He puffed out his chest like he had before in the coach. "My expertise and advice regarding Old World artifacts is sought the world over, you know."

"Uh huh." I didn't really understand what any of that meant.

"You must know that Blessing has one of the best-preserved Old World ruins on this continent?"

"Sure." My left leg—the leg made outta metal itself—twinged, but I ignored it. I didn't much want to talk about Old World ruins, or Old World tech.

"And many of the barons there have pieces that belong in a museum for all to enjoy … not hidden away in a private collection."

"Whatever you say, Professor." I thought of the giant cannon-gun Charlotte had stolen out of Baron Whittaker's manor and wondered what this man would think of that if he ever saw it. Charlotte had left it with me when she'd headed home, but I didn't use it myself. It was far too obvious of a weapon. And unwieldy. And … I didn't really understand how to work it, anyway. I mostly just left it packed away in a crate at our camp in Grave Gulch.

Professor Morton turned to look at me as I continued workin' at the knot. "Clearly *you* are not the one interested in that dialed lockbox."

My fingers paused in loosenin' that knot as my focus abruptly sharpened.

"Someone hired you to get it for them, didn't they?"

I squinted at him. "What makes you think that?"

"Young man, I've spent my entire life studying Old World technology. And most of my life around others who are … shall we say, *highly enthusiastic* about the subject. You strike me as someone who is anything but. And yet, you murdered those marshals and nearly killed me hoping to get that lockbox. So, you must have been hired."

I swallowed hard and met his curious gaze, only one fact out of his whole speech catchin' my attention. "The lockbox with the dials … it's … it's Old World?"

The professor nodded. "That's right."

My mouth went dry. So Nine-Fingered Nan *was* interested in Old World tech. And interested enough in this lockbox and whatever was inside it to ignore my metal leg and whoever had given it to me. Fer now. Unless I didn't bring her back that lockbox. Then I guess she was gonna take the next best thing.

"The person who hired you didn't tell you that?"

I cleared my throat and went back to workin' at the knot around his wrist. "No."

"Who was it that hired you, anyway? Was it another one of those barons? You weren't the first one to try and ambush us, you know. Those men who were escorting me said the barons are always trying to murder each other, steal from each other. I thought perhaps they were exaggerating … but now I'm beginning to think they weren't exaggerating at all."

I shook my head, rememberin' Baron Whittaker's cruelty clear as day. "I don't think they were exaggerating."

"So it *was* another baron who hired you?"

"I didn't say that."

"Really? Who was it, then? I haven't found many in this country very knowledgeable about the Old World except those barons … and I'm sorry, but if I'm to be frank, even they really aren't much more than thugs dressed up like gentlemen."

"I'd have to agree with you there, Professor."

"Are there other collectors besides them around here somewhere?"

I stopped tuggin' on the knot again and looked at him. "I'm

not at liberty to say." That weren't exactly true, I didn't think, but Nan *had* said she'd wanted everyone aboard the coach dead, so I figured that was close enough.

He frowned at me. He was quite pale, and I imagined all this time in the sun was gonna give him a nice burn, seein' as he had no hat. Sweat trickled down his face.

"What's in that lockbox, anyway?" I asked, tryin' to change the direction of the conversation and also sound casual. "Seems a lot of people want it." Nan mighta instructed me not to open it, but she hadn't said anythin' about askin' questions.

He shrugged. "No one knows."

I barked a laugh. "*What*? All these people after a lockbox and no one knows what's inside? That don't make no sense!"

Disappointment etched his sweaty features. He looked pointedly to his wrist, then, the wrist that was still tied.

"Oh, right." I started pullin' at that knot again.

The professor sighed. "The fact that it is an Old World artifact gives the item value in and of itself to some people," he told me then, as if it should have been obvious. "But there is a widely held belief among Old World scholars that that particular lockbox just might contain a key to navigate through the Valley of Lightning safely."

I chuckled again and shook my head. I'd heard of plenty of crazy people over the years believin' this or that would get them through that death-trap … but they'd all ended up just as dead as all the others who had come before. Once, as a boy, I'd been fascinated by those stories. But now … now that Mama and Pa had been murdered, our homestead burned down, my sister kidnapped, and every day since become its very own struggle to survive … it all just seemed a bunch of nonsense.

My concern at Nan's interest in this Old World lockbox eased a bit. If she were fool enough to buy into that madness, too

.... let her spend her time chasin' fairy tales. Might keep her occupied while I worked on bringin' down her empire and found my sister.

"Laugh if you want," Professor Morton grumbled. "But if it's true, it will be the greatest discovery of our time."

"Sure," I said. "Sure. And yer tellin' me this super important lockbox ain't on that coach?" I jerked my head in its direction. "Anywhere? Not in another hidden compartment or anythin'? 'Cause the person who hired me sure thought it was. And if you were ambushed before, seems they weren't the only one under that impression."

But the professor shook his head vigorously. "Oh no. No, no. Baron Haas knows it's a piece Her Majesty is particularly interested in. And he's a suspicious sort. He wouldn't trust me to ride with it, certainly."

I wanted to laugh again. Of course. I gave a hard tug on the knot in my frustration and the professor gave a cry of joy as his arms dropped, free at last. He pulled his hands into his lap with a wince and rubbed at his wrists.

"Where is it then?" I rasped.

He looked to me sharply, and I realized my tone had not sounded casual at all. And I was still tied to that rock. Couldn't afford to scare him off now...

I swallowed, tried to keep my frustration in check. "Just curious, is all. Wonderin' how so many people could be wrong about its whereabouts."

His eyes narrowed, and he scrambled up to his feet, still rubbin' at his raw wrists. "You still want to find it." He didn't seem too pleased about that fact.

Fer a second I just stared up at him, and the urge to lie warred with the urge to just tell him the truth. Which would he be more inclined to trust, I wondered? I tried to wet my lips, but

I was even more thirsty now than I had been before. "Look, Mister … the person who hired me is just about as bad as those barons. If I don't get that lockbox fer 'em, if I don't try like hell to get it, at least, a lot of people are gonna die. A lot of innocent people. I don't want that to happen, understand? If you know where it is … I'll escort you to Blessing and all, keep my end of our bargain … I just need to know where it is."

All right, so I'd given him half the truth and half a lie. Maybe he'd believe 'em both.

"So you can steal it?" His eyes were hard.

"Like I said, Professor … innocent people will die if I don't get that lockbox. You want that on your conscience?"

His expression darkened. Maybe that had been the wrong thing to say. "Oh no," he said, shakin' his head, his voice harder than it had been all day. "No. You don't put that on me. Innocent people have already died because of that lockbox, and one of them was almost me!" He pointed back at the bodies of the marshals, now attended by several vultures. "*They* were innocent, weren't they? And you didn't seem to have any problems gunning *them* down! So no, you don't put that on me. That's on *you*, young man, and only you. Understand?"

I opened my mouth to protest his accusation, but he didn't give me a chance.

"You want to know where that lockbox is?"

I shut my mouth abruptly. If he was gonna tell me without further promptin' on my part, I'd let him tell me. What he thought me guilty of or not guilty of didn't matter.

"As far as I know, it's already at Baron Haas' estate!"

All the hope in me died at those words.

But the professor didn't seem to notice. "I'm going there to negotiate for its purchase, among other Old World pieces, as I said. That kind of discovery should be handled with care, studied judiciously, treated with the significance it deserves! Not displayed as a show of arrogance and power ... or sold off to the highest bidder who might destroy it and whatever's inside of it in their eagerness to open it!"

Clearly this was a subject he was passionate about, indeed. But all I could think of, sittin' there tied to that boulder in the afternoon desert sun, was how much I didn't want to go back to Blessing. How much I didn't want to ever see any of those barons again.

"You think you'll just stroll on in to his house and steal it out from under his nose?" Professor Morton scoffed and spread his arms, the rope danglin' off his right wrist. "Then be my guest. But I will not be an accomplice to your crimes!"

I blinked up at him. The cloudless blue sky was dazzlin' in the heat. Maybe the sun was gettin' to him. Maybe the sun was gettin' to me. "I never asked you to—"

"You think I believe you won't kill me as soon as I set you free?"

Oh no. No no no...

"You think I believe you'd take me to Blessing and I'd ever get there alive? When you've made it abundantly clear what you'll do in efforts to find that treasure?" He waved again toward the marshals' bodies. "I don't think so, young man. You'd kill me first chance you got, and then kill who knows how many more trying to get that lockbox. And *that's* what I can't have on my conscience." He turned away from me then, and marched over toward the remains of the coach.

"Professor..." It was hard to find the words. The true realization of how dire my situation would be should he leave me here kept chokin' off my air. "Professor ... we had an agreement!"

"One I am quite certain you had no intention of keeping." He bent down to pick up my gun belts, and fear cut through me like a knife.

But the anger came after it, as I watched him buckle my belts around his own waist, drownin' out the fear, leavin' only that buzzin' rage. "Professor. You don't even know how to handle those things. You run into any trouble on the road, you'll be dead before yer hand even starts to drop! You think you can make it to Blessing by yourself? After you've already been ambushed more than once along the way?"

"I'm not going to Blessing," he said calmly. "I'm going to the nearest town. What'd they say it was? Sonoita, I think. Said it was only a few miles further. I'm sure I can manage that far."

My heart beat faster, crawlin' up into my throat. I pulled at the rope still holdin' my arms to that rock, but it wasn't goin' nowhere without outside help.

Professor Morton surveyed the mess of his trunks and wardrobe and sighed, then picked up the canteen left sittin' there and uncapped it, takin' a few big gulps.

I wanted some of that myself, real bad. I tried to swallow, and tried again. "Professor … all that stuff I told you before, about the mountain cats and the sun and other *less generous* souls wanderin' by … all that is still true. You leave me here like this and I'm as good as dead."

He turned to look at me, then walked back in my direction, and I hoped against hope he'd had a change of heart. He held the canteen down fer me, and tilted it so I could take a few good gulps of my own.

"I'm not going to leave you here to die," he said.

Relief flooded my limbs. Maybe I wouldn't kill him when I got free, after all.

"I'll get to Sonoita fast as I can, and then I'll send the sheriff back for you. I'll be sure he hurries."

All that hope inside me died again. Shriveled up into somethin' dry and hard and bitter. I stared up at him, wishin' my hands were free so I could wrap 'em around his throat. Pull *my* guns off him and put him out of his misery. I tried to surge to my feet, but I didn't have enough leverage with that rope holdin' me to that rock, and all I managed was a futile little lurch.

Professor Morton jumped back with a yelp, anyway, givin' me a little satisfaction, and then he glared at me in indignation as he recapped the canteen and slung it over his shoulder. He cleared his throat. "Well. Like I said ... you *did* free me, even if I suspect you planned to murder me later, so I won't leave you here to die. I'll send the sheriff back to rescue you."

"Some rescue," I spat, and the burnin' ball of rage and frustration and loathin' livin' in my chest made my voice sound not my own. "They'll hang me fer sure."

He looked down at me in silence fer a long minute, but there was no remorse on his face. No sympathy. Just the flat conviction of a man who believed he was unquestionably in the right. "We all make our own choices in life," he said finally, quietly. "Perhaps you should have considered where yours were taking you before you acted on them."

He turned from me again then, takin' my guns and the water and goin' to retrieve one of the harness horses.

"You don't know nothin' about my choices," I growled after him. "Nothin'!"

He didn't reply, concentratin' on fashionin' some proper reins from the harness lines. Then he gripped fistfuls of the horse's mane and swung up on its back like he'd been doin' such a thing his whole life. So he was better at horses than he was at guns, clearly.

And he really *was* gonna leave me here.

"Professor," I choked out, strainin' to see around the curve of the boulder as he kicked his chosen horse into motion. "Professor! Please—she has my sister!"

That slowed him up. He reined the horse back around to face me.

"She has my sister," I repeated. "And she's gonna sell her off unless I bring her that lockbox."

"Who?"

"Nine-Fingered Nan."

A pause. He walked the horse a little closer.

Yes. That's right. Please come back... I just needed him to get me free of this rock....

"And you think that justifies the murder of countless others?"

The question took me by surprise. Did I?

Yes. No? I suppose I didn't rightly know. I'd never stopped to do the math. I didn't much care fer math. The math didn't matter much anyway when her face kept hauntin' my sleep. When all I could remember was how I'd promised her I'd come back just as soon as I could ... but I hadn't come back soon enough. "She's all I have left," was all I said in answer. Guess he was gettin' the real truth outta me, after all.

Another pause. "Then I suppose you should tell the sheriff about that too when he arrives. Maybe they can do something about it through proper means."

I closed my eyes. Slumped back against the warmth of the rock behind me. *Proper* means? Maybe where he came from the law might do somethin' about every poor kidnapped soul ... but not here. Not here.

Especially not against someone like Nine-Fingered Nan.

"I'll have someone back here as quickly as I can," he said, and then I heard him take off at a gallop. The other two horses followed for a bit, but it didn't matter.

None of it mattered.

If he didn't make it to Sonoita, I was gonna die out here.

If he *did* make it to Sonoita, I was gonna die there.

Weren't a question of *if* anymore. All that uncertainty had turned certain awful quick.

The only question left to answer now was when. *When* was I gonna die ... sooner or later?

I supposed I wouldn't have to wait too long to find out.

IX

SOME LUCK

By the time I heard hoofbeats approachin' again, I didn't care who was comin'.

I didn't know how long it'd been, exactly. Long enough fer Professor Morton to have reached Sonoita, I figured. Long enough fer him to have told his whole story to the town's sheriff. Long enough fer the sheriff to have gathered a few more men and headed out this way. Long enough fer that posse to be arrivin' right about now.

The vultures were still feastin' on the dead, lots more of 'em here now and sometimes fightin' amongst themselves fer the best bits. A few of 'em had a peck or two at me, but I yelled out and kicked at 'em, and that dissuaded 'em from tryin' too hard to eat me.

The sun had moved across that dazzlin' blue sky some, and I'd managed to slide myself into what little bit of shadow the boulder was throwin' out now. It weren't much, but I would take it. I'd take any kinda small mercy at this point.

My shoulders ached, my wrists rubbed raw from the rope, and I was hot and thirsty as hell. I didn't move as the hoofbeats came closer, didn't look up, didn't open my eyes. I just listened and tried to count the number of horses. More than a few, sounded like.

Coulda been the sheriff and some others. Coulda been a gatherin' of vultures of the human variety. Either way I hoped they'd just put me outta my misery quick. I'd had plenty of time now sittin' out here in silence, alone, tied to a rock, thinkin' of all the ways I'd failed my family. All the ways I'd failed Ethelyn.

"Holy Mother," someone breathed as the horses came to a stop next to my boulder.

"Get those buzzards out of here," another voice ordered. "And start gathering up the bodies."

"Yessir."

If they were concerned about the bodies, they surely weren't scavengers themselves. Must be Sonoita's sheriff, then. Guess the professor had made it, after all.

I heard 'em all dismount, several of 'em, and start about their business. The vultures weren't none too happy about it, protestin' loudly as they flew off, reluctant to give up so much meat.

Slow bootsteps approached me then, spurs janglin'. Then someone kicked at my foot, and the voice that had given the orders spoke up again. "Hey. You still alive?"

I sighed and roused myself, openin' my eyes to squint up at him. He was the sheriff, all right. A badge glinted on his chest in the sunlight. Looked all shiny and new. He was an older man, with skin deeply tanned and weathered, but younger than Sheriff Jennings. Had a moustache himself, but also a thick carpet of gray stubble across his jaw. He'd pulled his duster back to show the grip of the revolver at his hip. As if he'd need it with me tied like this, and the professor havin' taken my guns.

"Does it matter?" I asked.

He smiled a little. "Depends. You do all this?" He turned to look out over the bodies and the sideways coach and the trunks with their contents strewn all over the place.

When he turned back toward me, I shook my head. "No, sir."

One of his eyebrows lifted. "That a fact? We got a man back in town who says otherwise."

I grunted. "You believe every story you hear?"

"Only those that sound sensible."

"And that man's story sounded sensible to you?"

He shrugged. "As sensible as a tale of murder and robbery can sound, I suppose."

"I guess he told you I murdered these men?"

"Sure did."

I saw his crew pass behind him, carryin' the dead marshals to the extra horses they'd brought, but I kept my focus on him. They'd sure come prepared. "And what if I told you a different story? If it sounded sensible enough to you, would you consider believin' me instead of him?"

It was always a gamble out here in the Territories if the lawmen would bother to uphold the law. I usually assumed they wouldn't, since that was most often the case, but the fact this sheriff here had gone through all this trouble to retrieve the dead spoke to him havin' a conscience, which meant he weren't likely to be swayed away from proper justice.

But I had to try.

His eyes narrowed. They were an unusual mix of brown and green. "Don't matter what *I* believe, really. You can tell your story to the judge and jury if you want. They'll be the ones you gotta convince."

My eyebrows nearly lifted off my scalp. "A *jury*?"

"Yeah, that's right. You'll get a trial." He glanced at his men, who were tyin' the bodies to saddles now. "Even if you don't deserve it."

"My, my, Sheriff." I clucked my tongue and shook my head again. "A trial! Ain't you all such civilized folk up here."

He turned a glare on me and motioned for two of the posse he'd brought with him. "Cut him free, but then tie his wrists again. In front so he can get on a damn horse." He pulled his pistol and thumbed the hammer back, then aimed it at me fer good measure. "And you," he said, lookin' right at me. "You don't try anything or you'll be gettin' fulla lead instead of gettin' that trial, understand?"

"Sure," I muttered. "I got it."

Maybe he weren't convinced, or maybe his men weren't convinced, because two more of 'em came over and pointed their guns at me, too. Maybe Professor Morton had talked me up into bein' some terrifyin' monster.

But the truth of it was my arms were mostly numb now from bein' stuck in such an awkward position fer so long. And the days of waitin' on that coach, the nights of little sleep, the hours under the sun, had sapped most my energy. So when they cut me free, I only winced as my hands finally thumped to the ground, and didn't protest at all as one of 'em roughly grabbed my arms and pulled 'em around front to tie my wrists again.

Then they hauled me up to my feet and escorted me toward one of their waitin' horses. I stumbled a bit, stiff from hours of sittin' cramped against a boulder, and struggled some with gettin' the metal leg to cooperate. By the time we reached the horse, though, most the stiffness had worked out, so at least I didn't make a fool of myself as I mounted up under the watchful eye of no less than five guns.

"I got a mule," I told the sheriff as one of his men proceeded to tie my bound wrists to the saddle horn. "Up the hill from the road there." I nodded in that general direction. "And the rest of my supplies with him. Will you get 'em fer me? The mule, at least? Take him to town? He's tied, so … well, if I don't come back he won't fare too good."

The sheriff holstered his weapon and gave a nod. "Sure." He signaled out two more of his crew. "McGregor, Belmont, you go on up and get that mule."

"Sure thing, Sheriff."

They mounted up and headed off, and then the rest of the posse took to their saddles, goin' in turns so there was always a gun trained on me, just in case. I wondered just what exactly Professor Morton had told 'em about me.

Then we headed off at a trot, my horse ponied behind the sheriff's mount. There were two each of the posse on either side of me, and they led the horses holdin' the bodies behind 'em. The sheriff had come prepared, all right.

We rode in silence. Had to follow the narrow valley for quite a ways before the slope that shouldered the road to our left evened out enough for our horses to go up it without too much trouble. Then we followed the road the rest of the way into town.

We caused quite a commotion as we passed down the main street with our parade of dead, headin' toward the jailhouse. Most the townsfolk stopped their business to stare wide-eyed. Some of 'em started mutterin' and whisperin' to each other. Some of 'em signed themselves and started prayin'. Lots of 'em looked at me in horror … and anger … and disgust.

I tried not to look back at 'em. Me bein' tied to this saddle sure made me look guilty, all right, and if that jury was gonna come from these townsfolk, I didn't want to see their judgments already bein' made.

The sheriff instructed his men with the bodies to go on toward the coroner's, and he and I stopped outside the jailhouse. He untied me from the saddle and ordered me to dismount, which I did obediently enough. Still, he took my right bicep in a grip like iron and steered me quickly inside the building, where he showed me to a cell in the back corner.

He pushed me inside and swung the door shut after me. The lock clicked as I turned back around to face him, lookin' over the place. This jailhouse was bigger than the one in Bravebank. Had six cells instead of three, all currently empty except fer mine. And no windows at all. The inside was dim, lit with a couple lanterns. The sheriff's desk was across the way, along the wall opposite the cells … along the wall lined with bulletins of people's faces.

Wanted posters.

I shifted my eyes away from those quick as the sheriff pulled his knife from his belt and gestured fer me to hold my hands out between the bars. I didn't want him to follow my gaze. Didn't want to remind him to check his collection to see if my mug was up there. I hadn't seen my own face there, yet, but I'd only barely managed a glance at 'em.

He cut the rope from my wrists and I sighed in relief, rubbin' at 'em. "Appreciate it."

"Sure," he said. He tossed the cut rope into the corner and then crossed the room to a sideboard just behind his desk. He grabbed the pitcher sittin' on it and a tin cup and brought it over to me. Poured the cup full and offered it to me.

Water.

I took it and gulped it down, then wiped my mouth with the back of my hand. "Thank you."

"More?"

"Please." I handed the cup back to him, and he refilled it fer me. I drank down three more cups before the thirst finally seemed satisfied.

He took the pitcher then and put it back where it belonged, and I eased myself down onto the bench and thin mattress that served as the cell's cot. I sat back against the wall and watched him. He weren't like other sheriffs I'd met. Even Sheriff Jennings, who claimed to be an honest lawman despite his arrangement with Nine-Fingered Nan, hadn't offered me nothin' when I'd woke up in his jailhouse with my whole body achin'.

"You hungry?" this sheriff asked.

I nearly fell right off the cot in surprise. "Yeah."

"All right, I'll get ya some grub." He headed fer the jailhouse door, but paused with his hand on the doorknob and turned back to me. "Don't think of trying nothing, though. I'll have armed men in here in just a minute to keep an eye on you."

I held up my hands in a gesture of innocence. "I ain't goin' nowhere, Sheriff."

He only grunted and stepped out, and the door shut firmly behind him.

I sank back against the wall and closed my eyes, pullin' my hat down over my face. Behind bars fer the second time in a week … my luck had never been good, no matter the things people said about me, but it had sure taken an especially bad turn of late.

And this time … this time I weren't sure if I'd make it out alive. Hell, maybe I *had* been lucky up till now. Maybe this was just what shit luck I'd ever had finally runnin' out. Like I always told Holt, that was the problem with luck. Eventually, it just ran out.

Could I somehow convince a judge and jury I hadn't murdered those marshals? That man called Moses was right—at least I hadn't had that rifle on me when the sheriff had found me. That left the murder weapon missin'. And the professor had taken my pistols, so now I didn't even have those. I was entirely unarmed. And how could an unarmed man rob a stagecoach, or murder anyone?

Of course Professor Morton could tell 'em all what had really happened, but if I could manage to fashion a story just good enough to make that jury start doubtin', start questionin'…

Maybe they wouldn't hang me.

Weren't likely. But maybe.

Maybe my luck hadn't entirely run out just yet.

I heard the door open and shut again and some more boot-steps cross the dusty floor. Musta been those men the sheriff had sent to keep an eye on me. They came over toward my cell, but I didn't bother acknowledgin' 'em.

They didn't seem to care.

"You the one that killed those men?" one of 'em asked.

"Nope," I answered, loud enough to be sure they could hear me from under my hat. The darkness was awful welcomin' after so many hours out in that sun.

There was a grunt. Then the other one said, "Why don't you get that hat off yer face and talk to us proper?"

I sighed. "I've had a long day, boys. I just wanna enjoy some peace and quiet fer a bit. Yeah? Ya mind?"

My answer was the horrific clang of metal bangin' on metal. Sounded like one of 'em was probably draggin' the barrel of his gun across the bars of my cell, back and forth.

Back and forth.

I tried to ignore him, knowin' he was only takin' advantage of my situation, tryin' to rile me up, but it *was* an insufferable racket, and I weren't exactly the most patient sort, even on the days I hadn't spent chasin' down a stagecoach only to get robbed and tied up and betrayed myself.

I put on my best murderous glare and pulled the hat down off my face.

Sure enough, the one of 'em had been pullin' his gun barrel across the bars. He stopped as my eyes met his and grinned at me, showin' off yellowed teeth. "Oh lookie there. That's better, ain't it?" He was about a foot shorter than his companion, but they both looked to be the rougher sort: badly sunburnt, generally unwashed, their clothes threadbare in places. A far cry from the crew the sheriff had brought with him to retrieve me, in any case.

Maybe all the decent folk were seein' to the final arrangements fer those marshals.

Or too scared of me to come in here, maybe. Depended on

what Professor Morton had been tellin' people.

The taller one of the two was squintin' at me, leanin' close to the bars.

I switched my glare to him. "Somethin' wrong with yer eyes there, Mister?"

Both of 'em were close enough I could probably make a grab fer one of their weapons...

"Nah," he said, and stepped back.

All right, maybe I'd go for the other one's gun, then...

"It's just that you look mighty familiar." He pulled a rolled-up piece of paper from out of the back of his belt and unfurled it, lookin' back and forth from it to me.

Uh oh. I considered slappin' my hat back over my face, but, well, that woulda made it even more obvious. So I kept still and tried to look innocent, holdin' his stare.

"Ha!" He said, and he slapped his friend's shoulder and held the poster up in front of his face. "Look! I told ya! That's him, that's gotta be him!"

Fuck.

The shorter one peered down at the paper, then did the same thing as the other fella, glancin' back and forth between it and me. "You sure?"

"A 'course! Lookit! Looks just like him!"

I scowled. It was a fair enough sketch, sure, but sayin' it looked *just like me* was goin' a bit too far. The ears were too big, fer one thing, and the eyes too squinty.

"Shit," the shorter one said. He pushed the poster out of his face to look directly at me again. And his gaze dropped to my left leg. "You gotta metal leg there, pal?"

I scoffed. "A *what*? You been drinkin', friend? Ain't no one got a metal leg."

"All right then, prove it."

"Prove what?"

The shorter one grabbed the poster out of his companion's hand and shook it at me. "Prove you ain't got a left leg made outta metal! Prove you ain't this fella here!" He rolled it out and held it at me so I could see.

It was my poster, all right. This particular one was well-worn, the creases deep, the corners tattered. At least one of these men had been lookin' fer me since that bounty had first dropped, seemed like.

I swallowed and shook my head. "I don't know who that Charles Miller fella is, but he's a swindler. Playin' desperate people fer fools. There ain't no such thing as a man walkin' around on a metal leg." I never woulda believed it myself, not ever, if I hadn't been livin' it.

"Then you'll have no problem showin' us yer leg, will ya?" the taller one put in. "Go on … just roll up that pant-leg and let's see it."

"No thanks." I settled back against the wall again and pulled my hat back over my face. "I ain't gonna jump through hoops just to prove to a pair of idiots some tall-tale ain't true. Of course it ain't true. It's horseshit to begin with."

"Who ya callin' idiots?" one of 'em snarled.

I lifted the hat just enough to peer out underneath it. "You two. Clearly. And anyone else who believes such nonsense." I dropped the hat. There was silence fer a minute. I thought maybe I'd convinced them. Then there were steps movin' away from my cell, and I hoped they were leavin'.

But no such luck, after all.

The footsteps came back in my direction, accompanied now by the sound of jostlin' keys, and then a click as my cell door unlocked.

I sat up quick at that, and pushed my hat back onto my head just in time to see both of 'em step inside the cell, blockin' the doorway, with their guns drawn. The space was cramped with all three of us in there, and I had to admit they both looked a lot bigger at such close range, made of hardened muscle from some kind of manual labor. Their forearms bulged as they clenched their fists.

Well, I'd managed just fine before against worse, I supposed. Though my middle was still sore from the barfight in Bravebank ... and these were mighty close quarters for a tussle.

"You wanna say that again now that you don't got bars protectin' ya?" the taller one growled.

I held up my hands and stood slowly from the bench. They were less than two feet from my face. And they mighta just handed me my opportunity to get out of here ... if I could get past 'em first. "Now, now, gentlemen. I don't want no trouble."

I kept sayin' that, and yet it didn't seem to make no difference.

"Then stop insultin' us," the shorter one hissed through his teeth, "and show us yer left leg is made outta flesh." He lifted his pistol and thumbed the hammer back. "Else we'll figure it out through *other* means."

"I believe that poster specifically says the reward is only fer the target bein' delivered *alive*," I reminded 'em.

"Who says we're gonna kill ya?" the taller one said. "We're just gonna make you bleed some."

I smiled at him, but was also plannin' out my first move. Their throats were in nice, easy reach. I could probably throat punch 'em both before they got off a shot. "I'd prefer it if you didn't," was all I said.

He leaned forward a bit, comin' nose to nose with me. "Then show us yer leg. 'Fore this gets ugly."

I bit back the urge to tell him it was already ugly enough from where I was standin' and sighed instead. Nodded. "All right. All right. No need fer violence, boys. You wanna see my leg, I'll show you my leg. Fine. But I'm tellin' ya, that's all nonsense."

"Just get on with it already," the shorter one snapped.

I sat back down on the bench and bent over like I was gonna roll up my pant-leg. They both leaned forward eagerly, wantin' to see it up close, I suppose.

It was just what I'd hoped they'd do.

LOST AND FOUND

I sent my right fist into the throat of the shorter one and kicked out with my left foot at the taller one, gettin' him in the knee. The shorter one gagged, droppin' his gun as both hands went to his throat. The taller one yelled somethin' awful and crashed to the floor, flailin' around as he clutched at his leg.

I snatched up the short one's pistol and vaulted over the one on the floor. He reached out fer me as I landed on the side of freedom, and his fingers hooked my ankle just enough to trip me up. I went sprawlin' to the floor myself, but scrambled back to my feet quick.

And got tackled from behind by the short one. All the air went outta me as he landed on me, but I managed to twist around and pistol-whip him across the face even as his hands clawed fer my throat. He sagged sideways, dazed, and I shoved him off me.

I rolled over and pushed to my hands and knees just as the jailhouse door opened again, and a third man stepped in. He didn't look familiar, but he weren't no ruffian. His clothes were new and well-tailored, his complexion smooth and dusky brown, and he had a pair of pistols on his hips. But his boots and his coat were dusty. Fer a second we just stared at each other, him and I, while I tried to decide if I wanted to up my murder count.

He decided for me, goin' fer his piece.

I grabbed up my stolen gun, too, but a fist hit me like a brick in the side of the face and sent lights flashin' in front of my eyes. It knocked me spinnin' and then I was flat out on the floor again.

That short bastard pounced on me before I could recover my wits and got his hands around my throat good this time. He started squeezin' like maybe he didn't care about that fifty thousand dollars no more. I gagged and kicked, tryin' to throw him off, but he didn't budge. Blood trickled down his face from where my blow had split the skin of his temple and he looked real, real mad.

"That's enough!" the third man barked, his boomin' voice like thunder through the jailhouse. "Get off him. *Now.* I need him alive."

That loosened the grip around my neck. The man sittin' over me twisted around to look at the one givin' orders. "Too late, friend," he coughed. His voice was all rough and hoarse from that fist I'd landed in his throat. "If yer after that bounty, my brother and I got here first."

The third man strode across the jailhouse and leveled his drawn pistol at the short man's head. "Then it looks to me like you can't read. Mr. Miller wants him *alive*."

The hands tightened again, chokin' off my air, and I tried to dig my fingers down under 'em to loosen the grip. "I ain't gonna kill him," the man chokin' me growled, but I didn't much believe him at this rate. "Just gonna hurt him. I think he broke my brother's leg!"

"That's too bad," the third man said, though his tone weren't sympathetic. "But I suppose that's what you get for openin' his cell. I'll say it one more time, *friend*. Let go of his neck. And get off him."

Through the rushin' in my ears I heard the click of the hammer goin' back.

The short man scowled somethin' terrible and gave my throat one more squeeze I thought would crush my windpipe, but then he released me and rolled off, gettin' to his feet to face the stranger with balled fists.

I coughed and choked and rolled onto my side, gulpin' air greedily and wonderin' why so many people seemed to have a problem with me breathin'.

"That's better," the third man said, and he kicked the gun lyin' on the floor over into the far corner. Well outta my reach. Well outta reach of the brothers.

"We found him first!" the taller brother yelled from where he laid in the cell's doorway.

"Looks to me like you were tryin' to lose him," the stranger drawled.

The taller brother's face reddened, and he reached out fer his own gun, but the third man had his second pistol out in a second, and his shot made my ears ring. The taller brother yelped as the bullet buried itself into the floorboards just short of his hand.

"Why don't you just leave that?" the stranger said. "Go get that leg looked at. Go on." His dark gaze flicked from one brother to the other, and he emphasized his instructions with the barrels of his guns, flickin' 'em toward the door, which still stood open.

I pushed myself up sittin' and rubbed at my achin' throat. "No need fer all this fightin', gents," I coughed. "That ain't even me on that poster. Yer goin' through an awful lot of trouble fer nothin'."

"Sure," the third man said. "Hear that, boys? He ain't even that fella on the poster. So you can go on home now. Let me sort this out."

The short one's face went pale all of a sudden, all the anger meltin' away. "Wait … are you … you that bounty hunter? Duster, is it?"

I looked up at that man myself, then, just in time to see him smile in a way that didn't reach his eyes. I'd never heard of a bounty hunter called Duster, but it was clear these two brothers had. And apparently he had a reputation. If I managed to get out of this new predicament alive, I'd have to educate myself. There were plenty of bounties out fer me floatin' around the Territories … and if there was a bounty hunter good enough to have a reputation out here, too, I needed to know about him.

I needed to know *a lot* about him.

He held his pistols aimed at the brothers, one fer each of 'em. "That's me all right."

The shorter brother backed away slowly, but the anger came back to his face. "Look, Mister … we were here first. Don't matter who you are, that bounty is ours by rights."

The man called Duster shrugged. "Only if you can deliver this outlaw to Mr. Miller … and it don't seem that was goin' very well for you boys. But I'll tell you what. Why don't we settle this outside in the street at twenty paces? Last one standin' gets to take him in?"

I lifted my brows. Damn, this Duster fella was serious. I eyed the gun in the corner. Could I possibly edge over to it while they were all conversatin'?

The two brothers had both gone pale now. The shorter one glanced to the one on the floor. Then he swallowed visibly and went to help the taller one to his feet. "He may not even be the fella on the poster," he muttered.

"That's right," I said. "I told ya, I ain't that man. All this trouble fer nothin'."

"You shut up," Duster snapped, "and don't even think about goin' fer that gun." He lowered one of his pistols toward me and

I frowned. Had I been that obvious? But he kept his eyes on the two brothers. "So? What'll it be, boys?"

"I'm takin' my brother to the doc," the shorter one scowled. His eyes blazed hatred as he glared at the bounty hunter. "But don't think we're done here."

"I should hope we ain't," Duster quipped.

The brothers limped away like kicked dogs, tossin' hooded glares over their shoulders as they left the jailhouse.

They passed the sheriff as they went out, who stepped inside quick, a bowl in one hand and his gun in the other. He took in the sight of my open cell door and me on the floor and the man standin' over me with guns drawn, but then, to my surprise, holstered his weapon. "What the blazes happened in here?" he demanded.

The man called Duster put away his right gun and reached down to grab my arm and pull me to my feet. "Greed makes some people stupid," he said. He nodded back to the sheriff. "Shut the door, would you?"

The sheriff did so, and Duster dragged me back into my cell and shoved me down onto the bench. I opened my mouth to protest his manhandlin', but that's when he drew his knife and slashed it downward at my left leg, so fast I didn't have time to react.

"Hey!" the sheriff barked, clearly as surprised as me.

But then that blade was at my throat, and instead of comin' up to my feet and punchin' that Duster fella right in the chin like I'd been plannin', I only froze, still sittin' on the bench, glarin' at him eye-to-eye.

He gave me one of those cheerless smiles. "Careful, Delano. I'd like you to stay alive probably as much as you'd like to stay alive."

Alarm went through me at the mention of my name, and his

smile widened. "That's right. I know who you are." He straightened, but kept the knife at my throat. Glanced down to my left leg and the slash he'd made in my pants, right over my shin. "Well, would you look at that? No blood."

"Duster," the sheriff said, "you better tell me what the hell is going on here or I'm locking you up too, understand?"

"Sure thing, Sheriff." The man called Duster withdrew his knife and sheathed it, but kept his left pistol trained on me while he backed out of my cell. Then he swung the barred door shut and locked it, tossin' the key ring to the sheriff, who caught it mid-air.

I gave 'em both my best glare, but I didn't like the way things were shapin' up here. Not at all. My heart beat too fast, too hard, and I'd lost my appetite. The sheriff slid the bowl of stew through the small openin' in the bottom of the cell door, anyway, givin' me a curious look, but I ignored both it and the food.

He turned to the bounty hunter as he stood, who had gone over to the sideboard and poured two glasses of whiskey. Duster held one out to the sheriff as the older man crossed the room.

"All right," the sheriff growled as he took a glass. "Start talking."

"Came out here to start askin' some questions and caught sight of you paradin' down the street with a mighty familiar face in tow," Duster said. "You found a real prize there, Sheriff." He threw back his whiskey and nodded toward me.

Clearly these two knew each other. Clearly they had some kinda history. Great.

The sheriff glanced over at me, then downed his own whiskey and poured them both another glass. "That so? He worth something?"

"You could say that." Duster reached into the inside pocket of his coat and pulled out a whole stack of folded papers. He set 'em on the corner of the sideboard and pulled 'em off one by one, unfoldin' 'em and layin' 'em out in front of the sheriff as he explained. "This one's got posters in several states. All the way from Alabama to Dakota. Everything from murder and robbery to cattle rustling."

The sheriff perused the stack of posters, then glanced over his shoulder at me and lifted an eyebrow. "Looks like you've been mighty busy—" he checked the topmost poster—"Mr. Delano. You still wanna tell me you didn't kill those marshals?"

I slumped back on the bench and crossed my arms. So this Duster fella was a professional, trekkin' across the whole country lookin' fer the next face that might bring him his next payday. Well, that didn't mean I was gonna freely admit to another crime. "I didn't," I insisted.

Duster actually laughed. He shook his head and threw back his second whiskey. "I've had all these for awhile," he waved his hand at my stack of bulletins, "but there's been worse folks out there worth more money. However … I happened to come across *this* one the other day." He set one last poster atop the stack. "Caught my attention right quick. Not many folk out there worth *that* much, Mr. Delano. Not no one, in fact."

The sheriff squinted down at it, then muttered a curse. "*Fifty thousand*?"

"That's right," Duster said. He started foldin' up all the posters again. "And I aim to collect."

"There ain't no name on *that* poster," I reminded 'em both.

Duster turned to smile at me. "There sure ain't. But it sure looks like you … and coincidentally, you got a left leg that don't bleed when cut. I ain't never found a leg made out of flesh that don't bleed when it's cut."

The sheriff stared at me like maybe he'd seen a ghost, then threw back his own second whiskey. When he spoke again, his voice was rough. "You're … you're telling me he's actually got a leg made out of metal?"

"That's what I'm telling you," Duster said.

The sheriff poured himself a third whiskey, and his hand shook, just a bit. "That's … that's something I coulda done without knowing. Look, I'm real sorry, Duster, but I can't let you take him. Metal leg or not."

The bounty hunter swung around to face the sheriff, the smug expression on his face wipin' clean off. "What now?"

I straightened on the bench and unfolded my arms, though there surely weren't nothin' I could do from inside this cell. But I hadn't been expectin' this turn of events, fer certain.

Sonoita's sheriff straightened from the sideboard and cleared his throat. He was several inches shorter than Duster, but he stood his ground, anyway, and I saw he'd flicked back his coat to show the grip of his revolver again. "I can't let you take him."

Duster drew himself up, too, but didn't draw his weapons. "And why the hell not?"

"He committed murder in *my* jurisdiction—"

"Allegedly," I grumbled, but they both ignored me.

"And *I* got him. He's here, in *my* jailhouse. I got to prosecute him here, for the crimes committed in my town. Whatever he did anywhere else ain't my concern. You understand."

The man called Duster drummed his fingers against the top of the sideboard. "Prosecute? Damn it all, Longley … you still insisting on holding those trials?"

Least I weren't the only one thinkin' this sheriff were out of his mind fer such a thing.

"That's right," Longley said, soundin' defensive. "I've already sent someone out to fetch the judge. This man will be tried for murder here, in Sonoita. And if he's found guilty, then he'll be hanged here. In Sonoita."

I swallowed despite myself. I could almost feel that noose around my neck already.

Duster let out a dry chuckle and shook his head, then

grabbed up the whiskey bottle and took a swig direct. "God damn, Longley. You sure don't make my job easy. So you're tellin' me you're gonna take that *fifty thousand dollars* right outta my hand ... you're gonna pass up splittin' it with me, even ... you're gonna say *fuck you* to Charles Miller ... just so you can pretend there's some semblance of civilization out here in the Territories?"

"Somebody's got to try and bring it out here, don't they?" Longley countered. "Might as well be me."

Duster muttered more profanities and slammed the whiskey bottle back to the countertop. "Damn fool is what you are," he scowled. "And you're gonna end up a dead damned fool, too, if you ain't careful. Don't you know who Charles Miller is?"

The sheriff shrugged. "Sure. But the only reason those damned barons got so much influence in the first place is because we let them. 'Bout damned time someone stands up to them."

The look on my face just then musta mirrored Duster's. We both looked at Sheriff Longley in disbelief, highly skeptical that he really had any good idea of what exactly it might mean to "stand up" to one of those barons. I'd tried it, indirectly, even, and it hadn't turned out so good.

I couldn't imagine what might happen if a person tried to do so more directly. Not unless they had a whole army at their disposal, maybe. And I didn't see no army at Sheriff Longley's disposal. I only saw one old man who liked the idea of tamin' the wilds of the west.

A damned fool old man, just like Duster had said.

Before the bounty hunter could manage to explain to the sheriff just what a terrible idea that was, Longley spoke up again. "And anyway, Mr. Miller ain't even a baron by rights. Ain't he just a bastard? They got what, dozens of those running around out here between all of them? Hard to keep track of them all."

I frowned at the mention of a bastard and remembered Charlotte sayin' Baron Whittaker had a harem. How many children did he have, exactly? And how many of 'em might be considered legitimate or illegitimate? I also remembered how Baron Whittaker himself had told me I should have killed him first thing, and all the rest of his family, too. But if he had dozens of children around these parts, and bastard children to boot, that seemed just about as possible as diggin' out a colony of fire ants without gettin' stung.

"Yeah," Duster said. "He's a bastard, all right. In more ways than one. He's even crazier than his father, if you ask me. Awful bitter about bein' cut off from the family fortune and all. Likes to take it out on other people."

Sheriff Longley picked up his third whiskey. "That so? If he don't have access to the family fortune, how's he fronting this bounty?"

Duster shrugged. "Guess he got backed by some of the other family members. But trust me, he's the one drivin' for Mr. Delano, there. And you don't want to get on his bad side."

Longley tossed back his drink and set down the glass with a heavy *thunk*. "That's just too bad. Civilization's got to start somewhere, Duster. I'm keeping Mr. Delano here, and he's gonna have a trial here, and that's the end of it. Got it?"

Duster stared at the lawman fer a good long minute, and I braced myself fer a shootout.

Honestly, I was rootin' fer the sheriff at this point. A trial woulda given me at least some kinda chance at goin' free, however small. And even if I ended up swingin', that sounded much preferable to meetin' any of Baron Whittaker's family, legitimate or otherwise.

But then, at last, Duster exhaled a long, hissin' breath, and his shoulders sagged. "All right. All right, Longley, fine." He rubbed at his face, like all of this was suddenly so exhaustin'.

I rolled my eyes. Surely his day hadn't been nearly as awful as my own.

"Have it your way," he said. "But if your jury sets him free, he's mine. Agreed?"

The sheriff pulled the whiskey bottle from the bounty hunter's grip and poured them both yet another shot. Then he held up his freshly filled glass, and Duster lifted his in turn. "Agreed," he said.

They made a toast to my fate, sealed either way now, like it was nothin' more than another business transaction, and all I could do was look on. Helpless.

Guess what little luck I'd had was up, after all.

I groaned and dropped my head into my hands, scrubbin' my palms over my eyes.

"But look," Duster said then, "if you're gonna insist on keeping him here for a trial, you'd better get it done just as soon as you can—"

"Judge can be here in a week," Longley said.

"—and you'd better keep him under heavy guard until it happens." Duster jabbed a finger toward me. "And only by those you *really* trust, Longley. Like I said, greed makes people stupid. There were two idiots in here who nearly let him go when I first came in. They were after that bounty, too."

The sheriff spat a string of curses. "So much for my volunteers," he muttered.

"If it's gonna be a week till the judge arrives, you need to keep him in here, unseen as much as possible, and don't go around talkin' about who he is. Keep it all as quiet as you can manage. That bounty's high enough you'll have *everyone* goin' after it. And I've heard some other things circulating recently."

Sheriff Longley let out a frustrated growl, then left the sideboard with the whiskey bottle and walked over to his desk, where he collapsed heavily into his chair. "Let me guess, more good news?"

"Some folk are sayin' Mr. Delano here is a demon."

The sheriff barked laughter at that, shakin' his head. He pinched the bridge of his nose and squeezed his eyes shut, then snapped them open again, lookin' over at me. "Well? What do you think of that, Mr. Delano? You some kind of demon?"

I raised my head and lifted my eyebrows, sittin' back on the bench again. This was news to me, but I was already wonderin' if I could somehow take advantage of it. "Not that I know of, sir."

Sheriff Longley gave a snort and took a good long swig out of the whiskey bottle.

Duster crossed the room to stand in front of the desk, leanin' forward over it. "You know how those people get," he said, voice pitched low so I could hardly hear him.

"Sure," the sheriff scowled.

"His metal leg has them all up in arms."

"That's … ridiculous," the sheriff spluttered. "No one should take that claim as serious without seeing it for themselves!" His gaze flicked up to Duster, then shifted back to me, and that look went over his face again, the one like he might have seen a ghost. He swallowed, and I got the sense that somewhere in his head he might be entertainin' the idea that I *was* some kind of demon.

On account of my metal leg, maybe.

Funny how that whole stack of posters hadn't seemed to convince him of such a thing. But a leg made outta metal … well now *that* he found downright unsettlin'.

He cleared his throat and turned back to the bounty hunter. "So what you're telling me is that I gotta guard this man against greedy idiots *and* the devoutly religious, both."

"That's right. If you want your trial." Duster spread his arms to the side. "Unless, of course, you'd like to just hand him over to me. Make him my problem." His grin flashed white teeth.

But the sheriff was not amused. He narrowed a glare up at Duster, then slammed the whiskey bottle onto his desk and stood fast from his chair. "Damn it all to Hell. You stay here and watch him. Don't let anyone in here till I get back. I'm going to go round up more *trustworthy* men." He turned toward me as he stomped toward the door. "And you. You'd better eat that stew before it gets cold. It's gonna be a long week."

XI

TROUBLE

Turned out bein' locked up was all kinds of borin'.

At this rate it was gonna be a long week, all right.

Least I weren't the only one stuck here against my will. Turned out that good-fer-nothin' Professor Morton was still in town, and it seemed the sheriff weren't gonna let him leave until after my trial, bein' that he was the only key witness and all. He weren't locked up in a cell, no, but the sheriff had assigned some men to watch him, to be sure he wouldn't go nowhere without permission. And apparently the professor was real sore about it, yellin' about how he worked for Her Majesty the Queen and had important business to see to that he couldn't be late fer. It was the best news I'd heard all day, and I had a good laugh at his expense.

I hoped he *would* miss out on his *important business*. I'd had important business, too, damn it all, business a lot more important than acquirin' some rusted old relics fer a monarch, and he'd sure put a wrench into my plans good.

Sheriff Longley had rounded up lots more people, sure enough, men and women both, and I hoped they were trustworthy. There was always a few of 'em inside the jailhouse with me, and he posted more of 'em outside around the building. The bounty hunter called Duster took on a few shifts, but the sheriff insisted on takin' point himself that first night.

I'd managed to choke down the stew … it weren't a bad stew, it's just that I weren't much in the mood fer eatin' anymore. But I managed it, and later that evening the sheriff brought me another plate of roast chicken and greens, and I managed to eat that, too. He even passed me a cup of whiskey, though he eyed me in a suspicious way as he did so, like maybe he thought I was gonna use some kind of demon magic to spring myself from my cell.

If only I had such magic.

But I took the whiskey with a nod of thanks. Maybe this town weren't really so bad.

I didn't sleep much, though, on account of several factors. Mostly I weren't convinced Sheriff Longley's new crew were as honest as he thought they were. I kept expectin' one of 'em to try and break me out and take me to Mr. Miller. Or I expected Duster to try it, maybe when his good friend the sheriff fell asleep.

But he didn't.

And neither did any of the others.

There was also the troublin' thought that I wouldn't get out of this one, no matter which way the trial went. If I even made it to the trial at all. Longley said the judge was supposed to be here in a week … but that was a long time fer me to be trapped here like a sittin' duck, waitin' fer greedy folk to make their move.

Holt was way back in Bravebank, or Grave Gulch by now, most like, or maybe wherever that bank was he'd wanted to rob. He didn't know where I was … probably didn't even care. Charlotte was nearly a whole country away, but I didn't want her here anyway, certainly. I didn't want to chance her gettin' mixed up with any violent idiots or devoutly religious types. And I really didn't want her to see that stack of posters featurin' my face. Didn't want her to see all those bad things I'd done.

Let her go on thinkin' I was a good person.

It was a small comfort I could take, lyin' there on that bench and starin' at the flickerin' shadows of the lantern light on the ceilin'. A small comfort to know she didn't know the whole truth of it. That she only knew I was tryin' to free my sister, and didn't know any of the other things I'd done to get this far.

But then ... this Mr. Miller fella could have been after her, too. I needed to send that message. To warn her. That worry kept me up most the night, tossin' and turnin', that and wonderin' what would become of Ethelyn if I didn't get back to Nine-Fingered Nan.

She'd be sold off to who knew where.

She'd think I'd abandoned her. Left her to that horrible fate.

The agony of it ate me up from the inside, and what little sleep I did get only brought me bad dreams.

In the mornin', bleary eyed and groggy, I asked Sheriff Longley to send a telegram to Charlotte fer me. I'd looked over all those bulletins on his wall durin' the long hours of the night, and I didn't see her up there. It was another small comfort I could take from this whole nightmarish situation, and I'd take whatever I could get.

This bull-headed fool of a man who'd rather hold a trial than take half of a fifty thousand dollar bounty was probably the most honest person I'd ever met, except fer my own mama, of course, and maybe Charlotte herself, so I figured he'd be my best chance at gettin' the warnin' out. I figured he'd relay my message to the telegram operator without readin' it, himself. Though I supposed even if he did read it, it wouldn't much matter. He'd already promised me a trial ... was riskin' his own life to hold it, and had already said whatever I'd done in other places didn't matter to him.

Even still, I tried to be vague in the wordin', but get the meanin' across. And the urgency. I wrote it out on a scrap of paper the sheriff provided me, then folded it up nice and tight and handed it to him through the bars. He nodded as he took it from me and tucked it into his shirt pocket.

He left right then to get it sent off, leavin' me under the watchful eye of some of his other people.

I sat back down on the bench and sighed. Well, that was Charlotte taken care of best I could. And the sheriff had told me last night his men had retrieved my mule and my supplies, and settled Joe into the livery and kept my stuff safe. Fer now. Till it was decided what was gonna happen to me.

Then they'd probably auction it all off, includin' Joe.

Maybe I shouldn't have named him, after all.

Least he weren't gonna get shot, I supposed. He'd go on to be useful to someone else.

Which was more than I could say fer myself. I stretched out on the bench and resumed my starin' blankly at the ceilin', turnin' over the whole of my life again and again in my mind.

Lots of regrets, there. Not much I was proud of.

If only I'd managed to find Ethelyn … all of it might have been worth it.

The day passed slow, with me takin' stock of all my sins, and workin' on the story I was gonna tell that jury. I dozed on and off a few times despite myself, but everything stayed quiet. I started to wonder if maybe that Duster fella had been exaggeratin' in an attempt to convince the sheriff to hand me over.

But it turned out he weren't.

Trouble came on the second night.

And it started with a fire.

All the shoutin' made me sit up, lookin' in question to those in the jailhouse with me. They'd set up a little table along the back wall and were deep into a game of poker, but they abandoned the cards right quick and readied their weapons at the sound of the ruckus.

There weren't no windows, so we couldn't see nothin'. But one of 'em went to the door and opened it a crack, peerin' out. Duster had left a few hours ago, claimin' he was off to the saloon and the brothel, but Sheriff Longley was still here. He'd been readin' the paper with his boots propped up on his desk, but dropped 'em to the floor at the commotion and looked to the man at the door, too.

A gunshot rang out on the street, and the man at the door jerked back, blood flingin' across the walls. He sprawled to the floor, a hole through his head.

Then the outside erupted into a whole hail of gunfire, and I guessed it was all those people the sheriff had recruited to guard me goin' after whoever was tryin' to spring me.

I came up to my feet along with the sheriff, who ran at the door and shouldered into it just as someone on the other side tried to open it. It slammed shut again, and he dropped the bar across it to lock it good.

The other men and women in the jailhouse hurried to take up defensive positions, all aimin' at the door.

That's when the back wall of the jailhouse exploded.

The force of it threw me back into the corner of my cell and then I crumpled to the floor, ears ringin' and coughin' in the haze of dust that billowed out from the hole. Half the lanterns in the place had been blown out or blown up, and the shapes of three men stepped through the resultin' gloom. The muzzle flashes of their guns lit up their eyes, their hat brims, the bandanas coverin' the lower half of their faces.

Those in the jailhouse guardin' me—those not killed or knocked unconscious by the blast—scrambled to return fire. But they didn't stand much chance in all the confusion.

I stayed on the floor with my hands coverin' my head, deafened by the dynamite and all the shootin'. Saw my hat lyin' there only a foot away, all covered in dust with its new bullet hole curtesy of Professor Morton, and snatched it up, stickin' it back where it belonged.

The shootin' stopped.

My ears were still ringin', but I risked a glance upward to see who'd won.

Someone was stickin' a key into my cell door. And it weren't the sheriff.

I hadn't seen what had happened to Sheriff Longley, but there was a part of me that hoped he was still alive, somehow.

Another shadowed person came up to my bars, and he pulled down his bandana as he glared at me. I only caught a glimpse of his face in what weak lantern light was left, but it was enough to recognize him.

The shorter brother.

Certainly not a person I wanted to see right now. He grinned down at me, teeth gleamin' in the dim lantern's glow.

The other fella yanked open my cell door and stepped aside, and I jumped to my feet in a hurry, plannin' to make a run fer it. Or a fight fer it. If they thought they were draggin' me off to that Mr. Miller easy, I was gonna change their mind right quick.

I charged at the brother, but then somethin' bright and blue flared in the darkness, and it hit me in the chest.

My whole body seized, my teeth snappin' together as I crashed back to the floor. It was a sharp, hot, clenchin' pain, everywhere, takin' away all my breath. The place where the flesh of my thigh met my metal leg burned like a ring of fire eatin' at my skin, but I couldn't scream. My mouth was locked shut, my lungs crushed.

Then it was gone.

I gasped, relaxed, saggin' into the floor. Hands grabbed me, rolled me over onto my stomach, and yanked my arms behind my back. I heard the clink of metal, felt the cold touch of iron against my wrists. If I was gonna get out of this, it had to be now.

My muscles were still half-numb, but somehow I managed to twist myself around sideways, yankin' my wrists out of the one man's grip. The manacles clattered to the floor and he swore, and I kicked upward with my metal foot as he was bent over and caught him right in the face.

There was a crunch and he staggered backward with a cry, hands over his face and blood seepin' through his bandana.

The other masked man gave a yell and brought up his gun as I rolled to my feet, but then that blue light flared again and I finally recognized what it was: a cattle prod. Pa had had one of those to help move the cattle sometimes. The shorter brother jabbed it at his partner, sendin' *him* down to the floor this time. "Don't shoot him, you idiot!" he snapped.

I took the chance and charged him again, and he didn't have time to swing that rod back around before I crashed into him. It flew out of his hand and bounced across the darkened room as he hit the ground, but the hotshot didn't concern me.

I only wanted his gun.

I grabbed it out of his holster just as he seemed to realize my intentions. His fist cracked into my face and I saw stars again, but rolled off him with the momentum of the blow and came back up to my feet. I staggered, head spinnin' as I tried to orient myself. Goddamn, that man could throw a punch, all right.

He and the man he'd zapped both scrambled to their feet, and out of the gloom I saw the third man had recovered himself enough to come lurchin' at me, eyes waterin' somethin' fierce. He had his gun in-hand, bringin' it upward.

I fired three times, the muzzle flash searin' my vision.

Everything still sounded like it was comin' from underwater, but I heard three vague thumps and blinked. It took me a minute to realize those men weren't comin' at me no more. To realize nothin' in that jailhouse was movin' no more.

'Cept me.

Three good shots, and they were all dead.

I stumbled over to the corner of the sheriff's desk and sank down onto it, feelin' light-headed and dazed. But I didn't have time fer this. Didn't have time to recover my wits. There was still shoutin' outside, that fire down the street still ragin'. But it wouldn't last forever. And I didn't think all the men and women the sheriff had recruited to guard me had been killed by these three men ... didn't know if these three were the only ones involved in this scheme, neither.

And Duster was still out there. Wouldn't be long before more people turned their attention to what was happenin' at the jailhouse, and I needed to be gone long before that.

I shoved myself off the desk and unbuckled the nearest man's gun belt, cinchin' it around my own waist, though I kept that brother's gun, too, and tucked it into my waistband. Then I grabbed an unbroken whiskey bottle from the floor—it'd been knocked from the sheriff's sideboard by the blast—and moved fer the hole in the wall. I glanced back as I stepped through it, surveyin' the bodies, and caught a glimpse of the sheriff's star shinin' dully in the remainin' light.

Fer a second, I hesitated.

But then I gritted my teeth and went on through the hole and out into the night. He mighta been a fair and honest man, but that still meant he'd have been happy to see me hang. And I didn't have time fer that.

I still had work to do.

There was an old buckboard wagon waitin' out back of the jailhouse, probably what they'd been meanin' to transport me to Mr. Miller in, and a few more dead bodies. Looked like most of those who'd been set up out here to guard me had gone to help put out that fire, though. And the rest shot down.

Didn't see anyone else out here left alive to take me to Miller, either, so I figured the three who had made it inside musta been the only ones to survive the part of Longley's crew who'd stayed behind.

I stepped over 'em all quickly, and left the wagon. It was too big and too noisy fer my purposes.

I couldn't risk goin' to get Joe, neither, nor any of my stuff.

I crept around back of the buildings, movin' away from the glow of the fire and all the commotion around it, stickin' to the shadows, till I reached one of the saloons. There were several horses hitched out front, and all those sober enough to notice a stolen horse were preoccupied by the flames roarin' down the street, most runnin' to help with the water brigade.

I chose the horse nearest to me, a short bay with a scruffy coat, and stuck the bottle of whiskey into one of its saddlebags. Then I swung up into the saddle with only a little wince. That spot on my left thigh where the metal and flesh met still stung, and my jaw ached from the force of that brother's blow, but the rest of me felt all right, considerin'. I urged the horse into a trot and went off down the street, reinin' it around the nearest corner before headin' outta that town at a canter.

We rode off into the night, but I had no idea where I was goin'.

All I knew was that I needed to put as much distance between me and Sonoita as I could, as quick as I could. Unfortunately, the land around here didn't offer much in the way of cover. Weren't many good spots to hunker down and lay low. And as soon as that fire was put out, and the townsfolk realized what'd happened at the jailhouse … what'd happened to their sheriff … I imagined they'd be real angry. I imagined they'd blame me fer all of it.

I imagined they'd send out search parties and a big ol' posse.

I imagined Duster would be ridin' out soon, too, and awful keen on findin' me himself.

So I kept that bay horse at a canter longer than I should have, till he was lathered up and blowin' hard, and then I only let him walk with great reluctance. And I realized I'd been headin' south without even really thinkin' about it.

South toward Blessing.

South toward Bravebank.

But I couldn't go back to Bravebank yet. I couldn't go crawlin' back there to Nan like a dog with my tail tucked between my legs, empty handed and beggin' fer her protection. Just like that first time we'd met, when she'd sent me off into the desert to die, it was clear now she'd given me a task she figured I couldn't survive.

She was probably back at her hide-out now, laughin' about it all. Part of me wondered if she really even wanted the lockbox, or if she just enjoyed makin' threats and settin' tasks to see if I'd jump through her hoops.

A puppet on strings... Was that all I was now? Just like Holt had said?

I sighed heavily and scrubbed a hand over my face. I was too tired to sort any of this. In the end, it didn't matter, anyway. Didn't do no good to ponder any of it, neither. I was gonna jump through Nan's hoops as long as it gave me a chance to free my sister. Long as it bought me time to find her myself, or to buy her back.

And that was that.

So I weren't goin' back to Bravebank without that lockbox.

I wondered if Professor Morton was right about it already bein' at Baron Haas' estate. But if that were the case … I'd have to go back to Blessing. I'd have to walk right back into that viper's nest. Into the heart of the place I was most wanted right now. Into the home town of Mr. Miller himself, Baron Whittaker's unstable bastard son.

And I'd have to do it all by myself this time. No Holt. No Charlotte.

I twitched the reins, aimin' my tired mount in the general

direction of Blessing. I cut across country, stayin' well away from the roads, and didn't dare stop to make any kinda camp. Not that I had any supplies, anyway.

I rode on through the night, keepin' my eyes and ears open fer trouble best I could around the exhaustion steadily buildin' in my mind, and prayed I'd come up with some kinda plan by mornin'.

XII

ON THE SAME SIDE, MAYBE?

I didn't.

I watched the sun come up from atop a small rise to the southwest of the town of Blessing, and still had no idea how in the fuck I was supposed to go in there and find out if Baron Haas had that lockbox.

I'd circled around the town from a distance most the night, mostly to try and keep myself awake in the saddle. And mostly because I was afraid that if I stopped fer too long, someone would find me. That bounty hunter Duster, or someone else from Sonoita. Or maybe just any other folk goin' about their normal business who had just happened to have had a good look at the bounty posters recently and wanted to take their chance on ringin' in a mighty good payday.

Of course, I was armed now, and I'd started makin' a decent reputation fer myself as a gunslinger around these parts, so maybe there wouldn't be as many folk as I feared willin' to risk dyin' to bring me in.

Like Duster had said, though, greed made people stupid. I couldn't afford to lower my guard on account of hopin' folk would know better than to pick a fight with me.

And anyway, I couldn't shoot no one if I were asleep when they found me.

So I tried not to sleep.

I just kept my horse pacin' a real big circle around Blessing, and kept tryin' to think of a plan that wouldn't land me killed or dumped at the feet of Mr. Miller. And I kept lookin' fer a good spot to hide. I was gettin' tired … real, real tired. I was gonna have to sleep soon.

But all the cover was too close to Blessing fer comfort. Down in the valley by the river, where it was all green and fulla trees. Woulda been a real good spot to hide out. 'Cept I didn't want to get that close.

Which meant I was stuck out here, in the blazin' sun and the rocks and sparse brush and the cacti. None of which woulda done much to hide me and my mount from curious onlookers.

So we stood up there on that ridge, and I looked down at the green of the valley and the bustle of Blessing and the gleam of what remained of those Old World ruins above the surface, and I muttered a lot of foul words. Maybe I *should* just head on back to Bravebank. Maybe I could at least tell Nine-Fingered Nan her contact from up north had been just as fulla horseshit as her man Taggert, and suggest that maybe she be more selective in who she took on as part of her trusted circle. Suggest that maybe if she wanted to send me off on an errand fer her, fine, but she could at least give me good information to do it on.

But then I remembered her threat about takin' my leg. And about findin' out where it had come from. And I remembered Dr. Balogh and the boy Radley and the girl Fanni, who'd been terrified of me, and the doctor's wife Hannah with her ever-present choppin' knife.

No … if I went back to Nan now, without that lockbox—whether or not she actually wanted it—I had no doubt she wouldn't bother to hear my suggestions, or my excuses. And I had no doubt she'd follow through on her threats.

I sighed and slumped in the saddle. Urged my scruffy stolen horse onward again. I went southward, but I weren't goin' back to Bravebank. I'd head a little further that way, sure, maybe get closer to Nan's circle of influence, where maybe more people hadn't seen that poster of my face worth fifty thousand dollars. I'd dare to venture a little closer to the river then, where I had better cover, and find a spot to get some rest, and maybe hunt somethin'. Even a stringy jackrabbit woulda been a welcome catch at this point.

My stomach was growlin' awful loud now, and all I had was that bottle of whiskey I'd swiped from the sheriff, and some jerky I'd found in these saddlebags.

So I went south, and then I went toward the river, and both the horse and me were mighty happy to finally pass under the shade of those cottonwoods. The horse fell to grazin' almost immediately, and I had to fight him fer every step until I found a suitable place to make my camp. Then I let him drink and graze all he wanted, makin' a picket line to tie him to. I settled into my spot up against a small bluff, back behind some thicket.

It was late afternoon now, and I was still hungry, but I couldn't hold off the sleep no more. The huntin' would have to wait. I dropped down onto the ground, pulled my hat over my face, and let myself slip away.

Voices woke me, and I came up sittin' with strange guns in my hands. I blinked hard in the darkness as I oriented myself. Behind the thicket, against the bluff, near the river. South of Blessing. That's right.

It was night now, and dark under those trees. The moon's light hardly reached me despite bein' almost full, though I could see it up above, turnin' some of the leaves silver. Damn, I'd slept hard. Musta been more tired than I'd thought.

The voices came again and I held my breath, glancin' out through the underbrush toward the horse I'd stolen. He lifted his head and pricked his ears fer a second, but then went right back to grazin'. I exhaled slowly, fer once grateful I hadn't had the chance to get Joe from that livery. He woulda surely called out to these newcomers, whoever they were, and given away my hidin' spot.

This horse didn't seem to care in the least.

But I used his momentary curiosity to help pinpoint where the voices were comin' from. Up above me, atop the bluff I leaned against. I kept still, kept quiet, and listened.

"You gotta piss every goddamn hour, we ain't never gotta get there!" a voice hissed.

"Ah, shuddup," another voice snapped. "You in some kinda hurry?"

"Yeah, matter of fact I am. I'm tired of listenin' to all the cryin' and whinin', and the wagon is startin' to smell."

Cryin' and whinin'? Just what kind of business were these men dealin' in, exactly?

"Just hit 'em a few more times with that rod. That'll shut 'em up."

The first man scoffed. "I'd like to shut 'em all up *permanently*. But then we wouldn't get paid, would we?"

"Guess not." There was a short pause, then, "Ya mind? I'd like to take a piss in peace. Why you followin' a man who's tryin' to take a piss?"

"To press upon you the urgency of our journey," the first man growled. "To make you hurry the fuck up. I want a drink and a goddamned bed. This is the last time we're stoppin' till Blessing, got it?"

The second man only grumbled, and I heard the first stomp off through the undergrowth.

I relaxed a bit, but only a little. So these weren't any kind of bounty hunters. Nor anyone from Sonoita. There *was* a road up there, a ways off, I'd seen it from atop that ridge earlier. It led into Blessing, sure enough, comin' in from the east.

The second man relieved himself, mutterin' and grumblin' the whole time about how he weren't gettin' paid enough to deal with all this shit, then I heard him turn and move away, back toward the road.

I exhaled long and slow, and crept out from behind my thicket. I checked on my horse again, but he weren't payin' me any attention. So I made my way quiet as I could along the bottom of the bluff until it tapered off and I could move up on top of it. I went quicker now, hearin' the second man's footsteps fade, but didn't get too close.

I weren't exactly known fer my stealth, and even if these men weren't bounty hunters, that didn't mean they wouldn't be if they happened to see me and recognize me. So I went from tree to tree, flattenin' myself up against the trunks, until I could just make out the wagon on the road.

As much as I'd been missin' Holt back in Sonoita, now I was glad he weren't here. He'd be complainin' somethin' awful about me comin' to take a look at this wagon. He hated when I got *nosey,* as he called it. Nosey, or playin' Good Samaritan. Or sometimes it was *actin' the hero*. He liked to call it all those things. Said it only got me into trouble.

That coulda been true. Gettin' involved in Charlotte's plight had nearly got me killed, after all.

I mighta done a lot of bad things myself in my life, sure ... but that didn't mean I was gonna turn a blind eye to other atrocities committed out here in the Territories. Even I had my limits. Lines I wouldn't cross.

No matter those lines seemed to be gettin' blurrier of late...

Still, there was somethin' about how these men had been talkin' that had set me on edge.

And now that I could see that wagon, I knew why. It was fulla *people.*

They were crammed in tight, and lots of 'em were cryin' and whinin', all right. The wagon itself looked like one giant cage, and there were six armed and mounted escorts along with it, three on each side. Four men and two women. Every now and then, one of those mounted escorts would stick a prod through the wagon bars, and I saw the familiar blue flare, heard the snap, and someone in the cage would yelp, and the wailin' would escalate.

The man who'd been takin' a piss climbed back up onto the driver's bench.

Anger flooded heat through my blood. My heart quickened, beatin' hard in my ears, and I thumbed my hammers back. They outnumbered me by a lot. But they also didn't know I was here. And it was dark. I could probably shoot down half of 'em before they even figured out what was happenin'—

I heard somethin' sounded like a whisper, and one of the armed escorts on the side facin' me gave a little grunt, then slid off his saddle and thumped to the ground.

Behind the trunk of the tree I was usin' fer cover, I straightened. Squinted at him. *The hell?*

More whispers, and more of the guards on horseback fell off their saddles. Finally, the two on the bench and the two remainin' escorts realized somethin' was goin' on. The driver yelled and slapped the reins, and the two guards fired wildly into the woods on both sides of the road. I ducked back behind my tree as bullets went whizzin' by.

Then … the shadows beneath the trees around me *moved.*

I swallowed back a yelp and hunkered down. Thought at first I was seein' ghosts, or maybe even demons. Shapes like people formed outta the ground and the trees, black as the night itself, and slid forward toward the wagon.

I stayed behind my cover, not wantin' to risk bein' caught in the hail of bullets, or bein' seen by the movin' shadows … whatever they were.

The wagon picked up pace, the horses whipped into a frenzy by the driver, but a knot of those shadows surged after it, and the two guards went down next. One of 'em was in a patch of moonlight brighter than the rest, and I saw what looked like the shaft of an arrow go right through his throat and halfway out the other side.

I didn't see what got the other fella, but by the time I looked back to the wagon again, the driver and his pal were dead too, slumped over each other on the bench. And I hadn't heard a single gunshot, hadn't seen a single muzzle flash from the trees.

Despite my initial horror, I stepped out from behind my tree to watch, mouth hangin' open as one of the black shadows caught up to the back of the wagon and leapt up onto it, then scurried over the top of it to drop down into the driver's seat and rein up the horses.

They snorted and pawed and danced around, but more black shadows clustered around them and seemed to be soothin' 'em.

So … not ghosts, then. Or demons.

"Who are you?" a quiet voice demanded, and I fair near leapt out of my skin. I whirled around to see a person-shaped shadow loomin' right there, right in front of me, and instinctively brought up my guns.

There wasn't a sound—was hardly a flicker of movement—but my left pistol jumped outta my hand like it was alive with the ring of metal strikin' metal, and my right arm got jerked backward and trapped against the tree. I tried to yank it free, but my sleeve was stuck, and stuck good. Just as I was movin' to grab my right pistol with my left hand, that shadow stepped up real close, and the point of a knife pricked the side of my neck.

And there was another blade at my gut, its sharp point bitin' into my skin through my shirt.

I stopped tryin' to reach fer my gun. Stopped movin' at all.

"Shhh," the shadow whispered. "Stay quiet. And drop your piece."

Their hooded head nodded fractionally toward the gun in my right hand. All I could see of 'em was their eyes, glintin' in the dim moonlight. The rest of their face was swathed in black, and their whole body, too. Couldn't tell if it were a man or a woman, but I guessed it was a woman, bein' as they were several inches shorter than me, and their frame lighter than most men.

The knives pokin' at me poked harder. I winced and let go of the pistol, and it thumped into the undergrowth.

Knives. That would explain why I didn't hear no gunshots. This person was also wearin' a bow over their shoulder, and a quiver fulla arrows on their back, though it was all hard to make out, since the weapons were entirely black as well, all of 'em.

They whistled suddenly, sharp and shrill, but kept their eyes and blades on me.

I heard murmurin' from back at the wagon, and the people inside of it were still cryin' and whinin'. They sounded awful scared. I couldn't turn to see what was happenin' over there, though, as I didn't want this person in front of me to decide to slit my throat.

"Who are you?" she demanded again, still in a whisper.

I swallowed. "No one important."

Her eyes narrowed, and her blades pressed a little harder. "What are you doing here?"

"I was just … camped nearby. Heard a commotion. Came to investigate."

"Investigate. You mean rob?" She said it like she was some kinda lawdog tryin' to get me to confess.

I snorted a laugh despite my situation. "No. But even if I *was* plannin' to rob those men … you people *murdered* 'em. Which is a good deal worse than robbin'."

The knife in my gut twitched and I sucked in a breath, pretty sure I was bleedin' now.

"Not that I care any," I blurted quickly. "If you—if you wanna know the truth of it, I was thinkin' about murderin' 'em, too. And not to rob 'em. Just took issue with people bein' caged and hit with hotshots is all. So really … don't that make us on the same side? Maybe?"

Unless these shadow folk were plannin' to cart off the wagon-load of people fer themselves. My stomach clenched at the thought. If that were the case, I sorely needed my guns back.

"Are you alone?" was all she said.

That gave me pause. Which answer would let me live, I wondered? Or maybe she planned to murder me no matter what I answered.

Before I could decide on what exactly to say, more black-robed people appeared next to her. And behind her. And all around me. They formed a circle around the tree, watchin' me through the narrow slits of their hoods. They moved under the trees with hardly a sound, and everything on them was black. Made 'em almost impossible to see clearly. But now that they were closer, I noticed they were all heavily armed. No guns, though. Just arrows and knives. Lots and lots of knives, sheathed all over their bodies. Across chests, arms, legs…

Not the big knives, though. The little ones. Throwin' knives.

"Who is this?" one of the new arrivals asked. Sounded like another woman.

"Found him sneaking around," the one holdin' her blades to me said.

"I weren't sneakin'—"

"Watching our business."

"Which matters to me none at all," I reminded her.

"Wait, wait … hold up a minute," another voice spoke up from within the circle. One of the shadows moved, makin' her way through the others till she stood at the front. "I think I might know this cowboy."

I couldn't turn my head to look at her, but I moved my eyes her way. Didn't matter any, though. She was robed in black same as the others. Her voice sounded mildly familiar, but I couldn't place it, and so couldn't be sure if her knowin' me might work for or against me here.

"That so?" the one with the blades on me asked. "Well then … he trouble or not? Do I cut his throat or let him go?"

The casual way she asked the question made me swallow. My heart quickened again, pulsin' against the point of that knife pressed to my neck. I started makin' plans fer how I was gonna escape this knot of knife-laden shadows should the answer come back unfavorable … though I suspected I wouldn't get very far before havin' enough blades in me to look like a porcupine.

Didn't mean I wouldn't try.

The woman who had claimed to maybe know me fumbled at her belt, and the rasp of a strikin' match sounded before the little tongue of flame brought a glow of light to all the shadow. She held it up toward my face and I squinted.

And held my breath. Waited fer her answer.

"Hey," said another shadow. Another woman. Were they all women? "I recognize him now. Ain't he the one who—"

"Yeah," the one with the match said slowly. "Yeah, that's him, all right." She shook it out as the flame neared her fingers, and plunged us all into an even deeper darkness than was there before. "He's the one who helped that redhead slave who escaped about a month back. And who wrecked Baron Whittaker's estate."

Numb confusion raced through me even as more murmurs passed around the circle of shadows, and I forgot I'd meant to try and escape myself right about then. Instead I only stood there, frownin' into the dark, tryin' to piece together how she could have known about Charlotte. Baron Whittaker's estate, sure, that was all on that damned wanted poster. But Charlotte … that didn't make no sense…

The knives pokin' at me withdrew, and I blinked.

Not what I'd been expectin', considerin' most others who knew about the baron's place so far wanted to bring me in fer that fifty thousand dollar reward.

The one who'd recognized me first lit another match and pulled back her hood to reveal familiar features, though the night's darkness deepened the rich sepia tones of her skin. She flashed me a grin. "Well howdy there, Mister," she said. "So nice to see you again."

She looked a lot different than the first time I'd met her, no matter how brief that had been, but now that I could see her face, too, it all came rushin' back to me. "Sally?!"

TPARK
2023

XIII

FREEDOM FIGHTERS

"That's right." She extinguished her second match, then stepped across me to put one boot up against the tree trunk, bracin' herself to yank out one of the blades that pinned my sleeve to it. She handed it back to its owner, then did the same for the second blade, handin' that over, too.

Then she reached down to pluck my guns up off the ground and gave 'em a little twirl before holdin' 'em out to me, butts-forward.

I took 'em from her, but then just stood there, starin' at her and the rest of the black-clad gang that surrounded us. "That's, uh … a lot more than seven knives," I husked. She was fair near bristlin' with 'em.

She laughed and gave some kinda signal to the others. They dispersed, gradually, meltin' back into the natural shadows, until only a few remained.

"Sure," Sally said, turnin' back to face me. "I carry seven at the saloon and most everywhere else. It's all I usually need. Except for this business." Vague shiftin' of her silhouette indicated her gesturin'. "Then I usually need a few more."

I shut my mouth with a click. I blinked and then also realized I was still standin' there with my guns in hand. So I stuck 'em back into their holsters and cleared my throat. Looked around at the woods, and saw some of her group had re-materialized back at the wagon. I lifted my fingers to brush at the trickle of blood slidin' down my neck. Those blades had broken the skin, all right. I felt gingerly at the stingin' spot in my middle. Well, it coulda been worse. A whole lot worse. "What . . . what exactly *is* this business?" I asked.

To my surprise, she hooked her arm in mine and turned us toward the wagon, then led me in that direction.

"We're in the business of rescue, Mister…" She paused. "Hrm. I don't think I ever got your name."

"You didn't."

"I see. Well that's a shame. I believe we're on the same side, after all. This wagon-load of folk was headed to the new Baron Whittaker's estate. To replace all the slaves you helped set free."

I drew up short, my arm reflexively clampin' down on hers.

"Easy there, cowboy," she drawled. "Don't get your dander up. If we'd wanted that reward, I wouldn't be here strolling through the trees arm-in-arm with you, would I?"

That was true enough, I supposed. I relaxed a little. But then the full meanin' of what she'd said finally registered and a cold dread slithered through my gut. "Wait. The *new* Baron Whittaker?"

She huffed a sigh, and pulled me onward toward the wagon again. "That's right. His eldest son took over the estate. He is now the new Baron Whittaker, picking up where his father left off. Trying to rebuild what you . . . destroyed."

I lifted my free hand to rub at my eyes, then pinched the bridge of my nose. "Great. He as *wonderfully pleasant* as his father?"

Sally gave a little grunt. "If you are referring to the former baron's penchant for torture, this new baron seems to be a little saner, truth be told. Certainly better than some of his siblings."

"Like Charles Miller."

"He's probably the worst of them."

I rubbed at my eyes harder.

"Unfortunately," Sally continued, "the new Baron Whittaker

still prefers slave labor to mine his ruins. So he's not all that much better than his father. And still leaves us with plenty of rescuing to do."

I opened my eyes and dropped my hand, and we came to a stop at the wagon's side. Sally's pals had unlocked it, helped people climb out of it, and were busy distributin' canteens and some scraps of food to the newly freed folk. There were all kinds of 'em … young and old, men and women, in varying states of physical condition. My stomach rolled at the sight of all of 'em, then growled at the sight of the food.

I ignored it. "You said all these were meant to replace the ones I freed?" The ones *Charlotte* had freed, in truth. But if she weren't on any posters, I weren't goin' to implicate her, even if Sally and her folk seemed friendly. Couldn't risk word gettin' out, gettin' around. Not if this Charles Miller fella was as bad as he seemed.

The stories about his pa had turned out true enough … I didn't doubt the stories about the bastard son were similarly accurate.

"Yes."

"So … the new baron never found the others? They all escaped, free and clear?" Despite all the trouble I'd endured the last few days, all the agony I'd endured at the hands of the old Baron Whittaker, my heart lightened a bit at that thought. Maybe somethin', *somethin'* had finally gone right.

Sally's face sobered somewhat then, and my brief hope faltered. "Well, most of them," she said quietly. "There were some that were re-captured. And some … *examples* made in the town square." She winced, and again that anger warmed in my belly, flarin' up to burn in my chest.

As much as I never wanted to lay eyes on another of those damned metal barons so long as I lived … another part of me wanted to ride into Blessing right that moment and burn everything they had to the ground.

Sally turned toward me before I could get words around that anger and took my hands in hers, givin' 'em a squeeze. "But most of them did escape, yes. Free and clear. We helped those of them we found, set them on their way back to wherever they came from, or to start new lives somewhere else."

I looked down at her, strugglin' to comprehend everything she was sayin'. She made it sound like they had a whole operation here. My eyes lifted to look over her shoulders, to the number of black-robed folk goin' about with quick, efficient movements. They ushered those from the wagon off the road, into the trees, and in the dim, dappled moonlight there I saw horses waitin' now where there hadn't been before. I wondered where they'd stashed the animals. Wondered who had gone to retrieve 'em.

They *did* have a whole operation here. That was clear enough. Sally's gang knew what they were doin'. They had a plan, a plan they'd practiced a great number of times, from the looks of it, and they went about it with a unity and precision I hadn't seen many other folk able to execute.

Certainly their plan was a great deal better than mine had been. I hadn't really thought any further ahead than just killin' the drivers and the guards.

Holt was always yellin' at me fer that, too. Not thinkin' my plans all the way through.

"So," I said, shovin' Holt's reprimands outta my head, "that's what you'll do fer these folks, too, then? Help 'em get back home? Or somewhere safe?"

I thought of Ethelyn, then. Like these folks, only worse-off, probably, bein' directly in the clutches of Nine-Fingered Nan. The one person I wanted to free more than any other ... and I couldn't seem to get to her. Couldn't seem to find her...

"Yes," Sally said, turnin' back to watch her people work and pullin' me from my worry. "We may not be able to act so boldly as you did—not yet, anyway—but we do what we can when we can." She extended an arm outward to indicate the wheeled cage. "Like this. We hit their transports as often as we can. Disrupt the trade. Stay a thorn in their side. Rescue as many of these poor souls as can be managed."

My brows lifted. They had a whole operation, all right. And were either very brave or very stupid. Another realization hit me, then.

Freedom fighters.

These were the people Baron Whittaker had thought I was allied with, that night he'd caught me burnin' down his barns. It all made a lot more sense now...

The sound of another wagon approachin' on the road snapped me from my musin's and Sally gave a surprised yelp as I shoved her around behind me and spun to face it, pullin' my right pistol, ready fer it to come around the bend.

"Stop," Sally hissed. She grabbed the wrist of my gun-hand and pushed it downward. "That's *our* wagon."

I glanced to her over my shoulder. "How do you know?"

She pursed her lips. "We have lookouts stationed down the road in both directions. If someone else was coming, we'd have already heard the warning."

"You sure? What if they got ambushed? Overpowered? Gunned down?"

She tilted her head to one side. "You hear any gunfire from down the road lately?"

I frowned. Let my arm drop under the pressure of her grip. "No."

"Then I'd say that's unlikely."

"Better safe than dead," I muttered.

"True enough, Mister." She stepped up beside me and put a

hand on one of those throwin' knives tucked into her belt. "Let's be ready, then, but not shoot on sight, yeah?"

"Fair enough," I agreed.

So we waited, side by side, me with my gun and Sally with her knives, alone in the road now. The emptied cage stood open behind us, but all the others had moved into the trees, out of sight.

The second wagon came around the bend at last, a big buckboard pulled by a pair of horses, and Sally gave two high-pitched whistles.

The driver of that wagon gave an answerin' whistle, long and low, and two short trills.

Sally dropped her hand from her knife and put it on my arm. "That's them, all right. They're fine. No ambush."

I shook my head and rolled my eyes. A whole language made of whistles. All right, then. But I waited to holster my iron till the wagon reined up to a stop beside us, and no one tried to shoot us. The others emerged from the trees then, too. The situation was explained to the freed folk: some of 'em would go on horseback, some of 'em would go in the new wagon, all of 'em escorted in some way by a few in the black robes to wherever they wanted to go.

Some of the freed folk nodded and seemed grateful and relieved, but some had been tricked or misled into captivity, and now didn't trust Sally's gang any more than they trusted the bastards who'd gotten 'em into such a predicament. There was some shouted, angry words, and they ran off on their own into the darkness, either on foot or by horseback, but Sally's friends didn't stop them.

I asked Sally if that was a wise idea, but she only shrugged. "We can't force them to stay. They each have to make their own choice. If they want to go it on their own, that's their decision. Some are plenty capable of taking care of themselves."

"And what about those who ain't?"

She shrugged again. "Least we gave them a choice in things, which is more than they had before."

I pondered that as I watched 'em all ride off in different directions, and the wagon disappear on down the road, where I was told it would turn back east again before runnin' too awful close to Blessing.

The bodies of the slavers were dragged away into the underbrush, the wagon with the cage in back was driven off the road and into the trees, and its horses unhitched and led away. And then the night was quiet again, no evidence of what had happened here remainin' except fer a few new blood stains in the dirt.

Only me and Sally were left now. I turned to her and was startled to see her already lookin' at me, and lookin' at me in much the same way she'd looked at me that day I'd first walked into her saloon and taken a stool at her bar.

I shifted under her scrutiny and cleared my throat, hopin' I didn't look quite as much like death as I had that day. "Well?" I ventured. "Ain't you gonna escort anyone to safety?"

She smiled slyly. "Sure. *You.*"

I barked a laugh that echoed out into the night. "I beg yer pardon?"

She crossed her arms, and those dark, shinin' eyes of hers ran me up and down again. "What are you doing out here, anyway? The Whittaker family is *furious* about what you did ... and that price on your head is obscene. The town is all up in arms over it. Lots of folk just up and left their professions to go on the hunt for you."

My heart sank right down into the pit of my stomach, and all I could manage was a grunt.

"I would have thought you'd have cleared the area by now. That would have been the wise thing to do. Unless ... you gonna go after another baron? Because I'm not so sure that's a great—"

"No," I blurted. "No. No more barons." Not if I could help it. "It's just … I got … I got some other business I need to take care of here before I can go." I didn't exactly want to give her any more specifics. I'd just told her I weren't goin' after another baron, after all. And maybe I wouldn't be. But I *did* need to find out if Baron Haas had that lockbox, or if it were still out there somewhere else.

"Hrm." Her eyes narrowed. "Other business. In Blessing?"

"Unfortunately."

"The very town where your face is right under one of the highest bounties I've ever seen?"

I hissed out a breath through my teeth. "That's right."

"That's risky, Mister. Real risky."

As if I didn't know that already. "And if the business weren't urgent, and important, I wouldn't risk it. But I don't got no choice in this."

"That so?"

"That's so."

She tilted her chin upward, gazin' at me from under long lashes. The moonlight splashed silver across her skeptical expression. "And you think you should just walk right on in to Blessing to carry out this other business of yours?"

I shook my head. "No, ma'am. No I do not."

"All right, so what's your plan, then?"

I looked down to the dusty toes of my worn boots and rubbed at the back of my neck. "I … well I don't exactly have one yet."

"Sounds to me like you need that escort, then."

That brought my gaze back up to her quick.

"You got a ride around here somewhere?"

"Yeah … down on the other side of the bluff … wait, you sayin' you'll help me get into town without bein' seen?"

"Getting *into* town ain't the hard part, cowboy. It's not being seen once you're there for … however long you'll need to do your business. You can hole up at the Seven Knives, if you'd like. I've got ways in and out of there a person can go secret-like." She smiled. "For use in my own business, you understand." She held out her arms to encompass the now-empty road and the blood stains in the dirt.

"I see. That's … that's mighty kind of you, ma'am—"

Her smile soured.

"—but I wouldn't want to impose. Or endanger you, if someone were to find out you were harborin' a fugitive."

She rolled her eyes and snorted. She hooked her arm in mine again, rather forcefully this time, and marched us off the road and under the trees, headin' back fer the bluff. "First of all, Mister," she said, "no more ma'amin' me. My name is Sally, so use it, would you?"

Her brisk tone and brisk pace left me a bit bewildered, and I nearly struggled to keep up with her despite my longer stride. She moved through the dark as if she had eyes like a cat, and in the absence of an urgent need to run, my metal leg liked to lag behind my natural one somewhat. The limp was less pronounced these days, sure, but it weren't gone entirely. Not by a long shot.

Sally hardly seemed to notice. "Secondly, *I'll* decide what company I'll keep in my own saloon, thank you very much, fugitive or not. You think I haven't kept wanted folk in there before? Ha! Been doing it for years. After all, no one found out you were hiding that redhead in there, did they?"

I stopped walkin' at that and grabbed her arm, pullin' her around to face me. Her eyes flashed dangerously, one of her knives comin' into her hand seemingly of its own accord, but I paid it no mind, only carin' that she answered my next question. "Yeah, about that redhead. How did you know I helped her?"

Sally's rigid stance relaxed at the question. Her knife slipped back into its sheath. "Oh. That." She gave a little laugh and shook her head. "You weren't very subtle about it, were you?"

I frowned at her.

Her eyebrows lifted. "You didn't think it might be suspicious you booked a third room later in the same evening? Why would two men need a third room? The next morning you took three plates. And some of my girls were talking … said you'd traded them various things for some women's clothes. They thought it all quite amusing … thought maybe you were the type of man who sometimes enjoys dressing up in women's things, but I suspected a different reason."

I only stared at her, runnin' back over all of it my mind, heat growin' in my face as I realized she was right. We hadn't been very subtle at all.

She shrugged. "Of course I went on letting them think what they wanted. Better than having the truth get out. But if you would have tried that at any other place, Mister, you and her and your other friend would have all ended up hanged. So. I *insist.* Hole up at the Seven Knives while you're in town, yeah?"

I swallowed, wonderin' if she was right about the hangin' part, too.

Probably.

"All right," I said finally. "Sure. If you insist."

She grinned at me. "Very good. Now, my horse is just right over yonder. You go and fetch yours and meet me back here, and I'll take you in to Blessing and over to my saloon safely."

I touched the brim of my hat. "Much obliged."

She nodded and stepped away from me, then melded seamlessly back into the shadows in a way that made the hairs on my arms prickle.

I shuddered as I turned away to head back down fer my own horse, more thankful than ever she and the rest of her crew were on my side. I'd been in a lot of scrapes in my life, but I couldn't imagine tryin' to fight folk who were so good at bein' nothin' more than shadows, who could move and kill so silently.

Whose faces you couldn't see at all, unless they wanted you to.

I usually just stuck a bandana over half my face when I was gonna do somethin' unsavory. And sometimes I didn't remember to even do that. These people took hidin' their identities to a whole new level. I imagined the law wouldn't ever get any kind of report from a witness they could follow up on. It was hard to pin down just who or what a livin' shadow might be, after all.

My fingers drifted up to my neck again and the little spot of blood there, now dried, but sore. I'd had enough of nearly dyin' these last few days. I really *was* gonna have to be more careful ... with Nan's information all wrong, a sky-high bounty on my head, and every shadow possibly a pair of ears and eyes and fulla knives, the Territories were gettin' to be a mighty interestin' place.

My stolen horse was right where I'd left him, grazin' on that picket line. No wonder he was so fat. My own stomach growled somethin' awful as I saddled him up quick and rode on up to meet Sally; found her waitin' just where she'd said she'd be.

Her neutral expression twisted into confused horror as I approached, her eyes locked on my scruffy mount.

"He ain't mine," I said in defense, but then at the flash of alarm that crossed her features, felt a stab of panic myself. "I mean, he ain't my usual mount, is all," I tried again. So maybe horse thieves weren't among the fugitives she tended to hide. I suspected stagecoach and bank robbers might also not be on that list, nor murderers of innocents. "Got a mule," I muttered. "Back at … well, I had to leave him behind. Fer now. I'll go back and get him later."

Sally squinted at me, either in confusion or suspicion, or maybe both, and I decided I should stop talkin'. I shut my mouth and fell in beside her as we headed toward Blessing, weavin' through the trees and stayin' off the road.

To my relief, she only grunted at my ramblin'. "Well cowboy, if I'm going to be hosting you at my saloon, I should probably have something proper to call you. Mister…?"

"Van De—" I stopped myself abruptly, swallowin' back my real name. It'd nearly come on out without me even thinkin'. I hesitated, warrin' with myself over whether or not to tell her the truth. A reputation like the one I was gettin' could open some doors, sure. But it could close plenty of other doors, too. And I didn't want this particular door to close. Not yet.

"Er … Lynd," I said instead, fallin' back to an old alias I'd used before. Slightly modified to accommodate my previous blunder. "Van … Der Lynd."

"Really? That a Dutch name?"

I shrugged, tryin' to look casual. "Maybe."

"All right, then, Mr. Lynd. Let's get you to the Seven Knives. And I'm guessing you wouldn't be opposed to a hot meal once we get there?"

"Not at all, ma'—Sally." My stomach agreed wholeheartedly with another loud rumble.

"And a bath," she added. "You could most definitely use a bath as well."

I weren't so sure about that part, but I weren't gonna argue with someone who was willin' to show me any kinda hospitality at this point. "Sure. I suppose."

"No supposin' about it, cowboy. We'll get you a meal and a bath and a good sleep in a bed, and then you can tell me all about this other business of yours in Blessing."

I winced at those words. I didn't much want to do that. Maybe I woulda been better off stayin' out here on my own, after all. Maybe I shouldn't have accepted this invitation of hers.

Or maybe I could just keep lyin'.

I'd done it plenty of times before. And done it plenty of times to get just these things: a roof over my head, a bed, a hot meal … wouldn't be nothin' new.

So I made no protest to the notion, and only followed Seven Knives Sally silently into the dark.

XIV

THE RIGHT KINDA TROUBLE

We got into Blessing easily enough, all right.

Left the horses at the edge of town—Sally promised she'd have someone retrieve 'em soon—and went the rest of the way on foot. It was an unconventional route from there, mostly back alleys and rooftops, until we reached a general store a few buildings removed from Sally's saloon.

She unlocked the back door and waved me inside, then locked it again behind us. She took an oil lamp from the wall and lit it, then showed me the way to a trap door in the floor, behind the cashier's counter.

"Norman is a good man," she whispered as she pulled it open. "We have an arrangement." Then she climbed down inside the hole on a short set of rickety stairs, and I followed her down and shut the trap door behind me.

The room beneath was small and pitch black save for the light of Sally's lamp. The weak circle of yellow light illuminated the edges of some shelves, stocked with extra wares for the store above. The air was still and muggy from the day's leftover heat, but Sally kept movin'. She ducked into a tunnel at the back wall, and I fair near had to double over to pass through it myself, fightin' with my metal leg to maneuver in the cramped space.

I tried to keep my breathin' slow and even, though I felt the edges of that panic come back, closin' in around me like these packed dirt walls. I didn't much like tight places. I tried to focus on the bobbin' lamplight, on the slender curve of Sally's gloved fingers around its handle, on her lithe, shadowed form glidin' effortlessly in front of me … on anythin' but the nearness of this ceilin' and these walls. Anythin' but the thought of us bein' underground, with a whole town on top of us. Anythin' but the feelin' that this muggy air was thickenin', that it was gettin' harder to breathe…

A ladder appeared out of the gloom, then, and I exhaled in relief. Sally stepped up to it and knocked at the trap door at the top, another pattern, like all her whistles.

The sound of a bolt bein' drawn back came muffled through the thick planks, then hinges creaked and a square of light spilled down over us. We squinted upward at a girl.

A woman, rather. But young. Couldn't be much over eighteen. My face flushed as I realized she was only wearin' her undergarments, and I hastily found somewhere else to fix my gaze. But she only looked sleepy and bored. Dark, messy ringlets of hair framed her face as she yawned and waved us up.

"Thank you kindly, Nora," Sally said as she climbed the ladder and stepped out into the room above.

I followed her up, studiously avertin' my eyes from the half-naked Nora, but I needn't have bothered. There were more women in the room just like her, loungin' or sleepin' or smokin', all in various stages of undress. And some of 'em I recognized as those Holt and I had traded with fer new clothes fer Charlotte. Rememberin' what Sally had said they'd thought of me regardin' that, the burn already flamin' in my ears burned hotter.

These were Sally's whores, then. And this room a room most folk never saw.

I decided now would be a good time to study the stolen gun belt around my hips, maybe count the cartridges stuck in its loops. Might be a good thing to know, anyhow, in case I ran into trouble later.

"And how's business this evening?" Sally asked conversationally as she re-locked her side of the underground passage.

Nora shrugged as she resumed a spot on a red velvet chaise lounge and sprawled with legs spread and feet danglin'. "Lighter than usual. On account of the Whittaker upset and that bounty, I figure."

Her brown eyes locked on me, and I realized all at once I was starin' at her, instead of countin' the bullets in my belt like I'd been meanin' to. I dropped my eyes again in a hurry, goin' back to the countin'. Except I didn't remember how far I'd got. I started over.

"Still?" Sally sighed impatiently and straightened, brushin' gloved hands against her snug black pants. Now that we were in better light, I saw she'd wrapped herself in black from head to toe, and all of it hugged her close. Better to sneak around the wilds at night, I reckoned, without snaggin' sleeves or trousers on brush.

The handles of all her knives glinted in the room's electric lights. She extinguished the lamp she'd brought from the general store and set it atop a nearby cabinet. "Well, be patient. Men'll be back here soon enough. They always come back. Not even treasure chasing will keep them away forever."

For some reason she looked at me when she said that, and I remembered again I was supposed to be takin' stock of my ammo. Except I couldn't seem to drag my eyes away this time. There was a lot of exposed flesh in this room, pale and rosy, bronze and tawny, smooth and ochre brown, thighs and breasts and slender necks, and it was all beginnin' to properly trample my focus.

"Why, Mr. Lynd," Sally said, givin' me one of her sly smiles, "you're blushing like a virgin bride on her wedding night!"

The girls around the room giggled at that and I scowled, shiftin' uncomfortably on my feet. Heat bloomed up my neck now, too, and I only wanted to get out of this room, clear my head. I'd never really figured out how to act around whores. Always been taught to treat a woman like a lady, no matter her station … up till the day Mama and Pa were murdered, anyway, and I guess fifteen years was long enough to get somethin' stuck inside yer head so solid another nine years weren't long enough to make it fade away.

Holt had always found it amusin', and the whores usually did, too. Those that didn't find it off-puttin', at least.

Another reason I tended to seek the sportin' women only on occasion … only when it became a powerful need … when it was startin' to cloud my judgment and take my concentration away from other things. Away from more important things.

Maybe it was all the stress of the last few days, or the overly long interval since last I'd visited a brothel myself, or maybe it was the memory of the last time I'd been in this saloon, upstairs, disguisin' Charlotte as one of these whores, bracin' myself over the top of her while her nakedness pressed into my bare skin, but that need surged up in me now hot and urgent, its intensity catchin' the breath in my throat.

I gulped it back and grumbled somethin', turnin' away from her, from all of 'em, to search frantically fer the door.

"Now, now," Sally said, "don't get yourself all bothered, Mr. Lynd, I'll get you taken care of. Everything's on the house while you're here." Her voice shifted away from me, so I could tell she was talkin' then to her whores. "Girls, this is Van Der Lynd. He might look familiar, yes. That's because he's the one on that bulletin. The bulletin that turned a lot of Blessing's folk into bounty hunters."

I stiffened, questionin' the wisdom of her tellin' so many others that information. And yet, if she brought those she chose to shelter in her saloon through that tunnel and straight into this room with all these other eyes, well, I supposed she must have a mighty powerful trust between her and these other women. So maybe it was all right…

"And yes, he's the one who killed Baron Whittaker and freed all those slaves—"

Charlotte, I thought again. *Charlotte did that, not me.* But I clenched my teeth against sayin' it out loud. All I'd done that night was get the shit kicked outta me by the baron's men. Though Charlotte had said that was the distraction she'd needed to free the others, so maybe I'd played a necessary role in some sense.

The old pains flared up again at the thought of that night. The burns on my arm and my thigh, not-quite-healed yet, pulsed dully. The scar across my right temple ached and I brushed my fingers across it absently. But it had doused the eagerness of my lust somewhat, fer which I was thankful. A bit of clarity returned to my thinkin'.

"—he's the one who helped that redhead that posse was looking for when they came through here and busted things up," Sally continued.

At least that part was fully true.

A round of whispers and mutterin' circled the room at that.

I'd found the door, but I didn't exactly want to march out of here without my host, especially considerin' I weren't exactly sure what lay beyond. Would the faces on the other side be friend or foe? Would they have seen that poster too, or not?

"He'll be staying here for a little while," Sally told them. "So you know what to do. And like I said, thanks to the service he's done us regarding the Whittakers and helping out that poor young woman, whatever he wants during his stay should be considered bought and paid for." She paused. "Within reason, of course. Everyone understand?"

A chorus of "Yes, ma'ams" answered her. Seemed she didn't mind *them* ma'amin' her.

I kept my attention focused on the door in front of me with its worn brass handle and the blessedly woman-free space around it, and not on the other thoughts now creepin' into my head at Sally's mention of my stay bein' entirely free.

"Glad to hear it. Now … Nora, Nettie, would you go get a bath ready for Mr. Lynd while I fix him up some grub? In the suite. Give him the Double Special. He seems tense."

"Sure thing," Nora answered, echoed by another soft voice that must have been Nettie.

The aches and pains leftover from my night at Baron Whittaker's weeks ago were fadin' again now, but the heat in my face blossomed anew as hands touched the small of my back and I startled, whippin' around to see Nora smilin' up at me.

"Pardon me, Mr. Lynd," she said, and she slid around me to move fer the door, steppin' closer than was necessary so that her front brushed up against mine.

That need raged up again full force, damn her, and Nettie stepped around behind me, trailin' a hand lightly up my arm and across my shoulders as she did so. Then they both slipped out the door, and I made to go after them.

A hand on my arm stopped me.

"Mr. Lynd."

I pulled my stare away from the retreatin' forms of Nora and Nettie only with great difficulty and found myself lookin' down at Sally. I blinked hard. Her form weren't much less distractin' at the moment, but the shine of all those knives gave me somethin' else to look at, too. "Yeah?" I managed to croak.

"Not quite yet. You want some food, don't you? I could hear your stomach the whole ride here."

"I…" Truth be told, food had suddenly become much less of a priority. I coulda waited a bit longer fer grub. I weren't sure how much longer I could wait to catch up with Nora and Nettie.

My eyes drifted from Sally to look back down the hallway where the two had disappeared.

Sally gripped my elbow and guided me through the doorway, but then pulled me in the opposite direction.

I might have whimpered in protest.

"Come on now, Mr. Lynd. The bath won't be ready yet, anyway. Remember those standards I mentioned to you when you came here last? They haven't changed."

Standards? What did that even mean? Vaguely, I remembered some mention of standards and a place called the Iron Jewel, which I'd taken at the time to be the metal-made saloon down the street.

"And you've got the stink of a long time in the wilds about you, currently."

My driftin' focus narrowed into an acute self-awareness at her statement. Did I smell? I'd hardly noticed.

She took me through another door, and we ended up in the kitchen, where a flurry of scents more pleasant than my own made the hunger come back right quick. My stomach gave another loud rumble as we passed a long counter spread with meat and vegetables, attended by no less than four cooks.

They hardly glanced up as we went around 'em.

I wondered what they could possibly be cookin' this late at night. But the fire in the hearth was hot, and there was a big black pot over it simmerin' with somethin'.

A small, rickety table sat in the corner, complete with two stools, and Sally led me to it and pointed. "Here you are. Have a seat. I'll get you something."

"Thank you kindly." I took the stool facin' the cooks and another door which I suspected led out onto the floor of the saloon proper.

Sally moved off to inspect the spread of food on offer, and at just that moment, another woman pushed through the other door. Plump and round, gray curls fallin' over her face, she carried an armful of empty plates.

I recognized her just about the same time she saw me, and she stopped short on her way to the wash basin already fulla dirty dishes.

Ginger. She'd brought me that second shot of whiskey up in my room last time I'd been here. Asked if I'd needed a doctor.

Surprise, then confusion, crossed her face, but then Sally appeared at my tableside with a heapin' bowl of stew and a chunk of bread, and Ginger's features smoothed into understandin'. She resumed her march toward the wash basin.

And I dropped my attention to the food Sally had set in front of me, mouth waterin'. It was thick and savory, heartier and of better quality than the stew I'd been offered in Sonoita. I dug into it eagerly as Sally next set a mug and a pitcher of sour beer on the table, then took the stool across from me.

Ginger dropped off her load of dishes and sauntered toward us, wipin' her hands on her apron. "Well, well," she said. "Look who's back." She glanced to Sally. "He's our special guest now, is he?"

Sally nodded. "For the time being. Has some business to take care of here before he can move on. And clearly he don't want to be just moseying on down the street in plain sight these days."

Ginger's eyebrows arched, and she turned toward me. "Awful brave of you to come back here so soon, Mister. Town's already in quite a stir from yer last visit. Here to cause more trouble, are you?"

Sally shot Ginger a look, but I was too grateful fer the food and hospitality at the moment to take any offense.

I swallowed before speakin'. "Not if I can help it."

"Glad to hear, then. Business ain't picked up again yet from all that mess. Hate to see a return to normal prolonged any further by more shenanigans."

"Ginger," Sally began, but the woman waved her off.

"Just sayin' what needs to be said. You got a soft spot fer trouble-makers, Sally, don't pretend you don't."

I glanced up from the stew to Sally at that, and saw her shift on her stool.

She scoffed. "Only if they're making the right kinda trouble," she said. "The rest of them I poke holes in." She pulled one of her knives again, spinnin' it around in her fingers like it mighta been made of fluid instead of metal, then tucked it away so smooth and quick I almost didn't see it.

She handled those knives like I'd seen the best handle their guns.

I swallowed another mouthful of stew and wondered again what kinda trouble she defined as the "right kind". Hoped it was my kind.

"Speaking of those I poke holes in," Sally said. She turned on the stool toward Ginger. "You had any trouble tonight while I was out?"

Ginger shook her head. "Nah. Been quiet. Got the usuals at the tables still, though … guess they think their luck is better in here than out there, lookin' fer that bounty."

Her eyes drifted to me again, but I ignored her, stuffin' a hunk of bread into my mouth.

"They'd be right," Sally said. "Good you ain't had any trouble, though. Guess I'd better get changed and make the rounds one more time before calling it a night."

"Sure thing, boss. I was just doin' another round myself before turnin' in."

"Thank you, Ginger."

The older woman gave Sally a nod and whisked off again, lookin' over the cooks' shoulders and peerin' into the bubblin' pot before movin' on again.

Sally turned back toward me. "You can have the suite

tonight, but just tonight. After that you can have the cot we've got set up in my office."

I nodded. "Appreciate it. But yer sure my bein' here ain't an … imposition? Don't wanna cause you any trouble after what you've done fer me."

She smiled. "Not at all, Mr. Lynd. We have guests like you all the time. It's no trouble at all."

"All right, then. Well … thank you. Again."

Her smile widened. "Think nothing of it."

Across the kitchen, Ginger musta been listenin' to our conversation, 'cause she called out suddenly, "Should I get the suite ready then, boss?"

Sally glanced to the woman, brief annoyance crossin' her features. "No need, Ginger. I got Nora and Nettie making Mr. Lynd a bath in there as we speak."

Ginger rounded to face us, one arm wrapped around a big bowl of boiled eggs, and a pot of somethin' that looked like oatmeal in her other hand. "Eh? Nora and … but I thought you said last time you wanted to give him a ride yerself?"

I choked on my stew.

Across from me, Sally stood abruptly from her stool, face flushin' a rosy, russet brown. She cleared her throat and sent Ginger an awful accusatory glare. "That will be quite enough, Ginger, thank you."

I reached fer the mug of sour beer and gulped it down, tryin' both to clear my airway of food and mask the fresh occurrence of heat once again crawlin' up under my collar.

Sally smoothed at the hips of her snug-fittin' pants, palms runnin' over the multitude of knives sheathed there. "Excuse me for a moment, Mr. Lynd … I'll just go and … change … be back right quick. You finish up there, and let the cooks know if you'd like more…" She turned abruptly and strode across the kitchen to exit out the back door we'd come in through, tossin' Ginger another glare as she did so.

Ginger, fer her part, only looked highly amused as she watched her employer leave. Then she turned back to me.

And I turned back to the pitcher of beer, pourin' myself another mug-full.

"Well," Ginger muttered, passin' close to my table as she moved fer the door that led out into the saloon, "it ain't no lie." Then, louder, she said, "Do enjoy yerself, Mr. Lynd. And don't worry, Sally's quarters are right off her office, so if you two do decide to get to ruttin', you don't gotta do it on that cot."

I coughed into my beer and then I choked on that, too, but Ginger only tossed me a grin and pushed on through into the saloon, leavin' me to attempt to recover my air on my own.

I thumped at my chest and rocked back on the stool, then glanced furtively toward the cooks through waterin' eyes to see if they'd paid any attention to that conversation.

If they had, they surely showed no interest nor concern over it. Acted like they hadn't heard nothin' at all, though I couldn't imagine they'd not. Oh well. Nothin' to be done fer it now.

The coughin' finally quieted and I took in a few deep breaths before clearin' my throat and turnin' back to the food. At this rate, this place was gonna be the death of me, instead of some noose or gunfight somewhere. I poured myself yet more beer and struggled to scrape together what was left of my wits.

And my dignity.

Sally returned a short time later, seemingly much more composed herself now, and clad in a simple white blouse, brown corset, and layered skirts. I'd finished my bowl of stew and the bread by then, and she asked if I wanted more, but I declined.

It weren't so good to gorge yerself after a long time of little food, I'd learned. Better to ease into a more normal meal schedule gradually. And anyway, I was satisfied enough, fer now.

"Glad to hear it," Sally said. "Then if you'll come with me, I'll show you to the suite. Got a back staircase that goes up to it, for … *discreet* business. Just checked on the room myself and it's all in order. Should be fine to head up now."

"Sure." Now that the food and beer were settled in my stomach, the exhaustion had kicked in again. It had been an interestin' few days of late, fer certain. Hard to believe just the night before I'd been in a jail cell awaitin' trial, and then sprung and nearly carted off to meet the Charles Miller I'd recently heard so much about.

I followed Sally out the kitchen's back door once more, and down the softly lit hallway and up a narrow staircase to another, wider hallway lined with doors. Looked mildly familiar, but we were on the opposite side of the building from the room I'd taken last time I'd stayed at the Seven Knives.

There were double-doors set into this end of the hallway, and they were carved all fancy with flowers and vines windin' around the edges and over toward the brass knobs.

"Here we are," Sally said. "The suite. Usually reserved for our most distinguished guests. All yours for tonight." She unlocked it with an iron key, then handed the key over to me. "I suggest you stay hidden away within as much as you can, and keep it locked. I'll retrieve you in the morning to get you moved into the other, less extravagant arrangements for later."

Her mention of the "mornin'" made me grunt, and I looked around fer windows, but there weren't none in the hallway. "Mornin'? Ain't it already almost daylight now?"

She shrugged. "Perhaps. But I'll give you the equivalent to a night's stay in hours, anyway. Now…" She turned toward the double-doors and pushed them open dramatically, then gestured grandly into the room. "Make yourself at home, Mr. Lynd."

It was the biggest room-for-rent I'd ever seen, and certainly the biggest I'd ever gotten to step foot in, myself. It was richly appointed, the wallpaper not peelin' like in the other room I'd stayed in here. The bed was also the biggest bed I'd ever seen, and had all four posts. Drapes hung from it, and heavy curtains covered the windows, so I suspected there'd be no way to tell what hour it was anyway so long as they were drawn.

A small desk and velvet-upholstered chair rested up against the wall to my left, and to my right, a small alcove set with a copper, claw-footed tub.

There was that bath Sally kept talkin' about, all right. The water steamed, the air heavy with the scent of lavender and rose. Across the tub lay a wooden tray set with soaps, sponges, and a bottle of whiskey. The good kind. Her *medicinal* variety.

And then, from behind the changin' screen in the corner, emerged Nora and Nettie. Both pale, with dark hair and dark eyes. And they wore nothin' at all on their top halves, and even less than before on their bottom halves.

The breath pushed out of me at the sight of 'em. That need roared to life again full force, blazin' white-hot and burnin' away any thoughts of anythin' else.

"Mr. Lynd," Sally purred from beside me, "I'll leave you in their capable hands. I'll see you in the morning."

I hardly noticed as she stepped backwards, out of the room, and shut the doors behind her.

XV

AHEAD OF THE STORM

Nora and Nettie padded across the floorboards toward me on bare feet, each offering soft smiles. I weren't quite sure what to do, then. I'd only ever hired whores who'd turned out to want to rob me, or who just wanted to get things over with as quickly as possible.

It'd never been anythin' like this, with all this set up, and build-up, and women who seemed keen to do more than just lay there.

"All right, Mr. Lynd," Nora said, comin' close and hookin' her fingers into my gunbelt. "Let's get you washed up."

Fuck. I hadn't felt the pull of it like this in a long, long time ... maybe not since that first time.

She flicked open the buckle with expert hands and pulled the belt loose.

Another pair of hands slid around either side of me from behind, pressin' into my stomach ... and slidin' downward. Nettie.

But the fallin' away of my guns' weight from around my hips sent off a faint warnin' in my mind. Small, and strugglin' hard against the nearly overwhelmin' flood of lust, but enough to drag some sense back into me, kickin' and screamin'. I pulled back a bit from Nora's attempts at the buckle of my second belt, the one that held up my pants, and forced my eyes away from the roundness of her breasts to assure myself she'd put my pistols in a conspicuous spot. Somewhere within easy reach. Somewhere safe.

And that she'd actually put them *down*.

Wouldn't forget that lesson so long as I lived.

Yes, she'd put them down. On the floor next to the—

Nettie's right hand reached my groin and I gasped. And then I didn't give a damn about those pistols. Didn't give a damn if these two wanted to rob me blind. Didn't give a damn if they saw my metal leg and decided they wanted to turn me over to Charles Miller, even.

So long as they let me finish this first.

My second belt came unbuckled, then Nora started on my shirt buttons. I weren't real sure what all happened after that, but I was stark naked soon enough, and lost in a haze of agreeable sensations I hadn't felt in far, far too long.

Made me wonder why I didn't do this more often.

Truth be told it was over faster than I would have preferred, though I suppose that was to be expected given my recent bout of rather lengthy abstinence. And once it was, and I stood there wrung out and pantin', my clarity of thinkin' came back. And I realized abruptly I was standin' there naked in front of two women strangers, my metal leg in its entirety in full view, from toes to thigh. The edges of panic fluttered in my gut, and I glanced reflexively to my gunbelt, coiled on the floor next to the bed.

"Itchin' for those again already, Mr. Lynd?" Nora asked. She'd grabbed a linen towel from a stack folded on the floor and wiped herself with it, but now followed my gaze toward my pistols. Fear etched lines into her face before she obviously tried to wrestle it under control and glanced back at me. "Whatever would you need them for, currently?"

She tried to sound casual, but the fear lurked there, under her words. Her voice shook just slightly.

And my own panic dissolved under the horror of causin' her to feel such a thing. Under the horror of realizin' her profession could often put her at the mercy of unsavory or violent types, and my stomach turned at the thought. Clearly, Sally tried to run a high-quality establishment here, likely thanks to those standards she'd mentioned earlier, but that didn't mean things didn't occasionally get out of hand. I wondered if that had ever happened directly to Nora or Nettie, or if their fear was only from hearin' stories second-hand.

Either way, at that moment all I wanted was to assure them they had no reason to fear me … and to end anyone who might have hurt them before.

"I … I don't need 'em," I croaked. "Just … well, there's been a lot of folk interested in … in this, of late." My left hand dropped down to my left thigh, grazin' against the lower half of it. The half of it made of gears and rods. It felt strange to have it exposed like this. Felt strange to have it exposed and yet not be fearin' fer my life. "Usually tryin' to cut it off me."

Nora's dark eyes widened, and Nettie stepped up beside me and took my right hand in hers.

"Don't usually let people see it, is all," I muttered. I shifted on my feet, feelin' awkward and lost again now that that ragin' desire had abated. I kinda wished they'd just leave, like all the whores I'd hired before.

But it seemed they had no intention of doin' so.

"Come now, Mr. Lynd," Nettie said, wrappin' my arm in both of hers. "We ain't got no interest in that. We see Old World tech all the time. Ain't no matter to us."

Nora came to take my left arm, and I blinked at both of 'em, but let 'em guide me toward the tub. "You … you seen other people with metal legs?"

"Well, no," Nettie said, "not that, exactly. But a lot of gadgets you wouldn't believe 'less you saw them yourself."

"Some of the area prospectors sometimes get lucky," Nora explained. "Find somethin' out in the wilds, outside of the barons' claims."

"And they can't wait to come in here and brag about it, show off their finds," Nettie finished. "Especially to us. Makes them feel all big and important, I suppose."

We'd reached the tub. The water still steamed, and dried rose petals and lavender leaves floated atop it.

"Won't you step in, Mr. Lynd?" Nettie gestured to the water.

"Can it get wet?" Nora asked, lookin' at my leg.

I hesitated. "I … don't rightly know." Another thing I hadn't chanced to ask the good doctor before high-tailin' it away from his place. I'd washed up a few times while stayin' at his homestead, of course, and I hadn't gotten it too wet, then. I'd kept the thing propped up on the side of the tub. It was more healed now, hurt less and worked better, sure, but I still weren't certain if it should go under water. So I figured I'd just do the same now as I'd done then. "Probably shouldn't get too much wet. I'll just rest it up on the side of the tub."

"All right," Nettie said. She picked up the tray holdin' the soaps and sponges and whiskey so I could climb in, and I tried to do so as gracefully as I could, given that I didn't want to submerge my left leg.

But eventually, I got myself eased down into the hot water, restin' my metal calf and ankle along the tub rim and leanin' back with a sigh. The water was deep enough it covered the seam where the doc had sawed off my natural leg and attached this one, but I thought that probably didn't matter, since that seam had been washed plenty of times before durin' my healin' process.

And anyway, it felt good there, surrounded by the water's warmth.

It all felt good. All of this. Better than I'd felt in a long, long time.

Nettie replaced the tray, and Nora poured me a generous dose of that good quality whiskey. She handed it off to me and then went around to kneel behind the tub, her hands slidin' over my shoulders and diggin' into the muscles there, but in a good way.

Nettie picked up the chunk of soap and a sponge. "You're smart to not let most people see that leg, though," she said quietly, also kneelin' beside the tub. "Those prospectors who brag about their gadgets … a lot of times they end up talking too much. The barons hear of their finds. And it usually don't end so well for those folk. One way or another."

I only grunted. I could imagine. But I didn't much want to consider the barons or their oppressive nature right now. Right now I only wanted to enjoy this bath, and this whiskey, and the way Nora's hands seemed to be unknottin' months of tension from my shoulders.

And the way Nettie's hands had now plunged underwater, and were currently workin' that sponge along my right thigh.

"But none of that matters here," Nora offered, as if she could read my thoughts. "You ain't got nothin' to worry about from us."

"That's right, Mr. Lynd," Nettie whispered. She leaned over the side of the tub for better access to my submerged lower half, her breasts nearly full in my face, and I swallowed as I felt the vestiges of that desire rouse again. She glanced at me from beneath dark lashes, wisps of hair fallin' across her face, and smiled coyly. "You just relax," she said. "Enjoy yourself. We got *all* night."

I slept the sleep of the dead.

Couldn't remember the last time I'd slept so sound, the last time I'd passed a night without a single nightmare.

Woke to the sound of hard poundin' at a door, and groaned in frustration at havin' such a nice slumber interrupted. My limbs were warm, languid, my eyelids heavy. I tried to pull 'em open without much luck.

The poundin' on the door intensified. A woman called out, "Mr. Lynd? You awake? You all right in there?"

She sounded vaguely familiar. I muttered somethin' and rolled in the bed, draggin' a heap of quilted bed sheets along with me.

The combination of unusual sensations finally pierced through my groggy contentment. Soft mattress. Softer linens. Quilted bed sheets.

And I was naked. Not a thread of clothes on me.

The last bit jolted me full awake in a hurry, just as I heard the turn of a key in the door, and it swung open. I sat up quick, disoriented, blinkin' the heavy press of sleep from my eyes even as I searched frantically fer my guns. The room was dark … unnaturally dark … only a thin sliver of white light slicin' through a crack in the drawn curtains at the window to my left.

I squinted in its searin' brightness and followed its line across the floorboards, only to see the vague shape of a woman—presumably the woman who had been shoutin' outside and who had unlocked my door—stride in with purpose, a tray set with tea service for two balanced on the hand which did not hold the key.

And that's when I finally saw my gunbelt. It was looped over the back of the chair at the desk against the opposite wall.

Far, far out of reach.

The woman drew up short at the sight of me sittin' there and exhaled a long, loud breath. "Mr. Lynd! You gave me a fright.

Thought maybe those girls had been too hard on you, made your heart give out, or something. I know, I know … wouldn't think it'd happen to a strapping young man like yourself, but I've seen it a time or two."

I blinked hard, and my blurry vision finally cleared enough fer me to recognize it was Sally standin' there in the near dark.

Those girls…

Slowly, the memories came back, piecin' together the hours before my dreamless sleep bit by bit. I swallowed.

Nora and Nettie. And the bath. And that whiskey.

And … everything else.

The whiskey bottle sat on the bedside table, empty. The tub was still half-fulla water, what I could see of it, anyway. The rest we'd splashed out, mostly. But that mess had all been cleaned up, looked like. And the pile of used towels was gone, too.

And … and my clothes appeared to be missin', as well.

I adjusted the sheets around my waist as Seven Knives Sally crossed to the lone desk and set the tea tray carefully atop it. Then she turned and went to the window, the one with the cracked curtains, and threw 'em wide open.

I cried out as the light stabbed into my skull and threw up my arm to shield my eyes. "Blast it all, woman, you make a habit of bargin' into people's rooms and blindin' 'em?!"

"Only if I think they might be dead."

"I ain't dead!"

"I can see that … now. In that case…" She marched back to the desk, fussin' over the tray. "I brought you some tea."

I scrubbed the palms of my hands into my eyes, tryin' to clear both the fog of such a long, hard slumber and the dazzle of the light. Then I opened one and peered across the room at her. "Don't you got any coffee? Or whiskey?"

She snorted. "I'm afraid there's a limit on the quantity of that whiskey you can imbibe without paying for it in real currency,

Mr. Lynd. And as for coffee, most certainly I got some, but I think you'll find this tea beneficial for clarity of mind. It's rather invigorating, if I do say so myself."

I opened my mouth to tell her I didn't much like tea … didn't like it at all, if I were to be honest … but then changed my mind and shut it again. Probably weren't polite to say such a thing after all the kindness she'd shown me recently. And probably weren't a *wise* thing to say, neither, considerin' my gunbelt was across the room and out of reach, and my clothes had gone mysteriously missin'.

So I kept quiet as she brought me a cup and offered it out. "Here you are."

I took the delicate piece of dishware from her reluctantly. It felt awkward and small in my hands. To my surprise, the sides of the ceramic were cool to the touch instead of warm. Perplexed, I sniffed at the pale liquid within, then coughed.

Peppermint. And very strong.

"Go on, drink up," Sally instructed, pourin' herself a cup.

I gritted my teeth and forced myself to take a sip. It was cold, all right. That, combined with the mint infused within it, sent a shock through me, sure enough. It cooled my mouth instantly, and went up through my nose into my head.

I coughed again, but there was a subtle sweetness beneath the powerful coolin' mint that made it not an entirely unpleasant experience to drink. I took another cautious sip.

"See, not so bad, eh?" Sally came to my bedside with teacup in one hand, then gathered up her skirts in the other hand to perch herself next to me on the edge of the mattress. She smoothed her skirts back out, arrangin' 'em neat and proper over her slender legs.

I lowered my right hand from the teacup to clutch a fistful of sheets myself, makin' sure they stayed in place while she situated herself. Makin' sure they kept me as decent as could be managed in my current situation.

Sally's brown eyes dropped down to that hand, and then she smirked behind the rim of her floral-patterned teacup. "So suddenly modest, Mr. Lynd. You are an enigma of a man, I'll give you that."

I frowned behind my own teacup. "How's that?"

She shrugged. "Just don't often see an outlaw that's got any manners. Or any modesty. Or that knows what the word *enigma* even means."

My heart quickened a bit at her use of the term *outlaw*, though I told myself that could merely apply to what I'd done at Baron Whittaker's manor. And that was somethin' she'd already more than shown her approval toward. Was, apparently, the "right kinda trouble".

Sally sipped at her tea and squinted at me while I tried to figure out what to say. My mind felt sluggish, disoriented. Maybe it'd been all that whiskey. Or the particular attentions Nora and Nettie had given me fer hours on end. Or the fact I was sittin' here unarmed and naked within arm's reach of a woman I was fair certain could be bad fer my health, if she so chose.

And there was also what Ginger had said about Sally last night. About her wantin' to have a go at me, herself. I hoped she weren't entertainin' the idea of doin' that now. Didn't think I had anythin' left in me fer that kinda business at the moment.

"You almost even act like a real gentleman," Sally said abruptly. "Sometimes."

I gulped at my tea. Maybe that clarity of mind would get here quick. I felt I was gonna need it soon.

Sally's teacup lowered to rest gently in her lap, cupped by her other hand. Her head tilted to the side as she studied me. "Almost like someone taught you once how to be a real member of society.

But then you got those reflexes … survival reflexes. Gunfighter reflexes. And some rough edges … like those fine manners you once had got all worn away over time. Like after awhile, you started to forget. Except sometimes, now and then, you remember again. It all comes back to you. Just now and then. Here and there. Making you, like I said, an enigma of a man."

I cleared my throat, shiftin' my gaze away from her toward the door. Least she'd shut it behind her. My eyes went next to my gunbelt, and I wished it were closer. That's not where it'd been when I'd fallen asleep, that much I knew fer sure. "Manners ain't worth shit out here," I muttered.

But even as I said it, I thought of Charlotte. And how I'd panicked at not knowin' how to act in the presence of a lady with proper breedin'. So maybe manners were worth a little somethin' out here. Sometimes. If you met the right kinda person.

Sally smiled at my declaration. "Now, now. That ain't true. They're worth something in some places. *Quality* places. They're worth something in my joint, I can tell you that."

My gaze went back to the empty whiskey bottle on the night table. "They worth more of that whiskey?"

Her smile widened into a grin, and she arched an eyebrow. "More like they're worth not getting a knife in the gut or swift boot to the ass sending you right back out into the thoroughfare."

"Ah."

"But maybe if you're especially sweet, I could rustle up another bottle for you."

"Mm. I'll think about it."

"You do that. In the meantime, I've got the cot all ready for you in my office. You can have that for the duration of your stay. Which will be … how long, would you say?"

"Hard to say, exactly."

"I see. Well, as a business owner in this fair town, I am

particularly sensitive to its ups and downs, as I'm sure you can imagine."

"Sure."

"So, if you *were* to be stirring up trouble here at some point during your visit, I would much appreciate being forewarned. In order to … stay ahead of the storm, you might say."

I shook my head. "I don't plan to be stirrin' up any trouble."

She squinted at me again. "And yet, something tells me things don't often go your way." She reached out to pat the shape of my metal leg beneath the sheets, and her eyes drifted pointedly to the thick bars of shiny pink scars lined down my right bicep.

I shifted in the bed, uncomfortable with the truth of that statement. "Yeah, well…"

Well shit. Seemed I had nothin' else to say about that. If my pa had ever had any real luck in his life, it surely hadn't passed to me when he'd died.

"More tea?" Sally asked, and I realized I was starin' down into my empty cup.

"Please." I handed the little cup over to her, relieved at the interruption to that path of conversation, and hopin' she'd drop it. That clarity of mind she'd mentioned hadn't come yet, and I wished it'd hurry up.

Sally took both teacups and stood from her seat on the bed, then moved over to the desk to refill 'em both. "Let me get straight to the point then, Mr. Lynd," she said, and her conversational tone turned all business.

Reflexively, I looked toward my gunbelt again. It hung right next to her and that tea service. If I didn't much like her point, there'd be no chance I could reach it before her, or before she could plant any of her seven knives in me.

She seemed unconcerned, her back to me as she poured. "Being a business owner in this fair town," she said, "and being particularly sensitive to its ups and downs, as I told you before, I've taken measures to protect my own interests here." She dropped a brown sugar cube into each teacup, and lifted a tiny silver spoon to stir them.

That would be the sweetness, then.

"Understandable," I said, curious as to where she might be goin' here.

"One of those measures is to extend a network of eyes and ears throughout Blessing, so as to report back to me the happenings and moods of the townsfolk regularly. To help me stay ahead of any oncoming storm, you see. If I have word of what's brewing before it breaks, I can take measures to ensure my establishment and my employees are protected."

"Smart of you," I offered. I wished she could have waited to have this conversation till I was more awake, and preferably fully clothed.

She finished stirrin' the tea and set the tiny spoon back on the tray. The memory of those manners she'd spoken of filtered back to me then, somethin' about not clinkin' the spoon against the side of the teacup. I had never paid much attention to those lessons, preoccupied more at the time with the things Pa was teachin' me about ropin' steers and shootin' rifles.

But I remembered the bit about not makin' the spoon clink when you stirred.

And Sally's stirrin' had been utterly silent.

She turned back to me, a teacup in each hand. "I am glad you agree. And so my point, Mr. Lynd, is that if your business here should require a network of eyes and ears about the town, or even, maybe, any eyes and ears within the barons' estates themselves, I should be happy to lend you the services of mine. It might prevent you falling into further trouble, is my thought. Being as it's not exactly wise for you to be wandering around the streets at the moment. And being as many of us business owners would prefer no further upset to our commerce … at least not for a time … as Ginger said in so many words last night."

She offered me the refilled teacup, and I took it from her, considerin' both her offer and what I suspected was the real meanin' behind it. She'd help me out, sure, on her own terms. And so long as my business didn't interfere with her own best interests.

I didn't think stealin' a lockbox from Baron Haas would do much to interfere with her interests, but neither did I feel particularly inclined to get her involved. Didn't want her to end up like Charlotte, too, hunted by the likes of Charles Miller.

She resumed her place at the edge of the mattress and looked at me expectantly, takin' another sip of her tea before speakin' again. "Or does your business here require more direct action? I have some in my service who could be employed for just such a thing, as well."

I looked at her fer a long minute, tryin' to judge her intentions. Did she suspect that by helpin' me out here, I'd feel inclined to owe her some kinda favor later, in return? I was already movin' quickly toward bein' in her debt, if I weren't there already three-fold, and I didn't feel much like owin' anyone else any debts.

I had more than enough already with Nine-Fingered Nan.

I dropped my gaze down to the full teacup restin' in my lap. It still felt awkward and small in my grip, and all kinds of wrong. "Will you … let me think about it fer a space? Truth be told, I'm not exactly sure what kinda action would best suite my business here just yet."

She nodded. "Of course." She sprang up standin' again, and went back to the desk and the tea tray. She finished off her second cup and set it down, empty, then faced me again, smoothin' at her skirts. "You just let me know when you decide, and we can go over the details then."

"All right." I had no intention of givin' her details. But if I owed her anythin' at this point, it was politeness and gratitude fer her kindness, at least. So I'd keep up the pretense as long as I could manage.

"I'll leave the tea for you. Please help yourself. And if you'd like a midday meal, take the back stairs to the kitchen. The cooks will have something for you."

"Midday…" I squinted toward the window, saw the slant of the sun anglin' across the street, and groaned, rubbin' at my eyes again.

"Indeed, Mr. Lynd. Now you know why I came to check on you. But I've other business to attend to for now, so I'll leave you be. I'll have Ginger come soon to show you to your new arrangements. Till then, do try to stay generally out of sight."

"Right," I said.

She headed for the ornate double doors, and that's when I remembered I had no clothes. "Wait," I called out.

Sally paused, one hand on the knob, and looked to me in question. "Something else you need, Mr. Lynd?"

"My clothes … seem to have gone missin'."

"Ah, that." A spark lit in her eye, and one corner of her mouth drew up. "I'm sure there are some who would not object to you wandering these halls just as you are, but we do have those standards to uphold. Yes, the girls took your clothes to be laundered. Should be fresh and clean for you by now. I'll have Ginger bring them up."

"I'd much appreciate it."

Her smirk widened into a genuine smile. "Most certainly, Mr. Lynd."

XVI

DON'T NEED NO NANNY

Ginger brought my clothes, indeed, not long after Sally had departed, and I clutched the sheets around my waist again as she bustled about the room, settin' the neatly folded stack of garments on the desk's chair and sweepin' away the tea tray.

She told me she'd wait outside the door while I dressed, then show me to Sally's office and my cot. I nodded to her, and she stepped out, pullin' the door shut behind her.

It took me a bit longer than usual to rouse myself outta that bed. Still felt I was movin' slower than usual, too, and didn't seem my head was much clearer than it had been before. Maybe I'd get some coffee down in the kitchen when I got some food.

I dressed quick as I could, grumblin' at the stiffness in the freshly washed fabric of my shirt and trousers. Then I grumbled at the strangeness of the stolen gunbelt and its irons as I buckled it around my waist and checked the guns, just to be sure everything there was all in order.

It was, so I pushed my hat down onto my head and went to the doors, exitin' that fancy room with more reluctance than I'd ever anticipated leavin' a room like that.

Ginger spun at the sound of the doors openin', the tea tray balanced on one hand. She smiled at the sight of me. "Well, lookie there! Ain't you just a vision of a man when you get all cleaned up!"

I halted, blinked, feelin' all sorts of awkward again.

"Come on, then." She waved me onward with her free hand. "Follow me. This way."

She led me down the narrow stairs and through the hallway that passed the kitchen's back door and the whores' room, and my eyes lingered on that door as we went by it and on down to the other end of that hall. Ginger opened the door at the far end and showed me in.

"Here we are."

It was a cramped space, mostly filled with a desk and a chair in the middle of the room and a cabinet on the back wall. There was one window, its curtains drawn, and a simple cot rested along the right wall. On the left wall was another door.

"There's the cot," Ginger said, pointin' at it. "Just make yerself at home. Sally'll be in to chat with you when she can." She started to retreat back out into the hallway, then paused. "And don't think of stealin' nothin'. Sally's got this whole room inventoried."

I turned to her in surprise. "I weren't gonna—"

She lifted her free hand to cut me off. "Just gotta say it, regardless. All right, then. I'll leave you to it." She stepped out then and again shut the door behind her.

Leave me to what, I wondered?

I didn't have nothin' to do, 'cept have a nice, hard think on how I was ever gonna figure out where that lockbox was. And maybe get some grub. My stomach growled at the thought, but I decided to take a quick poke around the place first. Weren't gonna steal nothin', not from Sally, not after all she'd done fer me, but I couldn't help myself. If I was gonna stay here fer the next few days, it wouldn't hurt nothin' to get a better idea of just who Seven Knives Sally was.

She seemed awful young to be a saloon owner. Couldn't be more than a few years older than me. But then, from what I'd seen of her abilities last night, and the quality of this establishment, I figured she had just the kind of steel personality and deadly skill with those knives to get her this place … and to keep hold of it.

I browsed through the room, quick and careful, takin' note of the valuables, though there weren't much. Probably on purpose, considerin' she hosted guests in here on the regular. Standard fare in the desk: paper, pencils, ink, whiskey, a ledger book fulla numbers, but I'd never been so good at numbers. A kettle fer boilin' water, a tin cup, a box fulla tea leaves … all right, that part weren't so standard, but it fit with the more refined part of her I'd seen earlier this afternoon. I put everything back where I found it.

One of the desk drawers was locked.

I decided not to pick it. Felt wrong to go that far.

I crossed the room and tried the door on the left wall. It weren't locked, so I pulled it open a crack and peeked through. A small, simple bedroom. The lights were off in there, so I couldn't see much, but I shut the door again, anyway, rememberin' Ginger's mention of Sally's quarters bein' off her office.

Felt wrong to go snoopin' around in there.

And so concluded my search of the place. I had no belongin's to stash, so I went ahead and slipped on out of the office, goin' to the kitchen fer that midday meal Sally had talked about.

I ate fast at that rickety table, helpin' myself to some beef roast, onions and beans, applesauce and fresh peaches, and coffee. Couldn't remember the last time I ate so good, or tasted anythin' so good, either, and I had the thought that if it weren't fer that sky-high bounty on my head and nearly everyone in this town wantin' to collect it … I might be tempted to stay here fer a good long while.

As it were, I had business to see to, and no time to waste.

So I left the kitchen soon as my meal was done and checked the office, but Sally still weren't in there. I glanced both ways down that back hall. It was currently empty; patrons weren't allowed back here and the girls were occupied or restin', I figured. There was another door to my right, at the very end of the hall.

A door that led out back of the saloon, if my sense of space was correct.

I ran my fingers over the tops of the cartridges tucked into my gunbelt. I hadn't ever got around to countin' 'em, but there were enough. I pulled my hat down low, lifted the collar of my duster, and went fer the exit door.

Sally had said lotsa people had left Blessing to go on the hunt fer me. That meant they wouldn't be around town. And anyway, who would ever think I'd be crazy enough to be walkin' around the town I was most wanted in? I'd stick to the alleys and back streets, have a look around Blessing myself. I weren't plannin' to do anythin' … yet. Just watch and listen, like she said her people did. Maybe try to find out where Baron Haas kept his residence. Maybe lurk around there a bit.

Wouldn't draw no attention to myself.

Would beat sittin' around doin' nothin' in Sally's office all day, anyway. And would keep me from feelin' inclined to tell her any details about why I'd really come back here.

So I stepped quietly out the back door of the Seven Knives, drew it shut silently behind me, and slipped away into the afternoon shadows.

I lurked. Listened. Watched.

But kept on the move.

Seemed to be even more lawmen out and about on the streets now than there had been the last time I'd been here, and I wondered if that was because Baron Whittaker had been murdered. Nan had mentioned that seemed an unlikely feat … maybe it had got all the other barons rattled.

The thought brought a grim smile to my face as I stalked down one back alley, skirtin' wide around a pig pen.

Good. Let 'em be rattled. Let 'em realize they were mortals just like anyone else.

I went from one end of Blessing to the other. There mighta been more lawmen around now, but the town was emptier of other folk than it had been before, that was fer certain. Though the regulars were still busy enough. Still plenty of saloons open fer business. And the livery. And the bank.

The ruins of Baron Whittaker's manor sat up on that hill, and I paused briefly in my walk to stop and take in the sight of it. Despite my sufferin' there, it brought me a great satisfaction to look upon the place now. The house was missin' its roof, and a good part of two of its walls near the back. Charred beams poked up into the hazy blue sky like the ribs of some great beast.

Some of the barn remains could be seen too, just over the hill's rise.

Too bad it looked like they were already rebuildin' it. There were fresh new beams up now in the places where the walls had burned, and several men hammerin' and sawin' at more.

I gave a grunt and moved on, circlin' around the outskirts of the town now. There were more fancy houses out a distance on the perimeter, lookin' much like Baron Whittaker's place, and I wondered if one of 'em might be Baron Haas' residence.

I saw one in the distance, on the west side of town, that had big blue and yellow banners draped over its wooden front fence at intervals. That was different. So I aimed fer that one, gettin' as close as I could without leavin' the cover of length-enin' shadows. I planted myself behind one of the less reputable brothels and leaned against its back wall, where I could have an unobstructed view of the big house and its banners.

Now that I was closer to it, I could see the bustle of activity goin' on around and within it. A wagon had pulled up at the end of the drive, and a buncha folk were unloadin' crates and sacks from it and carryin' 'em into the house. And there were more people out and about brushin' the place up, looked like. Trimmin' the hedges, sweepin' the porch, wipin' the windows.

Looked like they were gettin' ready fer somethin' big.

Curious.

A well-dressed older man stood amid a cluster of armed individuals at the base of the porch steps, one of 'em a woman with a long brown braid, clearly givin' some kind of instructions. He gestured to various places around the yard, and then over his shoulder toward the house. I could only barely hear some of what he was sayin', but I gathered from what I could make out that the group of armed folk were his security.

"...don't give a toss what that bastard thinks or what he says to you, you are *not* to let him step foot into my house, understand?"

Well, that part I heard clear enough. The folk around him nodded gravely.

I could only wonder if he meant Mr. Miller, the bastard I was so familiar with by now, or a different one. Or maybe he weren't referrin' to an actual bastard at all, but instead usin' the slur in a more general sense, aimed at someone he particularly didn't like.

Whichever way he meant it, his group of hired guns seemed to get the message. After a few more, less passionate orders from the older gent, they dispersed to go on about their business or take up their assigned positions.

The well-dressed fella had turned and was about to ascend the porch steps when a coach rattled up the road and pulled to a halt just behind the supply wagon, its horses all lathered up. He paused and turned back to face it.

I watched, too, curious about who might be in such a hurry to arrive at this estate. Curious about who this older fella was, and what he could possibly be preparin' for with all this stuff and all this security.

I couldn't see who came outta the coach at first, since the vehicle itself blocked my view of its occupants. But the older man's face changed at the sight of whoever it was. He seemed almost glad, his face lightin' up, and he threw his arms open as he made his way down the long front walk to greet the newcomer.

"Professor!" he nearly shouted.

And that's when the new arrival finally came into my view, havin' gone down the walk far enough himself to emerge from behind the bulk of the coach.

And I straightened abruptly from where I'd been slouchin' against the brothel's wall, my right hand goin' immediately to my gun, but then stoppin' there with my fingers curled around the grip. There were far too many witnesses around here fer that. Wouldn't do to murder a man in broad daylight in front of all these folk in a town I was already most wanted in.

But boy did I sure want to murder him.

Professor Morton.

He shook hands heartily with the older gentleman, and I noted he weren't wearin' my guns no more. I wondered if he still had 'em somewhere, or if he'd sold 'em off or some such. He better have still had 'em somewhere ... as I fully intended to get 'em back. Somehow.

My fingers tightened around the strange pistol-grip currently sittin' on my hip, but I resisted the urge to draw. Barely.

"So sorry I'm late..." the professor said, but the rest of his words were lost to me as he was ushered toward the big house.

I ground my teeth as I watched 'em go, talkin' enthusiastically amongst themselves, until they stepped inside and out of sight.

So the professor hadn't been lyin' about his Old World knowledge. Or about the fact he'd been expected at Baron Haas' place. Maybe he weren't lyin' about workin' fer Her Majesty, neither. He musta managed to slip away from Sonoita after my jailbreak. Guess if there weren't no outlaw left there to judge, there weren't no need fer a trial, and therefore no need fer a witness.

This must be the Haas residence, then. I'd found it after all. Still didn't know what all the fuss was about ... but at least I knew which house it was. And if the professor was here, I might just manage to get my justice fer what he did to me along the way.

I stayed there in the brothel's shadow as long as I dared, hopin' to catch some driftin' piece of conversation that might tell me what they were gettin' ready fer, or to come up with some decent excuse to wander closer and maybe find a way in.

But there was just too much activity at the place fer me to feel safe enough venturin' any closer. And all I heard was some complainin' about the heat, and complainin' about how the town's best butcher had gone off in search of that bounty.

At that, I scowled and tugged my hat lower. But I didn't think any of 'em could see my face well enough from that distance, anyway. If they even noticed me here, in the first place.

The sun dropped low to the western horizon, silhouettin' that big house and all its activity, and I figured I'd probably better start headin' back to the Seven Knives. The wagon of supplies had left, and another wagon shown up in its place. This one fulla flowers. Fresh flowers.

And ones I'd never seen before. Where in the world had they found *those*?

Maybe I could ask Sally if she knew what was goin' on here.

I sighed and straightened up from the wall, stretchin' out my stiff muscles. An afternoon of waitin' and listenin', and I hadn't learned much. Maybe I *should* take Sally up on her offer of help...

I turned away from the wagon load of fresh flowers and ambled around the corner of the brothel, grimacin' at the thick stench of urine in the alley there. I made my way quick as I could back toward the more respectable parts of Blessing. It was easier now, as the twilight grew more shadows fer me to hide in and the streets gradually emptied, the more respectable residents headin' home for their supper.

I was only a few blocks away from the Seven Knives when I realized I had a few shadows of my own, tailin' me. A sigh hissed out between my teeth, and I switched directions. No use bringin' 'em to Sally's place.

At least that poster made it clear I was wanted alive. That would buy me some time.

I led 'em around to the back alley by the pig pen, and then stopped. It was as good a place as any. Buildings on four sides, with only narrow paths between leadin' in or out. Nice and removed from the sight of any of those lawmen prowlin' the wider streets.

It was near full-on dark now, only a touch of light showin' over the roofs that surrounded me. I hoped I was in enough shadow to cover the motion as I slid my hands down to the grips of those strange irons in my stolen belt. "I know someone's back there," I said. "Might as well come on out and tell me why the hell yer followin' me."

Fer a minute I got no answer.

Then came the sound of boots in the dirt. A couple pairs of 'em.

They approached from behind, and went around either side, but didn't come too close.

I didn't move. Kept my eyes straight ahead, my hands on my grips, and just listened.

Somewhere far off, a dog barked. A wagon rattled by on the main street. The pigs grunted and snuffled about in their pen.

"We were just hopin' for a chat," a man said from directly behind me.

"Hard to chat with a fella when you don't announce yerself," I commented. From the corner of each eye I could see two of 'em. One to either side of me, both about my age. Both holdin' a pistol already bare, but lowered toward the ground.

"Well," the man behind me said, "wanted to make sure you were the fella we wanted to chat with, first."

"And?" I prompted. "What did you conclude? Am I the man you were lookin' fer?" I shifted just slightly to look back over my shoulder.

An older man stood there, blockin' the way I'd come in from. He had both a rope and a gun on his belt, and a hand poised over each. He shrugged. "Ain't quite sure yet. But the way you've been skulkin' around in the shadows makes you look mighty suspicious. And I couldn't help but notice your limp."

I resisted the urge to scowl down at my left leg. "Yeah. Twisted my knee up real good ropin' steers once as a kid. What about it? Ain't nothin' unusual about that."

"Maybe not," he admitted. "But the man we're looking for would have good reason to skulk around in the shadows. And he has a limp, too. You maybe wanna step out of this alley? Into the light so we can get a good look at your face? And a good look at that lame leg?"

"Why would I want to do that?"

The two young men on either side of me glanced to the older man behind me, but kept their guns lowered.

The older man sighed. "So we can make sure you ain't the man we're lookin' for. He's worth a lot of money. I'm afraid we can't let you be till we make sure you are or you ain't him, Mister. If you step on out here into the light so we can check real quick, we can all go on about our business."

I let my shoulders slump. "You know how many times I've been mistaken fer that man? Might go on the lookout fer him myself … and if I ever find the bastard, shoot him fer the trouble."

"He's only worth the money if he's alive," one of the young men said.

I scoffed. "Lucky fer me, then." I drew both pistols and fired 'em as one, one to each side, one bullet fer each of the young men. They both staggered backward as my shots hit 'em in the chest, their expressions morphin' into shocked surprise.

The man behind me yelled out, but I'd already dropped to one knee and twisted, and my two bullets hit him in the chest, too, just as he was raisin' his own gun.

I didn't wait to see him fall. I turned back around, lurched to my feet, and took off down the alley straight ahead, then pivoted down another to my left. The reports of my gunfire rolled away into the dusk, and there was already shoutin' and yellin' fer the law.

I needed to get away from there, and quick.

Unfortunately, my limp was only more pronounced the faster I tried to move.

I twisted and turned down the alleys and back streets blindly, not really knowin' where I was goin', and not carin'. As long as I put as much distance as I could between me and those men I'd just shot, I could work out what to do next later. Part of me wanted to run back to Sally's, all right, but I didn't think that was such a wise idea. Not yet. Not till I was certain there weren't no one else suspicious of my identity followin' me around.

I was so intent on listenin' fer sounds of pursuit and watchin' fer shadows on my tail that I failed to see the one that stepped out in front of me. Not till a hand caught my shirtfront, yanked me into a narrow side alley, and threw me up against a wall so hard all the breath crushed out of me.

"*The fuck you think yer doing*?!" an angry voice hissed.

My instinctive scramble fer my guns paused at the tone … I didn't recognize the voice, or the hulkin' shape currently holdin' me against that wall. But they sure sounded like they knew me. I squinted at the man who'd grabbed me, but his face was all in shadow under his hat.

"Huh?" It was all I could manage to get out in my confusion and bewilderment, and considerin' his huge paw of a hand pinned me to the wall and made it hard to breathe.

"Sally told me to keep an eye on you," he said, voice pitched low and soundin' an awful lot like Pa had used to sound when he'd caught me doin' something he didn't like. "And I thought, 'Nah, he ain't stupid enough to go wanderin' around outside the saloon, surely.' And yet, here we are. And you firin' off your guns, to boot. So I'll ask again: what in the fuck do you think yer doin'?"

I didn't much appreciate his tone. He weren't my pa, and I weren't no child. I shoved his hand off my chest and straightened from the wall. "I'm a free man," I spat back. "I can do as I damn well please. And I don't need no *nanny* to keep an eye on me."

"You ain't a free man," he shot back. "Yer a *wanted* man. And you'll be a dead man soon enough, too, if you keep on bein' so stupid."

"Fuck you," I snarled. "I was doin' just fine, till you stopped me. Anyone with any smarts knows we shouldn't just be standin' here, waitin' on the law to find us."

"Yeah, yer right."

He took a step back, and I took a step forward, anticipatin' movin' off into the dark again to get lost in the town's maze till the commotion over my shootin' died down some.

But instead, that big giant of a man clipped me on the temple with his big, giant fist, and I fell into a whole different kinda darkness.

XVII

THE CURSE OF CARING

"Those girls fuck all the sense out of you?!"

I winced at Sally's outburst, mostly 'cause my head was poundin' from where her man had hit me and knocked me clean out. I sat on the edge of the cot in her office, where I'd woken up groggy and disoriented only a few minutes ago. Sally had been there already, seethin', waitin' fer me to open my eyes. I had no idea how I'd gotten back here.

Now, Sally paced furiously back and forth in front of me, skirts swishin'.

And that giant goon of hers was there too, blockin' the door that led into the hall with his arms crossed. He was big, all right, but not exactly all muscle. Still, he was glarin' down at me, lips set in firm disapproval, and I got the sense he was the kind you didn't want to cross.

Of course, Sally weren't the kind you wanted to cross, neither.

"What in all blazes were you thinking?" she demanded as she rounded on me. "Taking an afternoon stroll through town when you're currently the most wanted man in the Territories?"

I groaned and dropped my head into my hands, scrubbin' my palms over my face. "I needed to take a look around. No one saw me."

"Oh, someone saw you," the man over by the door said.

"And then you *shot them*!" Sally hissed.

"Well…" I looked up at 'em, both of 'em, one to the other.

"It was either that or let 'em take me to Mr. Miller, I guess. What the hell else was I supposed to do?"

Sally straightened. "Hrm, let me think. Perhaps *stay put*! Stay here, perhaps? Perhaps let me send my people out to take a look around *for* you like I'd already offered? Perhaps not go strolling about town in plain sight like an idiot!"

"I weren't in plain sight," I snapped. "I was careful enough."

"*Not* careful enough," the man muttered. "You got seen."

"Not fer most the day," I said. "And I handled it."

Sally put her fists on her hips, her eyes narrowin' to slits.

I hadn't seen that expression aimed at me from a woman in a long, long while. I swallowed and shifted my seat on the edge of the cot, droppin' my gaze to my hands. Goddamnit. Why was I feelin' guilty over this?

"You didn't make sure those fellas you shot were dead," the man by the door said into the resultin' silence. "Livin' fellas can still talk. You want them tellin' the law who shot 'em?"

"They don't *know* who shot 'em," I countered. "Not fer sure. I shot 'em before they could *be* sure. That's the whole point. And anyway, why would they do that? If they want to collect that money, they gotta get me themselves, not send the law after me."

It was good enough reasonin', but neither the big brute nor Sally seemed to think it acceptable. Their stormy expressions didn't lighten at all.

I released a heavy sigh and prodded at the new lump on my left temple. "Why do you care what happens to me, anyway? My life ain't no concern of yers."

"I guess it ain't," Sally admitted. "But unfortunately, Mr. Lynd, as I've told you before, some of my business is in rescuing people. Which means, even more unfortunately, I have to live with the curse of caring what happens to strangers." She paused, then clarified. "The ones who ain't complete bastards, anyway." She turned away from me, goin' to her desk and pullin' out the drawer that held the whiskey bottle and two glasses. She uncorked the bottle and poured a finger into each glass. "And," she went on, "I live here. My livelihood is here. And if, Heaven forbid, you *were* to get carted off to Mr. Miller now, well … certainly he'd be asking you some questions before he executed you."

"Lots of questions," said her man by the door. "Under *extreme duress*, mind you."

Sally nodded and threw back one of the whiskeys before immediately pourin' another. She handed the second glass to the goon, who took it with a touch to his hat brim.

I couldn't help but notice she did not offer one to me. That guilt squirmin' around in my gut intensified.

"And under such conditions," Sally said, lookin' to me again as she leaned back against the desktop, "you might be inclined to tell him all about what you saw last night."

"Which wouldn't be too good," her man said. He tossed back his own drink.

"Not good at all," Sally agreed. "So. Please understand now the importance of keeping yourself safe while you're here, if you have to be here at all. Please understand the importance of *listening to me* in this regard, considering I know this town and its residents backwards and forwards and inside out. I realize now I should have been more to the point when we talked earlier today."

I lifted an eyebrow at her. I'd thought she'd been quite to the point already, myself.

She set down her second glass of whiskey and straightened off the desk, lookin' me square in the eyes, her face deadly serious. "So I will be as clear as I can possibly be now, Mr. Lynd. While you are here as my guest, under my protection, you will not leave the Seven Knives Saloon again unless you come to me first and arrangements are made for you to do so. If this proposal is distasteful to you, I will have someone retrieve your horse, and you can take your leave of this establishment and this town. Agreed?"

I looked at her steadily fer a minute, but her glare didn't waver. She didn't even blink. I didn't much like the thought of leavin' here, and not just because of her good whiskey and good food and good whores. And I most certainly couldn't take my leave of Blessing. Not yet. So I hissed out another breath and nodded, shiftin' my gaze over to the room's single window, which still had its curtains drawn. "All right," I muttered. "All right." My hat was sittin' over on the end of the cot, and in its absence, I raked my hand through my hair and then over the stubble on my jaw. I'd been so preoccupied with Nora and Nettie last night I'd completely forgotten to shave. "Fine."

"Then you agree to these terms?"

"Yes," I spat. "Yes, goddamnit, I agree."

"Good." She stopped starin' me down and turned to her man by the door. "You're the witness to Mr. Lynd's agreement of these conditions."

"Absolutely," he said.

I scowled and pushed myself up standin', then grabbed up my hat. "Don't need no witness," I said. "I'll do what I say I'm gonna do."

"I'm sure that's true," Sally said, and I noted some of the steel had gone out of her voice. She picked up the glass of whiskey from her desk and handed it out toward me. "So let's start again, Mr. Lynd. Let's start with *why* exactly you felt it necessary to venture out about town when you're currently the most wanted man in the Territories?"

I eyed the glass in her hand, aware that if I took it, she'd expect full honesty outta me. Not that I had to meet those expectations, of course, but I was already feelin' awful bad about slippin' out of the saloon and I weren't even entirely sure why. And she still didn't even know my real name.

I hesitated. Put my hat back on my head.

"He was watchin' the Baron Haas residence, mostly," the man by the door supplied at my continued silence, and I shot him a glare.

"I can speak fer myself," I growled. I snatched the glass from Sally's hand, mostly to cover my alarm at the fact he'd clearly followed me all afternoon and I hadn't seen him even once. He was awful stealthy fer such a big fella. "And who the fuck are you, anyway?"

He drew himself up, as if he needed to be any taller or bigger, and hooked the thumb of his empty hand into his belt. That's when I noticed the huge knife hangin' there. Sally and her people sure had a thing fer knives. He lifted his chin, lookin' down his nose at me. "Name's Bill. Bill North."

"He's my right-hand man," Sally said.

"Yeah?" I swung my gaze back to her. "He always go around knockin' out yer guests?"

Now Sally crossed her arms, and one of her eyebrows arched. "Only the difficult ones."

I grunted. Shot another glare over to Mr. Bill North, then threw back the whiskey Sally had handed me. "Yeah, I was watchin' the Baron Haas residence. He's got somethin' goin' on there soon, looks like."

"He does," Sally said, her tone suspicious. She uncrossed her arms now and glanced over to her right-hand man. "A showcase of his Old World finds, and an auction … for interested parties…" She turned toward me again, her dark eyes bright. Intense. "You an interested party, Mr. Lynd?"

I shifted under that sharp stare of hers and handed her back my empty glass. Then I paced over toward the far wall, toward the window. This room was too small, with too many bodies in it. It was startin' to feel claustrophobic. "I might be," I admitted. "He might have somethin' I need in there. In his house, I mean." I tucked my fingers under the edge of the curtain and pulled it back, just a sliver, peekin' through to the outside. The window looked out onto a narrow street. It was full dark now, though I couldn't quite tell the time. Yellow light from a few electric street lamps illuminated the far end of the alley. "I'll need to get in there. Somehow. Have a look around."

Bill gave a snort.

I let go of the curtain and stepped back from the window, glancin' over at him and Sally. They were both watchin' me, skepticism written all over their faces.

"I thought you said you weren't going after another baron?" Sally said.

"I ain't. I'm goin' after somethin' he's got. And I … I don't…" I paused, considerin' the cost of bein' fully honest. Maybe I could just keep on bein' *mostly* honest. "I don't exactly have the means to pay fer it."

I left it at that. Let 'em figure out the rest of it fer themselves.

Sally and Bill glanced to each other again.

Then Sally grabbed up the whiskey bottle and poured herself some more. She sat back against the edge of her desk and studied me. "You want to steal from Baron Haas?"

I shrugged. "If he's got what I want."

"*That's* your urgent business here? *That's* why you risked your life coming back here?"

I supposed it didn't sound too reasonable when you put it like that. But they didn't know about Ethelyn. Or about Nine-Fingered Nan. When you considered those two factors, it all made a lot more sense. But I didn't exactly want to share that part of it, so I only nodded. "That's right. There's a deal I made … a trade I've arranged… fer this thing Baron Haas has got. And in return, I'll get back somethin' real important to me."

Sally's eyes narrowed.

Behind her, from his station at the door, Bill shook his head.

I stood under their scrutiny, lettin' the silence stretch, and forced myself not to fidget. I hoped Sally wouldn't ask fer more details.

She didn't. Instead she stated flatly, "Someone's blackmailing you."

It was the last thing I'd expected her to say, but her words hit me nearly as hard as Mr. North's fist, and I felt like she'd somehow knocked all the wind out of me. I stood there gapin' at her like a fish, and couldn't find no words to say in return.

Unease prickled up my arms and under my collar at bein' so easily read. Denial flooded up my throat, but Sally lifted her hands and shook her head before I could speak.

"No, no, it's all right. You don't have to tell me. I've seen enough of it to know how it goes. I've seen that … look … on people's faces more times than I care to count. I know it ain't easy. I'm … I'm sorry." She swallowed her second whiskey and sighed. "All right. So you want to steal from Baron Haas. Can you say what, exactly, you're hoping to take?"

I breathed out long and slow, tryin' to slow my heart, relief washin' through me at her understandin'.

And now I felt even worse about sneakin' off this afternoon … about betrayin' her trust. She'd already done so much fer me … and was continuin' her kindness even still. She hadn't deserved my previous brusqueness. Didn't deserve my unhappiness with her conditions of my stayin' here. Didn't deserve my mistrust.

My throat felt like cotton as I tried to swallow and wet my lips. "A lockbox," I croaked. "A specific lockbox. Old World."

"Hmm." Sally twisted around to look at Bill, but he only shrugged.

"Don't look at me, boss. That old stuff is your wheelhouse, not mine."

"Hmm." Sally turned back to me. "And it's one of the pieces on display at his auction, then?"

"I … don't know fer certain."

She managed to look both surprised, dismayed, and discouraged all at once.

"It weren't where it was supposed to be," I clarified. "Weren't where I was told it was at first. But then I heard it was supposedly back here, at the baron's estate." That's what that Professor Morton had said, anyway. And he'd said it was a piece he and the Queen of Canada herself were interested in, too. And I'd seen him there, at the Haas residence, just today. It had to be there, surely. Ready fer this auction the baron was havin'.

"Hard to plan a robbery if you don't know the location of what you're trying to steal," Sally said.

"Yeah," I growled. "Yeah…" I paced again, back and forth in front of the window. And then it occurred to me I knew someone who had been inside that house, and just today.

I stopped pacin' abruptly and swung around to face Sally and Bill, a plan coalescin' in my mind all at once and dullin' the headache pulsin' in my temples. "I know someone who would know," I blurted. "And he's here, in town. Saw him this afternoon at the baron's place. I'll get him to tell me where it is."

And then I'd pay him back fer all the trouble he'd caused me. Pay him back fer leavin' me tied to that boulder. Fer gettin' me arrested and thrown in jail and nearly hanged. Fer takin' my guns.

Satisfaction warmed my insides at just the thought of it.

"Hmm," Sally said again. She straightened from her desk. "We'd best be quick about it then. That auction is happening tomorrow evening. Doesn't leave a lot of time to plan." She put the whiskey bottle and the glasses back in their drawer as she glanced to her right-hand man. "You take care of those fellas Mr. Lynd shot?"

"And left alive?" He looked pointedly at me, but I only scowled back at him. "Yeah. I took care of 'em. They won't be doin' any talkin' to no one."

"And no one saw you bring him here?"

"Nope. Put him in the wagon, covered over with canvas. No one was the wiser."

Well, that explained how I got back to the saloon, as undignified as it was. My scowl deepened.

"Good," Sally said. "What's the name of this fella you have in mind, Mr. Lynd?"

"Morton. Professor Christopher Morton."

"Do you know where he's staying?"

"No. But he shouldn't be too hard to find. He's a foreigner. Come all the way from Canada. Dresses fancy. Thinks himself awful important."

"All right." Sally moved over toward Bill and put a hand on his arm. "Go find this professor, would you? Bring him back here. And keep it *quiet*."

"You got it, boss." He turned fer the door.

"Wait." I stopped him as he reached fer the knob.

He looked over his shoulder at me and lifted an eyebrow in question.

"If he's got a pair of gun belts on him, or in his room, will you bring those, too? They're mine."

Now both his eyebrows lifted. He looked to Sally, who frowned, but then nodded. At his boss's approval, Bill shrugged. "All right." He stepped out and shut the door behind him.

That left just me and Sally in that cramped room. She stood over there by the door, lookin' across at me like she wanted to say somethin', but she weren't entirely sure what. In the quiet, the piano music carried over through the walls from the main room, and the general murmur of voices. Sometimes a shout or a burst of boisterous laughter.

I rubbed at the back of my neck and cleared my throat. "Thank you. Again. But I hope you ain't doin' all this just fer me."

She gave me a soft smile. "No, not *just* for you, Mr. Lynd. Don't you worry your pretty self none, I got my own reasons, too."

I nodded. "All right, then. And … I'm sorry. Fer … slippin' out. I just ain't very used to gettin' other folks involved in my business." 'Cept Holt, of course. He'd been involved in enough of it. And complained about all of it enough. "Don't like it much, to be honest. Involvin' other folks, I mean."

"We all have our flaws, Mr. Lynd. But I don't got no love for those barons, you know that by now. So I surely don't mind helping you rob Baron Haas. But we're going to have to be careful about it." She tilted her head to one side, lookin' me over. "You got any money on you?"

I dropped my gaze and sighed, suddenly afraid my wanderin' off had gotten my free stay privileges revoked. "Naw." What little I'd had before startin' off on this venture was still in my saddle bags in Sonoita.

"Well, you can do some work for me around here then to pay me back. You're going to need some new clothes."

XVIII

BY INVITE ONLY

Sally had Ginger bring us more whiskey and some supper, and we stayed holed up in her office while she laid out her initial idea fer pullin' off this robbery. She suggested goin' in herself, as an interested party, lookin' to buy some of Baron Haas' pieces.

"I think we can get you in, too," she said. "Now that you've cleaned up, and with a change of clothes."

I eyed her doubtfully across my emptied plate. "You want me to just … walk in the front door?"

She sat back in her chair. "Both of us. Yes. Baron Haas surely doesn't care about Baron Whittaker's murder. If anything, it helps his own position in town. He won't care about that bounty on you, if by chance he's studied those posters hard enough to think you familiar. Though I'd be willing to bet he hasn't paid those posters any mind at all. And the only reason anyone else around here is interested in that bounty is because they want that money. The people who will be at that auction, though … they won't need that money. Even a reward as high as the one on your head right now won't catch their interest."

I leaned forward in my chair, pulled up in front of her desk. "*Fifty thousand dollars* won't catch their interest?"

Sally shook her head.

I let out a low whistle. "Goddamn."

"So, yes. I propose we walk in through the front door. I'll pose as the interested party, and you can accompany me as my manservant."

"Yer … what now?"

"My manservant." She poured me more whiskey. "My servant."

I straightened in the chair.

"I'd suggest you could pose as my husband," she said, cuttin' me off as I opened my mouth, "but those manners of yours are a little too rusty to pass for that, I'm afraid."

I opened my mouth again.

"Unless you happen to know the proper way to address someone of greater or lesser social standing than yourself? The acceptable and unacceptable subjects of casual conversation? And possibly, how to waltz?"

I shut my mouth and sagged back in the chair.

"Didn't think so." She pushed the refilled glass of whiskey toward me. "We should probably say you're mute, as well."

I pursed my lips and growled in displeasure as I reached fer the whiskey.

"I thought you'd be relieved. Useless small talk is unbearably boring." She rolled her eyes and picked up her own glass. "This way, all you have to do is stay by my side and play dumb. Least until we spot that lockbox you want."

I mulled that over, and decided she was right. She was right about all of it. I didn't have the manners or the etiquette to fit in with a crowd of people who couldn't be bothered to take an interest in fifty thousand dollars. Didn't have a hope of even pretendin'. I sighed heavily and nodded. Scraped a palm over the stubble on my chin. "All right. Fine. I play dumb till we find that lockbox. Then what?"

She shrugged. "That … we'll have to figure out once we have more information from that Professor Morton you mentioned."

"You think your man will find him?"

A slow smile pulled across Sally's lips. "Oh, absolutely. Don't you worry about that."

And so we waited for her man Bill North to return with the professor. Sally excused herself to her quarters to rest while she could, and suggested I do the same. But there weren't much chance I'd be able to sleep, nor did I much feel the need, so I occupied myself by pacin' around the office some more, studyin' again the various items Sally had stashed there, and worryin' about steppin' foot in a baron's house.

It was nearin' dawn, by count of the pocketwatch on Sally's desk, when a hushed commotion sounded from outside in the hall. Anticipation jolted through me and drove out the weariness that had started to weigh down my eyelids. I turned from the window, where I'd been peerin' out, watchin' fer the rise of the sun, just as I heard someone knock on the door of Sally's quarters that faced the hall.

I held my breath. Heard her footsteps cross the room, the door creak open, muffled voices. Then the door shut again, and her footsteps came toward the joinin' office door. I straightened as it opened.

Sally swept through, clad now in a cream-colored dressin' gown with ruffles at the end of the sleeves and a low neckline. She'd loosed her hair, and it fanned out around her face wild and full, little ringlets fallin' toward her eyes.

I had opened my mouth to confirm Bill had found the professor, but my words got lost at the sight of her.

She didn't seem to notice, pausin' just inside the door to look right at me. She opened her mouth too, but then paused, takin' in the sight of me, I supposed, fully dressed with my hat and boots and gunbelt still on and everything. She huffed a sigh, but then said, "Bill found him. Got him in one of the boarding rooms meant for the girls' business. I'll…" She glanced down at herself. "I'll get decent and show you where."

I nodded, and she stepped back into her room.

Didn't take her long to get decent, and she emerged a few

minutes later in her customary blouse and skirts, though I noticed she hadn't bothered with a corset. She led me out of her office and down the back hallway to another row of doors. Bill stood outside one of 'em, arms crossed and lookin' smug.

He nodded toward the door as we approached. "He's in there. All trussed up for ya."

"Thank you, Bill," Sally said. She turned to me. "I suspect you'd like to be the one to question him?"

"Yes." The word hissed out with more force and enthusiasm than I'd intended.

"Oh yeah," Bill said. He uncrossed his arms and held one huge hand out toward me. Coiled in his fist were my two belts, with my two pistols in the middle of 'em. "Found these in his room. They yours?"

"Yes," I said again, and relief eased some of my coiled muscles to see somethin' so familiar. I took off the borrowed belt right then and there, in the middle of the hall, and put on my own, and havin' 'em back brought a strange sort of peace down around me. They fit just right, and the weight was balanced proper again, and I knew just how many bullets were tucked into those loops.

...unless the professor had fired any. I checked 'em over at that thought, doin' a quick count, and pulled the guns from their holsters to give 'em a careful look-over, too. If he *had* tried to fire 'em, who knew if he'd taken proper care of 'em after.

But they looked just the same as the last time I'd seen 'em, and none of the cartridges were missin' from the belts.

"You done?" Sally asked.

I startled, havin' almost forgot her and Bill were standin' there. Then I cleared my throat, heat risin' up under my collar, and nodded. I handed off the stolen belt to Bill.

He took it with an annoyed expression. "The hell am I supposed to do with this?"

I shrugged. "I don't care. Sell it if you want."

He muttered and grumbled at me, but I ignored him, squarin' off to face the door.

Sally stopped me from bargin' in with a hand on my arm. "We'll need to know if Baron Haas has what you're after in the first place, of course," she said softly. "But also, where it is inside the house. And how many the baron has employed to watch over his valuables while his guests are there. And the layout of the place, if possible."

I frowned. "That's a lot."

"If you want me to do it—" Bill started.

"No," I snapped, glarin' at him over my shoulder. "No. I got it."

He shrugged. "I'm just sayin' I got lots of experience with gettin' people to talk."

Somehow I didn't doubt that. Or the fact he also had lots of experience knockin' people out. But I was gainin' plenty of experience askin' people questions myself of late. I moved my right hand to the knife on my belt and drummed my fingers against its sheath. "So do I," I said, and then I swung open the door and stepped into the room before either he or Sally could say anythin' else.

And I closed the door behind me. Locked it.

And turned to see Professor Morton tied to a wooden chair in the middle of the room.

Or … there was a man tied to a chair in the middle of the room, but he had a burlap sack over his head. So I couldn't exactly tell if it was really Professor Morton or not. The room didn't have much else in it 'cept a small bed and a night table, and it was lit only by two oil lamps … one hangin' by the door, and one on the little table.

At the sound of my entrance, the man struggled against the

ropes and tried to say somethin', but I couldn't understand him. Clearly, he'd also been gagged.

Rollin' my eyes and scowlin', I crossed the room and yanked the sack off his head, tossin' it to the floor.

The man blinked, pale and sweatin', and his eyes got real, real wide when he saw me.

It was Professor Morton, all right.

He yelled somethin', but all his words were muffled into the neckerchief that had been shoved into his mouth and tied around the back of his head. He struggled more, makin' the chair creak. He had no shoes, and wore only a long, white nightshirt. A puddle of wetness spread in his lap as he pissed himself.

Well. Maybe this would be easier than I'd thought.

I ignored the pool of urine collectin' on the floor at his feet and pulled my knife.

He yelped, strainin' at the ropes.

"I ought to kill you here and now," I growled.

He shook his head vigorously, again tryin' to voice his protests through his gag. His eyes pleaded with me, wild and desperate.

"We had an agreement," I said, low and dangerous. Made it sound like I fully intended to carve him up real good. And a part of me wanted to, fer certain. I'd nearly ended up hanged because of him. Certainly come closer to it than ever before, even in all my years runnin' and robbin' with Holt. No one had ever gotten as close to bringin' me to justice as that Sonoita sheriff. "We had an agreement, and you just left me there. Left me to die."

He protested that statement, too, and I was sure he was tryin' to say he *didn't* leave me to die, he'd sent that sheriff back to retrieve me. But it was as much a death sentence as havin' just left me tied to that boulder, so I ignored his efforts to explain himself.

"*And* you stole my goddamned guns." I circled around

behind him and took a fistful of his thinnin' gray hair, pullin' his head back and lookin' down into his terrified face. "And that … that makes me real, real sore, especially. Last people who tried that … well, I murdered 'em. Left 'em to rot in the desert." And so I had. A man called Clint and his sonuvabitch friend. That seemed like a long time ago now, though it hadn't quite been two months since, in truth.

I brought up my knife, and the blade glimmered in the lamp light. The professor stiffened in the chair, his face gone deathly pale, hardly breathin'. He squeaked a little whimper.

"You want to die today, Professor?"

He squeezed his eyes shut, tears leakin' through his lashes, and shook his head as well as he could with my fist in his hair. He mumbled more nonsense.

I made a show of considerin', lettin' the silence draw out till he started tremblin'. "Well," I said finally, "there *is* somethin' you might be able to do fer me. Somethin' that might convince me not to murder you."

His eyes shot open.

"I need that lockbox, Professor."

He slumped in the chair and closed his eyes again, and whatever he tried to say next came out all high and whiney.

"What was that? 'Fraid I couldn't understand you. I know you were over visitin' with Baron Haas today. Saw you go into his house, I did. So? He got that lockbox like you thought he did?"

More mumblin'. Frantic. Clearly wantin' that gag outta his mouth.

"All right, Professor. I'm gonna take that gag out fer you. Then yer gonna answer my questions, or I'm gonna make you bleed. Understand?"

He stared wide-eyed at me, and sweat slid down his temple. But then he gave a nod.

I released his hair and pulled the neckerchief out of his mouth.

"Please don't kill me!" he blurted immediately. "I didn't leave you to die, I sent that sheriff back right away, and he got you to town before—"

I slapped him, good and hard across the face, and he cried out as the chair rocked. Truth be told, I wanted to punch him right in the nose fer what he'd done, but I got the sense he didn't have the strongest constitution, and I didn't have time to be sittin' around waitin' fer him to regain consciousness.

"Stop talkin', Professor. Unless yer answerin' my questions. I told you, I ain't gonna kill you if you tell me what I want to know. Got it?"

He nodded weakly, head hangin', hunched in the chair, and tears dripped off his nose.

"Good." I grabbed the back of his chair and turned him to face the bed, then sat down on the edge of the mattress. I kept my knife bare, turnin' it around in my hands as I glared at him. "Does Baron Haas have that lockbox? The one I want, with the dials?"

He made no answer.

I sighed. I didn't want to have to get blood on Sally's floor. "Professor." I slapped the flat of the blade against the top of his knee and he jumped as if I'd gone ahead and stabbed him. "Thought you said you knew how this worked?"

Silence. He stayed bent over with his eyes squeezed shut.

"Professor. Look at me."

Slowly, he cracked one eye open. Lifted his head incrementally.

I stared evenly into that one open eye of his. "I will bleed you out right here and now if you don't answer me. You think I won't?" I pointed at my own self with my knife-free hand. "Look at my face. You see how serious I am? I swear to God I'll do it. So

I'm gonna ask you one more time. And you better fuckin' answer me. Does Baron Haas have that lockbox?"

He was heavin' now, maybe tryin' to hold back sobs. But he gave the slightest nod of his head.

Relief surged through me, almost makin' me light-headed. I closed my eyes and exhaled a long, slow breath, lettin' myself soak in that feelin'. Lettin' myself appreciate somethin' goin' right fer once. But then I shoved it all away, back down deep with everything else, and opened my eyes again to glare at the professor. "All right. Good. That's better. Next question. Where's he keepin' it? Where's he gonna put it durin' that auction of his?"

Professor Morton opened his other eye, and his throat bobbed as he swallowed hard. "That piece ... that piece is critical to scholarly pursuits. Isn't there anything else you'd rather take, instead? Anything? Baron Haas has some very nice pieces ... I can give you an inventory of everything I remember..."

I shook my head. "Just want that lockbox, Professor."

He hesitated again, glancin' toward the door. He worked at his wrists, tied together around the back of the chair, but that Mr. North was experienced with knots, too. Morton gave an exasperated huff. "But ... but like I said ... it could be the greatest discovery of our time. You can't just ... you can't just *take* it..."

"Sure I can."

He lifted his head a little more now, squintin' at me through the glow of the nearest lamp. "Is it money you want? If you're just looking to sell it ... I have the Royal Treasury backing me, you know. I had intended to buy it from Baron Haas. Tell me what you're being offered for it. I'll match that price and add ten percent more."

I snorted laughter.

"Twenty percent more, then."

I tried to swallow back the laughin' and shook my head

again. "Professor, there are plenty of other, easier things I could be doin' to get money, if that's what I wanted. But no. This ain't about money." *Fer once.* "This is about that goddamned lockbox. So I need you to tell me where the baron is keepin' it."

There was another short silence, and I could almost see him thinkin', strugglin' fer a way to save both the subject of his scholarly interest and his own skin. "Who do you work for, then?"

I groaned and scrubbed a hand over my face. Fer a man who'd been blindfolded and gagged and dragged out of his room in the pre-dawn to end up here, tied to a chair, and who'd pissed himself at the first sight of me, he sure was persistent about protectin' that lockbox.

"Arrange a meeting for me with them," he went on. "I'll offer *them* the money. Then you can keep whatever other arrangement you've got with them. I'll make it worth your while," he insisted. "I'll make it worth *their* while. I swear it."

I'd had enough of this. Time was wastin'. I stood from the bed and he shrank back into the chair. "I'll just cut off a few fingers, then," I said. "You don't need all ten anyway, do ya?" But even as the words left my mouth, I remembered those fingers Nan's crew had thrown at me in the desert outside of Bravebank, and felt suddenly sick.

I braced myself against the back of the professor's chair, not hearin' whatever pleas he was currently babblin'. A sour taste rose to my mouth and I had to swallow back bile. Three fingers they'd thrown at me. One fer each of the three men I'd killed in the Stag Saloon. Three fingers I'd thought at the time were Ethelyn's, but instead they'd belonged to some other poor girl. Another young woman who'd died needlessly because of Taggert's cruel treachery.

She'd died in my arms, and I'd never even known her name. She was buried out there now, at the base of the Bone Spur

Mountains. Nothin' more than a pile of rocks. Nothin' more than a nameless grave.

I sucked in a harsh breath, strugglin' back to the present, strugglin' out of the memory of her warm dark eyes goin' cold, starin' up at the sky.

And then I didn't want to maim Professor Morton anymore. Didn't want to make him bleed. Not even fer leavin' me fer Sonoita's sheriff, or fer stealin' my guns.

"Surely we can talk this out!" he nearly shrieked, unaware of the fact I'd just lost my motivation to murder him. "We can come to some kind of arrangement, some kind of agreement!"

I took another minute to regain my composure, still standin' behind him like I meant to follow through on my threat of choppin' off some fingers. Maybe I didn't have the stomach fer that anymore, but I *did* still need that lockbox.

If I had to do it…

I hoped I wouldn't have to do it.

"Why would I want to make another deal with you, Professor?" I forced out the words before I could lose my resolve. Wrestled down the tangle of feelin's jumpin' around in my gut as I reached down and tried to pry one of his fingers free of his tightly clenched fists. "Nope. No more deals, Professor. You just decide if your scholarly pursuits are worth dyin' for … and decide quick-like, mind you."

I managed to wrench out the pinky finger of his left hand and held it fast.

He struggled hard, rockin' in the chair, yammerin' in a panic, talkin' so fast I could hardly sort what he was sayin'. Wasn't nothin' I wanted to hear, anyway. So I brought my knife blade to the base of his pinky, but only gently touched the edge to his skin. "How many fingers is it gonna take, Professor?"

I pressed just a little harder. Clenched my teeth against the wave of nausea. Braced myself to cut through that little bone.

"All right!" he barked. "All right, all right! Stop! Stop, God damn you, I'll tell you!"

I let out my sigh of relief slow and quiet, so he wouldn't hear it. But didn't remove the knife from his finger. Not yet. "Well?" I prompted. "I'm waitin'."

"It's … it's in his safe! Where else would he keep it?"

"What about the auction? He gonna keep it in his safe fer the auction, too?"

"Yes!" He twisted, tryin' to look at me over his shoulder. "For most the time, anyway … he's not putting that piece up for sale with everything else! He's holding a private auction for it later in the evening, by invite-only … I went to his residence today to try and work out a deal for it myself. Alas, his greed has blinded him. He refused my offer, said I had to bid on it like everyone else!"

I scowled at this news, and Professor Morton yelped as the knife pressed into his finger a little too hard, drawin' a line of blood. Wincin', I lifted the knife a space.

"I'm telling you the truth!" he said. "I swear to God that's the truth!"

"So … yer tellin' me he's keepin' that lockbox in his safe until it goes up fer sale itself?"

"Yes!" He was almost sobbin' now. "Yes, that's exactly what I'm saying!"

"And this invite-only auction … where's that gonna happen?"

"In his cellar! But no one can go down there unless they've been personally invited by the baron!"

I contemplated this development. Maybe it weren't all bad ... Baron Haas would have to take it out of the safe eventually, after all. And move it down to the cellar where the auction would be takin' place. "And these invites you mentioned," I said, "you got one?"

"Yes! Of course! Baron Haas knows I am the envoy for Her

Majesty, and he knows I'm backed by the Royal Treasury! Like I said, he is blinded by his greed. It wouldn't surprise me at all if he arranged this auction just to force me to pay through the nose for it ... much more than I could have offered him for it without such stiff competition ... and he also knows the queen will pay almost anything for it. He may have wealth and power here ... but he's a damn thief just like the rest of you!"

I grunted at his assessment. He'd meant it to be an insult, I was sure, but that didn't mean it weren't the truth. "Well, Professor," I said, and I sheathed my knife, movin' around to the front of him again. I hooked my thumbs in my belts as I looked down at him. "I might have a deal fer you, after all. You give *me* that invite of yours. And you pen a nice letter to Baron Haas, and you tell him you've been indisposed, but are sendin' along those you trust to act in your stead as far as acquirin' that lockbox, and those you trust are them that's holdin' that letter. You do those things, and I won't murder you. Agreed?"

He only looked up at me with wide, terrified eyes, and shuddered in revulsion.

Well, I felt the same about him.

XIX

DRESSED LIKE A TURKEY

I put the gag back in the professor's mouth and left him there, tied to the chair, while I stepped out into the hall again and told Sally and Bill what he'd just told me, about the private, invite-only auction and all. Then I told 'em my thoughts about gettin' the professor to give me his way in, and havin' him write a letter to explain it.

Sally looked thoughtful fer a minute. "Did he happen to say how many were invited to this private auction?"

I shook my head. "Naw. But I think I've softened him up. Sure he'll answer any other questions we got, if you want me to ask."

She pursed her lips, arms crossin' over her body like she were tryin' to hug herself.

"Boss," Bill said quietly, "you don't gotta go in there. You got no obligation."

His words took me by surprise, and I realized then her stance coulda surely been one of discomfort rather than contemplation. I didn't want to press her, not when she'd not demanded to know more about my own business here … but I also weren't gonna ask her to go into Baron Haas' place if she didn't want to. She'd done enough kindness fer me already, and I'd gotten enough people hurt by draggin' 'em into my trouble.

"He's right," I said. "You don't owe me nothin'. If anythin', I'm still in debt to *you*. I can do this myself."

Sally gave a little laugh. "No offense, Mr. Lynd, but I don't think so."

I straightened. "I can do it my way. With my guns and some dynamite. Forget all that invite nonsense."

She looked at me, her eyes shiftin' briefly to my right bicep, where she'd seen those scars earlier. "And what did I say before, Mr. Lynd? When Mr. North here had to knock you senseless and bring you back in the wagon to clean up your mess? I know this town. I know these people. That ain't the way to do this … not if you want to live through it. Subtlety is better here, trust me. And I might not have an obligation to you, true. But I *do* got an obligation to … others. I'll go." She straightened her shoulders and smoothed at her skirts, liftin' her chin. "*We'll* go. I'm overdue to call upon Baron Haas, anyways."

"You … wanna do more than just take that lockbox?" Bill asked. "Maybe burn his house down like Baron Whittaker's?"

Sally seemed to consider the notion, and I remembered her organization of black-clad, knife-wieldin' associates. If she'd wanted to do somethin' like that, surely she could … and have better success at it than I had, likely.

But she shook her head. "No. Not that. They'd put the town under lockdown if another baron got attacked so soon after the Whittaker incident. All of us would suffer. No, I'm thinking something more subtle. Maybe take back some of what should be mine in the first place."

Bill nodded, like he knew exactly what she were talkin' about.

I hadn't the faintest idea what she might be referrin' to, but again, I didn't want to press. So I pushed down the feelin' of bein' left out of a conversation and tried to contribute to the plannin'. "The private auction will be in the baron's cellar," I said. "Which is gonna make it harder to get in and out of. Seems the entrance will be guarded. Only those with invites let down."

Sally shook her head. "The private auction's no good. Not enough exits, and not enough people. We take the lockbox from there and Baron Haas will question everyone who was present till the end of time, or until he gets his treasure back. Such an exclusive event would mean he'd know exactly who was there, which would make his pool of suspects much too small for my liking."

Bill nodded in agreement.

I frowned. "Well then … how we gonna get it? Professor says it'll be locked in a safe till that auction, and if you don't want me blowin' stuff up…"

"We'll have to grab it while he's moving it," Sally said. "While it's going from the safe toward the cellar."

I considered the notion, but that didn't seem no better than the close confines of the cellar. "Won't there be more people around who might see us grab it, then?"

Sally shrugged and glanced to the lamp on the wall behind me. "Not if we make it hard to see in general."

Bill and I both followed her gaze, but it was Bill—again—who caught her meanin'.

"Electricity," he said.

My frown deepened. "How's that gonna help us get the lockbox out?"

The giant man smiled. "The baron's house runs on electricity. It's all wired."

I still didn't see how that could help. Lotsa wealthy, fancy folk had electric houses. "So?"

"So…" He shoved that stolen gunbelt back into my hands and then started to pace, one big hand fisted on his hip and the other in the air, index finger extended, wavin' around with each point. "Electricity is all connected to a central point. We cut that connection in the right spot, all the lights go out. Everywhere, all over the house."

"That … just might work," I admitted.

"When the lights go out, we grab the box," Sally said.

"What about us?" I asked. "We gonna be able to see to grab the lockbox in the first place? And find our way out? And what about his security? I saw an awful lot of armed individuals gettin' instructions over there."

"The dark won't be a problem for us," Sally said. "I got a way around that."

"A way around it?" I repeated, incredulous. "The dark ain't somethin' you just ... get *around*."

Bill snorted, and Sally gently patted my cheek. "It is for us, Mr. Lynd. You'll see soon enough."

I frowned at that statement, but then remembered how she'd slipped around in those dark woods like it was the middle of the day, and figured that was true enough, indeed.

"As for his security..." she began.

"We need a distraction," I said, seein' the glint in Bill's eye and wantin' to beat him to it this time. Of course. Of course that's what we needed. Seemed there was always need fer a distraction with this kinda thing.

"Yes, that would do it," Sally agreed.

"Dynamite?" I suggested.

Bill snorted. "That yer answer to everythin'? Blow it up?"

I glared at him and crossed my arms, shruggin'. "It's worked fine enough before."

"Not dynamite," Sally said gently. She put a hand on my arm, as if tryin' to ease the sting of Bill's derisive tone. "Too destructive. We'll need something disruptive, but that won't cause too much damage. Like I said ... we don't want the barons getting *too* cautious. Things are already hard enough around here after Whittaker's murder." She paused, then added, "As much as I appreciate his absence from this world, we need to be careful about how this plays out."

Bill paced again, both hands on his hips now.

I considered. Disruptive, but not too damagin'? That meant no fires, and no dynamite. Which were generally the most disruptive things you could get 'round these parts. Outside of that … maybe a buncha loose horses or cattle? Weren't a lot of cattle around here, though. Horses could work, I supposed…

"I got it!" Bill said, loud and sudden enough to give me a start. He clapped his hands together with his epiphany. "Firecrackers!"

I grunted in amusement. "Thought you were against explosives?"

His enthusiasm dampened at my question and he frowned. "Never said I was against explosives … this just ain't the time to be blowin' stuff up, is all. Firecrackers make a lot of noise. They'll draw attention, but not destroy nothin'."

"*If* you know how to use 'em," I countered. "You know how to use 'em?"

"Damn straight I do." He drew himself up and puffed out his chest, hookin' his thumbs in his suspenders. "Fair near an expert with 'em, I am."

Sally smiled at him, then turned to me, confirmin' his boast. "I do have Bill set some off every year, on the anniversary of the Seven Knives opening."

"We have a whole celebration," Bill added. "Whole town loves it. Well … most the town, anyway."

"True enough," Sally said. "And it's a good idea. It will sound enough like dynamite to cause concern, bring people running to see what's happening."

I nodded and did a little pacin' of my own. "So … we cut the electricity, grab the lockbox, set off the firecrackers, and get out while everyone's flounderin' around in the dark in a panic. That about right?"

"That's about right," Sally said.

"Sounds like a good time to me," Bill said.

I stopped pacin' and faced the two of 'em. "All right, then. Now we just gotta figure out when he'll be movin' it, where his safe is, where the cellar is, and what path he'll be takin' in-between so we know where to be."

"The *when* will be on that invitation," Sally said. "And I'm willing to bet he'll wait to move it till real close to auction time. But we'll want to be ready early, just in case."

"Leavin' the *where*," I said.

Sally and Bill looked to each other.

"Rose," Bill said.

"Rose," Sally agreed.

I was startin' to get real tired of feelin' left out. "What the hell does a rose got to do with this?"

"Not *a* rose," Sally said.

"A person," Bill offered. "Rose is a person. The Haas' housekeeper."

"Rose is my contact at the Haas residence," Sally said.

I blinked at her. "You … you got a person in there?"

Sally granted me a smile. "Well, *I* didn't put her there. She was already there. I only took advantage of an opportunity and created a mutually beneficial arrangement. As I said before, Mr. Lynd, I got eyes and ears all over this town. Rose will know where that safe is, and where the cellar is. I have a good idea she'll also hear wind of the route Baron Haas plans to take that lockbox in-between."

I straightened, tryin' to absorb the implications of this information. "And yer sure you can trust her?"

"Oh yes," Sally said without hesitation. "Absolutely." She stepped past me to lock the door of the professor's room and then looked back to Bill. "Could you head on over to the Haas residence? Check things out yourself and speak to Rose so we can straighten out all the particulars before tonight?"

Bill gave a nod. "Sure thing, boss." He touched the brim of

his hat, then ambled off down the hall, toward the saloon's back door.

Sally looked to me then, and I stared down at her. "He's just gonna go over there and have a chat with the housekeeper? And the baron won't think that odd?"

She let out a little grunt. "He won't even know. He doesn't keep track of all his servants' daily doings. That's Rose's job. She makes daily morning rounds around his grounds, anyway. Her and Bill have chats on the regular. And the baron is none the wiser."

"Huh."

"As for you," she said, lookin' me up and down, "we'll need to get something for you to wear. They'll never let you in looking like that, washed or not. I'll have Ginger fetch something. In the meantime," she took the extra gunbelt out of my hands, "there are dirty dishes in the kitchen that need scrubbing. If you'd be so kind? High fashion don't come cheap."

The notion didn't sound appealin'—scrubbin' dishes *or* wearin' high fashion—but I surely weren't gonna let Bill and Sally go to that auction by themselves, and I owed Sally more than a few hours of scrubbin' dishes by this point, anyway. So I only nodded myself, and gave her a wry smile. "Sure thing, boss."

I would rather have scrubbed dishes fer days than wear what I was wearin' now.

Ginger slapped my hand away from tuggin' at the collar. "Stop that. You're gonna get it all folded over!"

I didn't think that was possible, not with how heavily the shirt had been starched. The high collar hugged my neck uncomfortably close, its top edges cuttin' into the underside of my jaw if I moved my head too awful much. "I can't breathe," I muttered sourly.

"Nonsense." She moved to the front of me and straightened the gold bowtie from where I'd knocked it askew.

That was too tight, too. Felt like a noose. Felt like I was standin' on the gallows, about to be hanged. Instead, I stood in front of a full-length mirror that had been brought into Sally's office, bein' dressed and attended to by Ginger, while Sally was off gettin' ready herself in her quarters, attended to by another of her saloon staff. Bill had done his scoutin' and come back with a full report, then gone and retrieved the professor's things, so we could fish out that invitation. He'd been left in charge of Professor Morton then, usin' his intimidatin' figure to convince the man to do as we instructed.

It was approachin' evening, approachin' time to leave fer the baron's fancy auction, and I was wishin' I'd gotten more sleep than the few hours I'd managed earlier in the afternoon, after scrubbin' all those dishes. And I was wishin' I could think of a different way to get that lockbox now, too.

Goin' in with guns and dynamite blazin' sounded like a mighty good plan right about now. Anythin' would be better than sufferin' the torture of spendin' hours in this ridiculous outfit.

Ginger fussed about me, tuggin' at the jacket's hem, brushin' out its long sleeves, adjustin' the lay of its tails, givin' the toes of my shiny new shoes one last polish.

That was another thing. The shoes pinched my natural foot somethin' awful. Fer once I was glad that metal left foot couldn't feel nothin'.

The shoes sure were shiny, though. Shiny and black.

The navy blue trousers were pressed into crisp lines, the vest pale gold with a paisley pattern, and the jacket navy blue too, with a satin gold linin', and the same satin gold trim on its edges.

It was embroidered with flourishes in gold thread at the cuffs, around the standin' collar, and over the shoulders. Its two tails went down to my knees in the back, and it had three big, gold buttons in the front, which Ginger was now fastenin'. Or tryin' to.

"Would you hold still?" she grumbled.

"It's too small." It was all I could do not to rip it all off. Felt like it was squeezin' me. Couldn't bend my joints properly. Couldn't look around properly.

"Oh it is not. It's just that it's tailored to fit you proper."

"Well it don't fit. I can't fuckin' move. Can't fuckin' breathe."

"You come up with a different plan fer gettin' this thing you want, then? 'Cause I wouldn't object to Sally not goin' into that place, I have to say."

I glared at my reflection in that tall mirror. "Sure. Shoot 'em up, blow open the safe. Sounds good to me."

Ginger scoffed and shook her head. "Don't think so, Mister. That'd end bad fer all of you. And I don't want the boss to end up dead."

I only grumbled more.

"Just be thankful you ain't a woman," she said as she finally finished with the buttons and straightened. "How'd you like to be put into a corset and a bustle?"

"I wouldn't."

"All right then. So shut yer trap." She took a step back and admired the results of all her fussin'.

I looked over it, myself, in my reflection. I stood stiff as a board, scowlin' heavily, but admittedly, the costume made me look almost like a whole different person. I'd had a fresh shave, and they'd put pomade in my hair to make it all shiny, too, and slicked it back. The gold of my vest and jacket almost matched its dark blonde color, and without my hat to shade 'em, my eyes stood out more, lookin' an even darker shade of brown against all the shine on me.

"My my!" Ginger exclaimed. She nodded her approval. "If you ain't careful tonight, you might just come home with a wife!"

"Ha." I tried to shake my head. "That's the last thing I need."

Ginger arched one grayin' eyebrow. "On the contrary, Mister, I think that's the exact thing you need."

I was gonna argue with her further, but she turned away and moved fer the office door.

"You just wait here," she said. "I'll go see if the boss is ready yet."

She took her leave, and then I was left alone, standin' in front of the mirror in those awful clothes.

It took awhile longer fer Sally to get dressed, but when she was, Ginger came back to retrieve me, and we all met in the narrow confines of that back hallway. And I nearly choked when I saw Sally now.

If Ginger thought I'd find a wife dressed like this, well then, surely Sally would be comin' home with a husband. Or at least, any available man would be trippin' over himself to gain her notice. And maybe even those men who *weren't* exactly available.

She stood straight and regal, shoulders back, chin tilted slightly upward, clad in a dress of black and white. The bodice looked almost to be a black jacket worn over a white blouse, with sleeves to her elbows that ended in ruffles and black-and-white striped pleats, and a row of tiny black buttons all up her front. The buttons that should have closed the high collar of the dress up tight had been left open … exposin' the hollow of her throat. And despite the fact her regular-worn blouse often left more than that visible, my gaze stuck there at the base of her throat, unexpected feelin's rousin' in me.

Maybe it was the way the corset and bustle flattered her figure, which I supposed musta been the purpose of 'em to begin with. But she made a sight, all right, the striped pleats along the bottom half of her gown creatin' a mesmerizin' pattern as she walked. The main skirt of it was black, but all the layers of her bustle were striped like the pleats, and my eyes kept goin' there, too.

She wore a woman's black top hat, pinned slightly askew atop her oiled, ironed curls, and white gloves on her hands.

She paused when her eyes found me, and despite the intense displeasure I felt at bein' dressed up like a turkey, I didn't mind at all the way her gaze brightened at the sight of me. Or the faint flush I saw spread across her cheeks.

Maybe tonight wouldn't be so awful, after all.

"Oh my," she said, comin' to stand near, lookin' me up and down with an appraisin' eye. "Don't you look just positively *dashing*."

The brilliance of her smile made me wonder if sufferin' these clothes was maybe worth it. "Uh..." I shifted stiffly in my shiny, uncomfortable shoes and cleared my throat, strugglin' to sort my tumblin' thoughts. "I mean, er, thank you kindly. And ... and you look ... very nice, yerself."

Good Lord, good thing I was gonna be a mute this evening.

Her blush deepened, and she glanced down at herself, brushin' at the front of her bodice. "Why thank you ever so much, Mr. Lynd. You are too kind." Then she hitched up the right side of her skirt high enough that a flare of alarm went through me, questionin' her intentions, and questionin' more my ability to stay focused with her showin' so much leg. But then I saw the row of little knives strapped around her thigh there, and a flare of somethin' else entirely went through me.

"I'll have these on me all night," she said. "In case we run into any trouble. They won't allow weapons on the premises. At least, not any they can see." She flashed me a grin and winked.

"Just be careful in there, boss," Bill said quietly. He'd dressed up a bit, himself, clad in his best suit fer the occasion, bein' as he was gonna be our coachman. It weren't much compared to the duds me and Sally wore, but apparently it were good enough, considerin' he'd be stayin' with the coach all night. As fer Professor Morton, he was gonna stay here, tied, guarded, and under lock and key until we could finish our business at the auction.

Bill looked to me then, and I could read the warnin' in his hard, dark eyes as easily as I could read those disapprovin' looks Holt liked to give me. *You better not get her killed.*

I had a good idea Sally would fare better than me inside that baron's residence if things went sideways, given her familiarity with the populace and those knives strapped to her thigh, but I dipped my chin in acknowledgement to him, anyway. Nothin' was gonna happen to her, or even to him, in this endeavor if I could help it. I had enough lives on my conscience already.

He switched his gaze back to Sally. "You ready?"

She took my arm, and I could smell her perfume again, subtle and sweet. "Shall we?"

I nodded. Mute already, it seemed.

And so we went, the three of us, and boarded Sally's coach. It weren't nothin' too fancy, but was passable, Sally said. I still didn't understand any of this. Why we had to wear these clothes, or why it mattered what type of coach we arrived in, or why the coachmen were expected to wait hours and hours fer us while we were inside.

Not that I particularly minded that last bit, though, really. Havin' a ride waitin' outside ready to go in case anythin' went wrong before our planned departure was some small reassurance. Especially since I couldn't have my guns on me. They were up top, with Bill, hidden away. Along with a rifle, and pistols fer Bill and Sally too, just in case.

Later in the night, closer to the time we'd be makin' a grab fer the lockbox, another of Sally's employees would bring us some horses up this way, and have 'em waitin' out back of the baron's house. One horse fer each of us was faster than a coach, and that way we could split up, and lessen the chance of any possible pursuit bein' able to follow. That same fella was also gonna be the one to cut the electricity, right after he dropped off the horses. That way Bill had time to set up those firecrackers, and could be waitin' to set 'em off soon as he saw the house go dark.

It seemed like a good enough plan.

Seemed like it could work.

Now, inside the coach, Sally and I sat across from each other on the cushioned benches. And these clothes were more awful to sit in than they were to stand in. And they were hot. Sally had a hand fan at least, but I didn't have nothin'. And the closer we got to Baron Haas' residence, the more I was sweatin'.

Not just because these clothes didn't breathe, or because I didn't have my guns, or because I was suddenly havin' all kinds of doubts about our plan ... but because I kept thinkin' about the last time I'd gone to one of these baron's residences.

And how horrifically everything had gone wrong.

"Are you all right?"

Sally's soft voice pulled me back from the nightmarish memories, but it took me another minute before I realized she was askin' at me.

"You're awfully pale. Are you feeling unwell?"

"No." I shook my head, then pulled at that damnable high collar around my neck again. It was damp with sweat. I shifted on the seat and tugged at the bottom of the jacket, too, tryin' to swallow. My mouth was too dry. "Just ... these damn clothes don't fit right. I tried to tell that woman of yers—"

"Ginger?"

"—I tried to tell her it was all too small..."

Sally smiled and reached over to pat my knee. "You look very debonair, Mr. Lynd. It all fits just as it should. You'll be all right." In the coach's swayin' lantern light, shadows slid back and forth across her face. "Now remember, as my manservant, your goal will be to remain as invisible as possible. Unless it's to perform one of those duties we discussed earlier, stay by my side at all times. Shouldn't be too many people speaking to you, but if anyone *should* start a conversation with you, just give them the sign for mute. You remember it?"

"Yeah." That part was easy enough, at least. A closed fist at the lips, essentially. It was all the other things that were gonna be more difficult. And the *waitin'* was gonna be the hardest part of all.

"And please, don't fidget."

It was like she could read my thoughts.

"A restless servant will stand out something awful. Raise suspicion and make people wonder what kind of Lady I am and what kind of household I run."

I swallowed back the groan. "You sure we can't just shoot up the place and blow open the safe? Sounds like it might be easier…"

Sally lifted her eyebrows. "No. You'll be fine. You can do this." She leaned toward me, takin' my clenched fist in her gloved hand and pryin' open my fingers to give my palm a squeeze. "I have faith in you."

I opened my mouth to tell her that was a stupid thing to do, but the coach rolled to a stop in front of the Haas residence then, with its pristine wooden fence and bright blue and yellow banners. It was nearly dark now, and the glow from all its many windows lit up the night. Soft music drifted from the open front doors. Two men in tuxedos stood at the open fence gate, so motionless and expressionless they could have been statues.

Was that how I was supposed to act all night? Fuck me, this was gonna be the longest night of my life.

Sally jolted me from my musin's with a light smack to my knee and cleared her throat loudly. "The *door*."

"Shit, right." I stood from my seat and started to move past her to open the coach door for her, but she caught my arm.

"Don't be stumbling across my lap!"

"Oh, right. Sorry." I turned to disembark through the coach's left door and stepped down rather clumsily in all my stiff, tailored clothing. My hand went to smooth at the breast of my jacket, feelin' at the subtle outline of the strange glasses currently tucked into that inside pocket. Sally had given 'em to me to wear when all the lights went out. Said they'd help me see in the dark. I didn't really understand *how*, but I wanted to be sure they were still there, anyway, before I stepped into that big house.

They were, safe and sound, so I went around the back of the coach, tryin' to straighten my posture and adopt the same expressionless look as the two men in tuxedos as I came within sight of 'em. My heart pounded under that gold vest and starched shirt like I was goin' into a stand-off. I took in a deep, slow breath to calm it, and pulled the coach's right door open, then stepped back and offered up a hand.

Sally reached out to take it and smiled gratefully as she stepped down herself, a good deal more gracefully than I had done despite her corseted bodice and layers of bustle. Then she went on, and I shut the coach door and gave a salute to Bill, who nodded and clucked at the horses to move on to … well, wherever the hell he was supposed to wait.

I turned to follow after Sally as another coach rolled to a stop behind us. I was sweatin' again, but the two men in tuxedos didn't even seem to notice me, and I quickened my pace to catch up with my *employer*.

It was a long walk, and as we neared the front porch I saw

two more tuxedoed men, only these two were armed. They glanced over the two of us as we approached, and I sorely missed the weight of my pistols at my hips. But they only gave a nod to Sally and said nothin', made no move to stop us, as we stepped inside the place.

I squinted in the brightness of all the electric lights. The foyer was as big as most houses I'd seen, and a glitterin' electric chandelier in the top middle of it threw little rainbows down over everything below: walls, furniture, flowers, and people alike.

Another man in a tuxedo appeared in front of us so suddenly I startled. "No weapons allowed on the premises for tonight's event," he said. "If you have any on your person, I can take them now. They'll be returned to you upon your departure."

Sally gave him a gracious smile. "We have none, thank you."

"Very well. Any coats, hats, parasols, then?"

"Thank you, but no."

"Very well. The main auction is in the grand ballroom." He pointed the way with a white-gloved hand. "Other pieces are on display throughout the lower level, which you are free to peruse at your leisure." Now he made a grand, sweepin' gesture with the same hand. "The upper levels, however, are off limits. The baron requests that you respect his privacy. Anyone found wandering there will be asked to leave. I'm sure you understand."

"Most certainly," Sally said.

Asked to leave? That's it? Not thrown out? Or escorted out at gunpoint? Or tied to a chair and branded with the end of a hot prybar? This Baron Haas fellow sounded almost kinda reasonable.

Or maybe this was just how he treated those folk who had enough money to buy his trinkets.

Sally gave a delicate clearin' of her throat and stepped closer to the tuxedoed man. "And what about … the *other* auction? The one taking place at precisely nine o'clock?"

The man's eyebrows lifted and his dull gaze sharpened a bit. He seemed to regard Sally now with a whole different kind of interest. "Ah. Yes." He turned crisply on his heel to point down the wide hallway that stretched before us. "You will find the entrance to the cellar off the main kitchen. Straight through here, then your third right and first left."

"Thank you ever so much," Sally said.

Third right and first left. I repeated it to myself a few times and wondered if I'd actually remember it by the time nine o'clock rolled around. This whole place looked like a damn maze, with room after cavernous room all connected by wide, open doorways, and people movin' constantly through all of it.

"Do enjoy your time here this evening," this man in a tuxedo said. And then he was gone again, off to give the same speech to the next set of guests arrivin'.

"This way," Sally murmured to me over her shoulder. "Stay close." She made off toward the direction of the grand ballroom, and I made sure to follow close, all right. If I lost her in this sea of madness, I weren't sure I'd be able to find her again.

But it was hard to keep my focus on her, even with as radiant as she was lookin' this evening. There were a great many other ladies here in similar dress, and all the colors and feathers and jewels—and bosoms—were rather distractin'. The gentlemen in attendance, too, were all done up in suits and tuxedos and silk vests and more of those ridiculous neckerchiefs … er, no … cravats, they was called, or somethin' like that. Fancier than a neckerchief, they said.

But they sure just looked like neckerchiefs to me.

And in-between 'em all were the servants, or, if they were Baron Haas' people, more likely slaves, done up similar to me, but in varying colors, offerin' trays of drinks in tall, narrow glasses and little pieces of food no bigger than a bite. And those from the baron's household all easily identifiable from the same cut of their tuxedos … sharp and well-tailored, but subtly more plain than those of the guests.

If all the people here weren't overwhelmin' enough, there were all those other *pieces* on display as we meandered through room after room. More Old World tech than I'd ever seen before by far. All so strange lookin', full of dials and gears and tubes. Enclosed in locked glass cases. And all under one roof.

I gawked at 'em as we passed and tried to ignore the uneasy feelin' they settled in my gut. Was my metal leg really like these tarnished, rusted things? Old World?

Like somethin' from those bedtime stories and fairy tales … from a history so long gone no one could rightly remember it anymore?

I almost felt like I could hear my leg whirrin' suddenly beneath my pressed trousers, and thumpin' with each step in those shiny shoes. I was still limpin' … always limpin', but at least it weren't so obvious anymore.

Weren't nothin' more than a mild lurch to my step these days, somethin' like an old injury not quite healed. Not enough to draw much notice.

I hoped.

We arrived at the grand ballroom at last, and I almost forgot this was the same house we'd entered into at the foyer. Seemed we'd walked fer miles, and I'd already lost my bearings.

There was a stage at the front, set with a table, and upon the table were lined up even more Old World pieces. Some of 'em no more than a random part. Some of 'em a great deal more complex. Some of 'em made me think of that gun Charlotte had lifted from Baron Whittaker, and I wondered how much somethin' like that might fetch at an auction like this.

Maybe I should consider sellin' it…

There were couches set up along the edges of the room, and ladies sat on some of 'em, attended by their servants. More tuxedoed men stood at the entrance, holdin' fistfuls of little paddles with numbers printed on them.

"Will you be bidding tonight, ma'am?" one asked as Sally paused in front of him.

"I will, indeed."

"Here you are, then." He handed her one of the numbered paddles.

Sally nodded her thanks and aimed straight fer one of the couches, and I trailed after her. I went back to tryin' to be expressionless, like those gents out front.

It was more difficult than I'd expected, given the nature of this room, its occupants, and the items up fer auction. I kept bein' inclined to stare, and my mouth kept droppin' open … either from surprise at seein' somethin' so over-indulgent treated as if it were somethin' regular, or 'cause I was gonna say somethin' before rememberin' I was supposed to be a mute.

"Why, Ms. Wellman," came a man's voice, silky smooth in that false-pleasantries kinda way, "what a surprise to see you here."

I nearly ran into Sally's back as she halted abruptly, and only then did I realize the man was referrin' to *her*. To Sally.

And the man doin' the referrin' was Baron Haas, himself.

XX

BEST LAID PLANS

I recognized him from that photograph Nine-Fingered Nan had given me of him and his lady wife standin' next to that coach. And now that I saw him in person, up close, I realized it had been him I'd seen the afternoon before, givin' instructions to all those armed folk. He had his lady wife with him now, too, and she stood at his elbow in a shimmerin' green gown, drenched in pearls. She was smilin' toward Sally, but she also had that soft, pityin' look about her that I didn't much like.

"Didn't think you had the stomach for these old relics anymore," Baron Haas was sayin' now. "After the … *accident*."

Sally's face had gone cool, carefully controlled like all the folk runnin' around here in those identical tuxedoes. She pulled a fan from her sleeve and snapped it open with a flick of her wrist, then managed a smile and a small curtsey as she lifted it to her face. "Baron Haas," she said by way of greetin'. "Lady Haas. What a pleasure to see you again."

Again? I remembered how she'd mentioned somethin' about it bein' past time to call upon Baron Haas, and my stomach tightened. I wished I'd have gone ahead and pressed her a little then, found out exactly what she were talkin' about. The way the baron and his lady wife were lookin' at her now was a bit too familiar fer my likin'. If they all had some kinda history, it woulda been nice to know more about it.

"My dear, it has been far too long," Lady Haas said. "You really should come and visit more often!"

Sally's smile thinned. "As your husband mentioned, Lady Haas … I got out of the business, I'm afraid. But rumor has it you have some exceptional pieces up for sale this evening. I must admit, curiosity got the better of me. I could use a fresh relic or two for my establishment. You know the kind of draw they have to the … baser population."

The baron smiled, too, then, but it looked genuine. He was tall and thin, not nearly the imposin' figure Baron Whittaker had made, and his hair was full gray and recedin'. He could have been the perfect picture of a kindly grandfather, if I hadn't known better.

"Indeed we do," he said. He seemed about to say more, but then paused and looked over to me.

I straightened as his gray eyes found mine, and realized I'd been starin' at him.

No, not starin'. *Glarin'.*

His gaze narrowed, and I remembered belatedly I weren't supposed to be makin' eye contact with any of the fancy folk. I dropped my own gaze quick to the floor, cursin' myself. My shoes were so shiny I could nearly see myself in 'em. And the floor as well, which I now noticed was highly polished pink marble.

"Your man have a problem, Ms. Wellman?" Baron Haas asked Sally, and his genial tone had gone as cool as Sally's expression.

Shit. If I'd screwed all this up just 'cause I'd forgotten where I was supposed to be lookin'…

"No, Baron, he does not," Sally said. "But I fear he is new to the position. He's a fast learner though, I'm certain of it. That, or he'll soon be looking elsewhere for employment."

She put an edge in her words that was real enough. Maybe I weren't really her manservant, or her employee, but it was a warnin' nonetheless. A warnin' to remember the instructions she'd given me before we'd come here, or we might be asked to leave, and then our whole plan was nothin' more than horseshit, and I'd be hard-pressed to get that lockbox.

"I see. Seems he could do to learn some manners."

I tensed at that, wishin' I could show him just what kinda manners I had, all right.

"I believe he was just leaving to fetch me a drink," Sally said, facin' me then. "Something with bubbles. Go on now."

I usually didn't take too kindly to people orderin' me around like that, but I had a disguise to maintain, so I kept my eyes downward and gave a crisp nod, hurryin' along to do her biddin'. It was a relief, anyway. I mighta strangled the baron with his ridiculous cravat if I'd stayed there much longer.

As it were, I was free now … free to do some lookin' around on my journey to find Sally a bubbly drink. A big part of me wanted to go pokin' around the rest of the estate. Maybe find that safe. Maybe see if someone could open it fer me. But that was a stupid idea, and I discarded it as soon as I thought it.

I was dressed as a servant, and had not a single weapon. Weren't no one here who'd be convinced to do such a thing fer me. So all I did was hunt down that drink, which proved to be more of a challenge than it shoulda been.

Those waiters with the trays and the drinks kept movin' around, and they were clearly used to manueverin' around such large groups of people. Me, on the other hand, I weren't so used to it. And I had to be real careful not to bump into any of those fancy folk. Sally had warned me doin' that woulda been real, real offensive to 'em, apparently.

But, finally, I managed to wave a waiter down and grab up one of those tall, thin glasses. Didn't know what it was, but it had bubbles, just like she'd asked. Relieved, I turned to head back toward Sally … and then froze.

I weren't in the grand ballroom no more. I was in some other room. Smaller, but richly furnished, heavily decorated, and lined with a great number of things worth stealin'.

Holt and I coulda lived a lifetime off only a few of the items in Baron Haas' collection. Forget robbin' banks. Robbin' barons looked to be a far more lucrative option. And maybe easier, too.

Maybe. We'd see about that.

But first … first I had to figure out how in the hell to get back to Sally. Somehow, in my pursuit of this damned drink, I'd gotten myself all lost and turned around. *Goddamnit.* I wanted to say it out loud. Wanted to say a good number of things out loud right then.

But Sally had said swearin' was frowned upon here, too. And anyway, I was supposed to be a mute.

These fancy folk weren't no fun at all.

I bit back the urge to vehemently voice my frustrations and inhaled, instead. Then released it and willed myself to stay patient, stay calm. I started back in the direction I thought might be right, but as I went, the number of people I encountered dwindled, and I got the strong sense it weren't the right way at all.

And then, then I ended up in a kitchen. Waiters and cooks bustled about, readyin' all those drinks and all that bite-sized food.

Well shit. This surely weren't the right spot. I turned to head back the way I'd come and try a different route, but a low voice stopped me.

"Lost, are we?"

I looked over to see a man leanin' up against the kitchen wall, a lit cigar in one hand. He weren't no waiter or cook, surely. Not from the look of his black suit. His vest was silver, his cravat a snowy white. I remembered this time not to look him in the face, but he seemed vaguely familiar in my brief glimpse at him, anyway.

"Or maybe you were hoping to lift a thing or two off the premises?" He arched one black eyebrow at me, blue eyes accusatory. "Sneak away while no one was looking?"

My throat closed up, but I managed to shake my head so vigorously my starched collar chafed at my chin. He couldn't have known our plan to steal the lockbox, no way … but it was entirely possible he might mistake me fer a servant wantin' to snatch somethin' else. Anythin' else. There was surely plenty to snatch around this place, if I'd wanted.

He grunted and straightened from the wall. "I've told Edward countless times these ridiculous events of his are just asking for trouble. But does he ever listen to me? Of course not. No one ever listens to me."

He weren't much older than me, and not much bigger … maybe a little broader across the shoulders, is all, but there was somethin' ominous about his words. Somethin' about the way he purred them out, hardly more than a whisper. He stared at me with a hard, unblinkin' gaze that made my skin crawl. The intensity of it burned into my skin like that hot prybar Baron Whittaker had branded me with, and I stepped backward. I gave a hasty little bow and turned, hopin' fer a quick exit.

"Stop."

It was more than the word that made me go rigid. It was the way he said it. I'd heard that voice before. That cruel and commanding tone.

Baron Whittaker.

My skin went cold, and sweat slid down my temple to my throat to soak into that high collar.

"I didn't dismiss you, yet."

I just stood there, my back to him, stiff and motionless. I felt I should turn around to face him, but I couldn't get myself to move. My fingers gripped the stem of that glass so hard I thought I might snap it. That's why he looked familiar. He had his father's hair, and eyes, and nose. The new Baron Whittaker. He must have been.

"Just who do you belong to, anyway? I don't recognize you … or your colors. Usually see the same people, over and over, till I'm just bored to tears. But here you are … a fresh face … and sneaking around. How curious."

I shook my head again, managed to take a half-step around to face him. Lifted the glass as if in explanation.

The activity of the kitchen went on around us, though none of its other occupants seemed concerned in the least with our conversation. I weren't sure what the protocol was here, or what I could expect. I suspected none of the other people in this kitchen would care much what happened to me, long as it didn't trouble them or their duties none.

The new Baron Whittaker tilted his head. "Well? I asked you a question. I could take your silence as insolence, you know. Doubt your master would be very pleased to hear about that."

I swallowed back my retort, heat stingin' my face at my inability to currently act against these bastards. I decided I liked this one just as much as I'd liked his father … which was not at all. Least I'd be upsettin' their party here later, and stealin' that lockbox … long as I suitably managed to get out of this current conversation, anyway.

I made myself give him another bow, deeper this time, suspectin' he liked bein' groveled at, and put my fist up to my lips to show him I was mute, instead of sendin' it right into his chin, which is where I woulda much rather have put it.

His flat, even stare didn't change at my signalin'. "Ah, I see. Isn't that a shame? But not uncommon, for those in your position. There are not many places for mutes in this life, are there?" A corner of his mouth quirked, and then he came to my side and threw an arm around my shoulders like we were old pals.

It was all I could do not to squirm out from under it.

He turned us toward the kitchen's exit, herded me through the doorway and back out into the wide hall.

I'd never tried so hard in all the time since I'd lost my natural leg to walk without a limp. If he noticed my uneven gait now, he didn't mention it.

"Well, it's no matter," he said. "No matter at all. I know how it feels to be set aside. Discarded. To be seen as … *less*. At least you were able to find a place for yourself. At least people like you can find a role serving those better than themselves. Not a bad job, all in all. My place, on the other hand, was taken from me."

His fingers tightened on my shoulder, the hard press of 'em almost painful even through my velvet jacket.

"Ripped away from me, just as I nearly had it within my reach." He extended the arm he didn't have around my shoulders, and the hand that held the cigar, and made as if he were grabbin' a fistful of air. Then he heaved a sigh, and shook his head.

I had no idea what he was goin' on about. Wondered if he might be a ravin' lunatic, in truth.

"But! There is more than one way to skin a cat, so they say. I'll find my way again. Just as you managed to find your way, despite your … disability. You managed to find safe and secure employment, didn't you? Indeed." He nodded to himself, not waitin' fer me to make any answer. "Indeed you did. And so shall I. So shall I take my rightful place, soon enough. They'll see. Think they'll listen to me then, friend?"

He was mad. He had to be. He weren't talkin' any kinda sense.

Didn't matter though, as he didn't wait fer me to answer, again. He just kept on talkin'. "I always say, open and honest communication is one of the most important things to have in a household. To keep it running smoothly, you understand. To know who you can trust … or not." He shrugged, his arm still wrapped tightly around my shoulders.

I searched frantically fer some escape, tried to think of some excuse to duck away, but we hadn't reached the rest of the guests yet, and without words, I was havin' a hard time thinkin' of how to do that.

"Many in my position would hire translators." He seemed oblivious to my discomfort. Or he was just ignorin' it. "If they needed to understand what their dumb servants were trying to say, I mean. To convert the language of signs into the language of words. But that seems … an excess, doesn't it? Why not just learn the language of signs yourself? Why take the risk of any important details being lost to such a translation? How can you trust a person you can't speak with, directly?"

I didn't know what he was babblin' on about, nor did I care. I only cared that we didn't seem to be goin' in a direction that led back to the main event. He pulled me over into a side room, smaller than most I'd been in so far, but no less furnished or stuffed fulla valuables. There was a sword here, in this room, in a glass case on a table along the right wall, and I wondered if I could get to it, if I needed it.

And if I could get to it … was it sharp enough to be of any use?

The baron released me, finally, and faced me, takin' a long draw on his cigar so that the end of it lit up bright and red. He blew the smoke out in a thick cloud, and smiled with his lips but not his eyes. "So, my dear lost soul," he said, "go on. You can tell me. Use your signs. I'm quite fluent in them. Tell me who you belong to. And why you were wandering around back here unsupervised?"

I only stared at him. Use my signs? What signs? The language of signs? I didn't know no language of signs ... Sally had insisted no one of any consequence would deign to hold a conversation with a servant such as myself this evening.

Seemed she had not considered this new Baron Whittaker. A dire miscalculation.

"Well?" he prompted after a moment. "Nothing?"

I ... tried somethin'. Wavin' my hands around, gesturin', movin' my fingers like I knew what I was doin'. Pointed back the way I thought the grand ballroom might be—though fer all I knew I was pointin' out back of the house—and to the drink in my hand.

His flat look grew increasingly incredulous.

He weren't buyin' it.

"My heavens," he said dryly, once my gesticulatin' had finished. "That is certainly no language of signs I've ever seen. Didn't your betters ever teach you the real thing? The standard? It's usually a requirement for your position ... and certainly a requirement for your type to join any baron's estate. You don't belong to a baron, do you?"

I shook my head, grittin' my teeth against his repeated use of that phrase: *belong to*.

"Mmm, of course you don't." His blue gaze narrowed, scrutinizin' me with a critical eye, and I tensed. Sally had also said no one of any consequence would take any notice of me in this servant's role, and yet here this man seemed very keen to learn everything there was to know about me. And if he really were the new Baron Whittaker ... he might have a personal interest in that circulatin' poster with my name on it. It was his father we'd murdered, after all.

How close would he have studied that sketch?

I waited, still as a statue, hardly darin' to breathe, wonderin' what I'd do if he recognized me.

"Well," he said at last, "let's just go on back to the grand ballroom, shall we? I'll escort you there, since you seem to be so lost. You can point out your master in the crowd, then we can have a talk with them about your many shortcomings." He held out a hand and gestured with his fingers, like I were some kinda small child who needed coaxin'. "Come on, now. This way."

It was all I could do to keep from scowlin' at him. Took all my willpower to keep my face smooth and expressionless as I stepped forward to obey. I only needed to make it till that private auction … only thirty more minutes. If I could just suffer this nonsense fer another thirty minutes, I'd have that lockbox.

And then I could get Ethelyn.

He could say whatever he wanted to me, say whatever he wanted to Sally, none of it mattered. Just so long as he didn't recognize me fer bein' the man who had murdered his father.

I drew up alongside him, and somethin' stung the back of my left hand. I yelped and jerked away from it, half the drink sloshin' out all over the nice embroidered cuff of my jacket. I did scowl then, not even tryin' to hide it, and glanced down to see a circle of reddened skin where it hurt.

"Well now," the baron said, "seems you've got a voice, after all."

I looked up to him sharply, startled by his statement. *Shit.*

He was grinnin' at me now, bitin' on his cigar. The glowin' end of it sure looked like that reddened circle on my hand…

My eyes narrowed as I realized what he must have done: touched that thing to me on purpose, just to see if I'd make any noise when I yelled. *Bastard.*

He took another long draw off it now, then exhaled the smoke at me in one long stream, makin' my eyes water. "And I know you can hear just fine. So why don't you answer me another question, friend. Why the ruse? Who are you, and why are you really here?"

I stared at him fer a minute, sortin' frantically through my options. And then I did the only thing that seemed reasonable at the moment.

I sent a left hook right into his jaw, hard as I could.

He surely weren't expectin' that, and it dropped him cold. His cigar rolled onto the carpet as he hit the floor and I crushed it out quickly with the toe of my shiny shoe. Then I shook out my fist, swearin' softly, and peeked into the hallway to see if anyone else were around.

They weren't. Wherever he'd taken me, seemed it were the unpopular part of the house.

But that served my purposes just fine, too.

I set Sally's drink down on the corner of the nearest finely carved, decorative table and hurried back to the unconscious baron. I was gonna have to work fast, and hope this part of the house would stay empty fer awhile longer.

And I was gonna need that sword.

By the time I managed to find my way back to Sally—after havin' retrieved her a fresh drink—I felt I'd been lost in this damn maze of a house fer hours. In the end, the string quartet had started up their soft music again, and I'd used that to eventually find my way back to the grand ballroom.

My heart was still racin' from my dealin's with that baron, lodged in my throat as I frantically searched the crowd fer Sally's familiar face. I was out of breath from draggin' the man's unconscious weight into a closet, and from wanderin' all over this damn place.

And I was sweatin' somethin' awful. We hadn't even gone after that lockbox yet…

I found Sally, finally, over by the couch where I'd left her—I glanced at the big pendulum clock at the front of the room—nearly forty minutes ago. Was that all it'd been? Well, she was still probably wonderin' where in the hell I'd run off to.

She looked as lovely as ever, speakin' with a trio of other ladies done up in ruffles and lace. They fanned themselves lazily, ignorin' the auction takin' place now on the stage, even though they all held those little paddles with numbers on 'em, too. Maybe they just weren't interested in this particular piece.

I drew up beside her, and she turned to me in surprise. I proffered the bubbly drink and gave her a nod, riskin' a look straight at her fer just a second, hopefully enough to convey the urgency roilin' around in me like those bubbles in her drink.

"*There* you are!" She smiled and took the drink, but to my dismay, made no attempt to dismiss herself from conversation with the other women. "I was beginning to wonder if you had gotten lost." She made it sound like a joke, and the other ladies giggled, but I heard the note of true concern in her voice. If only I could tell her the half of it…

"My *goodness*, Ms. Wellman," one of the women said, but she was lookin' at me. She was blond, with a great heap of curls piled atop her head, and dressed in layers of pink silk. She fanned herself vigorously as she spoke, her cheeks flushed nearly as pink as her dress. "But you certainly did find a looker, didn't you?"

I kept my eyes on the floor, but a flush started up my neck. I tried to ignore it. Tried to ignore the woman and the heat of her stare on me, too.

"That's right." Sally grinned herself and sipped her drink.

Goddamnit. Was she encouragin' this?

"Didn't take you as one to hire on servants," another of the women said. She had a rich umber complexion and wore a gown of deep blue. "Even if you did have the means."

I frowned and fidgeted, impatient, wonderin' if everyone in this place knew Sally already, wonderin' why she hadn't mentioned that durin' all our preparin', and wishin' they'd all just shut up and go away so I could tell Sally we might need to change up all those best laid plans…

Then I remembered I weren't supposed to fidget and quieted myself, though I felt I might break with the effort.

"Well," Sally said, "I make exceptions, from time to time. For certain purposes." She cleared her throat and lowered her voice. "You should see him *out* of his livery..."

I whipped my head up to stare at her, wide-eyed, and she winked at me.

The three women let out shocked gasps, then fell into fits of giggles behind their fans, and my bewildered stare turned into a glare.

Fuckin' hell. She *was* encouragin' this.

Sally hid her grin behind her fan, but her eyes shone above its lace-laden rim, laughin' all by themselves.

Glad she was havin' a good time at my expense, then. Meanwhile there was an unconscious baron locked in a closet somewhere rooms away, who was gonna be awful angry when he woke up. I tried to tell her as much in my expression, and gave the slightest of nods back toward where I'd come from while the other women were still distracted by thoughts of me unclothed, apparently.

Sally's brows twitched, and she sobered, and I hoped she'd finally gotten my unspoken message.

This whole bein' mute thing had turned out more complicated than I'd expected.

She cleared her throat again and dropped her fan. "Yes, well, thank you ever so much for the chat, ladies. But I fear it is nearly my time to bid, and I must turn my full attention to the task."

A chorus of understandin' pleasantries from the three women followed this statement, then a chorus of sickenly sweet goodbyes and promises to catch up another time, and then they all curtsied to each other, and I nearly forgot to bow to them myself, and they giggled and fanned themselves more, battin' eyelashes at me as they slid off with a rustle of silks.

Soon as they were out of earshot, I turned to Sally with my mouth already open, the urgency wantin' to explode outta me in a tumble of words.

But then I stopped myself.

Sally looked up at me expectantly, and all I could think was how she'd told me we had to be careful tonight. And her whole speech about her livelihood bein' here and all, and how she knew the folk of Blessing better than me, inside and out, and I swallowed all the things I was gonna tell her about hittin' Baron Whittaker and tyin' him up and stuffin' him in a closet.

I couldn't tell her any of that.

At best she might stab me with some of her knives, and at worst she might demand we high-tail it out of that baron's residence to make our escape before the other baron worked his way out of that closet.

And I couldn't afford either of those outcomes.

One of her eyebrows arched. "So? What is it?"

I shut my mouth. Shook my head. And tucked my left hand casually behind my back so she hopefully wouldn't notice the new, circular red burn on the top of it. "It's … uh … it's nothin'."

Her brown eyes narrowed. "You made me run those girls off for nothing? You sure? You seem awful agitated."

I shrugged and tried *not* to seem awful agitated. "Just … had a time gettin' that drink of yers, is all." At least I weren't lyin'. That bit was true enough.

"I wondered. Started getting a little worried, truth be told. Why don't you just stay close the rest of the night? Don't want you getting lost. Not much longer till that private auction, anyway."

I nodded and glanced at the clock again. Only fifteen minutes till that private auction now, in fact. My eyes scanned the rest of the ballroom restlessly, searchin' fer the angry, disheveled face of the man I'd hit. But I didn't see him.

Not yet.

I prayed he'd stay locked in that closet till the lights went out, at least. Fifteen minutes … that weren't so long, really. It was a big house. And I'd tied him good with the length of his own cravat. And gagged him, too. And pushed a chair up under the knob of the closet door. Surely that would buy us enough time to get out of sight, into that back hallway Rose had said would be the place to grab the lockbox … and then there'd be no lights.

And we could get out in all the confusion.

It would be fine. We could still do this. I inhaled deeply through my nose and willed all the nerves jumpin' around in my gut to ease off. "Rose ain't signaled you yet?"

Sally shook her head incrementally. "Not yet."

The housekeeper was supposed to send a waiter to Sally with a tray of tiny lavender cakes and "warmest regards from a dear friend", and that meant Baron Haas was about to move the box. That meant we needed to head directly to the hallway behind the main kitchen.

Meanwhile, when the baron got close enough to that hallway himself, Rose would signal out the kitchen's back window … out to the kid who was waitin' to cut the electricity. Somethin' to do with a candle and the curtains. And that would tell him it was time to turn out the lights.

Then … then it'd be time to do our part.

"Uh oh," Sally said suddenly, and I jolted from my broodin'. "*That* could be a problem."

All those nerves flared up fresh and new again at her tone. She was lookin' to some point over my shoulder, and I hardly dared to ask. "What?"

"The new Baron Whittaker is here."

XXI

LIGHTS OUT

Shit.

How could he have gotten free of that closet so fast?

I turned stiffly, bracin' myself, but I didn't see him. "Where?"

Sally stepped closer to me, murmurin' behind her fan. "There. In the front, nearest to the auction table. Speaking with the lady in the cream dress. Red vest, silver cravat. See him?"

I saw the man she referred to now, sure enough, but it weren't the man I'd punched in the face. I frowned. "That … *that's* the new Baron Whittaker?"

"Yes. I didn't think he'd be here … the barons don't usually socialize with each other unless they have to…" She glanced up at me, then turned her attention back to him. "I don't think he'll recognize you dressed like that, but we should try to avoid him, anyway." She sighed. "This will complicate things."

I didn't understand. The man she referred to bore some resemblance to the late Baron Whittaker, sure … his eyes, the jawline, the black hair swept back … but if *he* were actually the new baron … who in the hell had I just locked in a closet?

Things were gettin' complicated, all right.

"Come on," Sally said, jerkin' me out of my contemplatin'. "This way. We'll just wait near that hallway. Should be safe enough there; Baron Haas would never let that lockbox go to another baron if he ain't gonna keep it himself. Whittaker won't be going anywhere near that cellar. Nor anywhere where he might not be the focus of a great deal of attention."

I followed her as she made way fer the grand ballroom's exit, none too disappointed to put distance between us and Whittaker ... any Whittaker. And luckily fer me, Sally seemed to remember that butler's instructions on how to get there. In all the excitement since first arrivin', I'd plum forgot.

We reached the cellar soon enough, without incident, and it was easy to spot. Was a thick wooden door right off another kitchen—a different kitchen than the one I'd stumbled upon earlier. This one was, unbelievably, even larger and busier than the other one. A single armed man stood to the side of the big wooden door, lookin' bored.

We strolled right on by him, and he paid us no mind at all.

Just past the cellar entrance was the intersection with that back hallway. Sally paused there and fanned herself, glancin' down the hall in either direction. Bein' that this weren't anywhere near the main attraction, it was sparsely populated.

"*You!*"

The shout roared out over the general din of distant conversations, the light music of the string quartet, even the far away barkin' of the auctioneer in the grand ballroom, and startled everyone nearby. A ripple of gasps and shocked murmurs from the kitchen behind us followed it, and both Sally and I whipped around.

The hired man standin' outside the cellar slid his hand to his weapon.

I looked toward the source of the boomin' voice, and grimaced. It was *him*. Course he had to show up now. Course he couldn'ta waited even one more minute, just enough time fer us to get around that corner and out of sight.

He barreled toward me, and people cleared outta his way like he was some mad bull. He sure looked like some mad bull the way he was chargin', face twisted up in anger, eyes blazin', his once-neat hair now all mussed, his cravat missin', and a trickle of blood from the right corner of his mouth bright on his bruised chin.

Fer a heartbeat I was frozen, not knowin' how to react. The urge to draw and fire ran through me, old muscle memory by now, but I didn't have no guns on me. My hand twitched reflexively, but of course that did no good at all.

The hired man near the cellar stepped in front of us then, eclipsin' my view of the angry baron—or … whoever he was. "Go on now," he told me over his shoulder. "Go on about your business. I'll take care of him. He's not supposed to be here."

He didn't have to tell me twice. I didn't understand it, but I'd take it. I weren't one to argue a rare stroke of good luck. So I turned and ushered Sally around the corner and into the hallway.

Just before I rounded the corner myself, I saw a woman dressed in regular range ridin' clothes intercept that man I'd punched, and she looked just as angry. But her anger was directed toward the man makin' a scene and scarin' all the guests. Her long brown braid was familiar, and I realized she must've been the woman I'd seen Baron Haas talkin' to with the rest of his security out front that day I'd been lurkin' around town.

"Mr. Miller!" she barked. "I've told you, in no uncertain terms, you are not welcome here!"

My mouth fell open just as someone grabbed my arm and yanked me around the corner. Sally. She fair near pushed me ahead of her, and we hurried down the length of the hall to where it ended, with the narrow back stair to our left and a closet to our right.

Sally gave a quick look around to be sure we were alone, then opened the closet door and stepped inside, draggin' me in after her and then pullin' the door shut behind us so only a tiny crack remained to see out of.

I sagged back against the shelves of fresh linens and waited fer my heart to stop tryin' to choke me.

Mr. Miller? As in Mr. Charles Miller? The man who'd put up that ludicrous bounty fer me? Fer Chrissakes, I'd been standin' right there with the man! Lookin' him right in the face, walkin' with him, talkin' with him … or, bein' talked to by him. I supposed it was another stroke of good luck he hadn't recognized me at that point. I still didn't think he realized I were the one he wanted fer the murder of his pa … but it sure seemed he wanted me now fer hittin' him in the face. Probably didn't appreciate bein' tied up and stuffed into a closet, neither.

Hell, if I'd of known he was Whittaker's bastard instead of the new Whittaker baron, I mighta just slit his throat with that old sword instead of only usin' it to cut up his cravat. Coulda saved myself a whole load of trouble and sleepless nights that way.

"Did she say Mr. Miller?" Sally hissed. "As in … as in *Charles Miller*? The bastard?!"

"Don't rightly know," I whispered back, breathless. "Couldn't hear her too well myself." That was a lie. The woman's voice was nearly as loud as Miller's had been. But we were too close to gettin' that lockbox. I weren't about to let it all fall apart now.

Muffled shoutin' carried through the kitchen, the hall, and the cracked closet door, but I couldn't make out any words. I wondered if Mr. Miller would tell the woman or any other hired security what had happened, and if Haas' people would believe him if he did. Or if they'd care at all. I figured a servant layin' a hand on any of these uppity folk wouldn't be tolerated … but if Baron Haas didn't want Miller here in the first place, and if Miller were a bastard child instead of a legitimate son … well, maybe no one here would care what'd happened to him.

I could only hope.

"Was he looking for *you*?" Sally asked. "Did he recognize you? How is that possible? He's not even supposed to be here!"

"He didn't recognize me," I said, and I hoped it were the

truth. At least in relation to the part about murderin' his father. Hittin' him in the face was another story, but I still didn't want to tell Sally about that part. "Don't think he was even talkin' to me just then. Musta been meanin' someone else."

I couldn't see Sally's expression in the dark of that closet, so I couldn't be sure if she believed me or not. But she said nothin' else fer a space, and we only stood there and waited, listened, and I held my breath, wishin' like hell I had a weapon.

The shoutin' moved off, grew fainter, and I dared to exhale, slow and quiet.

"Well," Sally whispered. "That was close."

"Yeah…" In the absence of a clear threat to my health, the ridiculous fact I was wedged into some wealthy baron's linen closet became suddenly apparent. "Ain't never stole nothin' before by hidin' in a closet," I muttered.

Sally gave a snort of dismissal. "Better than chance a confrontation at this juncture."

Well, she was probably right about that. I checked again for the outline of those slim glasses in my jacket pocket, but of course they hadn't gone nowhere since last I'd checked.

"You remember the plan?"

I scoffed. "Course I remember. You sure yer boys will come through? And Rose?"

She let out a little sigh, close enough in the tight confines of that closet that I could feel the puff of her breath against my cheek. "Of course. They've never let me down."

Must be nice to have people so reliable. "So Rose'll still signal when to cut the lights?" I pressed. "Even if she realizes you ain't where yer supposed to be to receive her warmest regards?"

Sally put a hand on my arm, maybe tryin' to reassure me. "Yes, Mr. Lynd. We made it clear. The lights go off no matter what. That way, even if we have to improvise, we'll get the cover of darkness to make our escape. Whatever happens. And whether or not we have the lockbox when we go."

"I ain't goin' nowhere without that lockbox," I growled.

She gave my arm a squeeze, but I supposed she knew better than to try and argue with me from my tone, 'cause she made no comment to that statement. Instead she only said, "Guess there's nothing else to do now but wait."

Sure, wait. Wait fer Baron Haas to come down those back stairs with the lockbox. Wait fer her man to cut the electricity. Wait fer Bill to set off those firecrackers.

I thought she was gonna move out into the hall again, then, but she stayed put. After a minute of her still not movin' fer the door, I ventured to ask. "You … wanna wait here, in the … in the closet?" I woulda much preferred waitin' out in the hall. The space in here weren't all that big to begin with, but the longer we stood in here, the smaller it seemed to get.

"Yes," she said, all matter-of-fact. "Safer that way. Won't due to be seen loitering around the area when there'd be no reason for guests to be doing so. Someone might remember seeing us milling about, and then tell Baron Haas about it later when he's trying to sort who stole from him. Not worth the risk. You understand."

"Er, sure." I swallowed. Reminded myself the baron would be comin' down those stairs any minute now. I considered puttin' those cat's eye glasses on now, but then figured seein' how close all the walls really were might make things worse. So I left 'em off, and focused instead on the pleasantness of Sally standin' so near.

But we didn't have to wait long, sure enough.

Several pairs of footsteps creaked down the stairs across the way from our closet, and I tensed. Sally reached out to grip my arm again, as if to dissuade me from leapin' out right then and there to grab the box … which, admittedly, was a notion I'd been entertainin'. If I'd had any weapons on me, I mighta already done it.

But as it were, I stayed put. I stayed still and silent, and strained to see through the sliver of open door out into the hallway. Two armed men, more hired guns by the look of 'em, walked past, followed by Baron Haas himself, and a single armed man after him. It weren't any of them that made my heart jump, though, it was the square shape the baron carried.

The lockbox. Had to be.

I exhaled quietly at the sight of it. It was there … *right there.* So close.

From what I could see of it through that little crack, it looked just like the sketch Nan had given me. Square-shaped, a row of five dials along the top of it. Made of some kind of metal that had gotten all rusted and greenish over so much time buried underground.

Didn't look so impressive, really.

All this trouble … over *that*? And no one even knew how to open it, accordin' to Professor Morton. I wondered if he might be right about what could be inside it.

Doubtful.

I moved my hand to my breast pocket to grab fer those glasses, and that's when all the lights went out. The closet plunged into absolute darkness. Shocked gasps and confused mutterin's came from the folk outside, includin' from the men escortin' Baron Haas.

The distant music of the string quartet and barkin' of the auctioneer fell silent.

"Everyone stay calm!" Baron Haas called from where he'd frozen in the hallway. "No need to worry … this happens frequently, I'm afraid. I'll have the lights back on in just a moment…"

I slipped the wire hooks of the glasses over my ears, folded out the lenses as Sally had instructed me back at her saloon, and then sucked in a breath as the closet brightened up fer me like someone had turned the electricity back on, just from what bare glimmer of light came in through the crack in the door. It was all in muted shades of color, and mostly shades of gray, but I could see everything ... the shelves of folded linens, the broom standin' in the corner, and Sally as she pushed the closet door open and stepped out into the hall...

Baron Haas dropped his voice, and to the men around him said, "Keep your eyes open. Get me to that cellar *now*. And then I want you finding out what happened to the lights. I don't like this..."

They answered him in the affirmative and moved off down the hall again, quicker than before, but Sally was already close on their heels. I followed her, and we caught up to 'em quick, our footsteps silenced by the thick carpet.

Sally hiked up her skirts then, and her blades were only a whisper of sound. The armed man bringin' up the rear was the first to fall, goin' down so fast and quiet none of the others even noticed. Then the two on either side of Baron Haas staggered, hands goin' to their necks in confused horror. The baron noticed that, finally, and clutched the lockbox to his chest as he watched 'em drop, spurtin' blood all over his nice carpet. His mouth fell open.

Of course, I weren't sure how much he could see, really, bein' that this hallway had no windows and no candles to offer him any light, but I sprang forward anyway just as he was turnin' toward us and socked him in the jaw same as I'd done to Mr. Miller.

My fist caught him just as unawares as it had Mr. Miller, too. I yanked the box from his grip as he went sprawlin' to the floor, but he weren't unconscious yet. So I dropped to a knee next to him as he rolled, hands over a bloodied mouth, and clipped him again in the temple.

He went limp.

Satisfied, I straightened and shook out my fist, lookin' to Sally. "Sure we can't kill him?"

She rolled her eyes behind those multi-lensed glasses, but before she could make any kinda reply, Bill's firecrackers went off.

And they sounded like cannons, all right.

Seemed the high-brow folk had managed to remain mostly calm with the lights goin' out, 'specially with the main floor havin' some candles lit here and there and light comin' in from the big windows. But when those firecrackers started boomin' fit to nearly make my ears bleed, the main floor erupted into chaos.

Just like we'd wanted.

There were screams, shouts, and everyone started runnin' fer exits fast as they could manage.

"That's our cue," Sally said, and I couldn't agree more.

She retrieved her three knives, wiped 'em on the shirts of the dead, and tucked 'em away again under her skirts. Then we moved quick down that dark hallway and turned left to head past the cellar and the main kitchen, joinin' a flow of folk rushin' fer the back exit there.

But we hadn't got too far with that mob before I heard Baron Haas shoutin' behind us, out of breath and furious, "Stop! Everyone stop! No one leaves till I find out who stole from me!"

Shit. He hadn't stayed asleep very long. Shoulda gagged him and tied him, maybe, like I'd done to Mr. Miller. Kept him from soundin' the alarm till we were good and gone from this place.

Too late fer that now.

But he might as well have been talkin' to a herd of panicked cattle. Not a soul slowed their rush toward the door—any door.

Outside, those firecrackers boomed and crackled.

I dodged further inside the group of people makin' fer a hasty exit, holdin' that lockbox close, bounced and jostled between bodies. I glanced back once, saw Sally likewise swallowed up, not far behind me, and then I focused on findin' the actual exit.

There was one up ahead … but a couple of the baron's hired security blocked it, guns drawn and lookin' ready fer a fight. They musta heard his shoutin', even over all the ruckus of panicked people and those firecrackers. The group of folks Sally and I were a part of drew up short in front of 'em and then milled around, talkin' excitedly amongst themselves like they weren't sure just what to do now.

I weren't sure just what to do now, neither.

ALL THAT IS OWED

"Quiet down, now," one of the men blockin' the door said. "Ain't nothin' to worry about. Just some firecrackers. Saw 'em myself out there ... real purty, they are."

"And you can see 'em for yourself after we search y'all," the other one said. "Make sure you ain't trying to take off with something you didn't pay for."

Many offended and aghast protests arose at that statement, and I bit back a swear of my own, glancin' to Sally again. She met my eyes, lookin' ridiculous in those multi-lensed glasses of hers, and nodded her head fractionally to our left. I looked that direction; saw a set of curvin' stairs leadin' to the second floor.

The floor we weren't supposed to be wanderin' around in.

But I figured I'd already stolen the baron's prized possession, surely violatin' his privacy couldn't be no worse. So I nodded back to her, then pushed through the people pressed close till I broke free of 'em, and headed fer the stairs.

Sally was right behind me.

It may have still been fairly dark in that big house, but the dim light shinin' through the big windows on either side of that back door was enough fer the two armed men to catch sight of us breakin' off from the herd.

"Hey!" one of 'em shouted. "Come back here! Don't be runnin' off!"

We only walked faster, till we broke into a jog and reached the stairway, then started up.

"Hey!" the man shouted behind us again, and I heard his bootsteps thump against the hardwood floors as he came after us. "You ain't supposed to go up there!"

Shit.

Sally drew up beside me and took my arm, pullin' me along. "Come on now," she hissed. "Time to move!"

I scowled at her. Easy enough fer her to say. She weren't constrained in unfamiliar clothes and hampered by a metal leg. In the absence of the initial surge of adrenaline, the damn thing had gone all heavy again, makin' my limp more pronounced. "If you woulda just let me bring my guns," I hissed back at her, "it wouldn't matter how fast we moved."

She gave a little *harrumph*. We'd nearly reached the second floor now, but that hired gun gained on us quick. He musta been leapin' up those damn stairs.

"Stop right now or I'm afraid I'll have to shoot ya!" He was only a little out of breath.

"Heaven forbid!" Sally said, even as we topped the stairs and ducked down the darkened hallway. Her skirts rustled, and she pressed somethin' into my chest as we hurried along, the plush carpet dampenin' our footsteps.

My free hand groped at it, and my eyebrows raised as I recognized its shape. A pistol. But not entirely familiar.

I frowned and glanced down at it. A pistol, all right, but like none I'd never seen before. More wood than metal, and with some kinda thin wires and tubes and little gears along the side. "What in the hell is this?"

"A gun," Sally said.

"Don't look like much of a gun to me," I muttered. "Where are the bullets? How you supposed to load it?"

She snorted. "The bullets are there. It's already loaded and primed."

"Primed?"

"Works like any other gun," she said. "You got twelve shots. Just pull the trigger. You'll see."

If we hadn't been in such a hurry, I'd have pulled her aside and demanded an explanation. As it were, we headed down a hall that seemed to have no end, passin' door after door, and more of those display cases and vases of flowers. And that hired gun still chased us. Outside, the noise from the firecrackers had ceased. I hoped that didn't bode ill fer Bill. I hoped our horses were out back, waitin'.

"And you've had this on you the whole time?" I asked. "All night? And you didn't think to give it to me till now?"

"Come on now, folks," the man behind us called out. "This is your last warnin'! I'm serious!"

I heard the click of his hammer even over the distance between us, and wondered how good his aim would be in such poor light.

Beside me, Sally shrugged. "You did well enough without it, didn't you? And anyway, I didn't fully trust you not to shoot Baron Haas, if you would have had it earlier."

I frowned, supposin' that was a fair enough point. My thumb fumbled at the top of the grip on the strange gun, but it had no hammer. *Just pull the trigger. Sure.* "What else you got under your skirts?" I mumbled.

"Ha!" Sally hooked a hand under my left bicep and yanked, pullin' me sideways just as the man chasin' us fired. She spun me around and pushed me back against one of the many doors, pressin' up close as he fired a second time, the bullet hissin' past to shatter one of the flower vases. "Wouldn't you like to know." She glanced to the pistol she'd given me. "You gonna use that thing or just hang onto it?"

My attention had gone abruptly to the feel of her pressin' up against me and her subtle floral scent, but I pulled it back with more difficulty than I'd have preferred, and put it on the man runnin' toward us and the smell of gunpowder, instead. I leveled the gun with no cylinder and no hammer at him, his figure bright enough through those cat's eye glasses fer steady aim. When I pulled the trigger, my weapon hardly made a sound. There was no muzzle flash. Only a soft *whuff* of air.

I woulda thought it had misfired or jammed, but I heard the bullet crack into the wall down the hall, and saw the man belatedly jerk away from it, lookin' as bewildered as I felt.

I'd missed. By a lot.

Sally was watchin'. "Haven't you ever fired a gun before, Mr. Lynd?"

I scowled and grumbled, and readjusted my aim to account fer the thing's minimal weight and lack of recoil. "It's too light."

"I'm sure."

My second shot landed in the man's right bicep and slowed him up some as he grimaced and swore, but then he was mad. He didn't bother with no more warnin's, and his aim was better, too, when he lifted his gun again, now that we'd stopped runnin'.

A click sounded from the door behind me and I nearly lost my balance altogether as it swung inward, the support against my back suddenly gone. I stumbled backward into the room and Sally came in after me, though it was clear from her lack of surprise or staggerin' that she'd been the one to open the door in the first place. She turned just as the hired man's third shot buried into the door frame and shut the door firmly, then locked it.

"What good is this gonna do us?" I demanded. "Now we're trapped!"

In answer, she only moved past me to the windows along the

opposite wall, and opened one up. The night breeze stirred the curtains. I could hear people talkin' down below, and the clatter of coaches and drivers shoutin' to their horses.

My shoulders sagged as I realized her plan. "Oh you gotta be—"

The door rattled behind us as that man threw his shoulder into it, and we both jumped around toward it, me with that pistol ready, and Sally with a knife in-hand. The knob jostled, but held.

"This way, Mr. Lynd." Sally tucked her knife away and gathered up her skirts, then hiked a leg up and over the sill, duckin' through to climb out. She looked entirely ridiculous, doin' that in her fancy gown, the little top hat pinned to her hair.

The door rattled again.

I sent two shots into it; heard the man on the other side give a yell. Maybe I'd got him.

But then, in answer, he fired through the door too, and wood splintered into the room as his bullet chewed through with more force than mine had.

I swore and ducked away from it, hurryin' over to the window, where Sally had disappeared out of sight. Leanin' out, I saw her climbin' down a lattice-work fulla vines. I vaguely recalled that Bill had mentioned somethin' about climbin' vines all around the house when he'd come back from scoutin' the place, but at the time I hadn't thought nothin' of it. Had thought it a strange detail fer him to mention. Guess it had proven relevant, after all.

Guess there was nothin' fer it ... I was gonna have to follow her down.

Another shot punched into the wall next to me just as I swung my natural leg over the sill, and then one hit the window, shatterin' glass down all over me. "Fuckin' hell..." I tried to shake it off, grateful then fer that high collar keepin' the sharp shards outta my shirt. Somewhere in the back of my mind, I knew that hired man had to be out of bullets. He'd need to reload.

Sure enough, silence fell across the room as I guessed he did just that.

I didn't waste the chance; I swung my leg back over the sill into the room and marched across the floor, unlocked the splintered door, and yanked it open.

The man in the hall looked up at me in shock, the cylinder of his revolver open. His mouth fell open to match it as I raised that strange gun of Sally's and sent two rounds into his chest at point-blank range. He staggered backward with that look of shock still on his face, then dropped dead to the carpet.

I shoved that strange gun into the waist of my trousers and turned away from him, crossin' the room again back to the window. I scrambled through it a great deal less gracefully than Sally had, even in her corset and bustle and high-heeled boots, since I had to keep one arm around that lockbox, and my metal leg still liked to misbehave, but I managed to get myself through and onto that lattice.

I started down with my one free hand and one good leg, descendin' it like a ladder, cursin' and swearin' the whole way.

"Come on, Mr. Lynd," Sally called up, just loud enough to be heard above the general commotion goin' on around the house. "Hurry up, now."

I cursed some more. What the hell did she think I was doin'?

I tried to climb down faster, slipped, and fell the last several feet, hittin' the ground with a grunt. Sally rushed over to help haul me to my feet, and I thanked her breathlessly as we took off through the chaos, aimin' fer the back of Baron Haas' property where our horses shoulda been waitin'.

"Well," she huffed as we went, "that could have gone better."

"Coulda," I agreed, but I was too out of breath from hittin' the ground to offer anythin' more.

The firecrackers had gone silent, but there was still plenty of confusion around the place. Folk milled about bewildered and lost, others yelled fer their coaches, fixin' to make a hasty exit themselves, and those employed by Baron Haas were tryin' to round up those outside, tryin' to keep anyone from leavin'. Didn't seem they were havin' much luck, though.

Sally and me cut through it all, me holdin' that lockbox cradled tight to my chest.

We hurried away from the general commotion, out into the dark, but I could see well enough through those glasses. I wondered if she'd let me keep a pair … they sure were provin' useful.

Baron Haas had a lot of property, and by the time we got close to the little copse of cottonwoods where our horses were tied, I was even more out of breath. But I saw 'em, waitin' there, and I didn't think I'd ever been so happy to see a horse. A feelin' came over me then, a kind of elation I'd never felt. Maybe this robbery coulda gone smoother, but I had the lockbox, and Sally's people had done just as they'd said, and we hadn't got shot.

I had what Nan wanted, and I was gonna get my sister.

We reached the horses. My awful little scruffy mount had been outfitted with the biggest saddlebag Bill could find, and I wedged the lockbox into it and buckled it up tight before mountin' up.

Sally hitched up her skirts again and started puttin' stuff into her own saddlebags—how exactly she'd stashed it under there, I had no idea—then finally mounted up herself and reined around to face me, catchin' me starin' at her. "What?"

"Er … nothin'."

"I told you, I needed to claim back some things that were mine."

"All right…" I didn't bother to ask when or how she'd managed to grab 'em, or what or how Baron Haas had acquired things that were hers to begin with. Not that it mattered, anyway. That was her business. I had my own business to attend to.

"Will you be at the meeting spot?" she asked abruptly.

I blinked at her, realizin' then she'd seemed to read my thoughts before I'd had a chance to take stock of 'em myself. I *had* just been thinkin' then of ridin' straight to Bravebank with that lockbox. Straight to Nan. Straight to bargain fer my sister. All I had back at Sally's saloon were my pair of clothes, and my pair of pistols were still with Bill.

The clothes didn't much matter. But the pistols did. "Yeah," I said finally. "Yeah, I'll be there."

Her smile was clear as daylight through those glasses. "Good. Do be careful, Mr. Lynd."

"You be careful, yourself, hear?"

She gave a nod. "I'll see you there." And with that, she reined back around and spurred her horse, and galloped off into the night.

I turned my stolen mount in the opposite direction and urged it into a gallop as well, lettin' the wind wash over me like that elation at finally havin' my hands on that damn lockbox.

Didn't take long, though, before I heard hoofbeats comin' after me.

A whole posse of 'em.

And I cursed again the fact I didn't have my pistols. All I had on me was that strange gun from Sally and six more bullets.

I urged my horse on faster, takin' him toward the edge of the valley Blessing was nestled into. At least I could see better than any man followin' me, and I tried to take advantage of that, hopin' the rough terrain would slow 'em up some.

Our meetin' spot was well outside of town, with the idea

we'd clear out any potential pursuit before gettin' to it. But I couldn't go there now. Not with these fellas on my heels. I weren't sure how they'd seen me leave, or, even if they'd seen me, *why* they'd decided to chase me down, and especially in such numbers.

No one who'd bothered glancin' my way in the baron's yard had got a good look at what I'd taken, I was sure of it. But the how and the why didn't matter now … all that mattered was that I lost 'em. Somehow.

My poor horse was blowin' hard already. I was pushin' him too hard. And I couldn't afford to slow up, not yet. The posse followin' behind me had dropped back a bit, but not nearly enough.

Then a new sound rose up outta the night … a sound I'd never heard before. Somethin' like the roll of thunder combined with the snarl of some great beast, but it made the hairs on the back of my neck stand up, and my horse threw his head and pinned his ears, eyes showin' the whites.

It got louder, and louder, till I coulda sworn it shook the rocks around me. Till it vibrated in my skull and drowned out all the sounds of hooves.

My horse nearly came unhinged, and it was all I could do to keep control of him, keep him on-course. I didn't know what in this world could be causin' such a ruckus, but if I could make it into the next stretch of trees, maybe I could lose 'em—the posse *and* that horrendous noise…

Somethin' roared over the rise to my left and went airborne, a big, dark shape made of glintin' metal and that awful sound, and my horse leapt straight sideways in mid-gallop. I clung fer dear life to the saddle, jarred as his feet hit the ground again, then came loose as he pivoted and sprinted the opposite direction … right back toward that posse.

I landed in the dirt with an *oomfph*, all the air goin' outta me.

That horrible noise quieted into a low rumble and came up beside me, a strange-lookin' wheel made of metal plates rollin' in front of me through the little black spots dancin' in my vision. I was tryin' to breathe, but my lungs didn't seem to work right. My strained, shallow gasps rose little puffs of dust as I willed my body to get up. To grab that pistol currently jabbin' into my belly. To run.

It did none of those things.

Thunderin' hoofbeats arrived then … the rest of that posse. They circled around me, and I heard their horses blowin' hard, and the chomp of bits, and ropes bein' slid from saddles and shook out. Lots of ropes.

"Go get his horse," a voice barked from over in the direction of that rumble, near that metal wheel. "It's got what you want on it."

No. No no no, not the lockbox…

"Maybe if you'd not insist on driving that *ridiculous* nightmare of a machine, his horse would not have spooked!" another man snapped back. But I heard a few of 'em peel off and go after my mount, anyway.

"And if I hadn't, you'd still be chasing him," the first man growled. "He had a good start on you, too. Would have reached those trees over there and then what? You'd have lost him."

My breathin' finally began to ease, and I focused on takin' in slow, deep gulps. My lungs stopped burnin'. That gun still pressed into my belly where it was smashed between me and the ground, and I inched my hand toward it, bit by bit.

"You underestimate my tracking abilities," the second man retorted.

The first gave a derisive snort. "And you severely overestimate them."

He sounded awful familiar…

"That's enough," came another voice, a woman's voice. "All of that is irrelevant. What matters is that we have him. So stop your bickering and secure him, would you?"

Several of the posse dismounted, then, and I watched their boots approach me. Least I'd recovered my air by now, but I hadn't managed to reach my gun, yet. I was out of time now, seemed like.

So I rolled, pulled the gun from the waistline of my pants, and fired quick at the bodies surroundin' me. There were five of 'em, and my six bullets hit 'em all in turn—three fell dead, two staggered back with shouts, still alive.

There was a lot of swearin', and then the two still livin' pulled their own guns, intent on murderin' me. But more shots rang out from the direction of the wheeled machine, and then those two fell to join the others in the dirt, no longer livin'.

Confused, I twisted around to see who had shot 'em … and found Mr. Miller. He stood next to a two-wheeled metal contraption with a saddle in the middle of it, in his black suit with his missin' cravat, his hair even more mussed now, and that thin line of blood dried on his chin. He holstered his smokin' pistol on the side of his machine, and smiled at me.

Well fuck.

"Goddamnit, Miller!" the woman yelled. "How many times do I have to tell you to stop wasting good men?"

I turned back toward her only to find her nearly on top of me, and I didn't have no bullets left. I brought the gun at her, anyway, hopin' she'd maybe think I might, but she didn't slow. She whacked her own weapon into my wrist and sent Sally's gun flyin', then brought hers back and cracked it into my right temple.

Pain shocked through my skull and my vision flashed white as I went flat to my back, and those fancy glasses of Sally's flung off my face.

She grabbed my arm and hauled me back over onto my belly

so I was face-down in the dirt again. Then she sat on me, and she was heavier than I'd expected.

Mr. Miller grunted. He leaned back against his growlin' machine, arms and ankles crossed, watchin' her try to truss me up, but he didn't lift a finger to help. "I think you and I have different opinions of what makes a good man," was all he said.

"I have no doubts about that," the woman muttered. She was tryin' to get ahold of my wrists, pull 'em back to her so she could tie 'em, but the pain in my head was only a fiery ache now, and I surely weren't gonna make the job easy on her.

I twisted and bucked and threw her off as neatly as my own horse had dumped me into this predicament, then rolled to sit on her chest and scrabbled fer her pistol.

She punched me in the jaw. A solid hit that snapped my teeth together and nearly knocked me off her. Then she wound that rope around my neck and yanked, simultaneously cuttin' off my air and pullin' me forward and downward, so that I lost my leverage.

She tossed me easy after that, and my fingers groped at the rope cuttin' into my throat as she staggered to her feet, pantin', makin' sure to keep it taut. "Thank you for your help, Miller," she commented breathlessly.

He shrugged. "Seems you have it handled."

I pushed onto my knees, then lurched at her, tryin' to put some slack in the rope so I could breathe even as black edged my vision. But she back-pedaled quick and pulled it tight again before I could get a full gulp of air.

I was gonna have to move faster…

Through the rushin' in my ears I heard more horses approach, then saw 'em. Three more men, and they were leadin' that scruffy mount of mine with its bulgin' saddlebag. He was unnerved and jumpy, eyes wide as he trailed reluctantly at the very end of his reins.

Fuck.

The new arrivals took in the scene at a glance, and Mr. Miller musta seen the looks on their faces same as I did.

"Easy there, boys," he called out. "We want him alive."

They hesitated, and in that moment I rushed the woman. Tackled her. Sucked in big breaths of air as the rope around my neck loosened. Fixed my hands around her own throat, nice and snug. Watched her eyes go wide.

The loop of a lasso settled around my shoulders then, and I'd only just released the woman's throat to try and free myself when it jerked me off her backwards so hard I lost all my air again. I was dragged several feet through the dirt, and by the time I stopped, the other two men were on me with more ropes.

I still didn't make it easy on 'em. It took both the men, and the woman, to finally get me tied, and by then we were all exhausted. I laid there gaspin' and glarin' up at all of 'em, covered in bruises and dust, while they all glared down at me. They'd got my wrists tied tight behind my back, my ankles tied, and left that loop tight around my shoulders, too. My head and my jaw both throbbed, and my heart raced fit to choke me.

This weren't turnin' out so good.

"Should beat the sense outta him for what he's done," one of the men growled.

"Should have shot him from the beginning," the woman said.

"Where's the fun in that?" Mr. Miller drawled, and the others turned to glare at him instead of me. Through all of this, he'd only stood there next to his strange machine and watched. Now, he dipped his chin in my direction. "Check his leg. The left one."

My racin' heart stuttered.

"You don't give the orders here, *Miller*," the woman hissed. "It's bad enough you dared show up tonight … bad enough you caused a disgraceful, disgusting scene! You should be ashamed of yourself!"

That made him straighten, and anger flashed across his features. "If not for me, Edward Haas would have never known who'd stolen from him. You wouldn't have known where the thief went. And you wouldn't have him now."

A long, brown braid hung down the woman's back as she faced Mr. Miller and squared her shoulders. So it was her again. The one who'd intercepted him inside when he'd been comin' at me, who'd told him he wasn't welcome there. Why would he have helped her now? And how could he have known I'd taken anything?

"And let me assure you," she growled, "that is the *only* reason I'm tolerating your presence at this moment. Let me also assure you that while I will inform Baron Haas of your assistance here, it will surely *not* make up for the embarrassment you caused him earlier tonight."

Mr. Miller smiled again. "Whatever would make you think I wanted to somehow make apologies to such a pompous waste of space as Edward Haas? Absolutely not. I had a right to be there tonight same as anyone else."

The men accompanyin' the woman with the braid looked to each other and shifted on their feet, and I got the sense this was a long-runnin' point of contention. If they could just keep arguin' about it, though, maybe I could scoot off into the brush, get out of sight.

"We grow weary of your delusions, Miller," the woman said. "Now, run along. Your part is done. I'll be taking this thief back for proper justice."

"Not yet," Mr. Miller said. His tone called back memories of Baron Whittaker, and dread stirred in my gut. "This man murdered my father, I'm quite certain of it."

The others hadn't been expectin' that, and they suddenly

looked uneasy. Even the woman's stiff stance softened, and she glanced down at me briefly before turnin' back to him. "How … how can you be sure?"

He nodded toward me again. "I told you, check his leg. The left one."

The woman hesitated, then turned and nodded to her men. They came at me, one pullin' a knife from his belt.

I rolled and tried to slither away from their reachin' hands, but it was a futile endeavor. They grabbed me, hauled me back, and the third man dismounted and helped hold me down while the one with the knife cut the left leg of my expensive navy trousers and ripped it open.

He muttered curses as he saw the metal rods and stood up quick.

The hands holdin' my biceps and ankles twitched, but they were already clutchin' hard enough to bruise.

"Would you look at that," Mr. Miller said into the silence. "The demon himself. Just as I thought. Guess I'll be takin' him myself, in fact."

The woman seemed at a loss fer words.

Miller finally stirred from his spot beside his machine, joinin' the others to stand over me. I kept my eyes on the woman, my gaze borin' into the side of her face as she stared down at my leg, and willed with every ounce of me fer her to refuse to hand me over. I'd face her … I'd face Baron Haas fer stealin' his lockbox … but I'd heard too much about Mr. Charles Miller to think I'd have any hope of livin' if he took me.

She hissed a sigh and looked to my horse. "Fine. Fine, you take him. I suppose we have back what he took from us, anyway."

"No," I choked out. It was the first word I'd spoken since they'd run me down, and it made 'em all look at me like maybe they'd forgotten I was a man who could speak fer himself.

The Haas woman finally looked at me, even, and arched one eyebrow.

"Oh good," Mr. Miller said. "So you do speak. That will make things easier. We have so *very much* to talk about, after all."

"Let's go," the woman said. "I've had enough of this filth. Be sure you get his horse. We'll come back with the wagon for the bodies." She signaled to her men, and they released me, goin' back to their horses.

Mr. Miller cleared his throat loudly, theatrically, just as the others were mountin' up. "About that…" he began.

She paused as she was about to step into her stirrup and turned, clearly annoyed.

Miller's right hand moved, and the pop of a firearm echoed out into the night, makin' me and the horses jump.

Four shots, and the woman with the braid and her three remainin' men were dead, slumped on the ground. Two of 'em had weapons in-hand, but they'd been too slow, caught by surprise, shot in the back.

"Well now," Mr. Miller said. He slowly pushed the spring-loaded pistol back into his sleeve. "That's better, isn't it? I've been wanting to do that for a long time."

I only gaped up at him, my mouth still open.

He leaned down to pick the cat's eye glasses out of the dirt. They were a little bent now, and coated in a fine layer of dust. He studied them fer a minute, then carefully folded 'em and tucked 'em into the inside pocket of his jacket. "That's some interesting hardware you have there, friend."

I said nothin', all my muscles coiled and braced fer … somethin'. Anythin'. I didn't understand this man, didn't know him outside of what I'd heard about him up till now, but it was quickly becomin' apparent he was dangerously unbalanced.

He reached down again and took a full fistful of my velvet, gold-embroidered jacket, then hauled me to my feet. I wavered there unsteadily—it was hard to stand with my ankles tied so tight together—and he brushed the dirt off my shoulders.

"There we are." He'd adopted that strange purrin' tone again. "So good to finally meet you face-to-face. Now I can give back to you all that is owed, at last."

XXIII

THE BASTARD OF BLESSING

He started by payin' me back fer what I'd done to him at Baron Haas' residence.

His fist came flyin' outta the darkness and cracked into my jaw, and I hit the ground again hard, havin' no way to catch myself. I rolled, reelin', and tried to catch my breath. Waited fer the ringin' in my ears to go away.

Miller turned and went to his machine. He had saddlebags on it, like it was some kinda horse. Ugliest and loudest horse I'd ever seen, certainly. He rummaged around in one of those bags, then came back to me. I couldn't quite make out what was in his hand now that I didn't have those glasses on no more, despite the fact the moon hung over the horizon fat and full.

He came and sat down next to me; pulled my shoulders up into his lap like I were some kind of injured man in need of care. My head was poundin' somethin' awful now, sure, and the rest of me was bruised up good, too, but the last person I wanted any care from was him. I made to sit up and move away, but his left arm hooked around my neck tight, and his right hand pressed a cloth to my nose and mouth.

I knew the smell immediately. Same stuff the doc had used to put me to sleep when he'd found me already half-dead in the desert.

I struggled against Miller's hold, turnin' my head in attempts to dislodge that cloth, but his arm squeezed at my neck like a trap, and I couldn't get my wrists free of those ropes fer nothin'.

He weren't suffocatin' me; I could breathe well enough, pantin' into that cloth, but I was gettin' awful dizzy. Black washed in across my eyes, and I couldn't tell if that were from him squeezin' my neck or from that stuff.

My body got heavy, my struggles weakenin'. Just like when Dr. Balogh had done this to me, and I'd woken up later with a new metal leg. Only I had a good idea Mr. Charles Miller did not intend to be such a helpful soul as the good doctor had turned out to be … if I woke up this time at all.

"Easy now," he said quietly. "It's just a little sleep. Just a little sleep and we'll be home real soon."

Terror shocked through me at those words, at the way he said 'em, and the jolt of adrenaline renewed my struggles. He almost lost his hold on me; my vision cleared fer just a second, but then he doubled-down. Clamped his arm like a noose on my throat and readjusted the cloth so a fresh wave of that sweet smell went full into my lungs.

The world spun circles, the darkness comin' on quick.

"Shhhh," he hissed. "Quiet down. You reap what you sow, friend, and it's time for the harvest. No need to be so upset about it."

I *was* upset about it. But I couldn't do nothin' about it, neither.

I fought as long as I could, long as I could hang on to a bare thread of consciousness, but eventually I couldn't hang on no more, and the sleep took me.

I had impressions of vibration and noise … so much noise. And bein' carried, and I came to enough to drag my eyes open once, but all I saw were shiftin' patterns of light and shadow, and then there was that sweet smell again, and I went back under.

But I did wake up, eventually, risin' up out of a deep, murky darkness like surfacin' from the depths of a lake. Consciousness broke on me like a wave, and with it came an acute throbbin' in my head. And then nausea. I retched and tried to sit up, couldn't. I vomited anyway, turnin' my head just in time to keep it from goin' all over me. Most of it went over the edge of … a table? Spattered against a hard floor below. I stared across now at a wall made of fitted stone, electric lanterns glowin' at intervals along it.

I frowned at it and spit, blinked hard, my mind sluggish and disoriented.

"Don't worry," said a voice, "it will pass."

I startled at the nearness of him, and my gaze shifted in his direction.

The bastard son of the late Baron Whittaker sat in a large leather armchair near a hearth set with a blazin' fire, one ankle crossed over the opposite knee, readin' a book. He'd cleaned up, too. Put his hair back in place, wiped that blood off his chin, donned a new suit, though one more casual than the one he'd worn to Baron Haas' auction.

Another armchair sat opposite him, empty. It looked fer all the world like he coulda been in the sittin' room of his own estate, enjoyin' a quiet evenin' … if not fer everything else around him. And the more I saw, the more I wished to go back into that blissful dark of unknowin'.

A basket near the hearth held an inordinate number of brandin' irons, and just the sight of 'em had my right arm burnin' like it was on fire again already. A sideboard had been stocked with various bladed utensils and knives instead of various blends of whiskey. Ropes, cords, whips, and chains hung from hooks along one wall. A shelf behind his chair held books … and the shelf beside that one held contraptions that were surely some kinda Old World tech, but their shapes were so unusual I couldn't even guess at their purposes. Sturdy wooden tables were set at intervals around the room, topped with sheets of pounded metal, and all fitted with thick leather restraints. There was a well in the far corner, a bucket of water next to it, and towels and rags stacked along its lip.

On one side of me was a small table laid out with items from a doctor's kit: stitchin' needle and thread, ointments, stethoscope, tourniquet, vials of medicine and syringes to inject them with. And on the other side of me was another small table with all my stuff lined up neat: the cat's eye glasses all clean, Sally's strange pistol … the dialed lockbox. And my fancy clothes, folded crisply like they'd just come back from a wash.

My … clothes?

I looked down at myself, and my heart quickened to see I was naked, all right, and strapped down tight to one of those tables. My metal leg gleamed dully in the light of the fire, fully exposed.

I groaned, closed my eyes, and thunked my head back to the table.

This weren't good. This weren't good at all.

A violent shiver racked my body and I retched again, addin' more vomit to the puddle.

Mr. Miller glanced up at me. Then he sighed, put the book's ribbon in his place, and closed it, settin' it aside on the arm of his chair. He shook his head and clucked his tongue as he stood. "Look at you. Making such a mess. And we haven't even started yet." He went to the well in the corner and brought over the bucket.

And dumped it directly on my face.

It was fuckin' *cold.* I gasped; inhaled some, coughed and spluttered and choked.

He turned and went back to the well, hooked the bucket on

the pulley, dropped it down to refill it. "You know," he said conversationally as he worked, "you should consider yourself lucky. I don't invite just anyone here. Only our most privileged guests ever see this place." He cranked the bucket upward again and looked back to me over his shoulder.

I was shiverin' more now, worse than before. Pain gripped my temples in a vice, and that nausea threatened to come up again. I tried to swallow it back, unsure of his intentions fer that second bucket, but preferrin' he not dump it on my face again. I watched him warily as he took it from the pulley and walked to stand next to my table, smilin' down at me.

"Most troublesome folk I relegate to the cellar. It's an ... unpleasant place."

My eyes shifted involuntarily to the multitude of unpleasant devices surroundin' us now on every side, and I wondered how any place could be more unpleasant than this.

"Here, however..." He lifted one hand to gesture. "Here we can be much more comfortable."

I figured he must have meant that ironically.

He lifted the second bucket and I braced myself, but the icy water still took my breath away as he poured that one all down the length of me, soakin' most everything except my metal leg. "Fuck!" I spat. "Ain't you ever heard of heatin' a person's bath 'fore you go spongin' 'em down?!"

A broad smile split his face at my retort, and he answered without missin' a beat. "On the contrary, I find a cold bath much more invigorating. Makes the body feel *alive,* don't you think?"

I didn't think I felt any more alive now than I had before. Only colder, and the pain in my head sharper. And anyway, I was pretty sure I wouldn't want to be feelin' anythin' at all here soon enough.

His gaze went to my right bicep, where the shiny pink scars from his father's torture had not quite healed, and one of his hands came up to touch them, fingertips brushin' lightly across the bars of new skin.

I recoiled from his touch, or would have, if not fer the restraints keepin' me still. But I pulled at 'em, anyway, intensely dislikin' the way it felt. The way it stung, somehow, and sent gooseflesh racin' all across my body.

He lifted his hand, and his smile faded. His eyes, the cold, calculatin' eyes of his father, had gone hard. "We'll get you warmed up soon enough," he said softly.

He turned away and put the bucket back in its place, then wandered around the room gatherin' various things from various places into his arms. "You sure have a lot of fight in you, friend. But I prefer it that way. Makes for a much better experience, in my opinion. So much more *entertaining*." He paused in his gatherin' to glance at me. "I've got quite a special week planned for you. Of course, I will do my best to make you last longer than a week." He went back to his perusin' and collectin', and I pulled hard as I could against those restraints.

They didn't budge.

"But I must confess, the longest Father or I ever managed to keep a *guest* of ours alive has been six days. I have been refining my techniques of late, though, in anticipation of your arrival. So … perhaps this time I could stretch your last days out to seven. Ten would be more satisfactory, of course, but I won't get greedy."

Ten days?! I tugged again at the leather straps at my wrists and ankles, but they were sturdy, the buckles thick. There weren't no windows in this place, and from the rock of the walls and floor, I got the sense we were underground. Of course. If this place were particularly constructed for this kind of grisly business … there'd be no easy escape.

And no way fer anyone else outside to hear the screamin'.

My heart pounded wild in my chest as he came back to my tableside.

"My father was going to give me his name," he said abruptly. He pulled a hammer from his collection, laid it down on my damp chest. "Make me a legitimate Whittaker." Pliers came next, set down alongside the hammer. "He was going to give me the whole Whittaker estate, in fact. Give it to *me*, not my half-brother." He held up a jar, gave it a good shake, and put it beside the pliers. The inside of it *moved*. Writhed.

Fire ants.

Fuck me.

"Not to the fraud who is currently the head of the family … to whom the estate was awarded upon my father's untimely death…" Now he put down a knife, a long, thin one made fer skinnin', and then two small pieces that looked almost like insects, only they were made outta metal. "Because he was *murdered* before he could make my induction into the family—my appointment as *heir*—legal and binding." The last thing he put down was a coil of rope with a noose in one end, and that one he laid on my belly.

I said nothin', my eyes locked on that jar of ants, but my breathin' gave away my opinion on all of this clear enough, anyway, especially with all that stuff lined up atop my chest. It all rose and fell, rapid and shallow, betrayin' my feelin's despite my silence.

"Now," Mr. Miller said, his hands grippin' my left forearm, "just how do you think I should repay the man who has taken so much from me? Who has, in fact, stolen away my very birthright?"

Still I said nothin'. I thought of Charlotte, then, and took solace in the fact she weren't here. He didn't have her. I'd already sent her that warnin'. She'd have had it days ago now. Even if he had people out lookin' fer her, she'd be ready fer 'em now, surely.

Maybe I wouldn't get to free Ethelyn, at this rate. Maybe I'd die here in this underground Hell … but maybe I'd have at least saved Charlotte from sufferin' this same unpleasantness. If Mr. Charles Miller wanted to take his vengeance out on me, so be it. Long as he never got to her.

He was right, anyway. You reaped what you sowed, like Pa had told me so often growin' up, and I'd been sowin' a lotta violence these last eight years. Some mighta said I deserved whatever Miller wanted to do to me.

Hell, I mighta even agreed with 'em, on some level.

But that didn't mean I wouldn't have preferred a different end, if given the choice. Somethin' a lot quicker, at least.

Despite my best efforts to stay distracted, my attention went back to Miller as he plucked the pliers off my chest. He turned them from side to side in the light, and his hand on my left forearm slid down to the cuff of leather around my wrist.

Reflexively, I clenched that hand into a fist.

"So many choices," he muttered. "But then … you *did* provide me the opportunity to end Baron Haas' bitch of a guard dog. She's been a thorn in my side for years. Head of his security, can you believe it? Been waiting for that chance a long time now … and it has been *so hard* to be patient. Now she's dead, thanks to you." He replaced the pliers, turned, and walked casually over to the hearth. He pulled one of the brandin' irons from the basket, and my breathin' went all harsh and ragged.

I tried to slow it, to calm my racin' heart before he came back close.

He stuck the end of the iron into the fire and rested it there along the floor. Then clasped his hands behind his back and paced. "I'll tell Baron Haas it was you who murdered her, of course. And that it was you who murdered the rest of them, as well. Imagine his delight when I tell him I found you. He will most certainly want to come retrieve you for himself. And when he comes, well…" He stopped pacin' and faced me. Smiled again. "I'll murder him, too. Teach him what happens to those who throw me out of their house like nothing more than a common wretch."

I remembered the scene he'd caused at Baron Haas' auction. So he'd been thrown out after that, then. Good riddance. Except it seemed he hadn't left the premises soon enough to spare me this sufferin'. Somehow he musta seen me and Sally goin' out the back, or else seen the woman and her posse head out after me and followed.

"Though I suppose if not for that," he went on, and I wondered if he particularly enjoyed hearin' himself talk, "I might not have seen those fireworks. And if I had not gone to investigate just who was setting those off, perhaps I never would have seen you and your little friend sneaking off with something that didn't belong to you. And then perhaps I would not have had the rather clever idea to kill two birds with one stone: apprehend the man who helped kill my father, and get the Haas guard dog to do it for me … thus luring her out to a place where I could, at last, eliminate her." He grinned down at me, and fear snaked through my belly at the thought of Bill and those fireworks. I hoped Miller hadn't recognized him. Hoped Miller hadn't abducted him, too, or killed him...

"But now that you are here," he said cheerily, "I can finally get answers to some of my *burning* questions. Questions like … wherever did you get that metal leg of yours? And … where is the woman Charlotte Harrison? And…" He went to the small side table that held my things—well, Sally's things, mostly—and placed his hands atop the lockbox. "And … whatever would you want with *this*?"

I didn't mind him talkin' so much, long as he was talkin' instead of hurtin' me … but I also didn't want to answer any of those questions. And I had a good idea that soon enough he was gonna stop talkin' and expect me to start answerin'.

"But let's not get ahead of ourselves." He took his hands from atop the lockbox and stepped away. "There will be plenty of time for conversation later. We have all week, after all. First we must decide exactly what kind of *motivation* your cooperation in our conversation might require." He stepped over to the shelf that held the Old Word contraptions again and browsed it as if it were his bookshelf. "I suspect you will be an exceptionally difficult man to wear down … given that Father had no success during your time with him. And that is … unusual, to say the least. Ah, here we are." He selected an object off the shelf, and it looked similar enough to a thing I was familiar with fer me to have a good guess at what it might do.

Miller brought it over to me: a short, thick metal rod with a trigger and a handle on one end and a circular pad on the other. He leaned his free hand on the edge of my table like it were a bartop and we were two old friends catchin' up. "You know," he said, "I can't decide if you are the bravest man I've ever met or the biggest fool I've ever met, coming right back into town so soon after what you did here. When I first saw you wandering lost in the Haas household, I didn't recognize you at all. The sketch is not quite accurate, is it? But it's close. It wasn't until we took a walk together, and I realized you had a limp, and that it was your left leg that was lame, that I wondered … was it possible? Was it possible the man I'd been hunting all these weeks had shown up *here*? Had walked, literally, right into my arms?"

He held up the contraption, gave the trigger an experimental pull.

I flinched as electricity buzzed, snappin' across the circular pad at the end, despite the fact that's exactly what I'd been expectin' from it. I just kept thinkin', with my body damp from that water, and that sheet of metal underneath me, and one whole leg of mine made of metal, too … I really didn't want him to touch me with that thing.

He released the trigger, and the electricity on the end of it went away.

I let out a slow breath.

"Still, if you had just kept playing your part … perhaps I would have let it go. Perhaps I would not have been so eager to prove out my suspicions, passing it off as merely a coincidence. But you could never have done that, really, could you have? I could see it on your face the whole time we walked. How much servitude chafed at you." He smiled, and I was startin' to hate his smile more than Nine-Fingered Nan's, even. Least hers was born of true glee, however cruel. Mr. Miller's smile, on the other hand, was like somethin' dead. Somethin' painted on. Like somethin' he thought might be socially correct, but somethin' he didn't understand.

I looked away from him and fixed my eyes on the bookshelf: the least disturbin' thing about this room.

He pressed the circular end of the rod to my left shoulder and leaned in close. I balled my hands into fists, braced fer what I knew was comin'.

"I suppose I'm grateful for that. Otherwise I might never have discovered who you really were. I suppose it's even all right what you did to me there, as disgraceful as it was." His left hand rubbed absently at the bruise on his chin. "It's all right that you dared to strike me. That you ruined one of my favorite cravats. That you stuffed me into a closet. Just fine."

"Yeah?" I growled, and I turned my head back to glare at him. "Then why don't you unstrap me? Let's make it a fair fight. I'll put you down again no problem. Won't need none of that doctor's stuff to put you to sleep, neither."

The corner of his mouth twitched. And then he pulled the trigger on that rod and a sharp, white-hot agony seized me from head to toe. My muscles all clenched and I strained against those leather cuffs, woulda rolled around screamin' if I coulda, every place my skin touched metal searin' especially hot. But I couldn't writhe around and I couldn't scream, my voice stuck inside my throat, my teeth clamped so hard I thought they might break.

The cry only came out after it stopped, and all my muscles finally, mercifully, released, and I lay there pantin' and shudderin', my body steamin'. The tools still lined up across my chest burned like brands of their own where their metal touched my skin, and belatedly, I realized the two of 'em that looked like insects were *movin'* now.

The urge to flick 'em away, get 'em off me, was nearly overwhelmin' … but my wrists were trapped, and my body slow to respond to my mental wishes.

Mr. Miller ignored the two things crawlin' over me and brought the rod up to study it like he had those pliers earlier. "I must say," he mused, "the people of the Old World were truly ingenious. You should see some of the things we've pulled out of those ruins. Not everyone understands how to make them work, of course. But over the years … I've become quite good at it. It does make you wonder, though … what could have possibly caused the downfall of their civilization? People so clever, who invented such wonderful and terrifying things, who built such large cities all across this continent … what happened to them? What brought about their end?"

He glanced down at me. "You ever stop and contemplate such things, friend?"

I hardly heard his question, too preoccupied by watchin' the little metal things explore the expanse of my chest. One looked somethin' like a centipede, a long, segmented body and all those tiny little legs, and it marched straight toward my face. I lost sight of it as it went beneath my chin, but I could feel it … a light tickle movin' up my neck.

My muscles were startin' to regain feelin' now, and I squirmed, turnin' my head around every which way in a frantic attempt to dislodge the thing now movin' past my ear and up toward my temple. "What does it matter?" I gasped finally, hopin' maybe Miller would pull it off me if I started talkin'. "They're all dead and gone. Don't much matter how."

"Of course it matters," he countered. "Haven't you ever heard it said: Those who do not know their history are doomed to repeat it?"

The metal centipede crossed my temple, aimin' directly fer my left eye. I squeezed it shut. "Can't say I have."

Mr. Miller clucked his tongue. "My, my. Perhaps you *are* just a fool."

The centipede's multitude of legs crossed the corner of my shut eye, and then it *bit* my eyelid, the pain sharp and lancin'. I jerked and yelped, and renewed my efforts to try and shake it off.

It clung to my skin with all its legs, and bit me again.

"Ow, fuck, what the hell!"

"Ah." Mr. Miller leaned forward. "If you'll hold still..."

I quieted my efforts to dislodge the thing, and to my great relief, Miller plucked it off my eyelid. He held it between thumb and forefinger, and it writhed around lookin' fer all the world like a real insect.

My stomach turned at the look of it.

"Not yet, little one," Miller said to it. Then he looked back to me, and held it down in front of my nose.

I reared back from it as best I could, not wantin' it anywhere near me. My eyelid stung somethin' awful, and a little trickle of blood ran down off it to slip down over my temple like a tear.

Miller leaned his elbows on the edge of my table and put the electric rod, so similar to a hotshot but with a much bigger kick, down by my side. "Take this creature, for example," he said. "Fascinating piece of machinery. Found a whole lot of them down in the ruins. We didn't know what they were for, or what they did, for the longest time. But after some experimentation, we discovered they are quite adept at creating burrows. Specifically, they gravitate toward the eyes. Then they dig in there ... make a nice little tunnel. I hear it's excruciatingly painful. Or at least, it seems that way, judging by the sounds people make when I set these loose on them."

I tried not to think about how much that would hurt, or about how close that one had come to doin' just that on my own eye just now, or about how that was likely to still happen at some point in my severely shortened future.

Mr. Miller reached down and plucked the second metal insect up off my chest just as it had concluded its exploration. That one was less insect-shaped and more like a flat rectangle with eight, spider-like legs. But it wriggled around same as the first in Miller's fingers.

"And this one," he said, indicatin' the spider-ish one, "this one will peel the skin right off you. It's so small, though. It takes a *very* long time, as I'm sure you can imagine. I could do it much more efficiently, but," he shrugged, "I do want to keep you alive as long as possible. So, perhaps I shall let this one have a turn later. But not today. These two are more advanced than we'll get to today." He took 'em back to the shelf where he'd gotten 'em, droppin' 'em down into a jar and screwin' the lid on tight.

"But this..." he said as he came back toward my table, and he put a hand on the shin of my metal leg, patted it. "This is something I've never seen before. Never in all my years of studying Old World machines." He stooped over it and frowned, and never had I wished more to bring up that metal knee so I could smash it right into his nose.

The leg twitched and whirred, and to my great satisfaction, Mr. Charles Miller cringed back from it. He regained his arrogant confidence almost immediately, but it had been enough.

Enough to know he was scared of it, at least on some level. Good.

He scowled, clearly unhappy with his brief loss of control, and went back to peerin' at it. His hands brushed over the rods and gears, and it was strange to know he was touchin' it, and yet feel nothin'. "It is not quite Old World, is it?"

"How should I know?" I said, and that was the truth. "I don't know, and I don't care. The thing's been nothin' but trouble since I got it. You want it? Take it fer all I care. And good riddance." That was the truth, too. The thing *had* been nothin' but trouble since I'd gotten it. And I could always get a new false leg. A different one that didn't make people want to cut it off me all the time. And maybe if I convinced him to take it from me, he'd unstrap that ankle. And then all I'd have to do was get the leg to do what I wanted it to do fer once, and maybe I could give Miller a broken nose or a broken jaw fer his trouble.

The thought made me happy, fer a little while. Till Miller turned his attention back to me instead of my leg, and I saw the look on his face. "Oh, I'll take the leg. Don't you worry about that. But not yet. Not yet. All in good time." He gave it another pat, then picked up the electrical rod again. "I have other work to do, first."

I opened my mouth to say somethin' else, to attempt to distract him further from inflictin' more pain, but he didn't seem interested in anythin' else I had to say. He lit up the end of that rod and pressed it into my shoulder again, and then all my words were gone, and all my thoughts collapsed into a world of hurt.

XXIV

ADVANTAGES

Fer days, he didn't ask me no questions.

I almost wished he would, just so I could have somethin' to focus on besides the pain. Least then I could occupy myself with thinkin' of creative ways to tell him to go fuck himself. Or concentrate on not speakin' at all.

But as it were, fer most of the first three days he only toyed with me. He'd threatened nearly every torture means I'd ever heard of, and several I hadn't ever heard of, but had only delivered on a few of those threats, stickin' to things that wouldn't leave no serious damage so long as they weren't applied too *generously*.

And he didn't apply 'em too generously. Yet. He measured it all out real careful-like, like he mighta been carvin' out some fine sculpture or puttin' together a rare delicacy of fine dinin' instead of just makin' a fella hurt. There'd been needles, and blades, and more of that freezin' water, and some of those fire ants, and he'd pulled off three fingernails from my left hand, one fer each day, and said he'd continue takin' one each day till the end, till I had none left. Ain't never felt a pain like that before; those had got the most yellin' and strugglin' outta me by far.

I'd almost—almost—pleaded with him not to take the third one … but I had a good sense that was just what he wanted me to do, so I bit it all back, all the yellin' and the thrashin', much as I could manage. Though just thinkin' of him doin' that seven more times made me sweat. So I tried not to think about it.

Nevermind the fact the fiery, pulsin' pain that still radiated from those fingers made it hard to forget.

And there'd been lots of that electrical rod. So much of that damned rod I'd blacked out a few times, lost most my sense several other times, and patches of red, angry skin lined my left arm and parts of my chest.

But worst were all the times in-between the pain. He'd sit in his chair and read while he waited fer me to recover myself. Sometimes he'd read aloud. Or he'd doctor me up some ... put ointment on the worst of the ant stings, stitch up the cut on my thigh that wouldn't stop bleedin', clean up my waste ... bring me food and whiskey.

I'd refused the food at first, no matter that it was better than most food I ate on a regular basis, and that the smell of it made my stomach twist in hunger. I weren't gonna accept such a thing from the likes of him. Weren't gonna make it easier on him to wring those ten days outta me. And he'd let me refuse it, at first. Didn't even make a fuss about it, fer which I was sorely disappointed. But I regretted it later, when he showed up with a funnel and a hose, shoved that hose down my throat, and poured some gruel down me.

Thought I was gonna die then, gaggin' and chokin'. That hose down my throat was worse than any of the rest of it, bringin' up a deep panic like I was bein' drowned. The next time he offered me real food, I took it. Let him spoon-feed it to me like I was some kind of invalid. And that's what terrified me most: the care he took in everything he did down here, his concern over seein' that I stayed alive, stayed coherent, fer as long as he wanted me that way. Like he enjoyed that part of it just as much as he enjoyed causin' the pain.

He was, by any measure, the most disturbed individual I had ever met.

I was sure now I'd die a horrific death at his hands, and yet

… there was still a part of me that struggled fer escape every time he left me alone. Still a part of me that kept thinkin' of ways I might get outta this, nevermind that I hadn't figured out how that might be yet.

It was the only thing keepin' me from losin' my mind entirely … that, and remindin' myself over and over again it was better me here than Charlotte, or Sally. Least Charlotte was still safe. And Sally … well, I was more concerned about her, bein' as Miller had mentioned he'd seen her leave with me that night. But she weren't here, at least. Maybe he hadn't recognized who she was. Maybe he didn't care. Maybe his glee at havin' me to torment was satisfyin' enough fer him at the moment. Or maybe he *had* recognized her, and he'd already told Baron Haas, and she'd already been dealt with accordin' to the law.

The thought gripped me with a horror stronger than any I'd felt facin' Mr. Miller's torture. But I had no way to know fer sure. And I dared not ask Miller himself. Didn't want him thinkin' I cared too awful much about her. In case he weren't concerned about her role in the robbery, or about the robbery itself—which I suspected he weren't, given he hadn't turned the lockbox back over to Haas yet—I surely didn't want to give him any reason at all to suddenly take an interest. And I feared he'd be all too eager to use such a thing against me if he knew I cared in the least.

Mr. Miller suddenly eclipsed my view of that dialed lockbox and I blinked. Hadn't even realized I'd been starin' at it. Dread stirred in my gut, so familiar now I hardly acknowledged it. Every bit of my bein' throbbed in constant, unendin' pain ... but each time he returned, he managed to find a new way to make it all so much worse.

He had a brandin' iron in hand tonight, and the end of it glowed white, havin' been in the fire all day. He put one in the fire every mornin', just to make me fret about it, I was sure, but he'd never used 'em. Not yet.

Now, I dragged my weary gaze up to his face, and through the heat shimmerin' off the hot end of that iron, I knew he meant to actually use it this time. The inside of me quailed, but I held my gaze steady, unblinkin'.

He turned from me, walked around to the right side of the table, and I watched him the whole way. When he stood by my shoulder, he held the iron down close to my face, until I had to turn my head away, and even then the heat felt blisterin' against my right cheek. My right hand balled into a fist—I didn't like to do that anymore with my left hand—and my body tensed. I clenched my teeth, wishin' suddenly he'd just get on with whatever he planned to do.

"They say my father had his eyes burned out," he said. The sear of heat left my face and traveled down the length of my body to stop over my groin, and my hands and feet jerked at the restraints, tryin' instinctively to cover myself.

But I couldn't, of course. I was strapped down tight and exposed and there weren't nothin' I could do about it. Nothin' at all.

"They say his genitals were badly burned, as well."

The heat got closer, hotter, and I gave a grunt of discomfort despite myself, fixin' my eyes on the ceilin'. Sweat beaded on my forehead, made the metal sheet against my back slick.

"I suppose it's only fair that I should repay you in kind."

I said nothin', rememberin' Baron Whittaker's shrill screams as Charlotte had shoved that glowin' crowbar into his face and into his goods. He'd deserved it, every bit of it ... his son deserved worse.

Then the heat drew away from my groin, and I dared to breathe.

"But maybe that wouldn't be entirely fair, after all," he mused. "I know you helped the woman free my father's slaves and burn down our estate. The redhead. Charlotte Harrison. But

I also know it wasn't you who actually killed my father. That was her doing, so I heard. Her that burned out his eyes and his...." The iron shifted downward, the heat drawin' far too near my groin again, and I sucked in a breath, held it.

"Yes," he said quietly. "I know what she did. So perhaps I should save that particular indecency for her, yes? What do you think?"

The breath I'd been holdin' hissed out in a snarl. "You ain't gonna get her," I said. "So you might as well save yer threats."

He smiled. Looked amused, even. And withdrew the iron again, to my great relief. "On the contrary, friend. I received a telegram just today. My men in Pennsylvania have located her family home. They assure me they will collect her tonight, and they'll bring her back to the Territories by train. Back to where she *belongs*."

My body went cold at that news, the sweat chill on my skin.

"Yes! All the way in Pennsylvania. Quite a distance to travel. Makes her almost exotic, doesn't it? My father was enamored by her. Couldn't bring himself to just put her down, not even when she proved to be more trouble than she was worth. But I assure you, I will not have that problem."

My heart pulsed in my ears now, and a fear sharper than any I'd felt over these last three days set fire to my limbs. I fought against the restraints in a renewed effort to free myself. I'd sent a warnin' to Charlotte, sure ... but if they'd found her ... would she have prepared properly? Would she have taken my warnin' seriously? Had she even got it in the first place?

And how many men had Miller sent? What kind of protection did her family employ in the first place? There were too many things I didn't know ... I couldn't be certain of her safety from here, almost a whole country away, and I couldn't stand the thought of him gettin' to her.

"My, my," Mr. Miller purred, watchin' me fight those straps.

"You don't much like that idea, do you? Interesting." He walked back to the left side of the table and pulled up one of the tall stools he sometimes used when his administerin' of pain was gonna take awhile. He took a seat now and peered down at me, and he still held that hot brandin' iron, though it seemed he'd forgotten about it fer the time bein'. "Tell me … who is Charlotte Harrison to you? Is she more than just a passing acquaintance, perhaps?"

"No," I choked out, suddenly realizin' what he must be thinkin', and knowin' if he kept on down that line of thought, it'd only make things more terrible fer me and Charlotte both. Hell, I'd been so intent on keepin' his interest away from Sally, I'd let my worry over Charlotte slip too easy. "Hardly know her. Only used her to help me get to yer father." Well … it was enough of the truth to sound convincin'.

"Hrmm." Miller turned the iron around in his hand absently, glanced upward toward the glowin' end of it. "Look at you. So talkative all of a sudden. What father did that night is starting to make a whole lot more sense now." He nodded thoughtfully. "I wondered why he'd sacrifice three perfectly healthy slaves. Now I understand." He kept on noddin', and then he stood from the stool and walked back to the fire, replacin' the iron.

I didn't understand what was happenin', why he'd suddenly decided against usin' it, but I was pretty sure it weren't because he was feelin' merciful.

"Father was always better at that than me," he admitted, comin' back to my table. "I learned quick how to make people hurt and how to make it last … but he was always better at finding the weak spots. He could always find just the place to *press* to make people come undone." Miller put his hands on the edge of the table and leaned forward, loomin' over me. He chuckled, lost in the glee of his own personal revelation, whatever it was. He shook his head. "He'd always tell me: not all pain has to be physical! I think I finally see what he meant. So. Why don't you tell me more about this Charlotte Harrison?"

I glared up at him and kept my mouth shut. But I also stopped my strugglin' against the leather cuffs holdin' me to the table. I'd already given him too much with my first response. *Stupid.* Shoulda kept calm. Indifferent. Now he had somethin' to work with. Somethin' real.

"Maybe we should put your treatment on hold until she gets here, yes?" He retreated, goin' over to the next table to my left and trailin' a hand along its surface. "I'm thinking … I could put her right here. Right next to you. And proper manners would demand I take care of her first. You wouldn't mind, would you?" He walked slowly around that table, and then back toward me, a malicious delight shinin' in his eyes.

I wanted to wipe that grin right off his face … with a fist, a bullet, a brandin' iron … I didn't much care, just anythin' that might change his twisted pleasure into the kind of fear he liked to bring about on other people. My own helplessness here was the most infuriatin' thing of all, bein' trapped and tied down and unable to do anythin' proper to put him in his place. The frustration, the rage, the hatred all roiled around inside with nowhere to go, gatherin' into a big ball of fire in my belly.

He perched atop the tall stool next to me again. "You wouldn't mind waiting while I exacted justice for my father's murder, would you? You could watch it all … I have some truly extraordinary things planned for her, of course, being as she was the one to actually mutilate and murder him. Even better than what I have planned for you. Just you wait. It will be glorious…" His grin turned lecherous then, and he leaned toward me and dropped his voice, as if sharin' some kinda secret. "I always have *particular* fun with my women guests, anyway, and Ms. Harrison will certainly be no exception."

My tenuous control snapped. I surged against those restraints hard enough to make the table shudder, and Mr. Charles Miller started. There was a strange whirrin', clickin' sound, and then my metal leg *shifted—opened*—and came free of its cuff abruptly. I recognized the shapes of blades stickin' out from it in multiple places at nearly the same time I swung it toward Miller.

He'd jumped off his stool and whipped around at the noise, and the calf of my left leg struck him in the middle as he moved to catch hold of it, givin' him a gutful of knives.

He grunted as the blades sunk deep, at least three of 'em, but then I yanked my leg back and pulled 'em all free. Crimson bloomed across his white shirt and painted his hands as he clutched at his stomach. I aimed the metal foot at his face and gave him a good solid kick in the jaw, hearin' a satisfyin' crunch as he went flyin' back into his bookshelf.

It rocked as he crashed into it, a few of the books comin' loose to rain down over him. He slumped on the floor, dazed, but I didn't think he was out yet … or dead. Yet.

Adrenaline pounded fierce through my veins, makin' it hard to focus, hard to think. My other ankle and my two wrists were still secured to the table … I had to get those free too, somehow. I forced myself to look close at my metal leg now, no matter that doin' so in its current state brought up an unsettlin' uneasiness. Maybe I *were* some kinda demon…

It had never looked natural, of course, bein' all made of metal, but at least it had been generally in the shape of a leg. Now … now it looked like somethin' else entirely. There was still a foot at the bottom, but everything between that and where it attached to my thigh had damn near turned into an arsenal.

Thin, narrow knives stuck out of it like spikes from ankle to knee, and the side of my thigh had opened and extended, offerin' out a bigger, proper knife, and a … a pistol. *What the fuck!?* How long had that thing been hidin' in there? I supposed it made sense Dr. Balogh hadn't told me about it while I'd been stayin' at his homestead ... but damn ... that thing woulda come in handy several times over by now if I'd known it was there.

Or if I'd known how to get to it.

I was surely gonna have to pay the good doctor another visit now. Have a little talk with him about anythin' else this leg might be hidin'. *If* I managed to get free of this damned table before Mr. Miller lurched up off that floor or called in reinforcements, anyway.

I heard him moanin' weakly down there, rollin' around.

I bent my left leg up, strainin' to reach fer the big knife holstered on my thigh with the sore, bloodied fingers of my left hand. I could only just barely touch the hilt. Grittin' my teeth, I pushed my wrist forward in its cuff until the leather bit hard into the already raw skin of my wrist. But I ignored it, finally gettin' my middle and index finger at the top of that knife hilt, hookin' it between 'em, and pullin' at it. It came free with little resistance and clattered to the table, and my heart came up in my throat as it nearly toppled over the edge.

My hand slammed down over the top of it just in time, stoppin' it. I gripped the hilt in my hand, turned it carefully so that the blade pointed backward and downward, and sawed awkwardly at that cuff.

The angle was bad, and the muscles in my hand and wrist burned with the effort of tryin' to keep it steady, tryin' to apply enough pressure to cut the leather, but not enough pressure to make it slip and cut my arm.

A blood-soaked hand rose up into my field of view and gripped the bottom left corner of my table, makin' me jump. I almost lost my hold on the knife. But then went back to cuttin' furiously, urgency cloggin' my throat.

The table creaked as Mr. Miller used it to haul himself up onto his knees. His face was good and bloodied now, and his jaw hung slack and a little crooked and I grimaced. He'd deserved that all right, but it sure didn't make a pretty sight.

He made some kinda noise, a furious growl that maybe he'd meant as a word, but I couldn't understand him. I kicked at his head again with my left foot, but he was out of reach. His left hand grabbed at my metal ankle below all the spikes, caught hold.

The cuff around my left wrist split, finally, and I pulled that wrist free with a cry of triumph, then wasted no time at all turnin' to unbuckle the one around my right wrist. With both wrists free, I sat up, then braced myself as the room swayed.

Mr. Miller struggled up to his feet, leanin' heavy on the end of the table and one hand around my metal ankle. His face was ashen gray, a sheen of sweat shinin' on his skin, but his eyes were clear … and real, real angry.

I reached down to work at the buckle around my right ankle, the big knife still clutched in my left hand. My fingers trembled somethin' awful, and Miller used the opportunity to lunge at me, grabbin' at my left arm. The blood made his hands slick, and I managed to wrench away from him, then sank that big knife down into his shoulder.

He yelled, and his hands went to try and pull that fat blade from his flesh, but I yanked it out instead, keepin' hold of it, and then that last buckle around my ankle came loose, and I rolled off the table to the right.

I stumbled as my feet hit the floor and fell to my hands and knees with a grunt. Didn't matter that Miller hadn't been wantin' to leave permanent damage these last few days … the torture had taken its toll, anyway. My body was stiff and weak, pain flarin' up fresh now that I was tryin' to get it to move.

Miller staggered around the table toward me and I scrambled up to my feet, reachin' fer that pistol holstered in my thigh with my right hand and prayin' the good doctor had put it in there loaded. I turned toward the Whittaker bastard and took aim at his chest, then pulled the trigger.

The hammer clicked on an empty chamber.

Fuck.

Miller limped forward and I went backward, riskin' a glance down to the gun. It was loaded ... the other chambers had bullets, I could see 'em right there ... I thumbed the hammer back again, watched the cylinder roll over to reveal the empty one, and gritted my teeth.

A safety measure, sure, which I supposed I appreciated given the fact the gun had been *inside my leg*, even if it were a metal leg, but I wanted all the bullets I could get right now, and I needed every shot to count.

Miller lurched at me and I opened fire, puttin' all five bullets into him. The gunfire reverberated off the stone walls and stone floor, deafenin', and the force of all those bullets knocked Miller stumblin' backward till he crashed to the floor, and he landed sittin' up against the lip of the well in the corner.

He sagged, his eyes not so angry anymore, but lookin' dazed and unfocused, starin' at the floor. His whole shirt front was soaked in red, and his breathin' rattled. Blood welled in his mouth, trickled out, and I took a few steps toward him slowly, the gun raised despite the fact I'd emptied it.

My ears rang and my heart thundered wild in my chest, my whole body achin', urgin' me to sit down and rest. But I couldn't. I half-expected him to get up again and come at me, like somethin' from one of those stories about the unnatural deeds of the worshipers of the dead.

But those were just stories, like I'd told Charlotte. And anyway, there weren't none of those necromancers here. Miller had taken three knives, five bullets and a good kick to the face ... he couldn't last. Not bleedin' out the way he was.

Didn't mean I was done with him, though. Not after what

he'd done to me these last few days. Not after what he'd threatened to do to Charlotte.

So I holstered the pistol back in my … leg … put the big, proper knife back, too, and forced my feet to keep movin', careful not to cut myself on the blades that still stuck out of my left leg at all angles. I went to the hearth and grabbed up that brandin' iron he'd discarded only minutes ago, then hobbled back to him.

He didn't look at me as I stood glarin' down at him, didn't even try to turn his head. He only wheezed and gurgled, tryin' to breathe through all the blood in his mouth. The light in his eyes was fadin' fast.

"Go to Hell," I spat down at him. And then I pressed the glowin' end of that iron right into his face. He choked and flailed as his skin sizzled, maybe he tried to scream, but I figured his lungs were all fulla holes. I held it there despite his noises and struggles and weak attempts to dislodge it. Then I pulled it away, and echoin' what Charlotte had done to his father, jabbed it up between his legs fer good measure.

All his noises changed pitch, but then I threw the iron away, lettin' it clang against the stone floor, and went to the shelf that held all his Old World trinkets. I picked up the jar of metal insects and the jar of real insects—the fire ants—took a few steps back in his direction, and smashed 'em both to the floor by his side. The bugs—both real and manufactured—were more than happy to be free. They swarmed toward him, up his leg and over his arm, coverin' him quick as I backed away.

"See how you like it," I growled.

He twitched as they found his flesh, bitin', stingin', or burrowin' in, but he didn't have much life left in him now. Least what little he had left would be spent in misery, which was still better than he deserved.

I left him to the insects and kept backin' away, around to the small side table lined with all my things. I grabbed up my stack of folded fancy clothes, the multi-lensed glasses, and the lockbox with the dials, but didn't take the time to dress just yet. I wanted out of here first. Didn't want to spend one more minute in this Hell-hole. I searched frantically fer the exit.

The room was larger than I'd initially thought, but I found a stairway leadin' up in the far corner, and ascended it in earnest. I had to balance myself against the rough stone wall with my free hand, feelin' woozy now that the adrenaline had calmed a little. At the top of the stairs was a heavy wooden door. I turned the handle and pushed.

Nothin'.

Oh come on. Come on, please. Please. I closed my eyes briefly and took a breath, set my clothes and the lockbox down on the top stair, and tried the door handle again, leanin' my right shoulder into it. Nothin'. Locked.

I clenched my jaw against the swell of exhaustion, terror, desperation. Leaned my forehead against the wood and tried to think through the risin' panic.

Locked, sure. Maybe he'd lock it in case any of his *guests* managed to get off their table. Wouldn't want 'em to escape. But he was in here, too, tonight. There'd be a key somewhere. Maybe he carried the key with him. Or else there was another way out. Had to be.

I gathered myself, takin' in another few deep breaths, pushin' hard against the tightenin' in my chest, the flood of dread through my stomach as I turned around, and went back down the stairs. I went slow and careful, so as to not fall on my face, or slice myself with my knife-leg. My left hand grabbed up the huntin' knife from its leg holster again and gripped it, white-knuckled, as I crept around the corner at the bottom and searched out the body of Charles Miller.

He was still slumped against the wall of the well, his head

drooped down on his chest now, and covered in his own blood and bugs both. Bitter satisfaction rose in me at the sight, though I wished I'd had the opportunity to inflict a lot more pain on him … somethin' less rushed and more akin to what he'd done to me these last three days … what he'd done to countless others before me.

Least now he was ended, one way or another. Least now he couldn't continue his twisted practices. Least now he couldn't hurt Charlotte.

Charlotte.

I needed to send her another warnin'. Needed to be sure his men didn't catch up to her … somehow. And that meant I needed out of this godforsaken room.

My goddamn hands were shakin' again, but I kept the knife as ready as I could in my right hand as I approached him, wary of gettin' close to the ants. I leaned over him, keepin' as much distance as I could, and swatted several bugs off his blood-soaked suit jacket, then pulled back the sides of it to check its inside pockets. The first one was empty, but the second one … the second one had somethin'. I slipped my hand down inside the bloodied silk linin' and closed my fingers around it. A key, all right. One of those big iron ones.

A few of those damn ants got too close, crawled up on my arm, and I yanked it back with the key in my fist and shook 'em off quick, before they could bite me again.

Then I turned away from the mess of a corpse that had once been the bastard Charles Miller and focused on those stairs, feelin' myself fadin'. By the time I got back to that wooden door, black spots wavered in my vision. I holstered the big knife; slipped the key into the lock and turned it, and the sound of it clickin' open was quite possibly the sweetest sound I'd ever heard.

I fell into the door more than pushed it, and it creaked open. The wash of fresh air startled me. Hadn't been expectin' that. I gathered up my clothes and the glasses and the lockbox again and stumbled through, then paused, strugglin' to orient myself.

It was dark, darker than Miller's dungeon had been, but my eyes slowly adjusted to the moonlight. A breeze ruffled my hair and brushed over my bare skin, raisin' gooseflesh. I took a deep breath of it, smellin' a town layered over the smell of a green valley, and lingerin' through that … the smell of old fire. Ash. So it was night, then, and I was outside now. I squinted as my eyes adjusted, and eventually I recognized the loomin' dark shapes that surrounded me, and I realized where I was.

Standin' in the middle of the burned-out bulk of the Whittaker estate. The house. All around me were blackened walls, burned-up furniture, piles of ash. And the new, fresh beams of the repair effort. Some of the original house had survived, one of which was the wall and the door I'd just come out of. And Baron Whittaker's torture chamber, conveniently untouched given its underground nature.

Well I sure as hell weren't gonna stay here any longer than I had to.

I limped out of the house wreckage and into the open night and sat heavily in the grass. Stared down at my metal leg in the dim moonlight and fer the first time … didn't exactly feel repulsed. Not even with all those things stickin' outta it.

If not fer that leg … Miller surely would have killed me. And maybe Charlotte, too.

I swallowed hard, thinkin' all those things stickin' outta it were probably what Dr. Balogh had really meant when he'd mentioned it had *advantages*.

Advantages. Sure.

Now if only I could figure out how I'd gotten it to open like this in the first place, maybe those advantages would be worth somethin'. I scrubbed my hands over my face and took a deep breath, then went about tryin' to sort how to close up the damn thing. I couldn't very well get any pants on with it lookin' like this ... and I didn't much want to go wanderin' into town full naked and with my leg lookin' like this, neither.

But the more I looked at it, the more I didn't even know where to begin. I thought maybe the thigh holster was spring-loaded, and tried to push it inward, but it wouldn't budge. Seemed to have locked into place, or somethin'. And the blades all over my shin didn't seem to have any dull parts where I could safely take hold of 'em and try to fold 'em in, neither.

I sighed and finally gave up. I was much too tired and sore fer such nonsense, anyway.

Guess I was goin' into town full naked and with a leg fulla knives, after all.

Least it was good and dark out, and awful late. Maybe the streets would be empty, and I could stick to the back alleys. Not like I hadn't done that before.

I almost didn't make it up standin' again, and those black spots were gettin' bigger. I wavered fer a minute till I got my balance back, tried to ignore all the spots of pain pulsin' in my body, and picked up that lockbox and my clothes and those glasses again.

I trudged down the hill toward the lights of Blessing, limpin' heavy, focusin' on puttin' one foot in front of the other. It weren't that far. I could make it. There was one safe place I knew I could go there ... one safe place I could stay till I recovered my wits enough to go on to Bravebank with this damned lockbox.

Long as Miller or Baron Haas hadn't gotten to her. Long as they hadn't burned down her saloon.

Sally.

I just had to make it to Sally...

XXV

NIGHTMARES AND RUMORS

It was all I could do to stay outta that tunnel of black as I shambled down the hill and into town. Then I fought to keep my mind on-task, fought to keep myself oriented, fought fer every step in the right direction. My mind kept wantin' to wander, float off somewhere, and my body kept wantin' to just collapse into the dirt.

I staggered like an awful drunk; had to keep leanin' up against the sides of buildings to keep from fallin' over. Gettin' free of Mr. Miller had taken pretty much everything I'd had left, clearly.

The lockbox was still tucked under my right arm, its metal corners diggin' painfully into my skin from clutchin' it so hard. But I weren't about to loosen my grip on it. All of this was because of that damned thing, and I surely weren't gonna chance losin' it now.

Those fancy clothes I'd stacked on top of it, and I'd put the glasses on, hopin' they'd help brighten my darkenin' vision.

Vaguely, I recognized the alley I'd stumbled into. I was almost there. Almost to the Seven Knives. I pushed on.

Fortunately fer me, there weren't many people out and about at this hour, and most that were stayed out of the back streets. I came up on a few people here and there, hurtin' too much and too tired to care if they saw me, but they were all drunk or outright passed out, and they didn't seem to care about me lumberin' by, neither.

The one fella coherent enough to take real notice of me straightened up from where he'd been slouched against a wall, and his mouth fell open. He dropped the bottle of liquor he'd been swiggin'.

I only glared at him through the waves of black swimmin' over my eyes, not in the mood fer anythin' 'cept a bed at the moment.

"Holy Mother," he muttered. He scrubbed at his eyes, blinked hard, then stared at me again.

I kept glarin', and kept on hobblin' by.

He slid along the wall to the corner, then dodged around it and ran off into the darkness.

I supposed I probably did make a terrifyin' sight at the moment. Good. I weren't in any condition to handle any trouble. That, and the pistol holstered in my thigh was out of bullets. I'd have to talk to the good doctor about that, too. A gun weren't much good without bullets.

Finally, after what seemed like slow, agonizin' hours, I reached the back of the Seven Knives Saloon, and thank God it was still standin'. I lurched up to the door I'd snuck out of only … what, days ago? Seemed like a good lot longer ago than that. The saloon's windows were all lit up, and I could hear the music and general merry-makin' even out here.

I pounded on the door with the flat of my left hand, then sagged against the door frame.

A minute or two passed, and I pounded on the door again, harder and more insistently this time.

It opened at last, and I saw Bill with a surly look on his face and a sawed-off shotgun pointed in my face before I realized I'd been puttin' more of my weight against the hand on the door than I'd reckoned, and I pitched forward over the threshold as he pulled the door open further.

Bill swore as he caught me in one arm. "What the fuck—what the hell happened to you?"

I murmured somethin' about bein' glad he was alive, and he dragged me inside the saloon's back hallway and kicked the door shut again with one foot. Surprised gasps and murmurs came from somewhere nearby … women. Some of Sally's girls musta been in the hallway, too.

"Go get the boss," Bill snapped at 'em. "Quick! *Now*!"

Their light footsteps darted off along the worn wooden floor, and I wanted to say somethin' else to Bill as he attempted to get me propped up against a wall. My mouth opened, but no words came out. Couldn't remember what I was gonna say, anyway.

Least Sally was here. Least she hadn't got ratted out by Miller, or grabbed by any of Baron Haas' men. Least she was still safe.

I cradled the lockbox to my chest in both arms, hardly aware of Bill fussin' over me, and unable to understand what he was sayin', though it mostly just sounded like a lot of profanity.

I let go finally, and the blackness swallowed me.

I went right back to Mr. Miller's basement, strapped to that table, only now he had Charlotte, too. And Ethelyn, even. And Mama and Pa sat in the two armchairs over by the hearth, readin' their books. I yelled out at 'em, yelled that Miller had us all trapped down here, that they should run while they had the chance, but they didn't seem to hear me.

A voice came from my right and when I looked, there was that girl who I'd thought had been Ethelyn, who Taggert's men had murdered for no good reason at all, and the front of her dress was covered in blood. She walked toward me, her brown eyes full of tears. She reached fer me, opened her mouth, but only more blood came out.

I couldn't get away from her, and I couldn't help her. I couldn't move at all, held to that table.

Then Mama screamed, that horrific, wailin', hair-raisin' shriek she'd let loose when Pa had got shot, and my gaze whipped back to her only to see Pa slumped backward now, his face made a mess by buckshot and parts of his skull and brain drippin' all down the back of his armchair.

My own cry welled in my throat, mixin' with horror and nausea both, but then Mama's skirt caught fire. She didn't seem to notice, kneelin' next to Pa's chair and shakin' him like she could wake him up.

The fire crawled up her dress, over Pa's chair, across the floor to my table.

I couldn't move. Couldn't breathe. Couldn't scream.

The flames snaked over my own skin, and everything turned into fire and pain and my Mama's screams…

I jolted awake with a yell and found myself sittin' up in a bed, starin' out at a collection of people who all stared right back at me, their expressions rangin' from real concern to outright terror. I glanced 'em all over in turn as I struggled to bring myself back from the nightmare, my own terror still burnin' hot in my blood. Sweat soaked me, my heart raced, and I gulped air in big, ragged breaths, my body still tremblin'.

"Easy," Sally said softly as she stepped closer to the bedside. "It's all right." She pressed a palm to my damp forehead. "It was a dream. You're all right now."

A snort came from my right. "One helluva nightmare, more like."

Bill.

I turned toward him, found him holdin' on to my right arm

with both hands. He released me and shrugged sheepishly. "Sorry. You were about to toss yerself from the bed."

The kid who had brought our horses the night we'd robbed Baron Haas was at the end of the bed, holdin' tight to my right leg under the sheets. He let go of me quick, too, and held up his hands as he backed away. "Boss's orders," he blurted.

I was about to look back to Sally when I recognized another of the people in the room.

Professor Morton.

He stood near my metal leg, which laid atop the sheets, and seemed frozen in place like a hare that might have sensed a predator lurkin' near. His eyes went so wide that monocle of his —this one unshattered—fell out of his eye to dangle against the breast of his vest.

"You," I growled. I made as if to jump off the bed and go after him, but several pairs of hands grabbed me and prevented me from doin' so at the same time as several voices raised in protest and told me to stay put.

"You don't need to be moving around just yet." Sally's voice cut out above the rest of 'em. "The doc ain't done with you yet. And anyway, the professor here is the one who managed to put that … that leg of yours back together. He's done a fine job of it, considering."

I shifted my glare from the professor's pale face down to my leg. The knives and the thigh holster had disappeared, all right, tucked back in to the leg itself, somehow. It looked just like it had the day I'd first gotten it.

"Now look," an unfamiliar voice said, and I looked up again to see an older man with big, bushy mutton-chops and small round spectacles step forward. "You've suffered a lot of trauma…"

"You think?" I snarled.

"… you need to get some rest, try to stay calm. Your injuries aren't life-threatening, but if you try to do too much too fast, you could aggravate them and make them worse, make them take longer to heal."

"You the doctor then?"

He straightened and smoothed at his rumpled shirtfront. "That's right. Dr. Alton Abbot, at your service. Those burns were pretty bad." He nodded toward my left shoulder, and I realized there was a bandage wrapped around it now, goin' down nearly to my elbow, and wrapped around my chest, as well. All those places Miller had pressed that electrical rod to my skin. Another bandage wrapped mid-thigh around my left leg, around the seam where my natural flesh met the metal leg, and the three fingers with missin' fingernails had bandages around 'em, too. All the little cuts Miller had made all over me were freshly medicated, the deepest ones freshly stitched. And the ant bite blisters had ointment on 'em.

"Be careful not to pull out those stitches," the doc added. "And change the bandages on your fingers daily. If you notice excessive heat or redness there, or any discharge, you let me know right away. As for your … er … false leg … well, I'm afraid that's outside my area of expertise. The professor here knows more about that nonsense than I do, so I leave it to him. I will return to check on you tomorrow."

"I'll be gone tomorrow." I said it reflexively, but even as the words left my mouth, I knew it weren't likely to happen. Not with the way I was currently feelin'. Might need a few more days, at this rate.

The doctor didn't believe it, neither. He gave a snort. "Most certainly not." He turned to Sally. "Under no circumstances allow him to leave these premises until I clear him to do so."

She nodded crisply. "Understood, Doctor."

"I'll leave when I damn well please," I muttered.

Sally glared at me and pursed her lips, and I effectively felt a little guilty fer my crassness.

I sighed heavily and rubbed at my eyes with the heels of my hands. "Fine. Fine. I'll … I'll give it a few days. Maybe."

"Thank you, Doctor," she said to him, and he nodded and turned to go before drawin' up short and turnin' back toward my bed.

"Oh. Almost forgot." He drew a bottle from his bag and held it out fer me to see, then set it gently on the nightstand. "To ease your sleep. You need to rest. One swallow before bed each night, understand?"

"Sure."

"All right then. I'll be back tomorrow."

With that, he nodded a farewell to each individual still in the room and then took his leave. The only others remainin' I hadn't yet acknowledged were Nora and Nettie, both pressed in close behind Sally and huddled together, watchin' me with a mix of worry and curiosity. When I looked at 'em, they blushed and looked away, then started whisperin' to each other.

I released a long, slow breath and leaned back into the pillows, suddenly aware of how *good* they felt. Soft and yeildin', and nothin' like that terrible table Miller had put me on. I relaxed into 'em and closed my eyes. "How long was I out?"

"Not too awful long," Sally answered, and I felt her palm against my forehead again. "Few hours or so. I called the doc right away." Her hand withdrew, and I heard her turn and urge Nora and Nettie to skedaddle and get back to work. She dismissed the kid as well, the one who'd brought the horses.

I opened my eyes again to see that Bill had stayed, and so had Professor Morton.

"The girls told me of your metal leg," Sally said once the others had left and shut the door behind them, "but I admit, it is nothing like I expected."

"Yeah," I grumbled. "It ain't what I expected, neither."

"It's … it's very unusual."

"I noticed."

"It's a wonder of engineering," Professor Morton put in softly.

He put a hand on the metal ankle, and I pulled the knee of that leg up to my chest to remove his hold, surprised when the leg actually did what I wanted.

Beside me, Sally pulled a bottle of whiskey and a glass from the nightstand and poured some, then offered it to me.

I accepted it with a grateful nod. Least it weren't that tea again.

"What happened?" she asked. The question was gentle, hesitant. "When you didn't show up at our meeting spot … at first I feared the worst, but we heard the next morning you'd murdered a whole posse, including Ms. Fields—"

I nearly snorted the whiskey through my nose.

"—and I thought maybe … maybe you'd decided to head on to where you needed to go right away, after all."

"No," I coughed, wincin' at the burn the whiskey had left in the wrong pipe. "No. I didn't murder that whole posse. I only murdered half of 'em. And it surely weren't me who murdered that woman, neither. It was Miller. Charles Miller."

Sally drew back, her eyes goin' wide as she pressed her hands to her sternum.

"Shit," Bill muttered from the other side of me. "I saw him get thrown out of the party, thought it awful amusin'. But then he didn't fully leave the premises. I thought he had, 'cept he showed up when I was settin' off those firecrackers and I had to get outta there quick 'fore he saw me. I wondered what he was doin' snoopin' around…"

"Apparently he was lookin' fer me," I said. "We had a … a run-in with each other inside, before he was kicked out."

"What!?" Sally barked.

I only nodded, feelin' foolish now fer not tellin' her about that before. Maybe if I had … maybe Miller wouldn'ta caught up to me outside. Maybe things woulda gone a lot different.

I told 'em all what had happened then, stickin' to the main points and sparin' most of the unpleasant details. But I mentioned Miller's two-wheeled machine and its horrific noise, how he'd murdered half that posse and the woman in charge of 'em, of the Hell that still existed beneath the ruined Whittaker manor, and that I'd only managed to escape because of my leg goin' haywire.

"It didn't go haywire," Professor Morton spoke up.

The rest of us looked at him.

"Huh?" I prompted. "The hell you talkin' about? Didn't you see the thing?"

"Of course I did. I studied it in great detail while the doctor was seeing to your injuries. I thoroughly investigated its structure and innards and I'm telling you, I saw nothing to indicate a malfunction."

"Meanin'?"

He blinked rapidly and shrugged. "Well … well I don't know! I've never seen anything like this before … but I'd say whatever it did was not a malfunction at all. More of … of a purpose it was built for. You didn't trigger the release of those weapons?"

I shook my head again. "Naw. Had no idea they were there. Or that the leg could open at all."

He looked confused, but I had no intention of explainin' myself or the leg to him. In fact, his particular interest in the workin's of my leg made me remember the lockbox and how he'd wanted that, too, and I sat bolt upright again. "Where is it!?"

Sally startled, her gaze followin' mine as I frantically searched the room. "Where is what?"

"The lockbox! The one with the dials ... the one we took from Baron Haas! I had it—"

"We got it," Bill drawled. "We got it, don't get yer knickers all in a knot. It's locked up in Sally's office right now. Safe as can be."

"I want it." I glared at Professor Morton as I said it, and his face reddened, his hands ballin' into fists. "Here. With me. Now."

In the corner of my eye I saw Bill glance to Sally.

Belatedly, I realized I'd been awful crass again, and these people had been nothin' but kind to me since Sally had first kept that woman from bleedin' me out in those dark woods. I cleared my throat and added, "Please."

Sally sighed. "Bill, would you escort the professor back to his room and retrieve the lockbox, please? Bring it up?"

"Sure thing." Bill lumbered over to Professor Morton and waved him toward the door. "Come on, you. Time to go."

The professor shook his head. "If you still insist on depriving the scientific community of that lockbox—and potentially a key across the valley—then I'd least like to further study this leg—"

"No." Sally, Bill, and I all said it at the same time.

"My leg ain't one of yer artifacts," I said. "You stay away from it."

"I'm the one who put it back together for you!" he blustered.

"For which we are grateful," Sally offered.

"Even if you only did it under threat of bodily harm if you didn't," Bill added.

"But that's enough for tonight," Sally continued. "You should go back to your room, get some rest. You have a long journey ahead of you."

At that, the professor's face turned a darker shade of red, and it was clear he woulda liked to protest further. But Bill grabbed his arm in one hand and patted at the knife on his belt with the other hand, and Professor Morton relented. He turned and stalked off toward the door, and Bill followed close behind.

When they had gone, Sally poured me more whiskey. "Charles Miller is dead, then?" she asked, and cautious hope rang clear in her tone.

"Yes." I downed the second glass of liquor, wishin' again I coulda given him more of what he deserved. The smears of his blood had been wiped from my skin now, and if it weren't fer the points of pain all over me, the bandages and stitches and the stiff soreness of my muscles, I might've thought the last three days of torture had only been another nightmare.

Already it seemed foggy, far away, unbelievable.

"Good." She took my emptied glass and poured more whiskey, then downed that one, herself. "But you're going to have to leave town as soon as you're able, I'm afraid."

Well, that was fine by me. Didn't want to stay here any longer than I absolutely had to, anyway. Weren't nothin' about this town I liked, 'cept Sally and her saloon. "I got no quarrel with that arrangement," I admitted. "Though I was under the impression no one around here much liked Miller."

"Oh, they didn't. It won't be *his* murder you got to worry about. He never reported the fact he had you. Or the fact he had Baron Haas' lockbox all this time. So those posters up over your murder of Baron Whittaker are still around. Course, once Miller's body is found, that might change up who is offering the reward … but Baron Whittaker the younger will still be out for blood, no doubts about that. And now you've got the murder of nine more people on you, too. That's … that's a lot of murder. And Ms. Fields, especially. She was quite well-liked around these parts."

"I told you, I didn't—"

"That won't matter. There aren't any witnesses left alive to dispute the story Miller started, are there? No one around here liked Miller, no, but they'll still be more inclined to believe him over you, especially being that you're already wanted for the murder of a baron."

I sagged back into the pillows again. If not fer Sally havin' her livelihood here, I woulda been sorely tempted to act on the impulse I'd had that night in the woods when I'd first come back here: just burn the whole town to the ground. Wipe it all away.

If only…

"And our getaway from Baron Haas' residence was not as clean as I would have liked."

"I'd say," I grumbled.

"But it doesn't seem anyone identified us on the way out. So … at least that part ended up in our favor."

"Sure."

"And since Miller never told anyone he had that lockbox, either … I took the liberty of starting rumors that it was stolen by the Whittakers."

I lifted my brows, considerin'. The new Baron Whittaker *had* been there. So had a Whittaker bastard. "Does anyone believe it?"

Sally shrugged. "It's starting to gain some traction. The barons already hate each other, anyway. But these things take time. We'll just have to be patient."

There was a moment of silence between us, and I became acutely aware then of the fact I was still naked. Least the sheets covered me to the waist now, only my left leg layin' on top of 'em. I shifted the sheets and slid my metal foot down under 'em to cover it, too.

"I'm sorry," Sally said abruptly. "For what happened. I can't imagine what you've been through. If I would have known—"

I shook my head and waved away her apology. "You couldn't have."

"But if I would have," she repeated firmly, "I would have found a way to get you out of there."

I stared across at the opposite wall, notin' the way the glow of the electric lights didn't flicker. A small vanity sat against that wall, and my clothes and hat were set on top of it. My gunbelts were hung over the back of a chair in the corner. And it struck me as strange then that I believed her. I believed she woulda come after me.

I weren't sure I'd ever been certain of that fer anyone, not since my own parents had died, anyway. Most the time I couldn't even be certain of that with Holt. Most the time I weren't sure if he were gonna show up and help or leave me fer dead ... or shoot me himself.

"I know," I said quietly at last.

"And I'm sorry to have to insist that you take your leave so soon, especially after what you must have suffered from Miller. But I do think it's in your best interest."

"I would have to agree."

"Well—" Sally began, but then the door opened and Bill came in, the lockbox tucked under his arm.

"Here," he said, "here's your damn box. Would be safer locked in Sally's office, but if you insist, then fine. Here it is." He brought it over and thumped it down next to me on the mattress.

I put a hand over the top of it. "Thanks. Mind bringin' over my guns, too?"

He gave me a look. "You think that professor is gonna come up here and try to steal it from ya? We're keepin' him locked up so he don't cause no trouble. And we're escortin' him far up north later today. He won't be botherin' ya."

"I'd prefer to have 'em close by, anyway."

Bill studied me fer a minute, then glanced to Sally. She gave an almost imperceptible nod, and then Bill gave a very overdramatic sigh as he marched across the room to the chair. "In case you haven't noticed, I ain't the maid." He pulled my belts off the back of it. "And I ain't yer lackey, neither. You want anythin' else, you can get it yerself." He tossed 'em to me, and I winced as the weight of the pistols landed on my bruised, cut up, and ant-bit right leg.

But at least they were close, now. "Thanks," I said again.

"You should get some rest," Sally said. "If you can. We can talk more later." She handed me the bottle of medicine the doctor had left behind. "One swallow of this. Don't forget. And would you ... would you like someone to stay with you? I could send the girls back up. Nora and Nettie, I mean. Think they've taken a liking to you. They know plenty of stories, songs, verses ... might be nice to hear some familiar voices while you drift off?"

I stared down at the medicine in my hand, if only so she couldn't see the way her offer had affected me. I didn't understand how she could so often know my feelin's before I did, but she was right. To my surprise, bein' alone right now was about the last thing I wanted. So I nodded wordlessly, unable to speak around the sudden lump in my throat.

"All right. I'll send them up. And we'll speak more when you've rested. Good night, Mr. Lynd. Or ... good morning, I suppose."

Mornin'? I looked closer at the small clock on the vanity, realized it read almost five AM.

Mornin'!? Charlotte! Shit!

XXVI

COMIN' WITH THE STORM

A strangled noise came out of me and I threw back the sheets, fair near jumpin' out of the bed before Sally and Bill both grabbed hold of me.

"Whoa, whoa now there, Mister," Bill said, and he rather easily tossed me back down onto the mattress, where I promptly scrambled to get back up again. He pinned me with one big hand on my chest, much like he'd pinned me to the wall the night he'd followed me around town, and pointed a finger in my face like he was scoldin' a petulant child. "Doctor's orders, you stay in bed."

"What the heavens is the matter?" Sally asked, and her face had gone a shade paler.

"Charlotte," I gasped, tryin' to pry Bill's hand off of me. For fuck's sake, he was a big fella. "Telegram. Gotta send a telegram. Gotta warn her!"

Sally glanced to Bill, but he frowned and shook his head. "Who is Charlotte?" she asked.

"The girl," I spluttered. "The redhead! The slave I helped escape who came through your saloon weeks ago." I stopped fightin' Bill's hold, exhausted and pantin'. I just didn't have the strength fer it … might not have had the strength fer it even had I not just spent three days stuck on a table bein' tortured. "Miller sent his men after her … said they'd found her family home … said they were gonna grab her tonight … last night … I need … I need to warn her they're comin' … may be too late already!"

"Dear God," Sally said.

Bill looked up at her. "Operator won't be there this early."

"Then where's he live?" I blurted. "I'll wake him the fuck up!"

"*You* won't be doing anything," Sally said, fixin' me with a stern glare. Then she turned to Bill.

He rolled his eyes. "Are you serious?"

She arched an eyebrow. "Use the telephone downstairs. It'll be faster."

"That operator may not be there this early, neither."

"Try it. If not, wake up Mr. Moeller. If he's reluctant to cooperate, you're the best one to manhandle him into compliance. But don't damage him. Bribe him, if you need to."

Bill gave another of his theatrical sighs and grumbled under his breath, but removed his hand from my chest and straightened. "Fine. Who do I call, and what do I say?"

Sally pulled out the nightstand drawer, removed a piece of paper and a pencil, and looked at me expectantly.

A telephone … that *was* a better idea. Surely Charlotte's family had a telephone, if they had the kinda money she'd talked about. And surely the operators in the area would know of the family if they had that kinda money, too.

I closed my eyes, pressed the heels of my palms into 'em, tryin' to think. Tryin' to remember. The note she'd given me with her address on it was in my pack with all the rest of my stuff in Sonoita. But I'd looked at it plenty of times before then, before I'd had Sonoita's sheriff send her my first telegram, even. I'd looked at it enough times the paper was gettin' all worn and creased, while I worried over the fact I had nothin' to write her about.

Well, I had somethin' to write her about now. And I needed to do it quick.

Slowly, hesitantly, I recited the address back as it came to mind, then dropped my hands from my eyes and opened 'em to be sure Sally had it all down. "Her family name is Harrison," I added. "Tell her Baron Whittaker's bastard son sent some more men her way to collect her and bring her back here. Tell her to take all necessary precautions to prevent that from happenin'."

Sally scribbled it all down, then handed the paper to Bill.

"Hurry," I urged.

"What if there's no one on the other side to receive this message?" Bill asked.

"Then we'll keep trying until someone answers," Sally said. "Go on now, quick!"

Bill grumbled some more but increased his pace as he went fer the door, then stepped out and shut it behind him.

I pushed myself sittin' again, but Sally put a hand on my shoulder. "It's all right. He'll get through to someone."

"What if he don't?"

"He will. The bigger city exchanges usually have longer hours. There will be someone there."

"What if her family don't answer their phone? What if Miller's men already grabbed her?"

Sally gave me a gentle, patient look, though her lips pursed, and I didn't understand how she could be so calm. "Then there's nothing you can do from here about either of those things. We'll just have to wait and see. One thing at a time, Mr. Lynd."

Another jab of guilt hit my insides at her callin' me that name. After all of this she'd done fer me, I was still lyin' to her. I fidgeted in the bed, tired and hurtin' and warrin' over whether or not to tell Sally my real name, worried over Charlotte, waitin' fer Bill to come back, turnin' that medicine bottle over and over in my hands.

It seemed to take him hours, and the time ticked by as I sat there, hatin' my helplessness just as much now as I had when I'd been strapped to Miller's table. Sally watched me like a hawk, like she could tell I wanted to go down and check on Bill's progress despite the exhaustion and pain. She'd move around the room periodically, straightenin' the paintin' on the wall, fluffin' the pillows, peekin' through the window's curtain; the only clue she might be feelin' nearly as anxious as I.

At last Bill's heavy footsteps came stompin' down the hall, and both Sally and I looked toward the door expectantly as he entered, a little breathless, but lookin' pleased.

I hardly dared hope.

"Telephone worked," he said triumphantly. "Got through to Charlotte's father. He said she's there, safe and sound. They got the telegram you sent earlier, and he hired more protection for the whole family. Some ruffians did show up last night, but they were handled. All of 'em in pine boxes this mornin', he said."

My breath came out in a big rush of air and I collapsed back into the pillows.

Sally smiled down at me. "There, you see? Everything is taken care of."

Relief clogged my throat, and I didn't have no words.

"Now … you get some rest while you can. I'll send Nora and Nettie up to keep you company. You let them know if you need anything else, understand?"

I nodded.

"All right, then." She turned to Bill and tipped her head in the direction of the door, and the both of 'em moved once more fer the exit.

Bill opened it fer her and waved her through, then followed her out, and the sound of the door closin' was loud in the resultin' silence.

I laid there starin' up at the ceilin', and I put one hand over the top of that lockbox, and the other hand over the top of my gunbelts. The bottle of medicine rested atop my chest, untouched fer the moment.

I closed my eyes against an unexpected swell of feelin's … breathed through it, slow and deep. All that mattered now was that I had Nan's lockbox. And I was goin' back to Bravebank with it soon as I could manage to sit upright in a saddle and keep my senses well enough to ride in the right direction.

Shouldn't be long.

Not long now till I had Ethelyn back…

It was three full days till I felt strong enough to ride.

By then, Miller's death had been discovered and reported. The new Baron Whittaker had found him, the paper said, drawn to explorin' the ruins of his family estate when those workin' on its rebuild had found his half-brother's strange two-wheeled machine parked out back of it.

No one had liked him much, true enough, but murder was murder, and the town was already up in arms over the senior Whittaker's death weeks ago, the Haas posse's deaths more recently, and the robbery at the Haas residence. The paper didn't question the nature of the room Miller had been found in, nor did it seem to care much what Miller might have been doin' to the person who had murdered him. And accordin' to the newspaper's editor, the law didn't care too awful much, neither.

Least no bounties had been issued fer Miller's murderer … yet. The article only begged that anyone havin' any knowledge of the incident come forward.

Fer questionin' only, they said.

They'd be waitin' a long time fer that one.

Still, Sally had me move to the cot in her office soon as I could, so as to make my presence as indiscernible from regular saloon business as possible. The cot weren't nearly as comfortable as her mattresses, but I'd slept on plenty worse, and I was grateful fer the refuge, anyway.

By dawn of the fourth day, she'd outfitted me with supplies enough to last me the ride to Bravebank, lent me a horse to replace the scruffy one we'd never found, and escorted me out of town and to the edge of the valley where the green started fadin' out into the reds and browns of the desert proper.

I'd said my goodbyes to Bill already three days ago, before he'd left to take Professor Morton up north. And I'd said my goodbyes to Nora and Nettie too, just the night before. All in all, I figured I owed Sally a whole helluva lot more than I could afford to repay right now.

The sun had just broke over the horizon, paintin' the sky a pale, pretty pink, when Sally reined up her horse, and I pulled my mount to a halt beside her.

"Well," she said. "This is as far as I go today. Guess this is goodbye, cowboy. Sure has been one hell of a ride."

"Yeah." I sat there fer a minute, searchin' fer words. I opened my mouth, closed it, and opened it again. "I … I can't thank you enough fer everything you've done fer me here. Guess I owe you a lot more dish washin'."

That made her smile. She wore different clothes today than I'd ever seen her in: a regular ridin' outfit, with leather chaps and a bandana around her neck, and a hat that looked a lot like mine, only minus the bullet hole. The soft dawn light framed her in a blush of rose as she shook her head. "Like I told you when we first met, Mister, I'm in the business of rescuing people. It's all in a day's work. But don't you worry none, I'll keep your tab open. You can pay me back someday."

I glanced over my shoulder. Back toward Blessing. "Might be awhile. Don't think I should come around here again any time soon."

"No, I don't think you should," she agreed. Then she

shrugged. “But you never know. Watch the papers. I might just have this place cleaned up sooner than you think.”

The statement made a corner of my mouth quirk into almost a smile, and it felt strange. I couldn’t remember the last time I’d smiled. “I believe you just might,” I said.

“All right, then. Safe journeys to you, Mr. Lynd. I hope you get what you need.” Her eyes dropped toward my saddlebag, where the lockbox had been stowed.

I sobered again and nodded. Swallowed. “Me too.”

She started to turn her mare around to head back toward town.

“Sally…”

She reined the horse to face me, instead. “Yes?”

“Did you … did you get what you needed from Baron Haas? That night we got the lockbox? Did you get what you were after?”

Her eyebrows lifted. “Why Mr. Lynd, how courteous of you to ask. I did, mostly. But I can be patient for the rest of it. I’ve waited this long … I can wait awhile longer. The barons’ days are numbered, mark my words.”

“I would help more, if I could. If I didn’t have … other business that needed my immediate attention.”

“I understand completely.”

“And…” I rubbed a hand over my mouth, shiftin’ in the saddle and questionin’ the wisdom in what I was about to say. But the urge to come clean with her was nearly overwhelmin’. I couldn’t ride away now, after everything she’d given me, without sayin’ it. The lie had been chafin’ at me fer days. “And … and my name ain’t Lynd. It’s Delano. Van Delano.”

To my shock, she didn’t seem surprised at all.

She just nodded thoughtfully. “Well, that’s all right. My name ain’t Wellman, either. It’s Clayton. Sally Clayton.”

At my stupefied silence, she gave me a wink. Then turned her mare toward Blessing again. "See ya around, cowboy." She kicked her mare into a trot, leavin' only dust behind her in the brightenin' dawn.

I puzzled over Seven Knives Sally Clayton fer the first few hours of my ride back to Bravebank. I'd never suspected she might not be usin' her true name, neither. Not that she'd ever given me her surname directly. But Baron Haas and others at that auction had called her Wellman. And she'd had some kind of history there, that was certain. The fancy folk there had known her. And he'd had somethin' that belonged to her. More than one thing, it seemed.

If I ever did get back to Blessing, maybe I'd go ahead and ask her to tell that story. If she were goin' to trust me with her true name, maybe she'd actually tell it to me.

Maybe.

The horse she'd lent me was an old, skinny mare, but sturdy enough, and I kept a steady, brisk pace fer most the first day. Though truth be told … I was wishin' I had Joe back. Guess I'd gotten more attached to that damned mule than I'd thought. He was still up in Sonoita, I reckoned. Maybe auctioned off by now. Maybe still waitin' unclaimed in its livery.

If I weren't in such a hurry to get back to Bravebank, I woulda gone back fer him. But time weren't on my side, here. I'd already been away too long, and I didn't know how long Nan would wait fer me to bring back her prize.

If not fer concern over pushin' my borrowed horse too hard, I woulda kept goin' right through the night. But as it were, I stopped to rest her and made camp, and as I sat starin' out at the stars on the horizon, my thoughts went back to Ethelyn.

How long had Nan had her, now? A few months, at least, musta been. I wondered how she was bein' treated. Wondered where she was bein' held. Wondered if Nan planned to ship her off on a boat by sea or a boat by air. Not that I'd ever seen an airboat myself, nor ever seen one pass over these parts, even, but I'd heard tales of 'em from drifters passin' through now and then.

There was a landin' field somewhere up north, somewhere in Utah, they said. If that were true, that was likely the nearest port. That was likely where Nan would take her. Maybe she was already there, waitin' on the next ship to come in. The thought made my heart wedge in my throat, and I had to fight down the urge to saddle up and ride on again.

She could just as well be somewhere else, somewhere Nan thought might be more secure fer safe-keepin'. All I really knew right now was that I needed to get this lockbox to Nan soon as I could, and that she'd better give me Ethelyn in return.

I laid back on my bedroll, starin' up at those stars, and didn't get much sleep.

I set out again just before dawn and pushed the horse as much as I dared all morning and into the afternoon. By then I was gettin' real close to Bravebank, and I also noticed the clouds startin' to knot together in the sky. They were buildin' up real tall, and the breeze had picked up into somethin' almost like a real wind, stirrin' dust and tumbleweeds.

A storm was comin', and comin' in fast.

I kicked the mare up into a trot, then into a canter. We rounded the base of a small rise, and the sprawl of Bravebank laid before me in the distance, dim through the haze. I kept the mare headin' straight fer it, kept nudgin' her to maintain her speed though she kept tryin' to slow up on me.

She was tired … but we were almost there now. So close…

We'd nearly reached the edge of town when I saw the wall of dust comin' at us from the northwest. I swore and dropped the reins to pull my bandana up over my nose and mouth and shove my hat down tighter on my head.

Then I grabbed up the reins again and urged that poor tired mare into a gallop, hopin' to close the rest of the distance to town in a hurry.

It chased us all the way there, that storm, and swept over us just as we passed by the outermost buildings, the gust of wind strong enough to cause a stagger in the horse's stride and nearly buffet me from the saddle. Dust and grit stung the exposed parts of my skin and the sky darkened quick.

The folk left in the street ran fer cover, the horses tied at the hitchin' posts milled about and nickered nervously. The wind whipped down the alleys and made store signs creak, awnings flap, and loose shutters bang.

I heard the rain before it reached us, a sweepin', thunderous roar, and then it hit, all at once and like a sledgehammer. A solid curtain of water, slammin' into all the hard surfaces and beatin' everything into submission. I gasped as it instantly drenched me.

The mare slogged on through it, and I let her drop back into a slow, amblin' walk, mostly 'cause I couldn't hardly see where we was goin' anymore, anyway. Water ran in streams off my hat brim, and now that the dust had cleared, I tugged my bandana back down around my neck.

I went in the direction of the Stag Saloon … I thought … the streets all mud now and runnin' with water like little creeks.

So much fer tryin' to beat the storm.

Lightnin' speared the gloom ahead, and the crack of thunder afterward made me flinch despite myself. This weren't nothin' compared to the storms I'd seen as a kid in Kansas, but it'd been a long time since I'd been around one of those. And these desert storms were becomin' bad enough.

More lightnin' came, lots of it in quick succession, and more thunder rumblin' like some great beast. Then, finally, I saw the weak yellow glow of the Stag's front lights up ahead, strugglin' to pierce the rain's fury.

I pulled the mare up to the nearest hitchin' post and dismounted, tied her, and dug the lockbox out of the saddlebag it'd been crammed into. Most of me was wet now, soaked through, my whole shirtfront and my pants, and the mud slurped at my boots as I bowed my head against the onslaught of water and headed fer the front door. Least my oilskin duster and my hat kept a little of me dry.

I stepped up onto the boardwalk, ducked under the shelter of the front awning, and put the box up under my left arm so both hands were free. The Stag's door was usually left open durin' daylight hours, but they'd shut it tight now against the force of this squall. So I pushed my duster back behind my right holster, rested my hand lightly on that pistol's grip, and shouldered roughly through the door.

Lightnin' lit the sky again behind me and thunder cracked as I stepped inside the Stag Saloon. It faded just in time fer the bang of the door slammin' back against the wall to echo out just as loudly across the room.

All sober eyes turned in my direction, just like they had the time I'd come in holdin' that big, unwieldy cannon-gun. The place was packed, fuller than I'd ever seen it thanks to the ragin' storm outside, and the raucous murmur of conversation quieted at my arrival. The card shufflin' stilled, the folks on the way to or from the bar or goin' toward the stairs paused.

I stood there in the doorway, soppin' wet and drippin', a puddle of water spreadin' out around me on the floor, and my gaze raked across all the faces starin' at me … and all those who weren't starin' at me, too.

Searchin' fer Nan, or either of those lieutenants she'd had with her last we'd talked.

I didn't see Nan. Didn't see those lieutenants, neither.

My glare landed finally on the barkeep. The same man who seemed to be here all the time. The same man who had spit in my coffee all those days ago.

But I'd surely been through far too much in my efforts to retrieve this lockbox to spend any more time waitin' around here fer Nan to show up whenever she damn well pleased. Or to suffer any more of that barkeep's disapproval.

So I narrowed my eyes, sent another murderous scowl out over all the gathered men of the Stag Saloon, and bellowed, "Where the fuck is Nine-Fingered Nan?!"

XXVII

PATIENCE IS A VIRTUE

No one answered.

Couple of the folk glanced to each other. Couple more folk suddenly found their cards or their food or their drink real, real interestin'. Couple of the saloon girls looked toward the barkeep.

I followed their gaze back to him, but he only met my stare in silence, his mouth firmly shut and turned down into a severe frown.

So I pulled my right pistol from my holster and stalked straight fer him.

People cleared outta my way in a hurry, some knockin' over their chairs or their drinks in their rush fer the door. Didn't seem to matter that the rain and lightnin' was still blowin' and howlin' outside, a good portion of the saloon's patrons fled out into it, seemingly more willin' to risk that kinda storm than whatever was gonna happen in here.

That suited me just fine.

The barkeep's eyes widened as I got closer to him, and his hands dropped below the bar.

But I had my gun up and aimed and hammer cocked before he could do much else but lay hands on the weapon he kept stashed back there. "Hands up," I ordered. "Where I can see 'em. Nice and slow."

He went real still and his face went real pale, but he complied.

The sound of more chairs scootin' back and feet runnin' fer

the door marked more of the patrons skedaddlin' out, wantin' no part of this trouble. 'Cept then I heard another sound, one not so friendly, the sound of sixguns clearin' leather and hammers clickin' back.

I stepped to my right at the same time I drew my left gun and spun, at the same time the guy behind me fired, and his bullets shattered bottles instead of my ribs.

The barkeep yelped and ducked behind his bar.

I fired my left pistol twice, caught the guy in the chest twice and he stumbled backward, starin' at me in surprise.

From the corner of my eye I saw the barkeep stand again, and now he had a sawed-off shotgun in his hand. I fired at him without lookin', got him in the gut, and he fell back against his shelves of alcohol lookin' even more surprised than the other guy.

The other guy finally gave up on livin' and dropped to his knees, then fell face-first to the floor.

More folk took that opportunity to get the hell out, and the saloon girls had all clustered together in the back corner, clutchin' at each other in terror.

I turned my attention back to the barkeep, but kept my left pistol leveled toward the saloon at large. "Hand it over," I said, noddin' at the shotgun gripped in his white-knuckled fist. "You might live through that shot. You won't live through another one."

His eyes burned with defiance, but he set his weapon slowly upon the bar top, slid it toward me. His other hand was pressed up against the bullet hole, and blood seeped between his fingers. Sweat beaded on his forehead. "Nan's gonna skin you for this," he spat.

"Let her try," I growled. "So long as she gets here quick." I holstered my left pistol and grabbed the sawed-off shotgun instead, albeit a bit clumsily with the lockbox still clamped to my side by my left elbow and bandages around three of those fingertips.

I turned toward the folk who remained in the saloon, then, most of 'em too drunk to know what was happenin', but some of 'em sober. Those few watched me carefully, but none made a move fer their weapons. "Well?" I barked at 'em. "Anyone else got anythin' to say?"

Silence. Only the storm answered.

Outside, the sky was dark and angry, makin' the inside of the saloon seem brighter than usual. The door had been left open in all the hurry to get shut of this place, and the wind blew sheets of rain through to stir the muggy air, almost makin' my damp clothes feel chill. The force of the rain and wind against the building was nearly as loud as the thunder itself, vibratin' in my bones.

But still no one moved. No one said a word.

So I swung my glare back to the barkeep. "Where's Nan?" I demanded again.

When he hesitated, I shook my head and shook the pistol still aimed at him, too.

"She's … she's conducting business," he finally ground out.

"Where? Here? Or somewhere else?"

"Here. In town. But I don't know where. I don't get involved in Nan's business."

"No?" I made a point of glancin' around the place we stood in. "But you run her saloon fer her, don't ya?"

His eyes narrowed. "She's in town somewhere. That's all I know."

"Then I guess you'd better go and find her."

He stared at me fer a minute, as if tryin' to figure if I were serious or not. But I was serious, all right, and I held his dubious gaze with a flat, even stare. He swallowed, his eyes droppin' down to the blood that stained his apron. "In case you hadn't noticed, you done shot me. And that storm out there—"

"Beats bein' dead," I said.

Another few heartbeats of silence passed, everyone else in that saloon holdin' stock still, like they was part of a photograph instead of livin', breathin' folk.

I thumbed back my hammer, and the motion roused the barkeep from where he slouched against his shelves. He straightened, grimaced in pain, and hobbled down the length of the bar toward the back door, glarin' somethin' fierce at me the whole way.

I glared right back at him, and tracked him with my pistol. "Tell her I got what she wanted. Meanwhile I'll have someone fetch the doc. He'll be waitin' fer you when you bring Nan back here. But I suggest you hurry. Don't want you bleedin' out on the way."

His only answer was another sour, hateful look over his shoulder, and then he pushed out through the door and stumbled into the storm.

Once the door had shut behind him I relaxed a bit, holstered my gun. I set the lockbox atop the bar and went around behind it myself, grabbin' up some whiskey and pourin' myself a healthy dose.

The doc. Fuck. Here in Bravebank, that would be Dr. Balogh. I needed to have a talk with him about my metal leg, sure … eventually. But maybe not now. I didn't exactly want him here now, not when Nine-Fingered Nan would be arrivin' so soon. And I didn't exactly want him to see the man I'd just murdered, or the man I'd almost murdered. Didn't want him to realize his wife had been right about me from the beginnin'.

I muttered a few curses and threw back the whiskey. Then noticed those left in here were still starin' at me. "What?" I snapped. "Go on, go back to your business. Stay outta my way and I ain't got no quarrel with you."

But they did not go back to their business. The girls took the chance to dart up the stairs, maybe decidin' to hide up there. The men remainin' with their wits intact picked at their food or absently arranged and rearranged their cards, but they didn't seem too eager to fully believe my claim. One of 'em stood up real slow, his hands held out at his sides and well away from his gun, and walked over to shut the front door against the force of the monsoon. Then he turned and walked back to his chair, givin' me a little nod as he sat back down.

Well, it didn't matter if they believed me or not. Long as none of 'em tried to cause any trouble, I didn't care what else they did in here while waitin' out the storm.

And that's what we did. We waited.

I drank more whiskey and tried to settle my nerves. Tried not to think about what I was gonna do if this exchange didn't go down like it was supposed to. Tried not to think about Dr. Balogh findin' out I was a murderer, after all. Tried not to think about what Sheriff Jennings had said about not shootin' people.

Outside, the storm hurled rain and lightnin', and thunder shook the walls.

It couldn't have been that long, but it felt like forever before the back door opened again, and the barkeep staggered in. He was soaked through, his boots and pants caked in mud, the stain of red across his apron larger where he still clutched at it with one hand. His face had gone gray now, his lips pale. He hardly made it into the establishment before he tripped and fell to his hands and knees.

He was alone.

A flash of anger lit in me that turned my insides hot, feedin' off the warmth of the whiskey. "Where the fuck is Nan?" I bit off.

He shook his head, rain water streamin' off his hair. "She … she's conducting business … like I said. Says … says … she'll come by here later."

"*Later?*" The word came outta me in a rasp.

The barkeep lifted his head weakly. "Where's … where's the doc?"

"*Where is she?*" I asked him again, ignorin' his question. "Where is Nan right now? Where's she conductin' this *business*?"

"She's … she's with the sheriff. At the … jailhouse. I need the doc … please. Need him now…"

"He's on his way," I growled. I left his shotgun on the bar, but snatched up the lockbox again and made fer the front door, pointin' at the most timid-lookin' of the sober men at the tables as I passed. "You," I snapped. "Go get the doc."

Then I flung open the door and faced the storm once again. Surely it couldn't last much longer. These summer monsoons came in hard and wild, but their fury expended itself faster than the storms in the heartlands. I could wait it out … could wait here fer Nan, too.

No. I'd waited on her long enough already. Waited on her three weeks to give me this damn fool errand in the first place. Waited on her to give me bad information so I could go out and get robbed, arrested, nearly hanged quick and almost killed slow.

No. I weren't gonna wait. Not fer this storm, and not fer Nan.

I bowed my head against the spittin' rain and turned down the boardwalk, toward the jailhouse. The sheriff was about the last person I wanted to see right now aside from Dr. Balogh, but even his threats weren't gonna stop me from makin' sure Nan kept her end of this deal.

So I stalked through the swirlin' gloom, holdin' that lockbox tight, grittin' my teeth in the gaps between the storefronts when the full force of the storm hit me. I almost couldn't see where I was goin' still, but I kept my head down and followed the line of buildings until the brick jailhouse finally loomed ahead, risin' from the tempest like a bulwark.

I marched straight fer it, went to the door, and barged inside with as much force as I had entered the Stag. A gust of wind came in with me, sprayin' water across the interior, makin' some of the men inside scowl and flinch away from the wet. I kicked the door shut behind me with a boot, my eyes locked on Nine-Fingered Nan.

She was there, all right. Sittin' in the sheriff's chair behind his desk. Her pale eyes lifted as the door slammed, and her men—four of 'em this time—turned to face me, hands slidin' toward their guns.

Sheriff Jennings stood to her right, and he looked awfully displeased, but he kept his arms crossed and made no move for a weapon himself.

I ignored him, ignored the four men clearly threatenin' to shoot me, and stomped directly toward Nan. Then took that lockbox and slammed it down onto the desk, right in front of her. Right on top of her spread of maps and papers. Water ran down off its nooks and crannies, trickled through its engravings, puddled underneath it. "There," I spat. "There's your damn lockbox. Now where is my sister?!"

Nine-Fingered Nan said nothin'. She only looked at me, her face unreadable. Then she leaned back in her chair and steepled her fingers, and her eyes dropped down to the strange metal box with its numbered dials.

Her four men closed in around me, standin' too close.

And some of the anger burnin' in me hot cooled off, dampened by an increasin' sense of apprehension.

Maybe I shouldn't have come here. Maybe I should have waited.

Nan nodded toward one of her goons and I tensed as he

stepped forward, but he only picked up the lockbox himself. He turned it over and around, studyin' it. Then he untied his bandana from around his neck and used the cloth to pat the thing dry. That done, he offered it out to Nan.

She took it. Looked it over much the same as her man had.

I held my breath. But that had to be it. That had to be the one she'd wanted. It matched her sketch. It was important, Professor Morton had said so. Baron Haas had clearly known so as well, or else he wouldn't have gone through all that trouble to hold a private auction fer it.

Nan finished her inspection of it, and one of her eyebrows twitched. She set it carefully on the corner of the desk, out of the way of the maps and papers.

"That's right," I said, and I realized suddenly things had gone eerily silent outside. The storm musta finally calmed down, but now everything seemed too quiet. And my mouth was too dry as I tried to swallow. "I got it. Got your damn lockbox. And no thanks to your source up north. He musta fed you a wagon-load of horseshit. That coach weren't carryin' it. Lucky I found it at all."

She smiled a little at that, and finally spoke. "That so? Thought luck was yer pa's forte?"

I clenched my teeth against her sneerin' tone.

She stood from her chair, slow and unhurried. "But maybe he's passin' you some from beyond the grave, because I will admit, Delano … I did not expect you to come back here alive. And I most certainly did not expect you to come back here alive and with this box." She put a hand over it.

"But I did," I said. "So where's my sister?"

She cocked her head to one side. "Saw you shot my barkeep."

I managed to hold her stare and hide the inward grimace. "He tried to shoot me first."

WANTED!
$50,000 REWARD
ROBBERY IN
BLESSING

"Heard you ran out a room stuffed fulla customers, too. Right out into that storm." She nodded toward the door, but kept her eyes on me.

Water dripped from my hat brim, and my wet clothes stuck heavy to my skin. Even still, the hair on my arms prickled. I kept my hands ready to draw, nevermind the fact I wouldn't win that one. "They did that of their own accord," I said flatly. "I didn't make no one leave."

"And yet they left because of you," Nan said. "A whole buncha men who could have been drinkin', gamblin', and whorin' durin' that storm … all run off because you wanted to start trouble."

"I didn't want to start nothin'." I risked a glance at the sheriff, thinkin' this conversation sounded awful familiar. But his expression was entirely unsympathetic, and I looked quick back to Nan. "You told me to get that box and bring it back here, bring it back to the Stag, and that's what I did. I was lookin' fer you. I kept my end of our deal. Now it's yer turn."

She leaned back a little. Shifted her hands to rest on her matchin' pearl grips, and I noted the two of her men who'd been standin' behind me shuffled more to the sides.

My breath caught, even despite all the anger I'd stormed in here with. I fully expected her to shoot me just then. All this trouble, all this time, just to be shot down now. The tick of a clock from somewhere in the room was loud as the thunder had been just minutes ago. I hadn't even known the sheriff had had a clock before. Now it pulsed out a rhythm to match the rush of blood in my ears as I waited.

Waited fer her answer, whether in words or in lead.

"Well, Delano," she finally drawled, "turns out I got a telegram just today from that fella who wants yer sister."

Heat flooded my face, and all that anger came rushin' back.

It was all I could do to stay still. To not draw. To not leap over the desk and throttle her.

"Ya see, I went ahead and told him there was another person interested in acquirin' the girl. As you can imagine, he was none too happy about that. He'd already sent his ship along this way, after all. Too late to call it back. Now, of course he does have other assets to retrieve once it arrives on this continent..." She shrugged. "But he's quite intent on collectin' yer sister along with the rest of 'em."

"That lockbox is worth more than she could ever be," I rasped.

"To some, maybe," she conceded. "But I ain't sellin' it, Delano. I'm usin' it. And as such, you've just been outbid."

I lunged halfway over the desk before her men caught me and hauled me backward, catchin' tight to my arms as I tried to go fer my guns next. One of 'em drove a fist hard into my gut, and I doubled over as all the air went outta me. Another of 'em kicked at the back of my knee and I went down, and I wrestled with 'em there fer a bit on the floor before they had me good, holdin' me on my knees with hands on my shoulders and both arms pinned behind my back.

"You sonuva motherless whore!" I tried to come up to my feet, to throw myself at her, wantin' nothin' more but to pummel her with my own two hands, but her men held me tight. "We had a deal!"

She had watched my attempt to tackle her and my struggle with her goons without so much as a flinch, without so much as lookin' like she might draw either of her guns. And even now she only looked down at me and smiled, seemin' more amused than anythin' else.

And that only made me angrier.

It swelled up in me so complete, so overwhelmin', I could hardly breathe.

"Sure we did," she said, her smile widenin'. "And now I've made a better deal with someone else. But I'm nothin' if not a businesswoman. So if yer willin' to make me a better offer, Delano, and, let's say, pay me back fer all the business you've cost me in the last month, well … I'd be willin' to listen."

"I … you …" It was a struggle to get the words out past the rage stuck in my throat. "One person can't possibly be worth that much," I finally choked out.

Her eyebrows lifted, and she feigned a kind of disappointed sadness. "Tsk, tsk, Mr. Delano. Discountin' yer own sister like that. She'd be heartbroken to hear it."

"I ain't discountin' nothin'!"

"Then yer willin' to raise yer offer?"

Thought my heart might slam right outta my ribs as I glared up at her smug, self-satisfied smirk and tried to sort what else she could possibly want from me. She was playin' me … usin' me fer sure … just like Holt had said. But it didn't matter … didn't matter till I had Ethelyn one way or another, either by gettin' her from Nan, or somehow trackin' her down and gettin' her free myself.

So I swallowed and gave a nod. "You know I am."

She grinned now. "Such a loyal brother. All right. I will write the buyer and let him know his offer has been met and raised. I will warn you though, he might just be willin' to go yet higher fer yer sister. She is … well, she's got the most strikin' eyes, don't she? And it's rare to find a woman of her age with her virtue still intact. That alone makes her worth more than most."

I tried to surge up off the floor again, but her four men held me fast, wrestled me back down to my knees.

"Now, now," Nan scolded, "don't throw away this opportunity, Delano." She gathered up the papers spread out over the sheriff's desk and rolled the maps. Even the one I'd made slightly soggy by slammin' the wet lockbox on top of it. She stacked the papers up neat next to the old metal box and handed the rolled maps to the sheriff, who took them without a word. Then she picked up that lockbox I'd nearly died several times over for. "I want my money's worth outta you, sure. But I ain't got no qualms about puttin' down a dog that bites, neither." She leaned forward over the desk to meet my furious glare with a flat, cold stare of her own. "So you just be sure yer on yer best behavior around here, understand?"

I ground my teeth, silence bein' the best answer I could manage at the moment.

She straightened from the desk, ambled around to the front of it, and her men pulled me around roughly to face her square again. She reached into her shirt pocket with her free hand and pulled out a folded square of paper, held it up in two fingers. "Got this a few days ago. Thought if you did show up here again, alive, you might be interested." She stepped forward to slide the paper into my own damp shirt pocket. Then she stepped back again, and her pale gaze flicked over to the sheriff. "Lock him up fer awhile. A good, long while. He could stand to learn some patience. You and I will conclude our business later. Fer now, I'm hungry. I'm goin' fer some grub. And to maybe find myself a new barkeep."

I struggled against the hands that held me even as they dragged me backwards, toward one of the jail cells. "Enough of these goddamned games!" I blurted as she made fer the door. "Just tell me what you want!"

She paused. Turned halfway around toward me. In the absence of the ragin' storm, the quiet rang in my ears. One corner of her mouth quirked upwards. "I want you to wait, Mr. Delano. After all, patience is a virtue." She touched the brim of her hat and turned her back on me, steppin' out through the door into the late afternoon, the sky already clear again.

I scowled and swore, cursin' her name with every foul insult I could think of and fightin' her men until they hit me again; another to the gut and one to my face hard enough to make me see stars, and then they relieved me of my gun belts, dumped me on a cot in one of the cells, and slammed the barred door shut behind 'em.

I laid there curled around the pain in my stomach and gaspin', head throbbin', and heard 'em all move away to follow after Nine-Fingered Nan, sneerin' and mutterin' till they finally took their leave of the jail house.

Then it was just me and the sheriff.

I said nothin'. 'Couldn't have, anyway, not till I got my air back. I just stared at the back brick wall of that cell, shakin' and numb with all the frustration, anger … rage. The skin all along my left shoulder and down the left side of my chest, the skin that had got all red and blistered from Miller's electrical rod, throbbed from so much manhandlin'. And I felt all those cuts and stings afresh, too, my three bandaged fingers raw and pulsin' from my struggles, my body sore and tired from the abuse at Miller's hands, the hard ridin' to get here, the blows from Nan's men.

All of that … everything I'd been through and done to get that goddamned lockbox … all of it fer nothin'.

Nan had what she wanted now. Would get more of what she wanted, too. And all I had was a debt that kept on growin'. A debt I was beginnin' to think could never be paid.

The rustle of papers drew my attention away from my self-loathin', and I heard the sheriff movin' around his jail house. Likely puttin' things back in order after Nan's visit. Then his footsteps came in my direction, but I didn't bother to acknowledge him.

Didn't move at all.

"Your sister, huh?" he asked, and his tone was gentler than I'd ever heard it.

Unexpected tears bit viciously into the backs of my eyes, so I closed 'em, squeezed 'em shut tight. "Yeah."

He grunted. Sounded thoughtful. But he said nothin' else, only moved off to putter around his jail house some more, and then he stepped out and left me alone.

Left me alone on that miserable cot in the near dark to wait. Wait on what, and wait how long, I couldn't imagine. And that was the worst part of it.

Eventually I remembered that paper Nan had stuck in my shirt pocket. I roused myself reluctantly, pushed up to sit against the bricks, and pulled it out. Unfolded it.

And as soon as I saw the ink scrawled across it, somethin' inside me broke.

My vision swam, the tears unstoppable now. I tried to blink them away, tried to read the words … the handwriting bringin' back memories from long ago. It was recognizably *hers*, though far more refined and elegant than it had been as a child. Mama had always praised Ethelyn fer her penmanship … it had always been a fair sight better than mine, despite the five extra years I had on her.

Van, dear brother,

They tell me you are still alive. They tell me they are bringing these letters to you. They tell me you are coming to get me. But it has been weeks now, and I am beginning to fear the worst. I fear they are lying, about all of it. I cannot fathom why they would tell such lies, except to torture me with the hope that it is all true … and brother, it has been torture of the worst kind. Except for that, they have treated me fair decent enough, though I am told daily that is only because the man who wishes to buy me absolutely insists I am given to him unmarked, and that if they should ignore that condition, he will not pay for me, and then that Nine-Fingered Nan would flay them alive. But even that is miserable to endure, as I do not know how much longer I will be here, or how much longer such people can stand to obey orders, even if from someone they fear as much as they clearly fear Nine-Fingered Nan.

Brother, if you are still alive, I pray this letter finds you, and I pray you are able to come for me as they say you are. But please be careful. These people are vicious and cruel, and I could not bear to think of you murdered, too, for my sake.

May the Grace of God and the Holy Mother be with you.

With all of my hope and my heart,

Ethelyn.

The agony came outta me in great, shudderin' sobs as I read, and when I'd finished I sagged back against the wall and let all the rest of it out, too. When I'd spent it all, exhausted myself, wrung it all out, I just sat there, the letter held limply in my hands as I stared unseein' at the opposite wall.

Nan *did* have Ethelyn.

Now I knew that much at least fer certain.

Nan did have her. And I *would* find her.

Nan could hold me in her debt fer as long as she wanted, fer whatever she wanted, I weren't gonna let that merchant outbid me. His money could only go so far. But if Nan wanted more Old World artifacts, if she wanted more banks or stagecoaches robbed, hell, if she wanted to cross the Valley of Lightning itself, all that I could do. Or at least I'd try my damnedest.

She wanted me to be patient? Fine. I'd play this fuckin' game of hers, sure enough. She clearly didn't know how stubborn we Delanos could be. But she were about to find out.

Feelin' more resolved now, I straightened up off the wall and folded the letter carefully, then tucked it back into my shirt pocket. I scrubbed my hands over my face, then wiped it with my bandana. Pulled off my hat and tossed it to the end of the cot. Raked fingers through my damp hair.

Then stopped abruptly as I caught sight of the newspaper that had been discarded near the waste bucket. The front page had a large photograph of a mighty familiar man. I woulda recognized those bushy eyebrows, hooded eyes, and grumpy expression anywhere.

I lurched off the cot to grab up the paper, and fear stabbed into my belly as I folded it out so I could read the whole headline.

NOTORIOUS OUTLAW HOLT HAGGERTY TO DIE ON THE GALLOWS

The fear clamped hard, cuttin' off my breath. Frantically, I searched out the date on the paper. Three days ago. Then I skimmed the article, hardly seein' the words, the small print all blurrin' together as I looked fer the date they'd set fer him to hang.

Finally I found it … fourteen days from the printin' of that article, they said. Wanted folk to have plenty of time to come from miles around to witness the spectacle, they said.

That gave him eleven more days. Eleven days from today.

In some town called Destry.

They were gonna hang him. They were gonna hang Holt.

And here I was, trapped in this cell fer who knew how long. I stood fast from the cot, crumpled the paper, and hurled it against the wall. "*Fuck!*"

EPILOGUE

A GILDED CAGE

She stood tall and proud, back straight, shoulders back, chin up, just like her mama had always taught her, and watched the airship lumber downward toward its designated landing field. She had always dreamed of seeing one, these airships, ever since she was a small child and had read about them in stories.

But there was no joy in her heart at seeing this one. No wonder. There was only a cold, bitter anger where her glee should have been. Where her heart should have been. She watched the airship land, alighting soft as a butterfly despite its bulk, and blinked away the tears.

They ran hot down her cheeks, overlaying old trails. She'd been crying for days. Quietly crying in the dark hours of the night and the early hours of the morning, knowing there was no one left to save her.

She had done well enough taking care of herself all these years. The Western Territories were no place for a young girl on her own, and yet she had survived. Not just survived, but *lived*. Had done all right for herself, considering. Until the day she'd let her guard slip, just enough, and Nine-Fingered Nan's web had caught her up.

And she'd been trapped ever since. Held close and secure, auctioned off to the highest bidder. The agent of the man who had won her stood beside her now, as straight and tall and stoic as she was, but dressed in colorful silk instead of colorful cottons. He had a long black braid like hers, too, all the way down to the small of his back.

Japan, he said. That's where they were going.

That's where they were all going. So many of them. Most of them women, or small girls and boys, but some young men, as well. All meant to board this one man's airship.

She couldn't imagine how much money he must have had, to afford to buy all of these people. She knew how much he'd paid for her alone. If any of the rest of these people had prices even close to hers … well, then this man from Japan was quite certainly richer than any person she'd ever heard of on the American continent.

The airship's boarding ramp descended, raising a cloud of dust as its bottom edge thumped into the barren ground of the airfield. This whole place was barren, she thought. Wide and empty, nothing but sandstone structures and dirt and an endless blue sky.

It might have been pretty, maybe, if it weren't the place her life would end.

A group of people descended the boarding ramp, their colorful silks looking as out of place against the drab landscape as the silks of the man who stood beside her. They hurried forward, toward her and the others. The others who had their hands bound like her, and manacles with a short chain around their ankles, and who were surrounded on all sides by mean-looking men and women with guns.

The man beside her, the agent, turned to her and swept out an arm toward the airship. As if inviting her to enter a party at a grand estate, instead of inviting her to board the contraption that would deliver her to a life of being some man's plaything.

She set her jaw. Blinked away more tears. And shuffled forward of her own accord, not waiting for Nine-Fingered Nan's brutal crew to coerce or push or shove her, like they'd been doing for the whole journey here.

She was met halfway to the boarding ramp by a cluster of women who had come off the airship, all Japanese, some gray-haired and some closer to her age, and they greeted her and the other terrified souls who followed her as if they were all long-lost family.

But the warm reception did not warm the coldness that had numbed her recently. Despite several efforts in the last few months, she had failed to save herself. And her brother was not coming for her. Perhaps he never had been.

They had told her he was. Told her he was going to buy her back from Nine-Fingered Nan. Soon as he got enough money, that's what they'd said he'd said.

She'd never been certain he was still alive to begin with … but then two weeks ago, just before they'd started this trek north to the airfield, they had come to tell her he couldn't pay.

No. Not that he *couldn't.*

He *wouldn't.*

No one was worth that much, he'd said.

The band of outlaws had sure had fun at her expense with that. Taunting and jeering over the fact her own brother had given up on her. Making sure she knew they'd certainly have paid the price to have her, if they could afford it. If Nan wouldn't have skinned them alive for it.

That night was the first night she had shed tears in all her time of captivity.

Perhaps it was all a lie. Perhaps Van had never been coming for her. Perhaps he thought she was dead. Perhaps *he* was really dead.

It didn't matter now, in the end, anyway. He'd left her once, after that horrific night when their parents had been murdered. He'd left her with the smell of their burning homestead thick in the air, in the dark of those woods, and he'd never come back.

She supposed she was a fool for believing he'd come back now, even if he were alive.

So she stood tall and proud, shoulders back and chin up, and shuffled up that ramp in her shackles, and refused to look back.

The inside of the airship was a great deal larger than she'd expected. She was guided along by several more silk-clad crew, until finally being ushered into a plush, well-appointed room. It had all the comforts of an expensive, high-class inn, only there were multiple beds, and they were stacked and small. Eight of them total.

A middle-aged Japanese woman bustled in, her robe breathtaking in its number of exquisite embroidered roses. Combs set with real flowers and trails of pearls were tucked into her jet-black hair. "Sit," she instructed, patting at a cushioned bench. "Sit here."

Ethelyn Delano did as she was told, confusion prickling at her neck. None of this was what she had expected. She startled as the woman pulled a slender knife from her sash, then only grew more confused as the ropes around her wrists were cut, pulled off, and thrown away.

The knife disappeared back into the sash, and the woman gestured at Ethelyn's ankles. "Let me see?" In her other hand, she proffered a small key.

Ethelyn straightened her legs, and the manacle chain clinked. The heavy iron cuffs had chaffed at her skin, and it was raw and sore.

The woman dressed in roses shook her head and clucked her tongue at the sight, but unlocked the shackles and pulled them away, too. She straightened and turned as more young women were ushered into the room, all looking as bewildered as Ethelyn felt.

But the woman welcomed them in much the same way, instructing them all to sit, and removing their ropes and chains one by one. "Do not worry, *mina-san*," she said softly. "You are all safe now. All safe. You will have food and drink, and warmth and comfort. We will take care of you."

Ethelyn blinked, wondering if all of this was some sort of sick joke. Wondering if this was how this wealthy man eased his conscience, helped himself sleep at night after condemning so many people to a life of forced servitude.

A gilded cage was still a cage.

She glanced to the other women who had come in, but they all seemed as lost as she.

Their Japanese host turned to a cabinet and removed a whole porcelain tea set beset with pale blue flowers and gold accents. She went about preparing a pot, and out in the corridor a man in a plain black robe passed by, said something to the woman in a language Ethelyn couldn't understand, and then shut their door.

A low rumble started up from somewhere, the floor vibrating beneath Ethelyn's feet, the walls humming.

"Ah!" the woman of flowers said cheerily. "We depart! We have a long journey ahead, but you will be as comfortable as possible. Now … who will have tea?"

Only silence answered her question as Ethelyn and the others looked among each other with many questions and no answers, and then Ethelyn gasped as the room shifted just slightly to one side.

They were lifting off, all right. Leaving the ground. Leaving the Western Territories and the American continent. Leaving the only place she'd ever known. She'd been kidnapped and sold, and yet this place and these people were already far different than she'd imagined.

If they were going to free her of her bonds, promise her

warmth and comfort, and offer her tea … maybe she had hope of freeing herself, after all. Eventually.

She'd done well enough over all these years.

And she'd done so by observing weaknesses and finding opportunity, no matter the circumstances.

Perhaps this journey … this new life, even if in an unfamiliar land … would be no different.

She cleared her throat, sat up straighter as she turned to face the woman, and raised a hand. She even managed a smile. The sugary sweet kind that had lured many a mark her way in the past. "I'll take some," she said. "I'll take some tea, please."

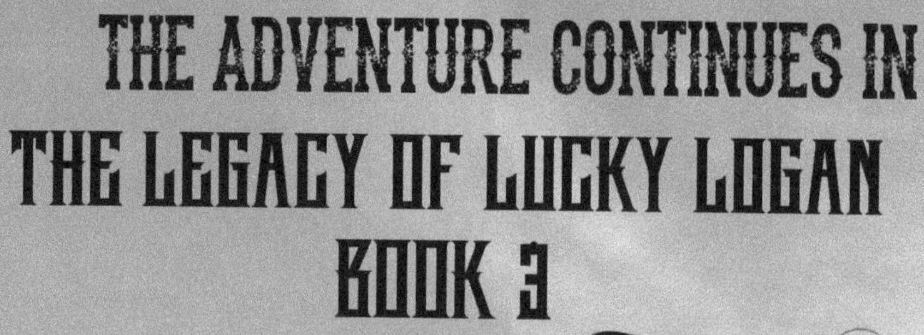

BONES IN BLACKBIRD

Special edition illustrated hardback of Bones in Blackbird coming soon to Kickstarter!

Enter this link in your browser and follow me the to be sure you get notified as soon as it goes live!
https://www.kickstarter.com/profile/jrfrontera

And don't forget your free book! Was Van's pa really the one to shoot off Nan's finger? Only one way to find out! Download your free copy of LUCKY LOGAN at the link below!
https://bit.ly/LuckyLoganFREE

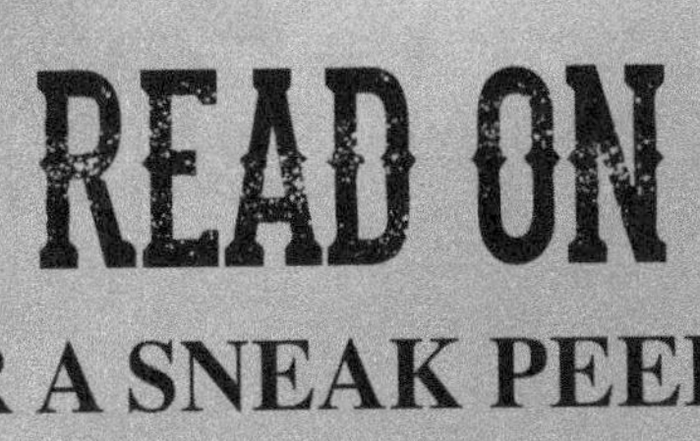

FOR A SNEAK PEEK AT
***BONES IN BLACKBIRD*! …**

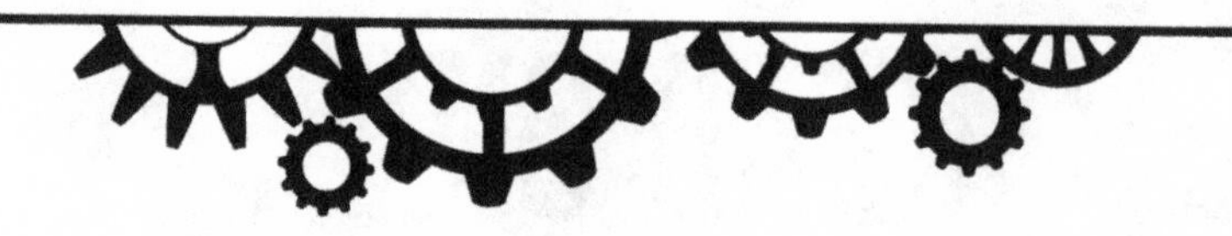

Don't forget, if you'd be so kind, to leave a review for this book on your favorite platform! The number of a book's reviews directly influences how visible the retail platform makes it to other readers! And leaving a few sentences about what you loved most about the book will help others decide whether or not this book might be for them, too! Also, you'll have my eternal gratitude!

If you didn't get the audiobooks through the last two campaigns, no worries! You can still purchase them for a discount at https://jrfrontera.com/audiobooks/!

THE LEGACY OF LUCKY LOGAN
BOOK 3

STORE

HANG 'EM HIGH

I couldn't see shit wearin' this bonnet.

Made me wonder how the women-folk put up with 'em.

I kept my eyes on the ground, mostly, bent over and holdin' a walkin' stick in my right hand. Partly to complete my disguise, and partly to help balance myself after standin' here fer hours. The crowd had arrived bit by bit over the course of the mornin', but I'd been one of the first ones here. Been here since dawn. Watched the sun come up over the town square … over the gallows. Watched the shadows of those nooses stretch out long across the ground, and then slowly shorten as the day wore on.

The cotton dress I'd donned over my usual clothes was startin' to get awful hot, but there weren't nothin' I could do about that.

The hangin' was set fer noon. And noon was comin' up awful fast now.

The crowd had swelled, all right. Fillin' in around and behind me, men and women and children, and vendors sellin' sweet cakes and rock candy and jerky, and tinctures and whiskey, too.

I ignored 'em, all of 'em, the spectators and the vendors both. Ran over this plan of mine again and again in my mind, tryin' not to calculate too awful much the odds of gettin' killed in this venture.

I couldn't afford to get myself killed. Not when I still had to get Ethelyn from Nan. But neither could I have stayed rottin' away in that jail cell back in Bravebank while Holt got hanged. The man was an insufferable, selfish bastard … but damn it all, he'd saved my neck too many times to count in the last eight years.

At least I owed him this. At least I owed him a try.

Sweat slipped down my face and I swiped at it with the back of my left hand, then brushed that hand against my hip, feelin' at the outline of my pistol beneath the skirt of the floral-patterned dress. I'd cut a slit in the fabric there along both holsters, so they could be covered up fer the most part, but still within easy reach fer when I needed 'em quick.

I'd never pulled a job dressed like a woman before, but it'd seemed the only way I was gonna have a chance of gettin' anywhere near this place without bein' recognized or lookin' suspicious. And so far, it was workin'.

Except fer this damned bonnet completely cuttin' off my peripheral vision. It hid my face, sure enough, but the narrowed field of view made me nervous, too.

I took a slow breath in, and let it out just as slow. Glanced up to look through the gallows scaffolding, across the square, to where I'd tied my mule Joe and the skinny old mare Seven Knives Sally had gifted me. I'd only barely managed to get Joe back from that livery in Sonoita in time to make it here before the hangin', and as luck would have it, I'd found Holt's horse in the Destry livery last night.

The hostler here was a downright drunk, so it'd been easy enough to sneak the horse out, but I didn't exactly want him tied in the middle of town now, considerin' the law had been notified of the missin' animal and tack this mornin'.

So I'd left him outside town a ways, along our planned escape route.

If this plan of mine didn't end with both of us dead, I imagined Holt would be mighty sore about havin' to ride that old mare outta here, but then, she'd be carryin' him to freedom, so surely he'd get over it.

I checked my line of sight to my distractions next, tryin' to only minimally turn my head so as to not reveal my very unlady-like features to the folk pressin' in close on either side. Didn't want anyone realizin' I weren't no old lady till I was good and ready fer 'em to realize such a thing.

But they were still there, my distractions, three small bundles of dynamite I'd planted in the wee hours of the mornin', wedged up along the rooftops of some of the surroundin' buildings. One above a dentist, one above the bank, one above the post office. Two to my right and one to my left. Fairly easy shots from my vantage point here at the front of the crowd, but I'd have to be fast.

And not miss.

I took another slow breath in attempts to quiet my hummin' nerves.

Too much feelin' threw off yer aim, and I was feelin' an awful lot right now…

A commotion rose up among the crowd to my left, where the jailhouse sat along that side of the square, and I glanced that way to see the lawdogs leadin' Holt out.

My hand tightened around the top of the walkin' stick and I sucked in a breath.

He looked as grumpy as ever, hands bound together in front of him, a decent-sized gash along his left temple still bruised and swollen. He was held by a deputy on either side, and had another man in front and behind him.

The crowd parted to allow 'em through to the gallows stairs, but booed and hissed as Holt passed, some shoutin' out that he was a murderer and a monster. A few flung pieces of rotten produce at him, fruit and vegetables that hit him in the chest with a wet smack, splattering a mess everywhere.

I shifted on my feet and clenched my jaw, eyein' my distractions again, memorizin' their locations. Then looked back to Holt to see him spittin' and yellin' insults at the town folk, which only earned him more rotten food and vehement invitations to go to Hell.

The sheriff and his deputies tried to settle the crowd some as they took Holt up the stairs, put him over the trap door, and settled the noose around his neck. And then they stepped back, positionin' themselves at the four corners of the stage. They didn't have their guns drawn, but they looked alert, all right.

It was generally known around these parts that Holt Haggerty didn't run with no gang, so they weren't likely expectin' a whole heap of trouble from any outsiders tryin' to save his neck. But it was also generally known that Holt Haggerty *did* often run with at least one other unsavory outlaw.

Me.

They were almost certainly expectin' me, and lookin' out fer me, too.

I tried to keep my head angled away from 'em, so all they'd see was a pretty floral bonnet and not my face while I ran more calculations in my head.

Four of 'em, the noose rope, my three distractions. I was gonna need both pistols. And every shot had to count.

Another man ascended the gallows stairs now. He was dressed in a rather nice suit and held a rolled up piece of paper in his hand. He motioned for the crowd to quiet, and to my surprise, they did. He stepped to the edge of the gallows platform and I dropped my gaze back quick to the dusty ground so he wouldn't notice my features as he scanned the masses spread out before him.

"Good people of Destry," he yelled out, "and all those gathered here from elsewhere in the Territories as witness! Today we will have, at last, the ending of a criminal outlaw who has terrorized our towns for far too long!"

The people cheered. Whooped and hollered.

He motioned them quiet again. "As mayor of this fine town of Destry, I must commend our Sheriff Bell and his deputies, who apprehended this criminal before he could make off with much of our hard-earned money."

More cheerin' and shoutin' from the crowd.

Holt scowled and grumbled somethin', but it was lost beneath all the ruckus.

The mayor waited till the noise died down some, then continued, "It will be my pleasure to oversee this execution, and I beg all of you here today to remember: crime does not pay."

It was my turn to scowl and grumble then, and I shifted again on my feet, my metal leg whirrin' softly beneath the skirts. Maybe crime didn't pay … but it had kept me fed fer plenty of years now. Fed, and sometimes warm and comfortable, too.

"Now…" the mayor said. He unfurled the rolled paper. "Holt Haggerty, for the crimes of capital murder, assault, robbery, arson…"

Well, that list was gettin' awful long. I wondered if my list were that long these days. Probably.

"… theft, kidnapping…"

Kidnapping? I didn't remember that one. But then, Holt had been an outlaw fer a long time. Certainly longer than just the eight years I'd been runnin' with him.

"… forgery, impersonating an officer of the law…"

All right, I *did* remember that one…

"… selling stolen goods, horse theft, and cattle rustling, I do hereby sentence you to hang by the neck until dead." The mayor gave a little nod of finality and curled up that paper, and another wave of murmurs and excited chatter circled through the gathered crowd.

The mayor squinted upward, to the stretch of blue above. Weren't a cloud in the sky. The merciless sun glared down at us full-bore, directly overhead.

High noon.

Time fer the hangin'. Time fer Holt Haggerty to die.

He looked back to Holt then, a rather smug look of satisfaction crossin' his pinched and sweaty features. "Well?" he asked. "Any last words?"

I risked a glance to Holt myself, lookin' up at him standin' on that gallows stage from beneath the shade of my bonnet, and I slipped my left hand through the cut in the skirt on my left hip to curl my fingers loose around my gun grip. The three middle fingers of that hand still had bandages around their ends where Charles Miller had pulled off the fingernails not so long ago. And they were still sore, too. But I'd been practicin' drawin' and shootin' with those sore fingers since I'd escaped the Bravebank jail, till I was comfortable enough with 'em that I could rely on 'em today.

I eased my right hand downward now itself, along the length of the walkin' stick, closer to my right holster.

My heart beat in my throat. Sweat slid down my temples to run down my neck.

Holt glared out at the crowd pressed in on all sides and they hushed as he opened his mouth. "Yeah," he grunted. But then his clear blue gaze found mine, and he paused. Surprise went over his creased, grimy features, then a cautious hope, but he looked away again quick before any of those lawdogs could take an interest in what he might have seen. His face went hard and angry again, and he focused his glare on Destry's mayor. "Yeah," he said again, one corner of his mouth quirkin' into a smirk.

"The best-laid schemes of mice and men often go awry, and leave us nothing but grief and pain, fer promised joy."

I rolled my eyes, cursin' him silently, hopin' his bein' cute wouldn't tip off those four armed men up there.

But the mayor only seemed perplexed, then shook his head. "Quoting literature will not gain you any sympathy here, Haggerty. Saying pretty words does not make you a civilized man."

Holt snorted in amusement. "You would know about that personally, wouldn'tcha, Mayor?"

The gathered masses booed at that comment, and shouts to get on with the hangin' already rang through the square.

The mayor agreed with 'em, 'cause he drew himself up straighter at Holt's insult and gestured to the sheriff. The sheriff nodded, pulled the black hood from where he'd had it tucked into his belt, and shook it out as he went to Holt's side.

"Goodbye, Haggerty," he said, and put the hood over Holt's head before Holt could snap anything in return. "And good riddance."

The mayor stepped over to the lever. All he had to do was pull it, and that trap door would swing open under Holt's feet, and he'd take a long drop on a short rope, his neck snappin' like a twig.

Unless I didn't miss.

I took in another slow, deep breath of the hot afternoon. Another trickle of sweat slipped down my face, but I didn't dare wipe it away. Not now. Not this close.

The mayor rested his hand atop the lever and affected a solemn expression. The masses around me went deathly quiet, their anticipation thick as mine, but fer entirely different reasons.

Someone across the square coughed, and a baby started cryin'.

A light breeze stirred, coolin' the sweat on my brow and shiftin' my floral skirts around my ankles.

"May God and the Holy Mother alike have mercy on your soul," the mayor said.

He pulled the lever.

COMING SOON TO KICKSTARTER!

ABOUT THE AUTHOR

J. R. Frontera has been telling stories in some form or another since she could hold a crayon and draw. Her love of science fiction and fantasy originated with her early exposure to the worlds of *Star Wars*, *Star Trek*, *Lord of the Rings*, and *Dune*. Exploring the potential and pitfalls of humanity in future or fantastical worlds is a temptation she's just never been able to resist. She loves to write rebel stories for rebel souls, and co-founded a local writing group known as The Wordwraiths. She's also co-owner of their publishing imprint Wordwraith Books. When she's not writing, momming, or working at her full-time job, she's often horseback riding, playing videogames, or cosplaying. She lives in rural Missouri with her husband, son, and more animals than she'd prefer to disclose. You can find out more about J. R. Frontera and her books by visiting her website at https://jrfrontera.com.

Printed in the USA
CPSIA information can be obtained
at www.ICGtesting.com
JSHW022358080923
47335JS00027B/13/J

9 781946 921390